PRAISE FOR
THE NeoG SERIES

"Wagers's inclusive worldbuilding contains an amazing range of personalities, while the fast-paced plot still gives time for meaningful character stories. . . . [They raise] the stakes with exciting action, terrific characters, and an expansive view on life in the universe." —*Library Journal* (**starred review**) on *The Ghosts of Trappist*

"As usual, K. B. Wagers delivers a rollicking space adventure, by turns serious and funny, full of witty banter, explosive tension, relatable characters, and families found and made. . . . I hope Wagers writes more in this series, or at least in one very like it: they have a wonderful knack for writing books that I find absolutely delightful entertainment."
—*Locus* on *The Ghosts of Trappist*

"Wagers lavishes a lot of attention on the internal conflicts and interpersonal frictions that accompany the more standard space battles and computer hacking intrigues. Readers who enjoy both the glitz of space opera and the conviviality of family dramas will be rewarded with as many embraces as EMP blaster pulses."
—*Publishers Weekly* on *The Ghosts of Trappist*

"Although the storyline is powered by an impressively intricate plot that features mystery, intrigue, and nonstop action, it's the deeply developed characters and the dynamic relationships among them that fuel this narrative. Wagers creates a cast of characters that are not only authentic, but endearingly flawed. . . . Top-notch character-driven science fiction."

—*Kirkus Reviews* (starred review) on
Hold Fast Through the Fire

"Wagers's second NeoG novel serves up buffet-size portions of everything their fans have come to expect: dug-in friendships, action, impossible odds, and clever dialogue that always hits home. . . . Wagers's characterization plumbs incredible depths, particularly with street rat–turned–engineering chief Jenks, a brain with vicious fists. Wagers's fans should snap up this fun, thrilling latest."

—*Publishers Weekly* (starred review) on
Hold Fast Through the Fire

AND
THE
MIGHTY
WILL
FALL

AND THE MIGHTY
WILL FALL

A NeoG NOVEL

K. B. WAGERS

HARPER Voyager
An Imprint of HarperCollins Publishers

This is a work of fiction. Names, characters, places, and incidents are products of the author's imagination or are used fictitiously and are not to be construed as real. Any resemblance to actual events, locales, organizations, or persons, living or dead, is entirely coincidental.

HarperCollins books may be purchased for educational, business, or sales promotional use. For information, please email the Special Markets Department at SPsales@harpercollins.com.

Harper Voyager and design are trademarks of HarperCollins Publishers LLC.

FIRST EDITION

Designed by Paula Russell Szafranski

Background image @ B. Coba/stock.adobe.com

Library of Congress Cataloging-in-Publication Data has been applied for.

ISBN 978-0-06-311524-8

$PrintCode

To Dex,
the Jenks to my Max.
With you until the end of the line.

CAST OF CHARACTERS

ZUMA'S GHOST
Commander Maxine Carmichael (she/her)
Lieutenant Commander Saqib Vahid (he/him)
Lieutenant Nell "Sapphi" Zika (she/her)
Senior Chief Petty Officer Altandai "Jenks" Khan (she/her)
Petty Officer Second Class Chae Ho-ki (they/them)
Petty Officer Third Class Rona Nkosi (she/her)
Doge, ROVER (he/him)

DREAD TREASURE
Commander D'Arcy Montaglione (he/him)
Lieutenant Commander Chaske Landon (he/him)
Lieutenant Heli Järvinen (she/they)
Master Chief Emel Shevreaux (she/her)
Chief Petty Officer Aki Murphy (she/her)
Petty Officer Second Class Lupe Garcia (he/him)

OTHER CHN MILITARY PERSONNEL
Senior Chief Yichen Lee (they/them)
Lieutenant Miles Compton (he/him)
Admiral Royko Chen (she/her)
Commander Nika Vagin (he/him)
Senior Chief Luis Armstrong (he/him)
Lieutenant Uchida Tamashini (they/them)
Captain Stephan Yevchenko (he/him)
Rear Admiral Scott Carmichael (he/him)
Captain Tivo Parsikov (he/him)
Lieutenant Opia Ruiz (she/her)
Vice Admiral Jackson Ford (he/him)
Captain Fábia Clark (she/her)
Captain Drani Jaishankar (she/her)
Spacer Lia Thorn (she/her)
Commodore Sameera Moussa (she/her)
Commodore César Lattes (he/him)

SEAL TEAM SEVEN
Captain Ella Giroux (she/her)
Lieutenant Commander Jordan Cerlio (they/them)
Lieutenant Ewan Ryan (he/him)
Chief Petty Officer Sy West (she/her)
Petty Officer First Class Mak Lee (he/him)
Petty Officer Second Class Steven Lynn (he/they)

FREE MARS
Sylvia Moroz (she/her)
Maria Ortega (she/her)
Clair (they/them)
Carlo Perez (he/him)
Mikhail Starov (he/him)
Josiah (he/him)
Wilke Johansson (she/her)
Mila Johansson (she/her)

ORPHANS OF WAR
Willis Hale (he/him)
Ralka Usova (she/her)
Anton Usov (he/him)
Dri Castle (she/her)
Charlie (they/them)

CIVILIANS
Elliot Armstrong (he/him)
Riz Armstrong (he/him)
Sergei Khan (he/him)
Anna Khan (undecided)
Parson Grady (he/him)
Cho Seo-Yoon (she/her)
Senator Patricia Carmichael (she/they)
Kavan Ying (they/them)

AND
THE
MIGHTY
WILL
FALL

AND
THE
MIGHTY
WILL
FALL

It is the mission of the Near-Earth Orbital Guard to ensure the safety and security of the Sol system and the space around any additional planets that human beings call home.

Eight Time Boarding Games Champion Carmichael to Facilitate Station Handover

PUBLISHED: SEPTEMBER 30, 2446 (EARTH STANDARD DATE)

Fresh off her eighth victory in the Boarding Games and her second triumph over her crewmate Senior Chief Petty Officer Altandai Khan in the championship cage match, Commander Maxine Carmichael is turning her talents back to her more regular NeoG duties: helping Vice Admiral Jackson Ford with the much-anticipated handover of the Mars Orbital Station (MOS) from NeoG control to Mars Civilian Command.

After a decade of focus on her Interceptor duties, Carmichael will be at the MOS for the next week to help with the final meetings between NeoG officials and their counterparts from Mars Civilian Command.

The MOS has been a strategic piece in the fight for Mars independence. Control of the traffic coming and going to the planet has long been in the hands of the NeoG, a move that many claim resulted in undue preference for Earth-registered freighters to the detriment of Mars businesses.

As the peace talks continue, putting the MOS into the hands of the people who know Mars best can only mean better things for both Mars's independence and its economy.

[*Read More*]

ONE

SENIOR CHIEF YICHEN LEE STRETCHED THEIR ARMS OVER THEIR head. The large main room of Mars/NeoG Ground Control, located at the NeoG base in the northern section of the major Martian city of Serrano, was quiet at this hour. Soon the day shift would start filtering in and it would be bustling with traffic and voices, but for now they were looking forward to wrapping up this quiet shift and then home for a nap before catching their kid's football match in the afternoon.

The normal day's traffic had been reduced to a few necessary flights that couldn't be changed. The handover of the station from the NeoG to civilian Mars control was only a formality at this point. An important one, no doubt, but it really was just a press opportunity under the guise of a handoff that should have happened long ago.

Yichen, however, had learned long ago to keep those opinions to themself.

"Don't know why we didn't just shut the lanes down completely for the day," Lieutenant Miles Compton muttered from his seat. "Hard enough to keep track of all these dignitaries, but add in even reduced traffic and it feels like a disaster waiting to happen."

"Good news is the dignitaries aren't our problem," Yichen replied. "Just the traffic. And they didn't shut it down all the way because people still need ground clearance." They kept their tone light, devoid of the annoyance they were feeling over having to once again tell a lieutenant how to do their job.

The blaring klaxon cut off whatever Lieutenant Compton had been about to say in reply, followed by a cool voice over the coms.

"This is Commander Maxine Carmichael. Code Bravo. All personnel on the Mars Orbital Station, evac immediately. Repeat evac immediately. Code Bravo. Unknown hostiles on board, command compromised. NeoG compromised. Ground Control, lock down. Repeat lock do—"

The transmission cut off and the two Neos stared at each other in shock.

"Shit," Yichen said, and scrambled into action.

This was *not* going to be a quiet day.

TWO

October 5, 2446, Earth Standard Date

JENKS: I heard from Doge; he said to tell you congratulations. Betrayed by my own dog.

MAX: I'll email him. Is he having fun with Pirene?

JENKS: Seems like. I miss him a bit. It was weird being at the Games without him.

MAX: Same. Hey, I figured next time we can tie one of my arms behind my back. It should give you an even shot at winning your title again.

JENKS: . . .

JENKS: You've been sitting on that one for a while, haven't you?

MAX: Maybe. :D

JENKS: *laughs* I am going to give you a beatdown the next time we spar. Lucky for you, we're about to lose coms. Have fun wrangling politicians. I'll be in the wilderness drinking and not having to watch my mouth.

MAX: You should be watching your mouth around those kids.

JENKS: Nothing they haven't heard. *grin*

MAX: Enjoy your vacation, brat. I love you.

JENKS: I'm the brat? Whatever. Love you too, sis.

COMMANDER MAXINE CARMICHAEL FLIPPED OFF THE CHAT screen with a quiet laugh and a shake of her head. "Jenks," she said when Lieutenant Commander Saqib Vahid gave her a curious look.

"You poked her, didn't you?" Even though he hadn't been privy to that chat, after two years on the team he was now familiar enough with Jenks's hijinks to guess at the source of Max's laughter.

"I just suggested the fight would be fairer if we tied one of my arms back." Max grinned at him when he sighed at her.

"Do I dare ask?" Her shuttle pilot, Petty Officer Aggy Bennet, was not as familiar with the situation, and they raised a curious black eyebrow in her direction.

"Family," Max replied.

"Enough said." They nodded. "My wife's family absorbed me—I didn't have much family when we met, and the ones I did have weren't great. Always wondered what it would be like to be from a big sprawling family like yours."

Max smiled again and smoothed slender fingers over the image of Pluto inked onto her brown skin, feeling the answering swell of emotion that always caught her unawares when she saw it, even so many years later.

Because Aggy didn't know the half of it. Max's biological family was complicated, and while it had grown slightly less so over the last decade, that didn't change the fact that the one she'd built for herself, with the NeoG, was what she thought of first when the subject came up. And what she'd meant here.

If someone had told her ten years ago that she would willingly share a tattoo with a rough, loud, hard-punching woman like Jenks, she'd never have believed it.

Moreover, she wouldn't have believed that that same woman called her sister with a fondness matched by the strength of the punches she threw at Max's head in the cage.

If someone else had told her she was a valued member of the Near-Earth Orbital Guard Interceptor team *Zuma's Ghost*, or a Boarding Games champion eight times over, or a two-time winner of the cage match. Or a *commander* in the NeoG . . .

She wouldn't have believed any of that, either.

She would have desperately wanted it to be true but wouldn't have dared to hope for something so incredible.

But it was true. And after all the moments where her parents had tried to stop her from living her life, Max was still here. That was the hardest thing for her to wrap her head around even now. Ten years. She was an officer in the NeoG because of her hard work and dedication, not her family name, and growing up that seemed like an impossibility.

So much is impossible until you try. Until you trust in yourself and, in turn, learn to trust others.

Maybe that would be her next tattoo . . . if she got through this assignment without causing an intra-system incident.

Not that she was too worried. She had been chosen to "wrangle politicians" as Jenks so wryly put it because her diplomatic abilities apparently continued to impress the higher-ups in the NeoG. And she *was* good at it—something she wasn't sure she'd have been able to say aloud the first day she'd stepped aboard *Zuma's Ghost*.

She'd learned so much since then. Yet the diplomacy was actually something that came from her upbringing as a Carmichael. Combined, it made her one hell of an asset for the NeoG to trot out for recruitment vid moments like this. So in the wake of their Boarding Games victory a few days ago, Max had been assigned to help oversee the beginning of the handover of the MOS, the Mars Orbital Station, as a gesture of goodwill to the people of Mars. It was the result of the ongoing peace talks between the CHN and the Free Mars movement, and meant they were one step closer to an independent Mars.

In terms of practical considerations, the NeoG would still be involved with the MOS, albeit in a limited capacity where they'd be responsible for overseeing and training Martian civilians for the next five years, at which point the station would become a wholly civilian venture and move to the newer station being constructed nearby.

All of which was to say Max just needed to ensure there were no blowups between the two sides that might send everyone back to their respective factions ready to start fighting again.

"NeoG Shuttle 443, this is Cho Seo-Yoon with MOS traffic control. We have you on the screen; please proceed to Shuttle Docking Bay Eleven." There was a pause from the voice on the coms. "Be advised there are media personnel in the bay."

Aggy chuckled at Max's quiet sigh. "We are advised, thank you." They flicked off the coms. "You had to know that was coming."

"Doesn't mean I like it," she replied with a shake of her head. "But you're right, I knew it was coming. Just bracing myself for the storm." Dealing with the press had gotten surprisingly easier over the years, every pregame interview and postgame press conference that slid by had somewhere along the line become just another day on the job.

She didn't love it like Jenks did, however, but she could manage it. She was even good at it. Which, Max had to admit, was probably another reason she'd been tagged for this particular job. Dealing with people had become increasingly easier over the years, occasionally even enjoyable. She wasn't sure this was going to be one of those times, but she could handle it. Again, that was more than could be said for just-graduated Lieutenant Max Carmichael.

The shuttle settled gently into its space and the familiar

whine of shutdown filled the cockpit. Max's fingers itched to help, but she kept them to herself as Aggy expertly ran through the sequence.

"I've got this, Max, if you want to go ahead."

"You just don't want to deal with the press."

"Neither do you. Great thing is, I don't have to. My job is to fly you two here and take you back to Earth when we're done. What I do in between is my business. So I'm going to take my time with the shutdown inspection, and then I'm just going to curl up in the back and sleep for twenty-four hours."

"You don't even have to do that. You could just head home, and Saqib and I will get a ride back to Earth from here."

"I would never abandon you. What would the media say?"

She chuckled. "I'd been meaning to ask you how you ended up with this assignment?"

"Bet the LT that you'd take the cage match championship. He thought Jenks wouldn't let it happen twice."

"Wait . . . and the *winner* got to fly me around?"

"Yeah. I got to meet you. Besides, better than core reactor disassembly back at the base. Do you know how long it takes to get that grease out from under your fingernails?"

Max laughed in startled amusement as she stood. "Well, that'll teach him, won't it?"

"Probably not—you know how LTs are," Aggy replied and Saqib choked back a laugh.

"I was one once." Those days were thankfully behind her, though again, Max sometimes could hardly believe it. No more awkward lieutenant. No more unsure Maxine.

Well . . . mostly.

She refused to think about the fact that she'd left a whole lot unsaid to Nika when he'd headed out last night. Part of her regretted not getting to stay on Earth with him for a while. The pull of a quiet space to finally say the words that were rolling around in her head had been strong, and she'd almost gotten them out, but duty won in the end.

Sometimes duty was all they had, and that bothered Max more than she cared to admit. Sure, the team had survived their first major shake-up two years ago with Max's promotion and Nika taking a new job on the ground at Trappist. And Tamago's exit to officer candidate school had been the best thing for their career, though Max missed them dreadfully.

Even the new members of *Zuma's Ghost* had settled in surprisingly well, and Max was glad Saqib had asked if he could join her on the trip to the MOS. The past two years had felt like a whirlwind of change, and she was looking forward to the chance to spend some time with the quiet man in a different setting.

But it was still a lot of change, and she knew she'd missed out on a chance to reconnect with an important part of her life.

Next time, Nika. I promise.

"All right. Well, you enjoy your downtime. I'll ping you when we're finished." She patted the wall of the ship and headed for the airlock, grabbing her bag from the narrow storage space nearby.

"You want me to run interference?" Saqib asked as Max stopped a moment to check her brown curls and straighten her uniform.

"Nah, I've got it. Probably a lot of the same faces we just saw." She took a deep breath, then tapped the airlock pad twice and crossed into the tiny space.

The blessed silence vanished as the outer door cycled open and she stepped from the ship into the sea of shouted questions and floating cameras. Max pasted a look Emel had teasingly called her "company smile" onto her face and stopped at the ring of reporters with Sabiq at her side.

"Bruce, didn't I just see you two days ago?"

Bruce Eamin, the reporter for TSN, grinned at her. "I get paid to follow you around, you know that. Are you taking some time off after this like the rest of your crew? I heard everyone else went with Nika."

"Probably," she replied.

"Where's Jenks? She dropped off the face of the Earth. Is she not headed back to Trappist with *Zuma* when you're done here?"

"Classified information, Bruce. You know I'm not going to tell you that."

"It'll be our little secret," the reporter wheedled. "Come on, Saqib, just a hint?"

The broad-shouldered man pointed at the camera hovering over Bruce's head with a shake of his own. "I value my life. Not a chance."

An unfamiliar man muscled his way forward, his handshake reading *Erik Murdoch, he/him,* Solar News Daily. "Commander, your parents seems to have backed off their public disapproval of you since the family blowup five years ago. Yet the NeoG brass obviously considers you one of their best young officers. What are your long-term plans for control of the Carmichaels?"

Several of the other journalists cursed and shot looks at the newcomer who'd asked the question, and Max studied him for a long moment before smiling. "Would someone like to repeat the rules for Mr. Murdoch?"

"You don't ask questions about the family," Bruce said. "Sorry, Max. FNG."

"No more questions." Max shook her head at the protests and put her hand up in the air. "You know the rules. You all should have vetted the new guy."

"All right, folks, back it up and give us some space." A short, muscular woman, whose handshake read *Lieutenant Opia Ruiz, she/her*, elbowed her way into the crowd. "Commander Carmichael? Lieutenant Commander Vahid? I'm Lieutenant Ruiz. I'm here to take you to Vice Admiral Ford."

Max hoisted her bag onto her shoulder and gave a little wave for the cameras as they followed Opia out of the bay and down the corridor.

"Sorry about that," the woman said with an apologetic smile to them both. "Vice Admiral Ford would have loved to keep them off the station, but with the event—"

"It's fine, Opia. I anticipated having to answer some questions, so if anything, I appreciate you getting me out of there as fast as you did." Max allowed herself a satisfied smile now that she was out of camera range.

Erik was probably getting yelled at by his fellow journalists right now. She refused to feel bad. He'd either learn or the others would keep him from asking questions in the future, at which point his publication would pull him for someone else.

She still couldn't believe how well her policy had worked. Five years ago she'd been terrified of the reaction. She'd been sure that she would get into some sort of trouble when she refused to answer a question about her family and then walked away, leaving everyone standing there in confused shock. After that, she'd laid out a slightly more polished version of Jenks's "I don't answer any questions I don't fucking want to" rule.

It was simple enough and the best part was she didn't have to enforce it, because the journalists who knew her were suddenly very good at making sure no one asked a question that would cut interviews short for everyone.

Most of the time, anyway.

SAQIB FOLLOWED ALONG BEHIND THE LIEUTENANT AND MAX, listening with half an ear as the two cis women talked about the upgrades the new station would have compared to this one. The time shift from Earth was always a killer, but coming on the heels of the Games, he was having a hard time waking up.

Their first round of competition together two years ago had been a whirlwind. Not unexpected, but still overwhelming in so many ways. It was a testament to Max's leadership, and the help of *Dread Treasure*'s solid presence, that they'd been able to walk away the winners his first year at the Games.

This time, though, he felt like *he'd* earned it. Even losing to D'Arcy in the championship sword fight hadn't dimmed that spark.

He'd thought he'd been happy at the academy, teaching sword fighting to sometimes awkward, gangling kids in their teens and early twenties. Every day pretty much the same as the last. His friend Coil's suggestion he apply for the newly opened Interceptor training slot had been met with laughter, amused surprise that faded into an unexpected *What if you do?* that hadn't gone away.

And now here he was. Life was weird . . . and exhausting.

But at least every day was different.

The interior of the Mars Orbital Station was showing its age, but the corridor leading away from the Shuttle Docking Bay shone with a fresh coat of paint and as much polish as the NeoG could put into it. This station didn't have the bulk of the one-off Jupiter or the newness of Trappist Station. It was little more than a traffic control point, a sleek, five-level tower spinning through space, designed for managing the flow around the planet. But it was maintained with the pride of a NeoG facility and would be until they were no longer in charge here.

Which was going to be pretty soon. There wasn't even a full contingent of Neos on board beyond the duty roster. Despite the failure of the more recent peace talks, the CHN had started shifting their military bases on Mars back to Earth and the moon. Now there were only a handful of smaller NeoG bases left along with the major one in Serrano. It was a gesture that had done little to soothe the anger of the Martian people, though Saqib felt in the long run it had been a good call.

Small steps add up, he thought.

He slowed to a stop with the others and looked down at the planet below. The outer ring of the station that led from the shuttle bays was designed with a wide window running the length of the ring. The view highlighted the beautiful red sands that the terraforming technology had preserved and the stunning blue of the Precioso Ocean ran along the western edge of Mars's major continent, Radona Marsa.

"She's a beauty, isn't she?" Opia asked, hitching a hip against the railing and looking down at the planet with a soft smile of her own.

"Were you born on Mars?"

"I was." She pointed to their left. "Just up over there, a little habitat off the Octavia E. Butler Landing site for the Perseverance rover four hundred years ago. Sort of our claim to fame given there is not much else there, even after terraforming. Lots of tourists liked to come see us, at least before the riots wrecked things."

Saqib frowned. There was a note of bitterness in the woman's voice, plus he'd never heard a Martian refer to the protests as riots. It was usually a clear indicator what side a person was on. He'd noticed Earth-born used it far more, while Martian-born people, like Commander D'Arcy Montaglione and Master Chief Emel Shevreaux, used the words and phrasing of Free Mars to a somewhat startling degree for CHN military members.

Saqib's knowledge on the subject was from both his Earth education and his activist mothers. They used to talk about how the victors wrote the histories and how carefully you had to interrogate those conclusions with other sources.

Obviously, some victories were good, some were bad, and some were more messy than people liked to contemplate.

Mars was messy.

Messy like learning to be an Interceptor after so many years buried within the structure of the academy. It had been fascinating to navigate his new team and the difference between what he'd known from the news versus working with them day in and day out. It was the same mix of projection and reality when you got right down to it.

The woman he was traveling with today was the perfect example. Max had made waves defying her famous family to join the NeoG, and though the press had talked a lot about her upbringing, it was clear that her time in the Interceptors had turned her into the leader she was today.

They also talked about her friendship with Jenks, but there was nothing like watching that dynamic in real time.

He took what he observed to heart and worked hard to not just react off assumptions. He knew, for instance, that Max wasn't just a by-product of her last name, but was instead more than aware that a whole other world existed from the one she'd grown up in. One where the lives of people who hadn't had the good luck to be born a Carmichael were a hell of a lot harder and sides weren't ever so clearly delineated.

Consider how she interacted with the rest of the crew. People like Jenks who'd grown up on the street and Nika who'd given up dancing because the NeoG would keep his family alive. People like Sapphi who'd had to overcome addiction. People like D'Arcy and Emel who'd ended up on opposite sides of the Mars conflict even though they'd grown up together. People like Chae who'd joined *Zuma* carrying a great burden. And people like Petty Officer Rona Nkosi, the other new member of their crew, who'd started off buried in an impressive amount of awe at the people on her team but seemed to have finally found her feet.

It's what Saqib strived for, even as his own upbringing had been safe and quiet comparatively, but filled with all the knowledge he was willing to cram into his head. *There's no easy answers*, he thought. *Only a lot of people trying hard to do the right thing.*

"Saqib?"

He blinked at Max. "Sorry, caught me wandering."

"Opia was just saying that the vice admiral is probably going to ping her any second, wondering if we got lost," Max said.

Opia laughed and held up a hand. "And there he is. No, sir. Sorry, we stopped so Commander Carmichael could take in the view. We'll be right there."

Max gestured and then followed the lieutenant to the lift. The station had actual elevators, in use before the low-grav tech for the travel tubes had been developed. They rode it up to the top, where the command deck and Vice Admiral Ford's office was located, pausing at the door to his office so Opia could press her palm to the door lock.

"I am looking forward to the security upgrades in the new station," she said.

"Jupiter was the same way. We've got some of the updated tech on Trappist-1d and it does make things easier," Max replied.

There the locks were keyed to everyone's DD chips, making the Intel headquarters all the more secure. The technology functioning the same as the palm readers, but with a unique series of rotating codes.

Lieutenant Nell Zika had gone over it all when the new locks had been installed, but as per usual, Saqib had only partially understood Sapphi's excited explanation. Computers remained an endless mystery to him, and he couldn't help but appreciate the simplicity of the security here.

"Maxine." Vice Admiral Jackson Ford smiled and opened his arms as they stepped through the opened door to his office. The lean man was more than twice Saqib's age, but with his LifeEx treatments his red hair was only starting to show bits of gray. His expression was bright and full of mischief. "Excuse me, *Commander* Carmichael."

"Hush." Max stepped into his hug with a laugh. "It's very good to see you, Jackson. I understand you know Lieutenant Commander Saqib Vahid."

"We are acquainted," Jackson said as he released Max and offered the same embrace to Saqib. "Though it's been a while."

"Vice Admiral." He greeted the man with a smile. Max had told him about her old academy instructor on the shuttle ride up and had been delighted to learn that Saqib's own time at the academy had overlapped Ford's slightly.

From what he'd gathered, the strategy professor hadn't cared she was a Carmichael, a refreshing change of pace for Max, Saqib was sure. He'd seen an unsure but brilliant (his words, not hers, Max was quick to point out) officer in training and had done his best to keep her head above water when all she wanted to do was sink in those early days. When they'd watched Max's first Boarding Games together in the faculty lounge, the now-vice admiral talked fondly about his former student and Saqib had been delighted to find out how much he undersold Maxine Carmichael.

Saqib knew Max held Ford in the same regard as retired Master Chief Ma Lěi, who'd filled an empty space for her when her own parents had all but abandoned her. That was something he still couldn't wrap his brain around. His mothers were extremely supportive, even if they weren't nearly as obvious about it as, say, Sapphi's wild family. So he'd never once had to worry about being dumped on the street just because of an argument.

That Max had gone through that to fulfill her dream of joining the NeoG made him respect her all the more.

"It's so good to see you again," Ford was saying. "I could barely believe it when Admiral Chen said she was sending the two of you. I've heard good things about your time with the Interceptors." His blue eyes sparkled with delight as he looked to Max. "And I always follow the careers of my students with great interest, but Max has done exceptionally well for herself. As I expected."

"Thanks to you."

"Not only me from the sound of it. How is your dangerous counterpart? Commander Vagin gave me quite a workout his first year in the academy."

Max laughed. "Did he now? You'll have to share those stories with me, I had no idea."

"He was, how do I say this politely, a handful."

Saqib couldn't stop the laugh, though he covered his mouth with his hand to muffle it as Max grinned slowly. The head of Intel's Smuggling Task Force was a deliberate and quiet leader, the complete opposite of his adoptive sister, Senior Chief Altandai Khan, and it was hard to imagine someone using the descriptor "a handful" on him.

Unless they were talking about in the sword ring. Saqib had thought his own skills were pretty good until he'd sparred with Nika the first time. In many ways the fact that he'd done so well in the Boarding Games was thanks to Nika's coaching.

Max rubbed her hands together. "I need you to tell us everything. To be honest I thought you were asking about his sister."

"She's trouble in her own right, but one of the best NCOs in the NeoG. Don't tell her I said that, though; she might start a bar fight just to prove me wrong." Jackson grinned back.

"In all fairness we haven't started a bar fight in years," Max countered.

This time Saqib was able to suppress the laugh, thinking of the extremely short brawl that had happened not even a week ago during the Games. They had *not* started that one, Navy had, but they'd certainly finished it.

"Why do I think that's only partially true?" Jackson asked.

"Years of experience?"

"Somehow I think you're making fun of my age, but I'll let it slide."

"Me?" Max asked. "Never."

Ford shook his head, laughing. "Jenks has rubbed off on you a bit too much, Commander." But there was definitely no rancor in his voice that Saqib could detect. The vice admiral continued, "The last of the Mars delegation is late, some sort of mechanical failure on the shuttle. So we've got some time. I'll have the lieutenant take you to your quarters so you can stow your gear and then bring you back. We'll have breakfast in half an hour?"

"Sounds great." Max hugged him once more. "It really is good to see you."

"Likewise." Jackson's eyes crinkled at the corners, and he waved a hand at the door. "Go get settled, and then you both can help me figure out how to get these two delegations to play nice during this ceremony and not ruin everything with their bickering."

"CHN SHUTTLE 310, THIS IS CHO SEO-YOON WITH MOS TRAFFIC control. We have you on the screen; please proceed to Shuttle Docking Bay Twelve."

"Thanks much, traffic control," Castle replied brightly. "Sorry for the delay, stupid mechanical mishaps."

"No worries, Vice Admiral Ford is aware of the issue. I'll let him know you're here and someone will escort you up."

Castle docked the shuttle and turned to Willis with a smile. "We're in."

"Not yet. Get me the security feed." He glanced over his shoulder at the others watching them silently. By his clock, the members of the delegations who were on station should be gathering on the command deck. "Ruiz, are you there?"

"Commander Carmichael and I are headed back to her quarters. Her companion stayed with Ford after the meal" came the reply over the com. Ruiz's voice was low, pitched to keep her target from hearing her, though the comment was vague enough to be easily explained if she was overheard.

"Good. Hold for my signal."

"I'm in the security feed. Looping. We've got five minutes until someone notices." Castle's voice was unusually smooth as she cut into the silence.

Willis pointed. "Ralka, Anton, take your team and clear the Shuttle Docking Bay now. Head for Main Coms."

They saluted and slipped from the ship.

Willis took a deep breath. "Attention, all strike teams—

ground and station. Carmichael is on the MOS. We will proceed with phase one of the plan on my go. You have your orders." He paused and his next words held no heat, only the sharp edge of a blade tempered by loss. "We bring justice to the orphans of war."

THERE HAD BEEN ALMOST NO ONE IN THE SHUTTLE DOCKING BAY because of the security for the handover, and the few people they'd run into had died without a fight. The corridor and stairwell up to the second level had been equally deserted, Castle's looping program covering their tracks. Ralka Usova looked around at her team, pleased at the lack of hesitation on any of their faces as she echoed Will's words and brought her fist to her heart. This was it—her chance for revenge, to hurt the people who'd taken almost everything from her. She felt Anton's hand on her other arm and looked up at her brother. "For the fallen and the forgotten," she whispered.

He echoed her with a nod.

"Mars Strike Team One, you are cleared to go," Will ordered.

"Roger that. We'll see you on the other side," Perez replied from down on Mars.

"MOS Strike Team Bravo, you are cleared to go." Simon and his team had come onto the station early, a risky proposition but the only way they could reach security on the command deck before an alarm was sent.

Ralka held her breath until Simon responded several moments later. "Security is ours. Moving to next target."

"MOS Strike Team Alpha, you are cleared to go."

Ralka moved for the door of the stairwell, the others

behind her as they swept down the empty corridor toward the coms office. The pair of Neos didn't realize they were there until it was too late. Ralka snapped the neck of the one on the left as Anton took the one on the right.

She shifted out of the way when the corpse slid from its chair and pulled the jammer from the pouch slung over Phanta's shoulder. "Strike Team Alpha, Main Coms secure. Moving to next target."

Will's voice came over the com. "Copy. All other strike teams—go. Repeat—go."

Ralka tapped Alex and Vadim on the shoulders as she passed them by. "You two, stay here. Hold this room."

"Yes, ma'am." Both men nodded sharply to her.

Ralka signaled to the rest of the team, and they moved out, weapons at the ready.

No one would stand in their way.

"DO YOU NEED ANYTHING ELSE, COMMANDER?" OPIA ASKED.

Max shook her head. "No, I'm fine. Please don't worry about me. I'm reasonably sure I can find my way back to Vice Admiral Ford's office on my own."

Saqib had stayed with Jackson after breakfast, ostensibly to keep talking about the way the handoff was going to work and the best way to smooth things over for the two delegations; but Max knew it was more to give her a little privacy so she could com Nika.

"I'll let you get sorted then. Just holler if you— Hello?"

She looked up at Opia's curious greeting and delight filled her face. "Pax! What are you doing here? Nobody told me you were coming."

"It's unofficial," her sister replied with a laugh, holding up her hands. "I knew you were going to be here, and we happened to be in the area so I thought we'd swing by." Pax gestured at the slender, black-haired person behind her.

"Kavan." Max smiled fondly at her sibling's partner. Pax had married their former bodyguard four years ago. Her defiance of their parents had caused almost as much of a fuss within the family as Max's now legendary standoff about the NeoG. "It's good to see you."

"Same," they replied with a dip of their head. "Congratulations on the win. I assume Jenks took the loss gracefully?"

"You know her," Max admitted with a laugh as she set her bag down on the nearby couch and pulled her sister into a hug. "She promised to beat my ass next time. I teased her about leveling the playing field. The usual. It is so good to see you."

"Same." Pax squeezed her hard. "I was—"

"Gun!"

Max grabbed for Pax and spun at Kavan's shout, deadly fléchettes hitting the spot where she and her sister been standing. She shoved Pax behind her, through the door of the bathroom. "Lock the door!"

Kavan tackled Opia and the pair went to floor. There was a muffled pop and swearing, followed by the spattering sound of more fléchettes slamming into the bulkhead. Max saw Opia roll sideways, gun still in her hand, and kicked at it as the lieutenant got to her feet. She only clipped the weapon, though, and Opia used the momentum to her advantage to line up a shot on Kavan, who was still struggling to get up.

Moving on instinct hammered into her from years of

fighting Jenks, Max grabbed Opia's gun hand before she could bring it around and twisted until she heard the bones crack. Opia cried out, but in Max's head Jenks's voice was loud, shouting at her to press forward, and she didn't let up. She drove the heel of her left hand into Opia's throat, and the smaller woman slammed back into the wall choking and gasping for air.

The alarms were blaring inside and out of her head, but Max forced herself to watch as the woman died.

"What the fuck is going on?" she murmured.

I just killed a fellow Neo. She was trying to kill us. The realization went to war in her head as Max stared down at the body.

"Kavan!" Pax's shout broke Max out of her daze.

"I'm all right. It just nicked me." They groaned. "Forgot how much getting shot hurts, though. Fuck. Max, are you okay?"

Before she could respond, Jackson came over the com, his voice calm and focused in her ear. "Max, Code Bravo. I can't raise Main Coms. Get over there and warn Ground Control. I'm sending you the station codes, lock it all down. Get to your shuttle and get your ass off this station."

"Jackson, Lieutenant Ruiz just attacked me. What is going on? Where are you?" Her heart thudded hard against her ribs. "Where's Saqib?"

"He's with me. So are the delegates. We're trying to hold the office. Ruiz?"

Max dragged in a breath. Trying to hold the office with seven civilians in the way was a recipe for disaster. "Dead. I'm coming to you."

"You get to Coms, then get off this station. That's an order, Carmichael." He grunted in pain and the com went dead.

There was no reply and Max cursed again as she turned. Code Bravo meant someone inside the station was trying to take over, and judging from what had happened, she couldn't even trust her fellow Neos except for Jackson and Saqib.

But she had to trust someone. Max hit her com, connecting to the shuttle on an encrypted channel, and hoped she wasn't making a mistake.

"Aggy, do you copy?"

"Max, what the fu— What is going on? My external coms just went to shit."

"I don't know. Code Bravo. I just got jumped by Lieutenant Ruiz; don't trust anyone." She swallowed. "I'm sending my sister and her partner to you. Get them off the station, Aggy, please."

To Aggy's credit, they didn't question or react to her orders. "Copy that. We'll wait for you, though."

"You'll do no such thing; that's an order, Petty Officer. You get out of here the moment you have my sister and the docking clamps are disengaged." Max looked up, trying to ignore her sister's tearstained face. "Kavan, can you run?"

They nodded grimly. "Code Bravo? Do we know who?"

"No. That's all Jackson said. Get my sister down to my shuttle. It's on the fourth level, bay eleven in Shuttle Docking. Don't take the lift; use the access stairs. I just sent Aggy a message to expect you. They'll get you off the station. Move fast; don't stop for anyone, even if they're NeoG." She sent them the coordinates as she pulled her sword free from her pack. The microsheath peeled away when her hand made contact with the hilt, revealing the matte black surface of the hooked blade.

"Max, come with us," Pax begged.

"I can't." She leaned over and pressed a kiss to her sister's temple. "You need to go. You're too valuable a hostage and I won't let them have you." She looked at Kavan. "I'm headed for Coms to warn Ground Control. Have Aggy try to make contact with Mars once you all are clear, too. They said there's some sort of interference on the external coms. I'll get to Flight Control to get the docking clamps disengaged. You keep her safe."

"You know I will." They nodded sharply to Max, then grabbed Opia's gun and slipped out the door, her sister following close behind. Max ran the opposite way down the corridor toward Main Coms, her heart pounding and her brain spinning. Even though she desperately wanted to race to the Command Deck and help Saqib and Jackson, she had to get the news out first.

Saint Ivan, I know Nika is the faithful one, but if I could beg a moment of your time to watch over my sister and Kavan? Watch over Saqib and Jackson. Give me the time to get to Coms and get everyone out safely. I would really appreciate it.

There was no way of knowing if the emptiness of the station was due to the now-aborted transfer ceremony or because of the attack, but Max didn't see a soul until she slid to a stop just outside the coms office and peeked around the edge.

Two large people in tactical gear rather than NeoG uniforms were facing the door, but they were thankfully looking at each other. No handshakes appeared in her vision.

She spotted a pair of bodies in the corner, dressed in NeoG blue, and fury surged.

There was a noise from the console, and both of the intruders turned toward it, giving her the opening she needed. Max moved before she even finished formulating the plan. She crossed the space from the doorway to the pair in three steps, driving her sword into the kidney of the one on the right and jerking it out through their side as the other person turned toward her in surprise. The tip of her sword sliced through flesh from collarbone to left ear in a vicious diagonal.

There was a moment of shock where their blue eyes met her brown ones and then the blood sprayed. Max turned her head to avoid the worst of it, spitting to clear her mouth of the copper tang as she scanned the office for any sign of other hostiles.

There were none, but the device plugged into the coms console obviously wasn't supposed to be there. Max reached down, yanked it loose, and crushed it under her bootheel. Then she slapped her hand down on the coms, queuing up both Mars Ground Control and the internal communication system simultaneously.

"This is Commander Maxine Carmichael. Code Bravo. Repeat. We have a Code Bravo. All personnel on the Mars Orbital Station, evac immediately. Repeat. Evac immediately. Unknown hostiles on board, command compromised. NeoG compromised. Ground Control, lock down. Repeat. Lock down." Max spat a curse when the coms went dead a second time and only the echo of her own voice came back at her.

She sprinted out the door, letting her brain deal with the issue of another jamming system somewhere on the station—Secondary Coms most likely? She had to make it to Flight Control, but first the Docking Bay, to get as many people loaded and locked safely on ships as she could. The stairwell access by the elevator was eerily quiet except for the slamming of her boots on the metal as she sped down the three flights to the Docking Bay.

Max slipped through the door, sword at the ready. The closer she got to the bay, the louder the screams were as people scrambled for ships regardless of who they belonged to. Several ships tore free from the docking clamps and Max swore. If someone punched through a stabilizing wall, the entire containment field for the bay would go down.

"Commander Carmichael!"

She couldn't stop the tightening of her hand around her sword at the sound of her name. The unfamiliar dockhand ran her way, but then they jerked and dropped to the deck. More screams bloomed along with the blood from a dozen fléchette wounds in their back, and Max ducked behind a pile of cargo as a voice echoed through the system.

"Honored guests! We will ask that all of you immediately lie down and put your hands on your heads. We want no further bloodshed, but do not force our hands. If you choose not to comply, you will be shot down."

Max stayed low as she scrambled back toward the door she'd come through, observing as the few people between her and her target followed the orders of the unknown voice. She slid through the door, straight into a surprised person holding an ugly-looking gun.

"Hold right there, little rabbit." Their grin morphed into surprise. "Well, well, well, if it isn't Carmichael—"

Max lunged forward with her sword, but her opponent twisted at the last moment and the edge of the blade only cut along their shirt, barely grazing their stomach instead of hitting something vital.

They hissed a curse, swinging the gun out, and a burst of pain shot through Max's head when it connected. She stumbled forward, avoiding the next punch out of luck more than skill, and spun, kicking out her leg in a move that had swept plenty of opponents in the cage.

They hit the floor and Max took off running.

Free Mars Hits NeoG; Civilians Killed
SEPTEMBER 17, 2411 (ESD)

Free Mars insurgents hit a group of Near-Earth Orbital Guard members doing reclamation work at Singing Brook, a farming community in the southern hemisphere section 133 near Chaimari habitat yesterday evening. Two people were killed and several wounded before the Neos were able to push back the attack and call in support from nearby Galileo Base.

Alexandar and Alina Usov had been working at Singing Brook for over a decade. The couple were well loved, and people gathered this morning to remember their lives and contributions to the community.

"Alex could coax anything up out of the ground," remembered Suni Risa. "We were working on a new version of red potatoes that he hoped would need less water and put less of a strain on habitats that have to bring water in to survive."

"Alina was a brilliant engineer who also had the most amazing sense of whimsy. I'm going to deeply miss listening to her delighted recounting of new designs. Mars—all of us, really—are poorer for her loss," said Roger Ulmori, head of Singing Brook's planning committee.

The Usovs leave behind two adult children who work and live on Earth. [*Read More*]

THREE

COMMANDER NIKA VAGIN SETTLED BACK IN THE BALCONY CHAIR, the warm cup of coffee in his hand steaming up into the morning air as he watched the sun rise over the Volga River. Sapphi, Chae, and Rona were all still asleep in the hotel room after a late night exploring the city of his birth. Nika had been both surprised and pleased they'd wanted to come with him. With Max and Saqib on the Mars Orbital Station and Jenks out in the wilds on a long overdue vacation with her family, he'd jumped at the chance to visit the place that had once been home, but he hadn't thought the others would join in.

It made him think they might actually like him. He laughed.

The funny thing was that home was now Trappist-1d, orange dirt and vistas that stretched for kilometers before disappearing below the horizon. So very different from

Ulyanovsk, a thriving city that survived the Collapse—much like London—despite its proximity to a major river.

He'd visited his grandmother's synagogue yesterday, because even though her faith wasn't his own, the place had always been a refuge. And wandering through the streets past their old house had dredged up a lot of memories. Including how a certain feisty teenager came into his life.

He'd never gotten Jenks to tell him the story of how she'd managed the almost two thousand–kilometer trek from Krasnodar to here, where a chance run-in with his grandmother had twisted their lives together irrevocably.

Nika laughed again, remembering their first meeting. Jenks had nearly taken his head off with a cast-iron pan before she'd realized who he was.

Once she had, she'd stuck to him like a burr, and even though he'd grown up an only child, Nika found he didn't mind having a not-so-little sister suddenly in his life.

Despite all the headaches.

Moving to Trappist the first time without her had been harder than he'd thought, though he'd kept so much of it to himself because he'd known Jenks was struggling. Coming back to the crew had been like coming home, despite his attempts to fuck it all up.

Their newest transition had been the easiest by far. When the Intelligence headquarters at Trappist had continued to grow as the habitats expanded, Stephan's infamous patience had finally run out. A little over two years ago, just after the Games, he'd stopped hinting and outright told Nika that he wanted him running the Smuggling Task Force before the year was out so he could focus his attention on a broader scope for the system.

And as much as Nika had loved his job, the idea of taking on a new challenge was appealing. So he'd agreed.

Max's promotion had seemed a logical step, and not too much of a stretch despite her shorter time in service. Tamago had fussed about the orders to officer candidate school, but had caved when everyone—surprisingly, Jenks included—insisted it was the best thing for them to do.

"I'll beat your ass black and blue until you can actually give me orders to stop," he believed his sister had said to Tamago. Though she'd probably been joking, the threat had worked. Nika missed them. He still saw most of his old Interceptor crew on a near daily basis, but Tamago had been too busy with work to even make the Games for a visit and there was no telling when they'd be able to meet up again.

Things changed. Life went on.

Even the new crew members who'd joined *Zuma's Ghost* had settled in stunningly well. Petty Officer Third Class Rona Nkosi had a deadpan sense of humor that had finally made an appearance once she got over her hero worship. And Lieutenant Commander Saqib Vahid's quiet presence was a fascinating complement to Max's, to the point of making people emphasize the ghost portion of the Interceptor crew's name even more.

Thoughts of Max brought a smile to his face, as they always did. Almost a full decade in her presence and he still couldn't believe it. How lucky he was. How his life had shifted so smoothly into her orbit.

He laughed softly, shaking his head. If someone had popped into Hoboins's office ten years ago and told him that his wild, streetwise sister would end up best friends with the brand-new, nervous as anything lieutenant who'd just saluted him, he'd have said they were full of shit.

Of course, he'd also never have guessed that he'd fall in love with that same lieutenant but here they were. Ten years later and still going strong, despite the job, despite his fuckups early on. They hadn't talked about anything formal, not since her mother's disastrous and dismissive comment about it a handful of years ago, but he wanted to. And avoidance aside, he was pretty sure she wanted to have that talk as much as he did.

"That is by far the sappiest expression I've ever seen on your face." Lieutenant Nell "Sapphi" Zika dropped into the seat next to him with a teasing look.

"Do you want me to tell Jenks you need an anime character nickname to go with that haircut? Because I will."

Sapphi rubbed a hand over the shorn side of her scalp and then flicked the straight-edged longer brown strands over her shoulder with a sniff. "You could try, but she went with Sapphi two seconds after we met and I doubt she'll ever give it up. Plus she's gotten soft since the kids."

"I'm so going to tell her you said that."

"Like I haven't already? You think I'm scared of her?" He quirked his eyebrow, and she had the presence to look a bit abashed before saying, "Maybe a little. Besides, we all know it's true that she's losing those jagged edges. Yes, she's still as deadly as a straight razor, but you won't get those incidental nicks along the way." She pointed both index fingers in his direction. "*Any*way . . . nice deflection attempt. What put that smile on your face?"

"I do like your new hair," he said, and Sapphi beamed at him, though she twirled a hand for him to continue. "I was thinking about Max. Remembering the first time we met? She saluted me and Rosa right there in Hoboins's office."

"She did *not*. How have I never heard this?"

"It just never came up, I guess."

"She was so different when she first got here." Sapphi shook her head. "I liked her then, but I was more worried about what Jenks was gonna do. You, though—you were sunk from the get-go, huh?"

"I don't know what you're talking about."

"Then why are you blushing?"

"I'm not!"

"Fine, you're not. But you *did* ask Tama to look shit about Max up for you," she singsonged at him, and then stuck her tongue out. "I miss you, Nik."

"Why do you say that?"

"Because I do? We're still working together, sure, but it's not quite the same. I knew things would change; it just feels weird sometimes. Not having you there on the daily out in the black." Sapphi looked away from him and out into the city with a soft sigh. "Like being without Tama. I knew they had to go, could feel it like a storm brewing. It was the best thing for them and their career. For us, too—the NeoG. They were too prone to just doing the job and pushing the rest of us to the front of things. Which isn't wrong, I guess, I just always wanted more for them."

"We can't grow when we're stuck in the same old patterns and roles," he said.

Sapphi nodded in agreement. "Exactly. Though I'm still a little surprised you didn't force your sister to OCS along with Tamago."

"Jenks never would have agreed to it," Nika replied with

a shake of his head. "I knew I could sucker Tama into saying yes, though."

"Tama loves and hates you in equal measure for it, believe me. They're doing great, by the way. Oh, and said they were sorry to miss us at the Games." She laughed. "No pressure, but are you gonna ask Max to marry you anytime soon?"

"Where's that coming from?"

"A decade of you pining and that silly look on your face?"

He couldn't argue with that. "What's the betting pool at?" he teased.

"I have absolutely no idea what you're talking about." Sapphi sniffed, even as he watched her doing some mental calculations—probably compounding whatever interest was accruing. "You two are good together; you remind me of my mom and dads."

"Now that's a compliment. You're going to make me cry, LT."

She snorted and leaned into his offered embrace. "Gonna make myself cry. What I really want is for you to make Max cry, so then we can all get drunk and teary at whatever parties happen. Even Jenks."

"Now that would be a sight to see," Nika replied. "The tears part—we've all witnessed the drunk part."

"Jenks cries, you know," Sapphi said softly.

"I do. I tease her about it, but of course she cries—her heart is bigger than all of ours."

They sat there together, happy to remember their companions. Happy to *be* companions. Nika patted her shoulder. "Let's roust Chae and Rona out of bed and I'll take you all over to my favorite breakfast place."

"Ooo, you know I'll never turn down food." Sapphi bounced to her feet and headed inside.

Nika got to his feet to follow, pausing when his DD pinged. "Vagin."

"Nika, it's Admiral Chen."

He frowned. "Good morning, Admiral. What can I do for you?"

"Approximately half an hour ago an unknown hostile force took over the MOS. Commander Carmichael got the Code Bravo out to Mars Ground Control before the coms went dead."

Fear gripped his heart in a vise, squeezing the air from his chest with brutal force.

Saint Ivan, watch over her. Please.

"I am enacting SSOP-47; we will follow all steps. A shuttle's on its way for you—it'll take you to your ship."

Not my ship, it's Max's ship.

Stolen Sun Operational Protocol was the CHN's plan for dealing with a takeover of a station. Given the nature of the liquid metallic hydrogen engines for most of the earlier stations, they were, effectively, large explosive devices. Blowing them up in orbit was dangerous enough. Crashing them into the planet they were orbiting was worse if the station in question was orbiting a rocky planet like Mars.

"I've already contacted Commander Montaglione; he hadn't left Earth yet. He will retrieve Senior Chief Khan and meet you at Serrano Base on Mars."

"Yes, Admiral." His feelings slipped free for a second, the words following after. "Is Max alive? What about Saqib?"

Her voice gentled from its usual no-nonsense tone. "I

wish I had an answer for you, Nika, but I don't. We haven't heard anything from the attackers. I'll send you the recording from Ground Control and what little information we have. I'm putting you in charge on the ground. Captain Fábia Clark will be informed of your arrival, and I'll be in touch with Stephan as soon as we can secure a link to Trappist."

"Understood, Admiral."

"I'll speak to you again soon."

He disconnected the com and strode back into the hotel room. The two petty officers' bleary greetings snapped off the second they got a look at his face.

"Pack your gear," he said, not slowing on his path to his room. "There's been an attack on the MOS."

They moved on pure instinct and training, and less than ten minutes later his crew was on the landing pad boarding the shuttle.

Saint Ivan, he intoned again, *keep everyone safe. Keep my crew safe.*

Because it didn't matter how many years passed, they would always be his crew.

They were greeted on the shuttle with the news that several ships had attempted to escape from the station and had been shot by the station defenses in the moments just after the attack.

Sapphi whispered a prayer to one of her gods, and Chae pressed both hands to their mouth, blinking furious tears away. Rona looked like she was fighting off shock. None of them were going to say out loud the fear that Max and Saqib had been on one of those ships.

Or the equally terrible possibility they were at the mercy of whoever had attacked.

We'll find out. We'll get them back.

And God help anyone who gets in our way.

MUSIC BLARED THROUGH THE EARLY MORNING AIR OF THE GYM, accompanied by the crashing sounds of swords, laughter, and the occasional swear from one of the two combatants dancing around each other in the ring.

"Come on, Jun! I wanted a workout this morning." Lieutenant Uchida Tamashini avoided the other Neo's thrust with a slight pivot of their body. Metal scraped along metal, and they dropped their sword just enough to catch Jun's blade with the wicked hook that curved back from the tip.

From there it was a simple matter to lift Jun's sword and tap her twice in the face with their left hand. In a real fight it would have been a punch to the throat or nose, but Tamago was trying to be nice.

"God, I yield, Tama." Lieutenant Jun Parker tipped her head back, short black hair falling from her face as she sighed in frustration. "That's three times. How? How are you doing that?"

Tamago laughed. "I can't even count the number of times Nika pulled that move off on me. You'll get it. It's just going to take some practice."

"Comes waltzing in here having trained with four of the best sword fighters in the NeoG and acts like I can pick it up no problem. I am not as good as you."

"That's not the point and you know it." Tama tapped Jun on the butt with the flat of their sword. "Believe me, I know the feeling. You just keep working at it and you get better; that's all you can do."

"Yeah, well, of the two of us only one will ever be a Boarding Games champion." Jun made a face. "That was rude, I'm sorry."

"You're fine. You could apply for the Interceptor course, you know?"

"I know. Would I be any good at it?"

"Yes." Tamago headed for the bench to grab a towel before their friend could see the emotions they couldn't quite keep under wraps. Missing the Games the last two years had hurt more than they'd anticipated, and the unpredictable schedule at the base in Kyiv had meant they couldn't even take the time off to go see their friends and former crewmates compete.

Tamago didn't regret the choice they'd made when Nika had offered to sponsor them for an OCS slot. Even if Jenks had needed to threaten them a bit to make them do it. They'd known it was a good career move, especially because the very idea had scared the shit out of them to contemplate it.

They'd loved their time as an Interceptor. Their time with *Zuma's Ghost*, but they also knew they'd been coasting, content to hang back in the shadows of their brighter starred companions.

"You can do more, Tama. I'm not judging if you don't want to, I just want to give you the opportunity if you do."

They suspected Max had had a hand in it all. She was too good at seeing all the angles of things and too aware of her own crew's health and well-being to let Tamago get away with settling because they'd been too afraid to make the jump on their own.

The friends they'd made at OCS and during the eight

months of intensive negotiation training after were all wonderful people, and Tamago enjoyed spending time with their new coworkers.

They missed everyone on Trappist, though, like a constant sharp pain in the chest.

"Parker! Uchida!" Kenta's voice rang out over the music, and they shared a look with Jun as Captain Hosaka waved at both of them from the doorway of the gym. "Get cleaned up. Grab your bag," he said as he joined them. "We're heading out in fifteen."

"What is it?" Tamago asked and the expression that crossed Kenta's face made their heart race.

He looked over his shoulder, dropped his voice. "Code Bravo on the MOS from Commander Carmichael before the coms went down. Several fleeing ships were shot by the station defenses before they could get clear. I don't have more than that. Get moving."

Tamago didn't have to be told again.

"PRESS DOWN." SAQIB DIRECTED JACKSON'S HANDS TO THE wound in his side, the cloth napkin quickly turning red with blood. He dragged in a breath and pushed to his feet, keeping his hands visible when the eyes and guns in the room swung their way. "He needs to go to medical. I can't stop the bleeding here."

"Maybe he should have thought of that before he killed Harvey. Sit your ass back down, NeoG, before you're bleeding, too." The shorter of the pair gestured menacingly with their gun, and Saqib tamped down the urge to jerk it out of their hands and hit them with it.

The seven civilians huddled by the opposite wall stayed his hand.

"Charlie, manners," came a voice from the doorway. Like the others, they didn't have an active handshake.

They were tall, broad across the shoulders, with short-cut blond hair easing into gray. They walked into the room with the easy rolling steps of someone who grew up in a low-gravity environment. Every nerve ending in Saqib's body fired off in warning. Whatever else happened, this person was dangerous.

"Lieutenant Commander Vahid. A pleasure."

"Not really." It was probably unwise to mouth off, but the words slipped free anyway. "Who are you?"

"Will, he/him. Free Mars," the man replied with a slow smile. "Your commander will be joining us shortly."

No, she fucking won't, Saqib thought. He'd heard Jackson's order, and the vice admiral had whispered through gritted teeth that Max had escaped their attack.

"I need better facilities to treat Vice Admiral Ford," he said carefully, keeping his voice low and calm. Exactly what they'd learned in the academy's negotiation training all those years ago. Low and easy to keep the person on the opposite side of the engagement at ease. "Whatever you want, killing the vice admiral won't help you get it. Let me help him and I can help you, too."

Will smiled slowly as he pulled the knife free from the sheath on his belt and flipped it between his fingers. "You want to negotiate, Neo? Convince your vice admiral there to give me the command codes for the station." His look sharpened as he reached out and touched the underside of Saqib's chin with the point. "Or I cut your throat."

Saqib stilled. He knew nothing about this man, hadn't yet had the time to figure out if he was reckless or thoughtful, if he had a plan or was just fueled by rage. He didn't know if the threat was real or just bluster.

The knife in his hand, however, was very, very real.

"It won't do you any good," Ford said, his voice thready. "I surrendered the codes to Carmichael. You missed your shot with her. She'll lock the station down and then she'll be out of your reach."

Will didn't look away from Saqib, so he focused on holding the man's gaze and keeping his face expressionless. The knife point wasn't pressing, but he knew how little force it would take to split the skin.

I really don't want to die today. The ridiculous thought that at least he'd kissed his mothers when he'd seen them at the Games filtered through his head.

"Ralka, report." Will tipped his head. "That appears to be the truth," he said, pulling the knife away and slipping it back into the sheath with a flourish. "Charlie, take these two to the medical bay. Lieutenant Commander Vahid is allowed to patch the vice admiral up and administer whatever medications are needed. Then bring them both back here."

Saqib moved to help Ford up, but Will caught him by the upper arm.

"A word of caution, Neo: don't take advantage of my kindness. The people in the docking bays and in here are the ones who will pay if you choose to be reckless."

"Jenks is the reckless one." The comment slipped out before he could stop himself.

Will's grin was wicked. "So she is. Good thing for us

she's on vacation and out of contact." He gave him a shove in Ford's direction. "Go on."

SYLVIA MOROZ, THE LEADER OF FREE MARS, HAD SURVIVED FOR seventy some years simply because she always expected things to go to shit. Still, when an old friend pulls a gun on you, there's bound to be some surprise.

This time it almost cost her.

"The NeoG sends its regards," Carlo Perez said, leveling the gun at her face.

Thankfully her head of security was even less trusting than she was, and it saved her life. Clair kicked the gun at the ceiling, shoving Sylvia to the floor as they threw themself at Perez with a shout of "Traitor!"

Chaos reigned for what felt like an eternity as several other people opened fire, though from her vantage point, Sylvia couldn't tell whose side they were on. Screams echoed through the room as her people fought off the unexpected attack.

Why now? Why would the NeoG do something so foolish?

Silence fell, Sylvia's rapid heartbeat pounding in her ears until it was broken by the cries of the wounded and echoing calls about targets neutralized. She dug in her pocket for her inhaler, the familiar pain lancing through her lungs with her too-quick breaths.

Sylvia gave herself the moment, knowing the medication would ease the scarring like it always did. First hit and the pain faded, second and it no longer felt like she was underwater.

Sylvia scrambled around the overturned table to where Clair had a still-alive Perez by the shirtfront.

"Talk to me, traitor! Why throw your lot in with the NeoG? Why now?"

"We'll have our justice for the orphans of war," Perez wheezed, blood trickling from the corner of his mouth. "All of you are complicit and all of you will burn." He dragged in another breath, but it slipped back out of lungs that no longer had orders to hold air. His eyes went blank, and Clair dropped the body back to the floor.

"Bastard Neos!" Clair shoved to their feet. "Are you hurt?"

"I'm fine." Sylvia lifted a hand. "I refuse to believe this was the NeoG."

"Your refusal makes no difference to the facts." Clair spit the words. "You heard him the same as I did."

"Fuck," Sylvia muttered. Grief and fury tangled together in her chest as she rubbed a bloody hand over her face. "What the fuck is this?"

Clair was right, and yet it was too easy. Too easy to give herself back to the hatred. They were right on the edge of peace and a path to a free Mars. Maybe not the one she'd envisioned originally but a path all the same.

What could the NeoG hope to get out of this kind of treachery? She couldn't believe the CHN had authorized it, and even if they had, there would be no proof.

The NeoG has created just as many orphans as we have.

"Sylvia!" Maria Ortega rushed through the door. The panic on the tall trans woman's narrow face at the carnage eased only slightly when she spotted Sylvia alive and unharmed. "Someone's taken over the MOS."

A frozen fist gripped her heart, and Sylvia could only stare at her for a minute, praying she'd misheard. "Who?"

Sylvia's DD pinged with the incoming message, and her

breath caught in her lungs again, freezing to ice at the sight of her own face staring back at her.

"Mars will be free. No matter the cost."

It was her voice. Her face.

It was her. But she'd never said those words; she'd always cared about the cost. About the people on the ground. Either way, she certainly wasn't saying them now.

"Fuck."

Maria tipped her head in agreement with the curse. "They issued that broadcast just before they went dark," she said.

Sylvia couldn't say where the sudden, cold certainty came from beyond all the years spent listening to her instincts and navigating the treacherous political landscape of a planet that needed its neighbor to survive, but wanted to be free.

"Something else is happening here. This was not the NeoG." She snapped a hand up before Clair and others could protest, and they fell into silence. "No more than we are responsible for what's going on up on the MOS. Don't you all see? Someone is trying to start a war here. They are trying to play us off each other. Perez had no reason to say that about the NeoG except he knew someone would overhear him. If he'd been successful in killing me, you all wouldn't have hesitated to blame them and the CHN for this. No, the timing is too convenient." She looked around. "And I don't know about you, but I am not willing to give up this dream all of us have worked so hard for, just so someone else can use us for *their* ends!"

A cheer went up from the assembled crowd. Clair put their fist in the air. "We follow you to the end of this. For the dream of a free Mars. Let no one stand in our way."

"Let no one stand in our way," Sylvia replied, thrusting her own fist into the air. She looked around at the bodies, her heart thudding painfully in her chest and her brain already grappling for a way to get out of the path of this meteor that was about to slam down on them.

"Nice speech," Maria murmured.

"Useless if we don't get on the air to refute this," Sylvia said. "They'll bury us if they think we're responsible for attacking the station. Have you heard from our contact?"

"Yes." Maria looked around. "Not here."

Sylvia resisted the urge to press. Even though she wanted to know. Free Mars was finished if anyone decided they were to blame for the attack, and there were far too many people out there who would gladly point the finger at her no matter how much she screamed they weren't responsible. Perez's final words teased at the corner of her memory, something just out of reach that slid farther away the more she tried to get a grip on it.

"Clair, lock the building down. Find out anything you can about who was involved. I want a comprehensive list as soon as possible and have your team start looking for signal patterns in the meantime."

They nodded sharply, understanding the meaning Sylvia hadn't been able to say out loud, probably because they were thinking it already. There might be others who hadn't attacked but had waited to see who came out on top. She wanted to know who she could trust.

Right now, that list was incredibly short.

"Maria, with me."

"Mikhail, go with Sylvia," Clair ordered, and the big man nodded, moving in front of them as they left the room.

It chafed but Sylvia didn't object. She would have to endure her people being overly protective for the next several months.

If she survived this.

"Any word from the NeoG? Or the CHN?"

Maria shook her head and then leaned in, her voice low. "Silence at the moment. I'm sure they're scrambling. Commander Carmichael was on station for the handoff, Syl. Our contact said she issued the Code Bravo to Ground Control just after the message was released. Said the NeoG was compromised. I don't have a status, can't get in touch with our operative on the station. The whole coms system went dark with the lockdown, and obviously our person at Ground Control is busy."

Fuck. She held in the curse, but only barely. The NeoG's darling, a fucking Carmichael, a potential hostage. Despite all the friction with her powerful family, Max Carmichael was a high-value target and Free Mars would get burned to the ground if she was killed—if not by the military, then by whatever private forces the Carmichaels could muster . . . which was probably quite considerable.

"They want to hurt both of us—that's one way to do it." Sylvia allowed herself a curse this time as she reshuffled priorities and then nodded. "Okay, public disavowal first, then we need to get in contact with Patricia Carmichael if we can. Quietly." She could only hope the former CHN senator was willing to still talk to her. Patricia had never seemed like the sort to let emotions overrule common sense, but with her sister in danger it was hard to know what the reaction would be.

"You really think the NeoG wasn't involved, Syl?"

"What sense does it make, Maria? The CHN has been moving toward peace both officially and under the table for the last several years. Why risk all that for a chance to kill me?"

"You are the leader of Free Mars."

Sylvia snorted. "I will not be the leader of *Mars*, though. Killing me only serves to perpetuate the violence. Think, Maria! Who stands to benefit if we are at each other's throats? I think Admiral Chen wants peace as much as we do. Furthermore, I think she would never authorize such a thing. Assassination is not her style."

"There are more people in charge than just Admiral Chen." Maria looked away, her mouth a hard line. Then she sighed. "But fine, say you're right. If we're doing unorthodox shit here, then it might be worth it to contact D'Arcy. At least to start. He could get in touch with someone at NeoG who'd listen to us. That is, if he's still in system?"

Sylvia dragged in a breath. She was surprised at the pain hearing that name caused, even more surprised that Maria would suggest him.

Unorthodox, indeed. Desperate times, I suppose, she thought with a choked laugh.

"All right," she said. "You see if you can reach him. Tell him I want to talk. Don't tell him about what Perez said, though—I want to look him in the face when I say it."

Maria nodded sharply and walked away. Sylvia watched her go and then patted Mikhail on the shoulder. "I guess you're with me."

"Always," he replied, and for some reason his grim smile eased the hammering of her heart.

AS FAR AS D'ARCY WAS CONCERNED, HELL WAS KNOWING YOUR friends were in trouble and being too far away to help. That thought and the relentless silent prayer to Allah, whom he hadn't acknowledged in far too long, for Max's safety, were bouncing around in his head as *Dread Treasure* sped through the upper atmosphere of Earth toward the remote spot where Jenks and her family were camping.

The elation of their Games triumph was gone, washed aside by the news about the MOS and the rising fear with each report of ships being shot out of the black in the space around the station. It was yet another reminder that although the Boarding Games seemed like the most important thing, it was really designed to hone the military branches so they could react to the real mission.

It did not get realer than this.

The perpetrators—Sylvia, damn her—had only issued a brief statement: *"Mars will be free. No matter the cost."*

An ominous message, even if one of the people he considered important in his life wasn't at risk.

He didn't know what the fuck Free Mars was thinking. The handoff was finally pushing things closer to independence than Mars had ever been. It wouldn't look exactly like what Sylvia had wanted, but wasn't that the point of agreements like this? Everyone walked away at least a little unhappy about the compromises, but in the end, it was better for them all.

Either way, it was a terrible choice on the part of Free Mars to actively attack something that was accomplishing that goal.

If he'd had a way to get in touch with them, he'd have said so to Sylvia's face.

"That's weird."

D'Arcy looked over at Lieutenant Commander Chaske Landon. It wasn't fair that his brain still expected to see Steve Locke over there even after the man had been promoted to an Interceptor crew of his own more than two years ago. All in all, D'Arcy liked the steady and unpredictably funny new pilot. But it was never easy to see family grow up and move out. "You know I don't like weird under good circumstances. Now is even worse."

Chaske chuckled darkly. "Me either. I'm getting a coms request on an encrypted channel. But it's not CHN. Coming from Mars."

"Put it through." D'Arcy crossed his arms over his chest and kept the curiosity hidden when an old familiar face appeared on the console. "Well, this is an interesting development. I was just thinking of you. Hello, Maria." His smile wasn't quite a baring of teeth, but it was close. "Knock over any space stations lately?"

"It's not us. It's a fake. Free Mars is not responsible for this attack." The words were said in a breathless rush that was very unlike her.

"Sure fucking looked and sounded like Sylvia."

"It was a fake, D'Arcy. I swear."

"I am not sure what makes you think that I'll just believe your word, but go on."

"Someone tried to kill Sylvia. Not twenty minutes ago. We are on the ground, not up on the MOS." She panned the camera around so he could see the landscape behind her.

Shit.

He heard Chaske's muffled curse, which was thankfully too faint for Maria to pick up, and kept his own face expressionless.

"Is she alive?" He didn't want to think about the chaos that the death of the leader of Free Mars would bring down into this mess. Bad enough if there was a fake message floating around, but if the whole of Free Mars lost their leadership at a time like this, it would be disastrous.

"Yes. She's broadcasting a denial now. This isn't us, I swear; it's not anything we've sanctioned. One of the people who attacked us said they would have their justice for the orphans of war. That all of us are complicit and all of us will burn. Sylvia wants to meet with you, in person. She says we need to work together against whoever is trying to kill our chance for peace."

D'Arcy hummed. "She's willing to turn herself in?"

Maria snarled at him and this time he did bare his teeth in reply.

"She's willing to *meet* with you."

"You going to be there? I'm reasonably sure you said the next time we were in the same room you'd kill me. That's not much incentive for me to agree to a meeting, if I had that kind of authorization to negotiate with you and even if Free Mars hadn't just taken over the MOS." He probably shouldn't be needling her, but he'd never been very good at resisting that where Maria was concerned.

If he was being honest with himself, he was pretty much a free-opportunity needler.

Focusing back on the matter at hand, he could see the logic of someone setting the NeoG and Free Mars at each other's throats to cause as much chaos as possible. But he knew all too well that poking at Maria was a good way to crack that stone composure, and he wanted to know anything else she might be holding back.

"I just told you, it wasn't us!"

"So you say. Again, even if I believed you, you think the CHN is going to take your word without some proof?" He stared at her. "And as amusing as it is that you think so, I am not in charge around here."

"We're offering to work with the NeoG, not the CHN."

"Putting aside the strangeness of *that*." D'Arcy's laugh was humorless. "We're the same thing, Maria, remember?"

She glared as he threw her last words at him back in her face, then visibly gathered her composure. "D'Arcy, Sylvia is offering to speak with you. I would think that counts for something."

He shrugged, old hurt bubbling up to the surface. "It counts for about as much as it always did after she hung me out to dry. Unfortunately for you, I've got friends in danger and not a lot of time for bullshit. Goodbye, Maria."

"Wait!" She held a hand out, muttered a vicious curse his Babel mangled in translation, but he'd heard it too many times before to not laugh at. Maria glared. "Damn you, D'Arcy. We have someone on the MOS. I don't know if they're even alive now. We've lost contact. I don't know if Commander Carmichael is still alive after issuing the Code Bravo, but if she is, she's going to need help up there. If you can make contact with the station, she'll at least have an ally."

There it was. Most of it. She was still hiding something.

D'Arcy stared at Maria for a long moment. If they did have an operative on the MOS, it would be in that person's best interests to help Max anyway. Never mind that with the coms blacked out, there was no way to get an order to them on Maria's end. D'Arcy wondered if she realized that she'd also revealed they had someone in Mars/NeoG Ground Control because the pool of people who knew that Max had been the one to issue the Code Bravo was very small.

Sloppy work from Mars Intel. He couldn't help the thought. Not after all these years of working with Stephan and all the lessons the man had hammered into his brain.

"D'Arcy, please." Maria had mistaken his silence for hesitation and the begging was surprising. "This wasn't us. We don't want a war, not when we're standing on the verge of peace."

"I hope you mean that. I'll talk to Commander Vagin. I can't promise anything; meeting with Sylvia is a decision beyond my pay grade, but I'll be in touch."

Maria nodded sharply. "I'll send you my contact information." She closed her brown eyes for a moment and then surprised him a second time. "Thank you, D'Arcy. I mean it. And . . . it's nice to see you again."

He swallowed the hundred pithy responses and just nodded back at her before he shut down the com.

"Never thought I'd see that," Chaske murmured.

"Tell me about it." D'Arcy blew out a breath and rubbed a hand over his face. "Let's go get Jenks and see if we can stop a war."

Whether Free Mars was responsible or not, someone out there wanted to put a spark to an O_2 tank and light this whole place up.

He wasn't about to let his friends and innocent civilians get caught in that explosion.

FOUR

JENKS LEANED AGAINST TIVO WITH A SIGH. LUIS WAS ON THE FAR edge of the camp, holding Anna up so they could touch the spiky needles of the pine trees that encircled their spot. Jenks couldn't make out the words passing between them, but the higher pitch of their child mixed with Luis's lower baritone made her heart do a delighted shimmy in her chest.

Their child. Was that ever going to not hit her with a wild mix of utter love and absolute terror?

Closer to Tivo and her, the three older kids fought to get their tent set up.

At the moment, it was a fight they were losing.

"They're going to need help," he whispered with a choked laugh when the entire thing collapsed on top of Riz. Gales of laughter and rapid-fire conversation between the trio followed.

"If they ask, it's good problem solving for them," she replied. He squeezed his arms around her and leaned down to press a kiss to the side of her head. "What's that for?"

"Do I need a reason?"

"I'm the only one around here who does things for no reason."

Tivo laughed. "You've got me there. I was just thinking about how you're really good at this parenting thing. I know you were worried about it, so I thought you should know it's nice to see how you've settled."

You could stick her head out an airlock and she'd never admit just how much that sort of praise meant to her. Tivo and Luis had both come from stable, loving households, and early on Jenks had felt like there wasn't anything she could offer to this little family that had—mostly unexpectedly—formed around her.

And yet the twins looked to her for . . . well, nearly everything, same as their fathers. They asked her advice. *Shit*, they listened to her advice sometimes. They followed her example.

It was wild.

As for the other two, Jenks felt a swell of emotion grip her heart the same way it had over a year ago when she'd spotted the pair of kids with black, curly hair holding hands in the entryway of the very orphanage she'd run from as a teen. They'd watched her carefully with solemn eyes, but when she'd sat on the floor to say hi, Anna had crawled right into her lap and wrapped their arms around her neck. Sergi had hovered nearby, his brilliant green eyes wide with curiosity and fear; but when she'd offered him a hand, he'd taken it.

Sergei and Anna's parents hadn't abandoned them like

hers had, but their deaths and the lack of any other family meant the kids had ended up in the same place she had—as wards of the CHN.

She knew all too well how lucky she'd gotten finding the Vagins, but the last thing she'd expected was the sudden, sharp desire to offer that same safe haven to the pair of children in her embrace.

There was little she could do beyond nervously bringing up the subject of adopting them to Luis and Tivo, then to the twins. Everyone had been on board with the idea, and she still wasn't sure why she'd been nervous at all.

"Your survival instinct was formed around trauma, Altandai. It's protecting you by expecting something to go wrong. Anticipating it means you think you can prevent it. Which isn't entirely untrue; sometimes that gut instinct helps. You've seen that in action. But that expectation doesn't ever really go away. When it feels unreasonable, all you can do is try to remind it where you are now. Safe and loved."

Jenks supposed that was the whole point of her therapist, but sometimes she really hated how close to home the woman struck with so few words.

"Pocket?" Tivo's voice dragged her out of her head, and his gorgeous blue-gray eyes were studying her with barely concealed worry.

"Sorry, what?"

"I lost you there. Okay?"

Jenks turned her head as she reached up and hooked a hand around his neck to pull him down for a kiss. "I'm more than okay," she replied when they separated. "You didn't lose me—you let me lose myself, and it's an amazing feeling. Have I told you thank you lately?"

"For what?"

"For not being an evil jerk. Navy though you are. Ack!" She squawked when he hauled her into the air. Jenks twisted and wrapped her legs around his waist, laughter spilling into the air.

"There are children present, you two!" Elliot called, sounding so much like his birth father that Jenks only laughed harder, clinging to Tivo's neck.

"I love you," Tivo murmured in her ear and Jenks tightened her grip. "Thanks for letting me into your life."

"I love you, too. Thanks for sticking around after I kicked your ass."

"Wouldn't have missed it for the world." He set her back down. "Let's go at least offer to help these kids before this tent eats them."

Jenks resolutely ignored the little voice in her head insisting this wouldn't last and instead focused on the joy in her chest as she took Tivo's offered hand and followed him over to the kids.

"MAX?"

"I'm here, Aggy." The words were thick in her throat. "Did they make it?"

"Yeah, but they're shooting down ships out there. I think it's best to hang tight."

Her stomach twisted. "Agreed. I've got a plan. I'll let you know when it's safe."

"For the record I disagree with your plan if it still includes you not getting your ass on this shuttle," they replied.

"Noted. Sorry, still going to do it. You can lodge a complaint with the admiralty when this is all over." Max took several deep breaths, trying to slow her racing heart as she moved swiftly down the corridor toward Flight Control on the third level of the station. She hadn't seen anyone else since the Docking Bay, the stairwells silent, but the relentless quiet made her grip her sword hilt so tightly it hurt her hand.

Loosen your fingers, Max. Nika's voice was soft in her head. *First time someone takes a swing you're going to lose your weapon.*

She took another breath and swapped the sword into her other hand, shaking out her right for a moment.

There was no sound from the Flight Control office, and she peeked around the corner into the still room. Two large people, dressed like the ones she'd taken down in coms, lay on the floor in a sticky pool of blood.

A third person in the civilian uniform of the MOS was draped over the console, and Max carefully reached a hand out to move them so she could get to the docking clamp controls. She swore and jerked away when the body came alive and thrust the wicked-looking knife at her. The blade missed and Max brought her sword up between them.

"Carmichael?" They blinked at her and then sagged back, the wound in their side was bleeding heavily. "Sorry, I thought you were one of those bastards."

"Easy, easy," Max said, laying her sword down and lowering them into the nearest chair. "Who are you? Why is your DD off?" There was no handshake, no indication of who the person in front of her was.

"Cho Seo-Yoon, she/her, Mars Civil Service. I was supposed to take over Flight Control from Master Chief Ilia

Porchenko. She was on break when the attack happened; I don't know where she is." She tried to sit up and then swore. "That hurts. Fuckers."

"You're lucky they only grazed you, but you are bleeding a lot." Max yanked the med kit from under the console and pulled a heal patch out. "We're going to need to clean that first."

"No time. They're tracking signals. Turn your DD off; we've got to move." Seo-Yoon pressed a hand to the bloody wound in her side and struggled to her feet.

Max shoved what she could from the med kit into her pockets and then hooked an arm around Seo-Yoon's waist, grabbing for her sword and easing them into the hallway. The sound of shouting and booted feet pounding on the floor echoed off to their left. "You been on station a while?"

"Three years."

"Tell me which way to go," Max replied.

Without her DD it was going to be hell to navigate unless she could flip it back on and get a map. Thankfully her DD chip was top-of-the-line and recently loaded with mods from Sapphi that were maybe running the edge of the legal line. Either way she could use most of them even with the active connection off once she had a minute to reconfigure things.

For now, though, she'd trust Seo-Yoon.

"Go right," she said. "Three doors down, there's a break room." She muttered a curse. "Blood trail's going to give us away."

"I'll deal with it." Max took the brunt of the woman's weight and hustled them both down the corridor, stopping outside the door. "Stay here."

"Oh sure." Seo-Yoon waved a hand. "Where else would I go? Maybe hurry, though."

Max took a wide step to the door, careful to keep the blood to a minimum as she tapped the panel and slipped inside. She grabbed a handful of towels and came back, tossing them down for Seo-Yoon to step on and over the threshold. "Find a place to hide; I'll be right back."

"Don't die on me, Carmichael. I'd like a chance to fangirl."

Max couldn't stop the surprised laugh that slipped out, and she pressed a handful of heal patches into Seo-Yoon's hand. "Don't die on me, either, okay?" She tapped the panel again and closed the door behind her. Then with the sounds of pursuit growing closer, she quickly mopped up the blood trail back to Flight Control. Max crossed to the console, typing Jackson's command codes into the system.

The code was accepted and immediately scrambled into uselessness. The lights went dim as the system locked down, red emergency lighting kicking in and the warning klaxon blaring as the massive doors shut between the five levels of the station. Every level was now sealed, containing the movement of these unknown attackers.

Max input a new code when the console flashed the prompt at her, saving it in her local memory. She could override the doors with her access, but everyone else was now effectively trapped where they were.

Then she sent a flash message to Aggie from the console with a quick rundown of what she'd done and to shut down their DDs until they took off. They answered in the affirmative and Max breathed a sigh of relief.

At least her sister was safe. That was something.

The shouting rose in volume and Max dropped face down behind the console in the corner of the room when the voices paused just outside.

"What a fucking mess. Ralka, what's going on?" There was a moment of silence broken by more cursing. "We've got two more down here at Flight Control. No, I don't know. Thomas spotted Carmichael at Shuttle Docking Bay Nine, but ships were already leaving so she can't be the one who released docking clamps. I don't think— Yeah, she got away from him. You can tell Will that if you want, I'm not going to. We're still rounding up Neos, slippery bastards. Should just kill them all now instead of waiting." The last bit was muttered to themself, and Max gritted her teeth against the rush of fury.

You stay down, Jenks whispered in her head. *Whatever those odds are you don't want them.*

"Kas, there's another body. Not one of ours." They snorted a laugh. "DD's not active. Looks like they died trying to stop the bleeding. Should I check for identification?"

Max held her breath.

"No, Greg, leave it," Kas replied. "We just got locked out of the station controls, but Ralka wants us to keep sweeping the level we're on until they get it sorted. I'm pinging four DDs ahead of us. Move out. Will said to leave everyone where they fall. It won't matter in the end."

Max didn't like the sound of that, but then again, she didn't like any of this. She counted to twenty after the footsteps had faded and then eased slowly to her feet and made her way into the corridor.

The smart thing to do was go to Seo-Yoon and figure out how to get her out of there, but once again Jenks's voice was in her head.

I'll be honest, LT, sometimes the smart thing and the right thing don't match up. You know as well as I do that going with the right one is always the answer.

Max loosened her grip on her sword and followed the hijackers down the hallway.

WILLIS HALE LEANED BACK IN THE CHAIR OF VICE ADMIRAL Ford's office and watched the Free Mars broadcast with interest. Ralka's fury was a palpable thing, but he had known the chances of Sylvia falling to the attack had been a long shot at best. She'd stayed alive this long for a reason.

It was fine; it didn't matter in the grand scheme of his plans. It had merely been another piece of chaos to sow in the hopes of holding off an official CHN response for as long as possible to get all the pieces into play. The counter in the corner of his vision was a steady reminder of what they were working against. Nothing mattered as long as everything fell into place before that hit zero. And after, Free Mars and the NeoG would be at each other's throats, tearing themselves apart in a fitting end for both organizations.

Sylvia was dead already. She just didn't realize it yet.

The feed cut off and the lights went down, replaced with emergency lighting that bathed the whole office in an ominous red.

"What the fuck is going on?" Ralka barked.

"Commander Carmichael is better than I anticipated," he murmured.

It seemed Ford had been telling the truth about the command codes. He'd managed to pass them on to Carmichael.

And she had somehow gotten them into the system. Locked them out of the station, out of Engineering.

Willis pushed to his feet. He could hear Castle spluttering in the front office. "Castle, give me a status report."

"I'm fucking locked out—that's your status."

He put a hand out, stopping Ralka before she could cross to the woman and exact whatever violence she had planned. "Something more than that, Castle, thank you."

"I don't *have* more than that. I was in and everything was fine, and now I'm not. Station is locked down completely. Every level sealed off. Doors offline. All controls are offline. Engineering included. We got people into the office section above but not into the core."

"We brought you here to figure out a way around it." Ralka's voice was as tense as the muscles under his hands.

"*He* didn't," Castle snapped, pointing a finger at Willis. "I need the command codes. That's it. I can't hack my way through this problem. Not for Engineering. I told you so repeatedly in the briefing. I should be able to get us back into station coms easy. I can unlock some of the other systems, one at a time, but I can't get into the whole thing. I told you I can't break through an official lockdown where Engineering is concerned—that's the whole point of the lockdown system!"

Ralka bit back her response when Will raised his free hand. "Patience, everyone. This was planned for; we move on to phase two. Ralka, tell the other teams to continue their sweeps and hold all our guests until we can get the levels unlocked. Castle, your team does what we brought you here to do. Focus on what you can unlock; save the rest for later.

"And tell everyone to keep an eye out for Commander Carmichael. I want her alive."

MAX FOUND HERSELF THANKFUL FOR CHAE'S INFLUENCE AS SHE followed the four guards down the hallway. Chae hadn't quite known what to make of her asking for "assassination lessons," but after their first discussion of tactics, they'd gotten really excited about the whole prospect.

It had paid off for the team in the Boarding Games, and now it was going to pay off here. She waited until the group went around a corner to strike. Max wrapped a hand over the mouth of the unlucky person at the rear, jamming her sword into their back and feeling their nearly silent gasp against her palm before they went limp in her grip.

She lowered them to the floor and darted across the hallway through an open door, slowing her breathing and waiting for the other three to realize their companion wasn't with them.

It took longer than it should have, and even better, only one came back, calling for Greg. She logged the name onto her list, crossing it out with a satisfaction she was a little ashamed of.

"Fuck. Kas—"

She struck before they could get the warning out, sword shearing through their neck and sending their head rolling down the corridor, leaving an ugly streak of blood over the gray surface.

Max swallowed down the bile that rose and forced herself to look away. *Think about it later, Max; right now you need to move.* D'Arcy's voice was gentle in her ear, and she dragged in a deep breath, then continued down the hallway toward the last of her prey.

"Jus, do you copy? What is going on?" The voice she assumed was Kas echoed ahead of her. "Eddie, go see what he's doing. I'll deal with the targets. I don't care what Will says about hostages; they're all dead anyway."

In retrospect Max knew she rushed. That she should have waited and taken Eddie down the same as their fellow hijacker, but fear for the four people ahead of her pushed her into movement.

Eddie's shout of alarm lasted only a moment before Max buried her sword into their chest, but it was enough to alert Kas, who came running down the corridor and sprayed the area she'd been standing in with razor-sharp projectiles. Max managed to dodge out of the way, but not quite fast enough as the hot sting of a fléchette cut along her shoulder.

However, the move that saved her life meant abandoning her sword, and the narrow corridor offered her no protection from the menacing whine as Kas powered up another shot.

"Carmichael," they said. "I should have fucking figured. Lucky for you, Will wants you alive. On your kn—" They broke off and whirled around, stumbling to the side with a regulation NeoG sword sticking out of their back. Max caught a glimpse of the tiny redhead diving out of the way of Kas's wild shot before getting her own legs to obey her screaming brain.

She rushed forward, hitting Kas hard and taking them both to the floor. They screamed as she drove the sword in deeper.

Max rolled free and up onto her feet in a move she'd practiced thousands of times with Jenks in the cage. She kicked the gun free, and it slid across the deck.

"Carmichael, sword!"

She caught her own weapon the redhead threw her way and brought it down near Kas's face. "Don't move."

"We'll have justice for the orphans of war," Kas replied and spat at her. The blood coated the toe of her boot. Then before she could stop them, they clamped their teeth together.

Max muttered a curse as they convulsed and died from whatever poison they'd just swallowed, taking any answers she could have gotten with them.

"Commander?"

She rolled Kas over and pulled the sword out of their back. "Turn your DD off. Who are you?"

"Spacer Lia Thorn, she/her." The Neo straightened, almost saluted before she caught herself. "I heard the shouting. There're three more hiding but I thought I'd come to help."

"You hurt?"

"No, ma'am."

"Good." Max knew her expression was grim, but she offered it up anyway as she flipped the hilt of Lia's sword over in her hand and held it out. "Thanks for the assist. Where are the others?"

"This way. They're all civies."

She followed the spacer down the hallway, hating she'd made the conscious decision to put herself at Lia's back rather than alongside her where the risk of attack was greater.

She did stab Kas; isn't that enough?

Maybe it was.

Maybe it wasn't.

Opia's lifeless eyes flashed into her head and Max hissed.

"Ma'am, are you hurt?"

"Not enough to make a difference." She chuckled. "You straight out of basic, Lia, calling me ma'am?"

The Neo flushed, pink staining her pale, freckled cheeks. "I graduated a month ago. This handover was my first posting."

"It's Max." She paused outside the door Lia indicated. "And I hope you'll forgive me, but this whole thing started when another Neo tried to kill me. So I'm having some trust issues, Lia. You going to stab me in the back if I go in first?"

Green eyes went wide, and Lia's freckles stood out in stark relief across her nose as she paled. "No, ma'am—Max—I mean. No. All I ever wanted was to be a Neo like my dad."

Max knew Jenks would yell at her, but her guard dropped a little. "Your dad, huh? What's his name?"

"Command Master Chief Galen Rost."

Max blinked. She knew of the man. He was the highest-ranking noncommissioned officer in the NeoG, but she didn't know him personally. She vaguely remembered something about him having daughters but not the details, so she had no way of knowing if Lia was telling her the truth.

Now was not the time to guess at it. "I didn't know he had a daughter."

"Two of us, actually. We're adopted. My mom . . . well, it's a long story. He raised me from when I was a baby; my sister was about two when she came to us. The last name is my mother's. It's a lot. Sorry, I'm babbling."

If Lia was lying to her, she'd picked a hell of a cover. Without her DD chip active, Max couldn't verify the info on the wider net, and she wasn't going to risk turning it back on here. But if she was telling the truth, it meant there was no way Max could let whoever had taken over the station get their hands on this girl.

"Come on, we need to move." She gestured at the doorway, and Lia didn't object but moved through it. She knocked on the wall in a quick pattern, and three heads popped up from behind a desk in the far corner.

"DDs off," Lia said. "This is Commander Carmichael."

"Follow me," Max said after introductions were finished and she'd confirmed their DDs were shut down. "Lia and I will stay in front. If we tell you to do something, you do it. Understand?"

The trio of civilians nodded. Max dragged in a breath and headed back out into the hallway. She stopped briefly to collect the fléchette guns from the dead bodies as she led them back to the break room.

"Seo-Yoon, it's me. You still alive?" she called after opening the break room door. There was a moment of silence, and Max's heart thumped hard in panic before a bloody hand waved to her from behind the counter.

"I'd stand up, Carmichael, but you'd have to catch me when my legs gave out," Seo-Yoon called. "Actually, that's maybe not a bad idea."

She laughed as she crossed the room. "Are you flirting with me?"

"Might be—my wife says it's a condition." Seo-Yoon blinked unfocused brown eyes at her that told the truth of her state better than her jokes. Then she looked past Max's shoulder and swore. "Well, shit. Heya, kiddo. When did you get on station? How's your dad?"

"Two days ago. I meant to come say hi, just hadn't had time. And he's good," Lia replied.

Relief at this corroboration rushed through Max even as she urged the woman to lay back down. "Let me see what kind of hack job you did on this wound." Seo-Yoon had actually done a good job getting the heal patches onto the wound in her side, which meant the loopiness was likely just from her previous blood loss. "You know Lia?"

"Oh sure, Rost and I go way back." Seo-Yoon hissed in pain. "I watched this one and her sister grow up. Lia, there's more heal patches right there—fix Carmichael's arm up."

Max gave the woman an annoyed look, but Seo-Yoon simply stared until she shrugged out of her long-sleeved duty shirt so that Lia could get to the cut on her shoulder.

"I want you all to stay here and stay quiet. I'm going to see if I can find you a better place to hide or a way off station."

"They were shooting ships down, Carmichael," Seo-Yoon said, brown eyes clearer than they had been a moment ago. "And don't think I didn't notice you not including yourself in that."

Max dragged in a breath. "I can't leave my crew, and Vice Admiral Ford might still be alive. I have to see if I can help."

"I know. Just be careful."

"I will," Max promised. "Does the phrase 'orphans of war' mean anything to you?"

Seo-Yoon frowned and shook her head. "No. Why?"

She pointed at her jaw. "One of them said it to me before he poisoned himself. 'We'll have justice for the orphans of war.'"

"I maybe heard one of the deckhands saying something similar?" Seo-Yoon muttered a curse, and her eyes flicked to where Lia was helping the three civilians get settled. "Does this have to do with why you were so tense until I said I knew her dad?"

Max nodded and dropped her own voice. "The NeoG lieutenant who met me at the shuttle dock tried to kill me."

Seo-Yoon whistled. "I'm thankful now that you stayed your hand when I took a swing at you, Carmichael. You don't have any reason to trust me."

"Well, if you're not on my side, you're doing a hell of a good job faking it." Max laughed, but then sobered. "I don't want to kill you, Seo-Yoon, so it's not too late to change sides here if that's not the case."

"Hey, I don't like a lot of the politics that fly around. That much is true. But there have been some real strides for peace lately, and this station handover was going to make a difference," Seo-Yoon replied and held out a bloodstained hand. "I'm on your side, Carmichael, and not just because I like you. I don't want these bastards on our station any more than you do. Whoever they are."

Max took her hand and squeezed briefly. "Since I'm pretty sure you're not going to shoot me, I brought you some fléchette guns. Figured the dead guys weren't using them."

"Now see, givin' me weapons as presents? You're gonna make my wife jealous."

Max laughed as she got to her feet. She gestured for Lia to follow her to the door and leaned in. "Keep an eye on her. You stay here until I get back or I send someone, okay? I'm going to lock the door from the outside, but you'll be able to open it." She tapped a quick pattern on the wall. "Only for this. If I find any others along the way, I'll send them to you."

"Yes, ma'am."

"Max."

"Max." Lia's expression was tinged with worry. "I should go with you."

"I'm trusting you to keep these people safe. That's our job. We keep people safe. So you stay here and do that. Okay?"

The younger woman took a deep breath and nodded. Max gave her what she hoped was a reassuring smile and then slipped out of the room and sprinted down the hallway.

"COMMANDER VAGIN. IT'S AN HONOR TO MEET YOU. WISH THE CIR-cumstances were better." Captain Fábia Clark crossed over to greet them as the spacer led *Zuma*'s crew into the main room of Ground Control. She was a tall, well-built cis woman with slicked-back, short brown hair a few shades darker than her skin.

Nika tapped his fist to hers. "Fábia, I'm not here to step on your toes. Admiral Chen thought I could help on the political side of things, given the circumstances. I am more than willing to listen to your recommendations for anything, given how long you've been on the ground here."

"I am very glad you're here then and more than happy to hand the politics off to you. Mr. Grady seems to think that my experience makes little difference. Maybe he'll listen to you when you explain that this is still NeoG property, which makes it our jurisdiction."

"Grady?"

Nika followed the finger Fábia pointed across the room.

A slender man in a suit, whose handshake read *Parson Grady, CHN Mars Oversight, he/him*, was in the middle of a heated discussion with a harried-looking master sergeant.

"Why is he here?"

"He was supposed to be headed up to the station for the handoff, but there was a mechanical issue with his shuttle that delayed him. Then the shit hit the fan," Fábia muttered. "Now he's our problem."

"Look, I don't know how many times I can explain this to you in a way that will make you finally understand I can't do what you're asking." Master Sergeant Roger Tran, whose handshake read *they/them*, was a short, stocky Marine with short black hair. Their voice was pitched low, but Nika could hear the thread of suppressed violence as well as everyone else could. Grady, however, seemed oblivious.

"I'm not asking, I'm *telling* you. As the ranking member of the CHN government here . . ."

Fábia let slip something that was suspiciously close to a snort before she pinched the bridge of her nose with a finger and thumb and muttered, "Take a deep breath, Rog," ostensibly over a shared com.

"First off, Mr. Grady, with all due respect to your position, this is a NeoG facility. Which means you're not my boss. She is." They jerked their head in Fábia's direction. "Secondly, it's physically impossible." They dragged out the last two words slow enough to make Grady's eyes narrow. "Procedure for a code of this level means that our side of things was locked down with Commander Carmichael's order, so even if I could access anything on station, it would require someone with more authority than you to lift that lockdown. Like Captain Clark, my aforementioned boss. She's not going to do that without approval from at least Admiral Chen. I promise."

They pointed upward. "And Commander Carmichael's message said she locked the entire station down on their end with Vice Admiral Ford's command codes—again as per procedure for an attack by an unknown force. Which means we can't do jack shit from here even if we wanted to."

"Listen, Sergeant—"

"Master Sergeant." Their voice was frozen.

"Thanks, Rog, we'll take over," Fábia said, smoothly stepping between the pair.

Roger shared a look with Nika before nodding to them all. Then they turned on a heel and stalked over to the other side of the room.

"Captain, I won't be spoken to like that!"

"Mr. Grady, as I will explain to you for the *third time*, this is a NeoG facility. Not a civilian one. Everyone here, regardless of what branch they belong to, is under my command. You are Mars Oversight, not NeoG. You do not have authority to order anyone to do anything and my people know their jobs, so I'd appreciate a little more co-operation from you. Understood?" She continued without waiting for an answer from the sputtering man. "This is Commander Nika Vagin of the Interceptor *Zuma's Ghost*. He's here on orders from Admiral Chen herself and will be in charge of the situation."

Nika kept a pleasant smile on his face as the man looked him over. "Mr. Grady."

"Commander. My people are up on that station. They are in danger."

"We are aware, Mr. Grady, and it's more than just your people in danger." Nika turned to Fábia. "What can you tell me about what we're dealing with here?"

"No one knows," the man sneered before she could answer. "Because you people won't get eyes back on the station and are just letting those Free Mars criminals do what they want."

Nika heard several people around them drag in audible breaths.

Fábia's reply was politely sharp edged. "Mr. Grady, I am going to need you to stop saying that."

"You saw her!" Grady thrust a hand at the frozen image of Sylvia Moroz that was still on a screen at the front of the room.

"We did," Nika replied. "We also saw the second message that claims this was a fake." He put a hand up at Grady's snort of derision. "I understand your concern for your people, and I share it. However, we will not rush into action without confirmation, and we will *not* spread false rumors that might incite rash feelings and decisions. As Master Sergeant Tran explained to you, we have no way currently of finding out what's happening on the MOS. We don't want to put anyone up there at risk, do we?"

Grady at least had the grace to look abashed. "I suppose not."

Nika smiled reassuringly. "Thank you. Now, I have procedures I am required to follow, and given your political experience, I appreciate your understanding of how delicate this situation is. Can I expect your cooperation?"

The older man finally nodded. "Fine, Commander."

"Nika," Sapphi whispered. "I'm gonna go talk to the master sergeant. I've got an idea."

He nodded, then lifted a hand to get Fábia's attention. "Captain, a word in private?"

"My office," she replied, and pointed across the room.

Nika glanced Chae's way, and they nodded once at the unspoken order to keep an eye on the civilian. Chae had the patience of a saint and could spend all day deflecting whatever Grady threw at them with a cheerful and extremely noncommittal response of "I'll have to talk to my commander about that."

"That was impressively handled, though I shouldn't be surprised he was willing to listen to you. Tell me it's not worth my career to murder that man," she muttered as they walked away.

Nika laughed. "Jenks would say not in front of witnesses anyway."

Fábia chuckled. "I'm admittedly both disappointed and relieved she's not here. Maybe more of the latter."

"Well, you can flip those emotions in a little while. Commander Montaglione headed to retrieve her as soon as we got word of what happened," Nika replied. He looked through the doorway at where Chae was distracting Grady and lowered his voice. "How big of a problem is Grady going to be?"

Fábia rubbed at her jaw. "I don't know. He's been an annoyance at this point but manageable. I could probably get him out of here on some flimsy excuse, though I'd catch hell for it later. Nika, my job is coordinating traffic between Mars and the MOS, not wrangling politicians and the biggest independence movement on this planet. I don't mind saying I am out of my goddamned depth, and I'm really glad that you're here."

He nodded. "I'm expecting another com—"

"Captain?" a Neo interrupted. "I've got an incoming com from Commander Montaglione."

"From that very person," Nika finished.

"We'll take it in here, Suz, thanks," Fábia said, and leaned over to close the door.

Nika leaned against the desk as D'Arcy's face appeared on the screen. "Nika. Captain Clark," he said, nodding in Fábia's direction. "We're almost to Jenks's location. Are we secure?"

Nika glanced at Fábia, who mouthed *Yes*.

"Clear, D'Arcy, go ahead."

"I received a message directly from Free Mars. They're claiming not to be responsible for this and also that some of their own people tried to kill Sylvia Moroz less than an hour ago."

"Tried?"

D'Arcy nodded again. "Failed, thankfully."

Nika frowned. "Before or after she put out the denial?"

"Before, she said Sylvia was recording the denial as we spoke. I hate to say it but it makes sense. If I were planning something like this, that's what I'd have done anyway." D'Arcy muttered a curse too low for the mic to pick up, but Nika knew the feeling.

And D'Arcy had a point, if someone wanted to make this look like Sylvia was responsible but she wasn't? Taking her out of the equation would have been priority one.

The question was why? Why did whoever was on the MOS want this to look like Free Mars?

Unaware of Nika's thoughts, D'Arcy continued, "She wants to talk, Nik. Whatever's going on up on the MOS and whatever that broadcasted message looked like, I don't think they're involved. In fact, I think it's shaken them. They're willing to work with us. I told them I needed authorization from someone higher up before I could agree."

Fábia's indrawn breath was almost imperceptible at the unprecedented news. While Free Mars had grudgingly agreed to negotiations with the CHN, their enmity with the NeoG over the crackdowns of the '09 protests and the violence in the habitats that followed had never wavered.

It was hard to blame them.

"You don't think they're just trying to play both sides?" Nika asked.

"I think we should see what they want. Sylvia's very obviously on the ground at Mars and not up on the station." D'Arcy made a face. "And despite the years, Nika, if she'd wanted to do this, she'd be taking full responsibility for it. Could it be a smoke screen? Sure, but I don't think so. My contact was scared." He paused, eyes flicking at Fábia briefly. "She's not the kind of person who gets scared easily."

To Fábia's credit, she didn't react, though Nika suspected by now D'Arcy's involvement with Free Mars prior to his NeoG service was more common knowledge than it had been for most of his career. Even Nika hadn't known about it for a good chunk of their friendship. But word spreads, especially when more than one person is trying to keep it under wraps.

He hadn't blamed D'Arcy for keeping it quiet, that was the sort of thing that kicked up all sorts of bad blood even decades later—like it had during the attack on Jupiter Station. He wondered how strange it must be for D'Arcy now to be seeing faces from his past, but also appreciated the level of intel it might be providing. That said . . .

"Do you think the offer to meet is a trap?" Nika asked, and D'Arcy shrugged.

"Could be. What's one more Interceptor crew in the grand scheme of things, though?"

Nika snorted. One more crew would be bad enough, but it wasn't just any crew. It was D'Arcy's, and his history with Free Mars made him a hell of a target—even if he didn't want to admit it.

Still, if Free Mars was telling the truth and whoever had taken the MOS wasn't acting on orders? It made this whole thing feel like a setup designed to put them at odds with each other. Once upon a time, Nika would have been frozen by this choice, but time—and Max's influence—had smoothed out the rough edges of his nerves.

"You've got your authorization. Pick up Jenks. Go meet with Sylvia," he said. "But be careful and keep your eyes open."

"Should I also make sure to close the hatch before flying in space?" D'Arcy replied.

"Point taken." There was no heat in Nika's glare.

"I'll be in touch."

Still Defiant
JUNE 3, 2435 (ESD)

Sylvia Moroz has never done anything the easy way. The infamous leader of Free Mars grew up in one of the poorest sections of the oldest habitat on the planet. Her parents died in a Red Lung outbreak that nearly took her life as well when the CHN refused to allow treatments through the quarantine perimeters in that area of Serrano.

Her rise to power and her spot as the leading voice of those calling for Martian independence in the months after the Referendum Protests is not without controversy, but no one, not even her detractors, can deny her bravery.

We sat down with Sylvia to talk during the twenty-fifth anniversary of the EM massacre—when unarmed protestors were assaulted and killed by members of the Near-Earth Orbital Guard in 2410. Time has not dimmed her fighting spirit, and this brilliant woman continues to push the CHN for a free Mars. Her vision of this ongoing fight for freedom is inspiring, hopeful, and honest about the problems that are on the horizon. [_Read More_]

FIVE

SAQIB KEPT ONE EYE ON CHARLIE AS THEY SPOKE QUIETLY WITH an unknown guard who'd stopped by the medical bay. They were both armed, though the weapons were currently slung across their backs. Sloppy. Out of reach if one felt like risking the odds of a fight.

He hadn't heard anyone else in the hallway, but Saqib was willing to bet there was at least one more person nearby. The strike teams seemed to be moving in groups of four or six, but everyone else was in at least pairs of two.

It spoke of professionalism and planning.

He was sure Will had sent Charlie alone as a test, and the appearance of the other guard not long after they'd gotten to medical was proof enough he'd been trying to set Saqib up. It was still tempting to try to escape, but not if it meant that innocent people would pay the price.

"If I create a big enough distraction, you could slip

away," Jackson said in a low voice, his thoughts clearly mir-roring Saqib's.

The lieutenant commander shook his head as he con-tinued to clean out the wound in his side. "Not leaving you or the civilians. That's bad form." More, even if he had the chance, he knew Max wouldn't want him to take it.

"So is dying here. I could order you to take the chance, Lieutenant Commander."

"You could." He allowed a tiny smile. "You know Max is my commanding officer, though, not you."

"She didn't order you to stay with me. Also, I outrank her."

"She didn't, she's just a terrible influence about *not* fol-lowing orders under certain circumstances. Which is how I know she's not getting the hell off this station like you told her to."

Jackson chuckled and then groaned, digging his fingers into the side of the table. "I'm admittedly surprised—she was such a good cadet."

"From what I understand you can't even blame Jenks for it," Saqib whispered. "First time Max did it was before they were friends. Of course, she did it to save Jenks's life, which is what kicked off the friendship. She also apologized to Commander Martín before she did it . . . although the commander still threatened to court-martial her if she ever did it again."

He'd appreciated that the members of *Zuma* went to great lengths to catch him and Rona both up on their inside jokes (though in this case, he knew part of it was simply because it was in Jenks's top three favorite stories used to embarrass her commanding officer). It made him feel welcome and truly part of the family they had cultivated on the Interceptor. More importantly, it provided him with the bigger lesson that Max would put the team above everything else—every time. It was a lesson Saqib had taken to heart.

"That's a story you're going to have to tell me later."

Saqib swallowed, hoping that things wouldn't take a definitive turn for the worse and he'd have the chance to actually tell Jackson the story. Or better yet, Max would.

He wished he could talk to Max, but as far as he could tell, her DD was off. He could still try sending something, but real-time contact wasn't going to happen. It was a good thing as it meant Will's people would have a harder time tracking her down, but also meant Saqib couldn't talk to her . . . and vice versa.

He knew the likelihood of Max leaving them was slim, even if she could find a way off the station without getting shot out of the black. Still, he sort of wished she would take it and get those command codes as far away from these people as possible.

He didn't know what they wanted with Engineering access, but it couldn't be good. He sent the list and all his information over to Max in the hopes the commander would come back online and get it. Maybe she could pass it along to Nika and the others.

Then there wasn't much else to do but wait. Saqib stripped off the dirty gloves and tossed them into the bio-recycler. It would sterilize everything before breaking it back down to component parts. He reached for the heal patches, carefully palming a wrapped scalpel at the same time and slipping it into his cargo pocket.

Jackson kept his eyes on the door. "I am serious, though,

Neo. They may not kill me, but you're probably slightly more expendable in their eyes and I don't want you hurt. If you have a chance to get out of here, I want you to take it."

Saqib didn't respond. Even if he didn't have civilians to worry about also, he wasn't going to leave Jackson, no matter what the vice admiral said. Max wouldn't do it; no other *Zuma* would do it, and he wouldn't, either.

Instead of outright refusing, though, he said, "Sir, I'm more use here. I've not only trained for hostage situations, I also have experience." Saqib frowned as the memory came back abruptly. "Which I'm realizing Will knew. He called me out about trying to negotiate with him. He knew Jenks was on vacation. He knew Max was going to be here." He paused, thinking.

"What is it, Neo?"

"Not sure yet. But I don't like the ideas that puts in my head."

"Your crew is fairly high profile. Assuming they knew who was going to be on station, it makes sense he would look up everyone on *Zuma's Ghost*."

"Maybe." But Saqib didn't think that was it. He just couldn't put his finger on what was bothering him yet. He smoothed the heal patch over Jackson's side. "You want a clean shirt? There're basics in the cabinet."

"Let's leave it," he said. "Might be better to have them continue to think of me as injured."

"True." Saqib scanned the room, wondering if there was anything else he could take without being noticed.

"Hey, are you finished?" Charlie snapped. "Get a move on."

"Almost done," Saqib replied. He helped Jackson off

the table and hit the console to start the sterilization cycle. "There, Pushy, we can go now."

"Watch your mouth, NeoG."

Saqib really wanted to ask what would happen if they didn't, but his patience was nearly as legendary as Max's, so he just made his way out into the corridor with Jackson leaning heavily on him.

"There are better ways to handle your grievances," Saqib said instead, and Charlie shot them a sideways glare.

"What do you know about our grievances?"

"Nothing. Which makes it hard for me to help. Why don't you tell me?"

He needed information from someone. Will was clearly in charge, and he was also obviously informed about the NeoG's negotiation tactics. But this person . . . it was a worth a shot.

"You all caused this mess," Charlie snapped. "You can't fix it. It doesn't matter, though. We're past fixing it anyway." That was muttered under their breath, and Saqib was pretty sure they hadn't meant to say it out loud.

"Past fixing what, Charlie?" he asked softly after a quick glance at Ford. The vice admiral nodded slightly, an encouragement to keep going.

"The war, conflict, operation—whatever the fuck you're all calling it now. You can't bring people back from the dead, so it doesn't matter. *Does it?*" Charlie's hands tightened on their gun as they spoke.

"I'm sorry. It sounds like you're really hurting."

"What the fuck would you know of it?" Charlie spat.

The punch that followed caught Saqib by surprise, sending

him staggering into Ford. Pain streaked through his face, but he kept a grip on the vice admiral when he tried to surge past him. "I'm fine," he whispered. "Don't give them the fight they're looking for."

"Keep moving," Charlie ordered, pointing down the hallway with their gun.

Saqib nodded and followed the order.

"SHIP, MAMA." ANNA POINTED UP AT THE SKY.

Jenks frowned and looked up as the Interceptor circled in and settled into the meadow a dozen meters away. "Shit."

That wasn't good, couldn't be good.

That's what you get for letting your guard down for two seconds.

She batted the voice away as her DD crackled to life. "Jenks, it's D'Arcy."

"I'm on vacation. Answer is no." Even as she tried to joke, the writhing of her stomach told her something bad was coming. He wouldn't be here otherwise.

"I know, I'm sorry. Possible group of hard-line Mars separatists took over the MOS a little under two hours ago. Nika sent me to grab you, with his apologies."

Fear gripped her before he even finished speaking. "Max? Saqib?"

"Max put the Code Bravo out. Then the coms went down. I don't know where Saqib is. I'm sorry. I don't have anything more than that."

"Shit." She muttered again. "Luis!"

"D'Arcy was on the main com. Tivo's packing your bag,"

he said, taking Anna from her and pressing a kiss to Jenks's temple. "Go do what you do best. I love you."

"I love you." She cupped his face and kissed him properly and then peppered Anna's round cheeks with kisses. "I love you, too, baby child."

"Shit!" Anna said brightly, and Jenks bit her lip to hold back the laugh when Luis shot her a sidelong glare.

"Boys!" she shouted, running back toward camp. Elliot and Riz came at her call, Sergei trailing behind, all three wearing their worry on their faces. "Gotta go rescue your aunt Max." She pulled them into a hug, the teens towering above her while their seven-year-old brother wrapped his arms around her waist and clung tight. "I'm sorry to mess up this vacation," she whispered. "I'll make it up to you."

"Come back," the twins replied too quietly for their younger brother to hear.

"Promise."

"Don't go, Mommy," Sergei whimpered.

Mommy. How the hell did I get so lucky to have someone this beautiful call me Mommy?

She got down on her knee and looked him right in the eye. "Our family is in trouble, love. What do we do when someone in our family needs our help?"

"Beat up the people hurting us?" he asked, eyes wide.

She laughed even as her heart broke and scooped him up. "Close enough, sweetheart."

She kissed them all, then threw herself at Tivo, who caught her and lifted her up to kiss her hard.

"We'll pack up and follow. Be careful."

"Hey, it's me."

Tivo laughed. "That's what I'm worried about." Then he sobered and set her on her feet, touching a hand to her heart. "Here, always."

Jenks put her hand over his. "Always." She grabbed her bag and sprinted for *Dread*.

TAMAGO WAS ON THEIR FEET BEFORE THE SHUTTLE LANDED and grabbed for the bar over their head to steady themself. Fear was crawling under their skin, a companion to their racing heart, but they kept their face expressionless.

The hurried briefing on the shuttle ride from Earth had only made things worse. Listening to Max's utterly calm voice on the recording, Tamago was sure they were the only one who could hear the undercurrent of panic that Max was so good at hiding.

They'd resisted the urge to message their friends, as painful as it was. Tamago knew the procedure, and the time before the news of the hijacking got loose was a precious resource. Once it broke that the MOS was on lockdown and that Max was on board, it was going to add a whole layer of complication into the mess.

Tamago followed Kenta off the shuttle, Jun behind them. The younger lieutenant was tasked with carrying most of the gear through the bright sunlight across the yard and into Ground Control, but Tama had their own backpack slung over one shoulder.

It was tightly controlled chaos inside the building, the kind Tamago had come to associate with hostage situations. Grim-faced Neos nodded at them as they passed, some of them allowing the relief to show when they spotted the Hostage Negotiation Team in their handshakes.

"Tama!"

The sound of their name called over the din of main Ground Control had them jerking in surprise, but the sight of Petty Officer Chae Ho-ki filled Tamago's heart with a burst of relief.

"Chae!" They embraced the smaller Neo, a double handful of centimeters shorter than Tamago's own height of 164 centimeters and pressed their cheek to Chae's with a shaky exhale. "It is good to see you. What are you doing here?"

"We were still on Earth. Admiral Chen commed Nika, put him in charge of coordinating things." Chae squeezed them tight and then stepped back. "You remember Rona?"

Tamago exchanged greetings with the Neo who'd replaced them. Rona was patient and kind, a natural with a sword in a way Tamago had never been. Her burnished brown curls were cut short, and her eyes were quietly sympathetic, showing her own worry for her commander and lieutenant commander without saying a word.

When Tamago scanned the room, they spotted Sapphi deep in conversation with a burly Marine, the expression on their best friend's face one equally of concentration and that slightly spaced-out look that indicated she was doing something on her DD even as she talked. "Where's Nika? That's probably who Captain Hosaka needs to speak with if he's in charge." Another thought hit them. "Where's Jenks?"

"Jenks was in the wilds with her family," Chae said, and then muttered a curse that was out of character for the normally quiet Neo. "Rona, fill Tama in, will you? I have to go wrangle Mr. Grady." They moved off at speed, intercepting the brown-haired man whose handshake marked him as a Mars official before he could poke his nose into the information on a nearby screen.

Politician babysitting duty. Sorry, Chae!

"Commander Vagin is in Captain Clark's ready room, Lieutenant," Rona said. "Over there. Commander Montaglione went to retrieve the senior chief; they should be here within the hour." She glanced around. "Do you need somewhere to put your gear?"

"Yes, please. Jun, this is Petty Officer Rona Nkosi with *Zuma's Ghost*. Hey, Captain," they called out, "we want to be over there."

Kenta nodded and followed them to the door in the corner. Tamago knocked twice and smiled at the dark-skinned woman who appeared. "Captain Clark. Lieutenant Uchida. This is Captain Hosaka with—"

"Tama?" If the sound of Chae's voice was welcomed, Nika's was even more so, and Tamago didn't even have time to get a greeting out before they were swept into a bruising hug.

They clung and whispered. "We'll do everything we can to bring her home safe, Nik, I promise."

"I realize how inappropriate this greeting is, but I am really fucking glad to see you," Nika murmured before he released them with a laugh. "Captain Hosaka, sorry for manhandling your crew."

"No worries, Commander. I know you and Tama go way back, and given the situation, it's understandable." Kenta extended his fist. "It's nice to meet you finally, wish it were under better circumstances. Captain Clark," he said, nodding.

"Captain Hosaka. Good to see you again. Did someone get you settled?"

"Partially. Nika's crew was finding a spot for us."

"Not my crew," Nika corrected with a smile that Kenta answered.

"Fair enough. I don't think Commander Carmichael would take offense."

Tamago caught Nika by the upper arm before their former commander could pull away. "How are you, really?"

"Holding on by a thread," he replied. "You know Max put out the Code Bravo?"

"I listened to it," Tamago said. "She sounded scared, Nik. Do you believe Free Mars is responsible? We're still running verification on both broadcasts."

He shook his head and Captain Clark reached out to close the door again, sealing them off from the rest of Ground Control. "D'Arcy said someone from Free Mars contacted him," he said. "Let's get you all caught up, then we can go from there."

SLIPPING THROUGH THE LOCKED DOORS WAS EASIER THAN SHE expected, and once Max was back up a level and far enough away from Seo-Yoon and the others, she dared to flip her DD back on just long enough to download a map of the station and scan for anyone near her.

While she did that, an alert from Saqib popped up and Max's heart surged with hope. But the file was only accompanied by a short message.

SAQIB: Bad guys have me, Ford, and seven civilians. Me and civies are fine. Ford's slightly injured, just

patched up in medical. Headed back to office.
Someone named "Will" in charge. Guard: Charlie. I
think a hacker in other room but no visual yet. Lots
of people in and out. No active DDs. Well-outfitted,
military guns, funded. Dangerous. Goal: unknown
despite claim of a "free Mars." No sign of Sylvia
Moroz or any other familiar faces with the movement.
Attached more detailed observations and images.

She downloaded the file, photos included, resisted the
urge to check on Pax, and shut her DD back down. They were
safer right where they were and with no one knowing about
them. She also resisted the overwhelming urge to head all
the way upstairs and find Saqib. The lieutenant commander
could take care of himself and the others if it came to it; she
had to trust in that and focus on the big picture.

So instead Max turned her attention to her objective—
Secondary Coms on the second level of the station. Turning
off the jammer, if it existed, would mean she could maybe
unlock the com long enough to get another message out.

*"You can also get a sense of how many people you're deal-
ing with if you use the com alert to scan for all active DDs."*
She could almost see Sapphi's mischievous grin in her
mind's eye as she remembered a long-ago conversation. *"Not
what it's supposed to be used for, LT, but it works in a pinch."*

Max followed the map she'd pulled, three doors up and
on the left, slowing as she approached, and the sound of
voices wafted out into the hallway.

"You keep an eye on that door, Harro. I don't like the
number of dead we're racking up, and I definitely don't want
to be on the list."

"Then stop flapping your mouth and do what Castle asked you to do."

Max eased backward, listening for the sounds of movement inside the room as she added names to her list. She could hear the two speakers, but the sound of extra footsteps filtered through the words, restless feet moving in place.

Three? Maybe four?

Four seemed likely given the previous team. She didn't want to take them all on at once. But how best to separate them?

You know how, Max—you've got control of all the doors on the station, not just between the levels.

She carefully backtracked, slipping into an office and casting around for a console. Finding it, she brought up her access, then grabbed an empty water bottle off another desk.

Max headed back to the door and pitched the water bottle down the hallway. It made a loud noise in the stillness as it rattled across the floor, rolling to a stop past the Secondary Coms office.

There was a moment of silence, then two people emerged, fléchette guns at the ready. Max counted to ten, watching as one went down on a knee by the water bottle, and then she hurried back to the console.

The startled shouts rang out, but Max merely eased back to the doorway of her office and waited.

"I don't fucking know what happened. The door just closed." The voice paused as a response came over their com. "You're the one trapped in there, you figure out how to get it open. Or call Castle."

"Harro, Levi is going to kick your ass when he gets out."

"Shut it, Eva, and keep your eyes open. A ghost didn't throw that bottle. Sweep these offices. You take that side."

Max logged the additional names onto her list as she listened to the footsteps approaching. The nose of the gun edged through the doorway first, but Max waited until the person holding it cleared the lip.

There was a fifty-fifty chance they'd see her.

Her luck held, and they looked left first, giving her the opening to slide her blade up and into their right lung. The gasp was low, too low to be heard by their companion in the opposite office, and Max grabbed them with her free hand over their mouth as she dragged them away from the door.

Max twisted her sword, driving it farther in, and her opponent jerked, then went limp. She lowered them to the floor and pulled her sword free, shoving away the writhing in her chest over the blood and the growing tally of dead.

Think about it later, Max; right now is for surviving.

"Eva?"

Max's heart redlined when the call was immediately followed by the larger of the pair of hijackers poking their head in the door.

"Fuck! Levi, it's Carmichael!" They swung the gun in their hand in her direction, but Max was already moving and the razor-sharp, hooked tip of her sword bit deep into the metal.

And stuck there.

Max dropped it as Harro barreled toward her, slamming them both into the console. Pain exploded through her even as years of training kicked her instinct into high gear, and Max brought her elbow down twice on the side of their head without any hesitation and as much force as she could manage.

Harro yelped and released her. Max, however, surged forward and wrapped her arm around their throat, catching them up in an arm triangle choke hold. She pushed off the console with a foot, driving them both to the ground and using all her weight to try to hold the struggling person down.

What felt like an eternity later—but was only about fifteen seconds—Harro stilled. Max scrambled off the unconscious person and grabbed for her sword, putting her booted foot on the gun so she could yank it free.

She turned, fully intent on driving her sword into their heart, but froze.

They were down. Unarmed. Not a threat.

I can't. I know I should, but I can't.

Max forcibly slowed her breathing and kept one eye on the door as she jerked several cords free from the nearby supply closet and bound Harro's hands behind them.

Because they were alive, their DD chip was still active and the risk of being discovered outweighed the possibility of finding the com channel they were all using. Max flipped her DD on, and the quick scan resulted in an explosion of noise in her head.

". . . We are under attack on the second level; all teams on level two converge on Secondary Coms!"

"I don't fucking know what's going on; we're locked in!"

"Harro, do you copy?"

"Everyone quiet now," a low, cold voice overrode all the others, and Max froze at the doorway. "Ralka, where are you?"

"Working my way through the fucking maintenance tunnel to Engineering even though Castle can't tell me if I'll even be able to get in. Anton's on two; he's headed for Levi's location."

That would be your location, Max—time to move.

Max switched her DD back off, silencing the chatter in her head. The noise was replaced by the pounding of booted feet, and she raced ahead for the door that led down to the third level, slipping through that one and heading directly for the fourth, where the docking bays were located.

Secondary Coms was going to have to wait. She turned back into the nearest room and grabbed the tablet off the desk. If she timed it right, she could piggyback a signal whenever they decided to open the coms with their demands to the NeoG.

She just had to hope they actually wanted to talk, but at the moment the odds were not looking good on that front.

SIX

WILL STUDIED THE NEOG OFFICERS SITTING IN THE CHAIRS OP-
posite him. Ford had walked back into the office under his
own power, even though the effort had clearly cost him and
the wiser thing to do would have been to lean on Lieutenant
Commander Vahid for support. These people, so proud even
in defeat, so certain of their righteousness.

He was going to make sure they all saw the folly of their
pride before the end of this. See that Gio and all the others
who had been lost to this endless conflict got their justice.

The thought of Gio brought a sharp stab of pain, as it
always did. Too many decades without him, when they were
supposed to spend forever together. His sweet, kindhearted
love. Gone in an instant because of the NeoG—because of
Free Mars.

They'd been so close to a resolution of it, but no one had
taken the necessary final steps for peace. Not Earth. Not

Mars. Now they would reap the crop they'd sown from the blood-soaked soil.

Judging from the mark on the lieutenant commander's face and the fire in the vice admiral's eyes, something had happened in the corridor. Will was reasonably sure it hadn't been an escape attempt or Charlie would have gleefully announced it on their return. Which meant he was going to have to make it clear to Charlie they couldn't just bash around people at their pleasure.

Will needed both men alive for the moment, and undamaged enough that the NeoG would be willing to waste time negotiating. There were still pieces of this that he needed to put into place.

"I've got door controls again." Castle stuck her head through the door right on cue. "Coms are almost up. Both internal and external."

"Excellent. Loyalty is an admirable thing," Will said, steepling his fingers together on the desk. "But one has to be prepared to make sacrifices, and that's where the NeoG falters, isn't it, Vice Admiral? You're fine if the sacrifices aren't your people. The lives of others mean less." He waved his hand in the air. "Transports with civilians mean nothing if there's a chance of taking out the leadership of Free Mars."

Ford frowned. "What are you talking about? The NeoG has never—"

"Save it." Will cut the man off, raising his hand. "Here is what's going to happen. When we have control of the coms again—and we will shortly—you are going to get on them and order Commander Carmichael to surrender herself."

"She won't."

"You'd better hope she does," he countered with a bland

smile. "Or things get difficult across the board. How many people are you willing to sacrifice?" He glanced at the seven civilians huddled together in the corner, and both men stiffened.

"Dead hostages do you no good," the lieutenant commander said softly. "What do you want, Will?"

"A free Mars." Will could see the disbelief in Saqib's eyes, but surprisingly the man didn't call him on it.

"We were headed that way before you took over the station," he said instead, gesturing around the room. "A handoff of the MOS into Mars civilian control would—"

"Spare me the speech, Lieutenant Commander. Handing off this station to a CHN-run government on Mars does very little, and we all know it."

"Where's Sylvia?"

"Otherwise occupied." Will flashed a grin. He knew what Saqib was angling at, had seen this all before, and he would play the game when it suited him. "What I want right this moment is the command codes, and since those have been passed to Commander Carmichael, we're all in a bit of a spot. This is in your hands, Vice Admiral. I suggest you decide if sacrifices need to be made or if Carmichael should do as she's ordered. You have until the coms are back up to make a decision."

"I won't help you." Ford's response was flat. "This was your decision from the beginning."

"Pity." Will snapped his fingers. "Anton, while we're waiting, I want you to hunt down Carmichael and bring her to me alive. Alive, but you don't have to be gentle about it."

"If she surrenders?"

"Even if she surrenders."

Lieutenant Commander Vahid's face was impassive, but Will could see the fury in the man's eyes. Ford, to his credit, didn't so much as flinch.

"HOW ARE YOU DOING?"

Jenks glanced away from the schematics and then smiled at Master Chief Emel Shevreaux. *Dread Treasure*'s engineer and senior NCO had come to Trappist and the Interceptors six years ago. Jenks had immediately liked the woman and was more than pleased when D'Arcy had managed to sort out whatever shit had been between them to make the crew gel and excel.

Working in close quarters with her for so long, not to mention their runs together in the Boarding Games, meant that rather than her usual deflection, Jenks answered her honestly.

"Not great."

Emel nodded and, even better, didn't give her the bullshit platitudes about Max and Saqib being fine, to have faith, or any of those other things people used to fill the sharp emptiness of uncertainty.

Jenks knew too well how life could shift. How good things could be snatched away. And how the bad guys could triumph no matter what kind of fight the heroes put up.

This wasn't a story. It was real, and one of the very select few people in the universe who truly saw her was in danger. Which wasn't to say she wasn't also worried about the other hostages, not to mention the lieutenant commander.

She'd been the same sort of wary with Saqib that she'd been with Max, but the man hadn't been the least bit insulted and instead had waited for Jenks to decide how to proceed. They'd settled into a comfortable routine over the last two years, and she trusted him. He was kind and friendly, very good at his job, and she was lucky to have someone like that on her crew. She couldn't imagine him being dead. But Max . . .

Max was— Losing Max would feel the same as when she'd thought Luis was dead. A great big hole in her chest and far too much pain.

Just thinking of it was too much pain.

"Do you need a hug?"

Jenks sniffed hard and blinked away the tears that had started. If Emel hugged her, she'd probably fall apart, and that was the last thing that would help the situation.

"Maybe—" Jenks cleared her throat. "Just give my shoulder a squeeze, would you?" The weight of Emel's hand settled on her shoulder, warm and comforting, and Jenks reached up to hold on for a second.

Quietly, the older woman asked, "What are you looking at?"

"Station schematics." Jenks pointed. "Depending on how many hostiles there are, I'm assuming they've got people in both Main Docking and Shuttle Docking, plus in Cargo." She highlighted each level in turn. "The airlocks won't be functional because of the lockdown. But there are maintenance tunnels with airlocks that access some critical outside equipment. Sapphi can probably hack those in her sleep. It's faster to get to than taking an EVA with a bag of tools. Though they usually do routine maintenance from a shuttle, it's more efficient—"

"How do you know all this?"

"Oh." Jenks grinned. "I dated a girl back when we were on Jupiter Station—she'd worked on the MOS crew for a few years before transferring. She liked to talk about her work, and I found it interesting."

"You didn't have anything better to talk about?"

"The other better thing we had going didn't involve a lot of talking," Jenks said, and Emel blushed.

Feeling just a touch lighter than moments before, Jenks pointed at the schematics. "The MOS is our smallest and oldest station. Old extra bit. Main stalk is a kilometer in diameter at the Command Deck and tapers down to half that size after the Docking Bay to where the engine core is at the bottom. Four engines, still running off liquid metallic hydrogen, stored in the tanks here." She pointed at the large mass at the very tip of the station.

"It's orbiting Mars about once every sixty minutes, give or take. The new station will be more like our Jupiter Station in construction with dual points—still a ways to go, though, as they've only got one stalk partially up at the construction point so far. That one is going to run entirely on solar, which is supercool, even if I don't entirely understand the mechanics of it just yet. There's sail things and something else . . . What?"

Emel chuckled. "You never fail to amaze me, you know that?"

"I'll be honest, I frequently amaze myself, too."

"Hang on, everyone—we're hitting atmo in fifteen seconds," D'Arcy said.

Jenks grabbed for the roll bar by the console, making room for Emel as the ship began to shake before the internals kicked in.

The Interceptor cut cleanly through Mars's atmosphere and made the descent to the coordinates D'Arcy had gotten from his Free Mars contact: a tiny NeoG base called Red Rock out in the middle of nowhere. One dinky little landing pad inside the fencing and a handful of buildings that had seen better days.

"Are we flying into a trap?"

D'Arcy looked over his shoulder at her. "I hope not, but if it comes to that, you're welcome to vent your frustrations."

"I'd rather be doing that on station," she replied, and watched the emotions flash across D'Arcy's face. Worry. Fear. Something else she didn't want to put a name to at the risk of making it real.

"I know," he said quietly. "One thing at a time."

D'ARCY HAD BEEN PRIVATELY SURPRISED AT SYLVIA'S WILLING-ness to meet him at a NeoG base, even if Red Rock was isolated and little more than a glorified research station. It was still technically NeoG territory with at least some trained personnel on the ground.

At least, he hoped there was still personnel there.

Red-orange dust puffed up around his boots as D'Arcy dropped to the ground, falling back to the black surface as gravity took hold. There'd been an explanation in OCS about how the terraforming also impacted the gravity both here and on the planets of Trappist. Truthfully, he hadn't understood it, but it was easy enough to believe that everything was close to Earth standard when you couldn't tell the difference.

He glanced in Jenks's direction. He'd seen the look in

her eyes as they'd shut *Dread* down, and the restless tapping of her right hand was a dead giveaway as to her unsettled state. "While I don't know what we're walking into there, do I need to worry about you picking a fight with Free Mars?"

"You said I could vent my frustration on them."

"If *they* start shit. Not you. Again—am I going to have a problem?"

"No," she replied immediately. "I don't have an issue with them. I don't even think they're entirely in the wrong."

He couldn't stop the surprised laugh that kicked out of him. "Really?"

Jenks shrugged. "People deserve to have a say in their lives—don't they? Earth, Mars, Trappist—it shouldn't matter where you're born. I won't even say I object to their tactics—kick ass if you need to kick ass, right? Anyway, you know me too well for me to feed you that bullshit." Her grin was sharp.

He smiled, too, but then went serious once more. "I have faith in Max and Saqib," he said, pitching his voice low. "It won't be easy, but they might get out of this."

"Faith doesn't keep the nightmares at bay, D'Arcy—you know that as well as I do." Jenks looked away, but not before he saw the sheen of tears in her mismatched eyes. "But I have faith in them, too. Fuck, I taught Max almost everything I know, and Saqib's a hell of a fighter. But I should be there where I can help, not down here," she muttered. "I'm useless down here."

He reached out and closed his fingers around her upper arm in a quick squeeze, releasing her as they hit the gate. "You are far from useless, Senior Chief. You *can* help here.

Keep an eye out for anyone who looks like they're about to do something reckless, no matter what side they're on."

"Aye, aye, sir."

"Brat." D'Arcy nodded to the officer who stepped up to meet them. "Commander Hoffman."

"Commander Montaglione, it's been a while. You've got friends on their way to see you. Scan picked up the vehicle just a few minutes ago." The shorter man pointed toward the gate.

D'Arcy snorted. "I think we stopped qualifying as friends when Maria said she would kill me."

"Well, for what it's worth, it seems like they're unarmed. Bet they're not happy about it, but if it was Sylvia's decision, they'll abide by it. I'll open the gate."

"Thanks. And make sure you tell your people to keep their hands loose."

"Ordered 'em once already, but I hear you. The last thing we need is a ruckus."

Not quite the word D'Arcy would have used, and he resisted the urge to tell Hoffman they were probably going to get one anyway. Still, he put a smile on his face as he walked toward the opening gate with Emel and Heli on his left and Jenks on his right. Chaske, Lupe, and Aki were behind them.

He recognized Sylvia and Maria straight off, as neither woman had changed much in the intervening decades beyond the obvious passage of time marked in hair and skin. Both of them were nearly as tall as him with dark brown hair and tanned skin. Sylvia's hair was threaded with silver and the lines in her face only starting to hint at her age.

The massive man behind Sylvia was also painfully familiar, with a shaved head, and pale green eyes. Mikhail

Starov had once been an old friend, but now judging from the glare he was sending the Neo's way, his feelings about seeing D'Arcy again weren't at all cordial. The slender redhead to Maria's left didn't have any handshake at all. They were young, though, or at least looked to be no older than Heli's twenty-five years.

They were also staring daggers in his direction.

Well, this will go great.

D'Arcy stopped a meter away. "Sylvia."

"D'Arcy." She dipped her head in greeting. "Been a while."

"Yeah. You wanted to talk?"

"Not here. Inside." She started forward, but the redhead caught her by the arm.

"I am not letting you walk onto a NeoG base. We have no assurance they'll let us walk out of here," they hissed.

"You've got mine," D'Arcy said, and sharp blue eyes snapped his direction while Mikhail snorted audibly.

"The oath of a traitor means shit to me."

D'Arcy knew they were trying to get a reaction, so he didn't give them one, not that he had time to before Jenks's laughter broke into the air.

"Something funny, NeoG?" The redhead turned their ire on her, almost successfully concealing the flash of surprise that rolled across their face when they registered who Jenks was.

"I don't believe you staged an attack on the MOS, and your boss thinks we need to talk or she wouldn't have asked for a meeting. Why don't we try working together since the bad guys clearly don't want us to?"

"*You* are the bad guys."

Jenks grinned and spread her arms with such drama

that D'Arcy had to clear his throat to keep from laughing. "Maybe. Way I see it, there's no clean hands here, no use pretending otherwise. Your boss wanted to talk, so let's talk. Don't waste time with your dick waving out here in the open where anyone could take a shot at you. Come with us or don't. We've got shit to do."

D'Arcy lifted a shoulder at Sylvia's hard look. "You are the one who wanted to talk," he repeated.

"Clair, enough," Sylvia said when the redhead sucked in another breath to respond. "You're not helping."

"I'm not here to help. I'm here to keep you alive," they muttered, and Jenks laughed again.

"I like you, Free Mars. For whatever it's worth *I'm* not gonna try to kill you," she announced, then turned on a heel and headed back through the gate.

D'Arcy resisted the urge to laugh at the look of utter confusion on Clair's face and gestured at Sylvia. "Come on, we'll find a conference room."

She fell into step beside him. "I am reasonably sure that's not how Clair wanted their first meeting with the infamous Khan to go," she murmured.

D'Arcy lifted a hand to hide his chuckle. "They're a fan, huh? Maybe we can get them an autograph after this."

Sylvia looked at him, a mix of a glare and amusement.

He shrugged again. "I'll be honest. I thought the trouble would come from our end, but I did tell Jenks to step in if anyone got twitchy."

"You'll have to forgive Clair; I'm asking a lot of them right now."

"I get it," he said easily. "And I'm not so naïve as to think everyone feels the same way, but there are bigger concerns right now and I'm not the only one who expects people to re-member that and keep focus on our priorities." Sylvia made a little noise, and he glanced her way. "What?"

But she didn't respond as they reached the door Jenks was holding open, and the senior chief said, "Hoffman says conference room 202, down the hall and to the left."

D'Arcy let the silence settle as they followed Jenks's di-rections. Even after all these years he was certain Sylvia wouldn't respond well to pushing.

"I see the NeoG did what I couldn't," she said finally as they paused at the open door. "Beat the impulsiveness out of you."

He smiled down at her. "Hardly. That's time's doing more than anything."

Sylvia studied him for a long moment, her brown eyes solemn. "I don't think I realized how much I missed you until you were right here in front of me."

Once upon a time Sylvia had been like a mother to him, his own long gone even as the ache for her comfort still re-mained. Sylvia had slipped easily into that spot—mentor, parent, leader.

Until D'Arcy had turned his back on everything she stood for.

"Holy Mother of God," Maria muttered, putting a hand on Sylvia's shoulder and gently pushing her past D'Arcy. "Al-most getting killed has made you ridiculous," she said.

"You didn't miss me, too, Maria?" Teasing her was the easiest way to deflect from the unexpected emotions clutch-ing at his chest.

"Like I miss a broken tooth," she shot back, and D'Arcy let his grin widen as she ushered Sylvia toward the far side of the table.

SYLVIA WATCHED D'ARCY LEAN OVER AND SPEAK QUIETLY TO THE tall blond lieutenant whose handshake identified her as *Heli Järvinen, she/they*. The lieutenant nodded at the orders and gestured to two other crew, all three of them leaving the room and closing the door behind them.

That left them even numbers—four on four—though Sylvia had zero interest in going up against D'Arcy or the senior chief even under better circumstances. Let alone the other two Neos with them.

Sylvia had seen enough of the news reports on Master Chief Emel Shevreaux coming out of her naval retirement and joining the NeoG to know she'd be a problem if it came to a fight. Some enterprising reporter or another had dug up the angle about her brother and the Mars protests nearly every Games cycle. What had been surprising was D'Arcy's ability to shoot those questions down every single time without so much as batting an eyelash.

He could deny it all he wanted, but the NeoG had made him into a formidable opponent in a way Sylvia hadn't been able to. Maybe if she'd had more time.

Maria's right: almost getting killed has made me ridiculous.

What could she do, though? She'd been unprepared for the ache that rose up when she'd seen him again and the way her fingers twitched of their own accord, wanting to pull him into a hug. He'd been the closest thing to a child she could ever claim to have—so angry, so driven, so fucking smart.

Then he'd left.

No, leaving would have been easier. He'd been taken in an operation that had gone to shit, and even though every cell in her body had wanted to mount a rescue operation, she'd known how it would end. So she'd had to leave him there. A martyr to a freed Mars.

Except the enemy had offered him a deal, and for reasons she still didn't know or understand, D'Arcy had taken it rather than staying true to the cause.

The leader in her still hated him for it.

The mother she'd become . . . well, she was relieved he was still alive.

Someone cleared their throat and Sylvia realized everyone was looking at her. Jenks's mismatched eyes held a surprising amount of understanding, while Emel's were carefully blank.

Sylvia took a deep breath. "First things first. Perez said the NeoG wanted me dead. Any reason to believe the word of a dead man, D'Arcy?"

The shock that rippled through the Neos was obvious and unfaked, though impressively none of them said a word. No one reached for a weapon.

They were waiting for D'Arcy, Sylvia realized.

He flicked his gaze away from her for just a moment, those dark eyes settling on Maria with unnerving intensity. "It seems an important piece of information went missing."

"Not missing. I told her not to tell you." She wouldn't apologize, despite the flash of hurt in his eyes.

"That's not a great way to start things off." D'Arcy looked away for a moment, jaw tight. "Because you wanted to see my reaction. You don't believe it, though, or you wouldn't have come onto a NeoG base. Wouldn't have offered to work with us."

She couldn't help the smile that slipped free as she nodded.

D'Arcy rubbed a hand over his shaved head with a soft sigh. "Bearing in mind I'm only an Interceptor commander and not necessarily in the loop on major decisions among the NeoG brass, I'm going to have to go with we were not responsible for the attack. If you give me some time, I can talk with Nika and get an actual answer.

"That said, I would ask you: What good would it do us? You're mostly out of the picture. We were supposed to hand over the MOS today. As Mars moves closer and closer to being a voiced part of the CHN, Free Mars is less and less relevant of a group."

Clair hissed a curse, but cut it off with impressive speed when Sylvia raised a hand. D'Arcy was right, of course— she'd said much the same thing to Maria earlier. That didn't make it any easier to hear, however.

"I suppose I deserve that for my withholding of information," she said. "I apologize. I needed to know."

"Accepted," D'Arcy replied easily. "Understand, though, that my comment about Free Mars isn't a swing at you, Sylvia. You've done a worthy job over the years representing the cause," he continued, surprising her again. "And you're about to see the fruits of your labor. But you also know you won't be welcome in whatever leadership they end up with for Mars. You're too volatile and have too much history. You've made your peace with it. I would think you wouldn't jeopardize all that you've worked for with something as reckless as taking over the MOS."

Sylvia dipped her head and then met his gaze squarely. "I promise you it wasn't my people."

"Again, if it's worth anything, I believe you. I think NeoG Command believes you, too. We ran the broadcast from the

MOS; it's a really good fake. The audio was pieced together from previous speeches." He grinned, suddenly boyish, and Sylvia resisted the urge to look Maria's way. "I'll trust you if you trust me."

Maria's huff was a thing of true beauty, and for a moment it was thirty-three years prior. Just before D'Arcy had been taken from them.

"Trust me. We'll be in and out before they even know we're there." D'Arcy leaned into Maria with that grin he always used to get his way.

"Damn you, this isn't about trusting you. The intel is still soft; we should wait." Maria shoved him away and turned to Sylvia. "We should wait."

Sylvia looked at the map again and traced a finger along the screen edge. She was always aware that people's lives rested on her decisions, but it was just a little bit heavier when D'Arcy was involved.

"Go," she said finally and held up her hand at Maria's protest. "Scout only, you understand? You pull back at the first sign of trouble."

"I will," D'Arcy replied.

THE MEMORY OF THAT SMILE HAD HAUNTED HER FOR DECADES, and now here it was in full view once again. Sylvia dragged in a careful breath through the tightness of her lungs before her next words. She didn't want to have to use her inhaler in front of these people; even if they were going to work together, showing weakness was a bad idea.

"Over the last year I've been in closed-door negotiations with several members of the CHN Senate and other people here on Mars. We were invited to the table by Senator Carmichael shortly after the vote on Trappist passed. Her hope was to find the same common ground they'd been able to with the Trappist Liberation Front and the people in system." She laughed softly and looked at the wall. "I admit I was skeptical about the offer. Trappist's history with the CHN is vastly different from Mars's, and there are a lot of old hurts that are never going to heal."

"Sometimes you don't heal, you just choose to move forward," Emel murmured.

"True." Sylvia forced a smile. "Though that's far easier to do as a single person than an organization like Free Mars. I have never pretended this to be a democracy, but I'm also not so misguided as to think I know what's best all the time. A lot of our younger members are in favor of a deal with the CHN. Their lives are entwined with Earth in a way that ours never were.

"But others aren't so quick to forgive," she said, and tapped two fingers on the table. "We've had four major splinters in the last decade and two more since the rumors started. None of them have made any public move to challenge me up to this point, but it's obviously happening now."

"Do you have names for me?" D'Arcy's question was loud in the stillness, and Sylvia could practically feel Clair's disapproval from where her security lead was leaning against the wall.

They'd argued about this on the way over, but Sylvia couldn't think of anything else that would convince the NeoG to accept their help and she couldn't afford for Free Mars to not be involved no matter which way this disaster shook out. Their press and the goodwill of the public had splintered in the last year even as they worked in secret toward peace to finally realize their dream of a free Mars. All thanks to the names she was about to give D'Arcy, the people who'd decided revenge and violence were better than any sort of concessions.

Now this.

"I have names for you," she said, and sent him the file.

NIKA HAD ONLY BEEN DEALING WITH PARSON GRADY'S PRESence for about an hour, and he was already contemplating how much damage his career could survive if he hit the man. He figured that he'd garnered enough goodwill for at least one punch to the face.

Probably should do it before Jenks gets here and does it for me, he thought and couldn't stop the laugh that followed.

"I'm glad you find this situation amusing, Commander."

He leveled Grady with a flat stare that he so rarely had to use on anyone. Sadly, the man had no experience with the potential consequences of such an expression and continued to berate him.

"We have several dozen hostages up there and you have done *nothing!*"

"What would you have me do, Mr. Grady?"

"I would have you do something other than just stand there."

"I could do jumping jacks if it'll make you feel better." That response was Jenks's fault somehow, Nika was sure of it.

Chae valiantly tried to turn their laugh into a cough, but Grady still glared in their direction for a moment before returning his gaze to Nika.

"Isn't this the point of the Interceptors?" Grady shot back and Nika stepped, very firmly, on his temper. "For all the talk about the NeoG's prowess at the Boarding Games these past few years, I would think that going up there and freeing people would be your priority instead of spending the last hour with your hands in your pockets."

The whole room went dead silent.

Sapphi and Chae turned to look at Grady, their eyes wide with shock. Captain Hosaka raised a black eyebrow, the expression of astonished disgust on his handsome face mirroring Tamago's. Fábia sucked in a breath as if to respond, but Nika reached back and touched a hand to her forearm before she could say anything.

"Mr. Grady, the Games are just that—games," he said softly. "While you are correct that part of our mission is rescue scenarios just like this, we do so with a great amount of care. We don't rush in like they do in a holo-vid performance. Given the current lack of intel and the possibility of bringing harm to those dozens of hostages you mentioned if we make a wrong move"—Nika didn't shift into the man's space, but the quiet venom in his voice was enough to make Grady take a nervous step back—"I will continue to stand here with my hands in my pockets, as you say, until such time as I know that I can pursue a course of action that won't put anyone in further danger. Am I understood?"

Grady opened his mouth, closed it again, and then nodded. "Fine, Commander."

Nika suspected it was very much not fine, but right now he didn't have the patience to continue the conversation. Whatever Grady's opinion on their state of busyness, he knew exactly what the people in the room were doing.

Sapphi was in the middle of figuring out how to get eyes on the station despite the com blackout. Master Sergeant Tran was coordinating the military ships who were now trailing the station. And Captain Hosaka's team was waiting on Mars Intel so they could move to the next step on their procedure list.

It was, he thought bitterly, a lot of "standing around with hands in pockets," but there wasn't anything else they could do.

All he could do was wait and pray.

"Captain Jaishankar is here. I've got someone bringing her to you now."

He nodded at Fábia and turned away from Grady, only dimly aware of the captain's murmured comments to the politician as she led him away.

SAPPHI: You're doing exactly what you should be, Nik.

The message was accompanied by a squeeze of her hand on his forearm, and he smiled softly. He appreciated the reassurance, but it didn't help the anxious writhing in his gut. What Grady didn't seem to realize was that Nika also wanted to be doing more, desperately wanted to get back in the Interceptor and fly to the station and find Max.

But that wasn't what was required, and they all knew it.

So he would stand here and do his damn job, even though it was killing him inside.

"Nika!"

He turned back with a welcoming look for the Mars Intel chief. "Drani, thanks for coming."

"Pfft. Of course. I saw Fábia and Grady. He's giving you

grief already, isn't he? Man thinks he knows everything." She clasped his forearm in a firm grip. "This is a mess and a ton, eh? Sorry for whatever ball I obviously dropped here."

"I'm not sure it could have been helped. I know security was high enough for the handover as it was. And yes, about Grady. I think he wants me to launch an all-out assault on the station with no intel. He hasn't even let Kenta and his team make first contact."

Drani waved a hand at Kenta, who spoke softly to Tamago and then headed in their direction. "Security was high. I had two people on station, but I haven't heard a peep from them since Carmichael put out the Code Bravo. There was a whole contingent of Marines also—ostensibly as escorts for the media, but they were also there for security. What's the plan to make contact?"

"Let me introduce you to Lieutenant Zika. Sapphi's got a plan that will hopefully get us some eyes in place." He gestured back to the coms. "After that you can take her, Kenta. We've cleared the room of all but essential personnel. I don't have the authority to boot Grady, though—Admiral Chen is trying to play nice with the CHN, and they've said he's the most knowledgeable one about the issues with Free Mars."

"They are unfortunately right," Drani admitted. "He's abrasive and biased, given some past history with Free Mars that tends to color his views. Like I said, he doesn't know everything, but he knows the politics of the situation. He's got history here and contacts. Sorry."

"It's fine," Nika said with a shake of his head. "I can work with difficult; he just needs to be reminded he's not in charge."

Every two seconds.

JENKS BOUNCED ON HER TOES AS CHASKE BROUGHT THEM down on the landing pad inside the perimeter of the NeoG base in the northwest section of Serrano. The largest and oldest habitat on Mars had been a full-fledged city for more decades than she'd been alive. It was weird that people on Earth acted like it was a dust pile newly scraped together.

They'd left Free Mars at Red Rock close to an hour ago with a promise of more contact once D'Arcy conferred with Nika.

She knew the information Sylvia had given them was potentially helpful; she just wasn't sure it was enough to push the NeoG to work with Free Mars.

Or convince Free Mars to come all the way here and willingly get on a NeoG base far larger than Red Rock.

Flippancy to Clair aside, Jenks understood the lingering trauma of almost a century of conflict, not to mention the somewhat ham-fisted distrust the people responsible for the attack had tried to sow among them. She was just furious it was going to get in the way of helping her crew.

"Jenks, go on," D'Arcy said with a wave of his hand. "We'll catch up."

She tossed him a salute before bolting out the door and down the ladder.

"Jenks?" Nika's voice came over her com, the unspoken question wrapped into her name.

"Ready to go, just give me an order," she replied. "Have you heard from Max?"

"We haven't heard anything. Sapphi's about to see if she can get eyes and ears on the station using a Fast Response Cutter. We're in the main Ground Control office."

"Okay, we're headed your way." She flipped the com to

D'Arcy. "Nika says they're waiting for us at main Ground Control. See you there." Jenks cut across the tarmac and ducked through the door of the main building, meeting the solemn faces of other Neos as she strode down the hallways. It felt like the entire base was holding its breath.

"Let me talk to Senator Johnson . . . No, the other one."

Jenks glanced into the conference room, spotting the speaker on the far side as they paced back and forth with a cup of coffee in their hand. Even if Jenks hadn't been able to read his handshake right after, the bureaucratic stink clinging to him was riper than a ship with a broken head.

Great, that's all we need here.

Parson Grady caught her eye and glared daggers as he stalked across the room and slammed the door. Jenks rolled her eyes and hurried down the hallway. She hit the Ground Control office and the scene resolved into a semi-contained chaos. People were rushing back and forth, urgency in their steps and on their faces. Groups of Neos were huddled around monitors in heated discussions.

She saw Tama first, her heart leaping out of her chest at the sight of them in deep discussion with a man whose handshake read *Captain Kenta Hosaka, he/him, NeoG Negotiation Team.*

JENKS: Hey, who's that shiny LT I see?

TAMAGO: Hey, you. <3

Tama glanced up, smiled, and went back to work. As much as Jenks wanted to go over and wrap them in a hug, she respected their decision. They *all* had work to do.

"Senior Chief." Chae dropped their chin along with the greeting and she squeezed their offered hand for just a moment when she joined them at Nika's side.

Nika's gaze flicked past her, and Jenks managed not to react as Grady returned and stepped just a little too far into her personal space. She reminded herself that Max and Saqib were the priority along with all the other people trapped up on the MOS and that keeping her mouth in check mattered if this guy was in charge.

She really hoped he wasn't in charge.

Nika was ignoring him, which was a good sign. He put his hand on Sapphi's shoulder. "You ready to go?"

"Yup. Hey, Jenks." She waved a hand over her head as she turned back to the console.

Nika's smile for her was real, if tight around the edges. "Senior Chief."

"You owe me vacation days," she teased because she knew it would take the stiffness out of his shoulders.

It did. The fact that it made the CHN flunky's scowl deepen was only a bonus.

Nika chuckled. "Duly noted. I'll make sure you get credit."

NIKA: You okay?

JENKS: I'll be better when we know they're safe.

NIKA: You and me both.

JENKS: Are *you* okay? What's this guy's damage?

NIKA: I'll tell you later. I'm in charge, which is what matters.

"What are our bad guys doing?" Jenks asked out loud.

"We're still working that out. Sapphi's got the FRC *Omar Tazi* out of range of station defenses, even though we haven't seen any other signs of them being active. That could just be because no other ships have tried to leave."

"Do we know how many people on board?"

"I'll send you the roster, but that's only an estimate. Captain Nier reported three ships shot up; we have a narrow window to go in for any escape pods or look for survivors. Another few minutes and we can move in safely again. Navy has two more destroyers and a cruiser en route from Earth."

Jenks nodded and held back the question about using the stealth program that *Dread*'s Petty Officer Lupe Garcia had put to use when they were fighting a rogue AI on the edge of the Trappist system. That was a secret their crews had kept under wraps, knowing all too well that tech like that didn't need to be floating around out in the black.

She made a note to speak to Nika about it in private, though. They could use it to get a ship to the station without being seen, and even to collect survivors—if there were any—from the ships that had been attacked.

If we don't use it for this, what's the point of even having that tech?

Sapphi conferred with the burly Master Sergeant Tran on her right for a moment. "The problem is we have no way of knowing what com the attackers are using, but we can be reasonably assured it's none of the encrypted NeoG channels. We know Max's shuttle is still on station. If I can get into its system using the linkup with *Omar Tazi*'s computer, I can maybe use the shuttle's sensors to scan for active DDs and also chatter on the coms."

Jenks was impressed at how well Sapphi was avoiding saying the word "hack" in front of Grady. Even if it was with full approval, she was pretty sure the man would have a hissy fit over the idea of them hacking into anything.

"Captain Nier, are you ready?" Sapphi asked.

"As we'll ever be, Lieutenant."

"Go ahead, then."

"Executing linkup in three, two, one. Showing successful connection on my end. How are you, Ground?" the FRC captain asked.

Sapphi nodded. "Looks good on our end. I have control of your computers, but if you need to, you can disengage. Starting scan now."

"I'm getting some DD pings," Tran said. "*Omar* is too far out, so it's only ID codes; we'll have to run them for names."

"I expected that. Here we go. Found it." Sapphi tapped the screen in front of them. "That's NeoG Shuttle 443 that Max flew in on. I should be able to—" She stopped talking as her fingers flew over the light keys. "I know it's because I know what I'm looking for, but that is too damned easy," she muttered to herself.

What the hell does that mean? Jenks shifted, the restlessness starting to claw at her again from standing still for a little too long. She was useless down here. Needed to be up on the station where she could actually help.

"Sapphi, keep the rest of us in the loop," Nika reminded her.

"Sorry, Nik. There are people in the shuttle. At least, I think so. It's just heat sigs, not DDs. Hello, can anyone read me?"

"This is Petty Officer Aggy Bennet with the NeoG," a voice responded. "Who is this?"

"Lieutenant Nell Zika, *Zuma's Ghost*. Petty Officer, I—"

"Sapphi? Is that—" The familiar voice was cut off before she finished speaking, and Jenks stiffened, unable to stop herself from reaching for Nika's arm.

"Ah, Lieutenant, are you on an open com?" Aggy asked, their voice tight.

"Yeah, sort of," Sapphi replied after a glance at Nik. "Give us a second."

"Captain, I want everyone out except for the Interceptors," Nika said. "Kenta, you and your team can stay."

To her credit, Fábia didn't hesitate and spun a hand in the air. "You heard him, clear the room, people. Now, move it," she ordered, and shuffled the protesting CHN rep out of the room, closing the door behind her.

Jenks slipped into chair next to Sapphi that Master Sergeant Tran had vacated. Tamago came up on her other side and wrapped their arm around her shoulders with a whispered "Hey, you." Jenks leaned into them and took a shaky breath.

"Captain Nier, Sapphi is going to lock you out of coms for a moment," Nika said.

"Roger that, we'll talk to you in a few."

"All right, Aggy," he said. "Room is clear and the com is encrypted. Let me talk to Max."

"It's not Max. It's me, Patricia." The video came up at the same time as her words.

Jenks had never felt such a tangle of crushing disappointment and utter terror hit her all at once in her entire life. Nika muttered a curse that D'Arcy and Captain Hosaka both echoed.

"Why are you on the station?" Nika asked. "Are you injured?"

"No, I'm not hurt," Max's sister and former CHN senator replied. "Kavan and I were with Max when Lieutenant Ruiz attacked her. Kavan was shot with a fléchette gun. We think that's mostly what these attackers are carrying."

"It's a flesh wound, I'm fine," her partner chimed in, leaning into the frame, and Jenks knew they were tracking all the people in view with a speed that impressed even her. "The gun I took is military issue. Max said the vice admiral called a Code Bravo, Commander. Someone—a lot of some-ones, I think, but I don't have a count for you—took control of the station. Max sent us to her shuttle and just a little while ago told us she was going to lock down the MOS. She also said the hijackers were tracking DD signals."

"That's why you're off. They're probably using the same method we tried? Maybe something more sophisticated, but I doubt it," Sapphi said. She rubbed at her chin in thought. "I'll send you the specs so you can do it yourself through the shuttle. It's not much, but it'll at least give you a heads-up that someone is nearby. I'm assuming the shut-tle is locked?"

"Yes."

"Sapphi, I don't think anyone knows I'm here?" Patricia said with a little shake of her head. "Ruiz is . . . well, Max stopped her. We brought a private shuttle that's under Ka-van's name. I mean, people could piece it together, but only if they've got a reason to look. Max told us to go at the first opportunity, but—"

"You'll do that here shortly," Nika said, cutting off her protest. "We've got a Fast Response Cutter nearby who can provide cover for you."

"You're asking me to leave my sister here." Pax's voice was frozen fury.

"I'm asking you to let your sister do her job. These people have enough high-profile hostages; if we can get one away from them, it matters, and you know Max would agree with me."

Jenks wondered if anyone else could hear the pain in Nika's voice. Something of it must have gotten through to Patricia, because she nodded once, looking as solemn and poised as the CHN senator she'd once been.

"All right, understood, Commander."

Death Toll Rises in Hellas Conflict

MARCH 29, 2414 (ESD)

Accusations continue to fly between Free Mars and the NeoG
in the wake of a transport crash near the heavily contested
Hellas habitat. All one hundred and seventy-four passengers
were killed when the transport exploded after being struck by
a missile and crashed into the Hellas Ocean just off the coast.
Body recovery is slow, due in part to the continued fighting in
the area and also the depth of the ocean floor.

The Hellas habitat has been a base of operations for
Free Mars for almost eight Martian months, despite several
incursions by CHN forces. Reports from inside the habitat
remain in strong support of the independence group, with
many posts on SocMed continuing the call for a free and
independent Mars. However, as the sanctions from the CHN
continue to hit the civilian populace hard, there have been
increasing calls for food and medical supplies both from within
and without the habitat.

There has also been a resurgence of support back on
Earth for the CHN to pull their military forces and allow
humanitarian groups access to the region, but officials
maintain that doing so would only allow Free Mars to get
a firmer foothold in the area and draw out the fighting. It
remains to be seen if this latest horrific loss of life will turn the
tide. Especially since unconfirmed rumors continue to spread
that members of the humanitarian group Hope for Mars were
aboard the transport, including their founder Giovanni Hale,
husband of Senator Willis Hale.

Senator Hale, who is a member of the Mars Oversight
Committee, could not be reached for comment. [Read More]

SEVEN

THE TWITCH IN PAX'S JAW WAS SO SIMILAR TO HER SISTER'S stubborn expression it made Nika's heart ache, but he wasn't going to budge. It was critical they get her off the station safely. Max knew that and so did he. The last thing they wanted was these people getting their hands on a former CHN senator, Carmichael or not.

The fact that she *was* a Carmichael only made it worse. Nika already knew the news was out and the clock was ticking down to when he got a com he did not want to answer. Though hopefully Admiral Chen would be able to keep the family distracted for long enough to let him do his job.

"Sapphi, can we tell if the MOS defenses are active from here?"

She frowned in thought. "We can, though I need to talk to Captain Nier again. The shuttle doesn't have the sensors to detect it—not unless they're being shot at. But I think we could patch in with the FRC's sensors, and maybe see if the nodes are hot."

"I would like to avoid anyone being shot at, so do it," Nika said. "Pax, if you will put Aggy back on-screen and stay silent?"

She nodded and the petty officer moved back into the frame as Sapphi brought *Omar Tazi*'s coms back up. "Captain, can I get you to do a long range—"

Static filled the screen for a moment, and relief rushed through Nika when it cleared and he saw her. Followed quickly by gut-cramping fear at her injuries.

"Max."

Surprise followed by a spark of happiness raced across her bruised face. "Not who I was expecting," Max replied with a sharp laugh. "But I'm not complaining. Hi, everyone." She looked around, and Nika saw the way her mouth wobbled when she spotted Tamago and Jenks together before she got control of her emotions.

"Gang's all here, huh? That means you've probably heard things have gone to shit. I didn't know if Ground Control got my message or not."

"They did." The fact that she was cursing would have told him the seriousness of this even if he hadn't already known. "What are your injuries? Where's Saqib?"

"Bumps and bruises." The deflection was easy—too easy—and Nika bit down on the demand to know how bad it was. No one else spoke, but Nika could feel Jenks vibrating next to him with the need. "Saqib is with Vice Admiral Ford and seven civilians. They're in his offices, with our hostiles. As far as I know, the members of the handoff delegations are also there. They should all be alive. I got a message from Saqib a little bit ago with some intel. I'll forward it along."

"Tell me what you know." He watched her switch gears from the shock, sliding into years of experience between one shaky breath and the next.

"The attack started about two and a half hours ago. I was jumped by Lieutenant Opia Ruiz. I'm assuming the intent was to take me hostage rather than kill me." Max cleared her throat and looked away. "Lieutenant Ruiz is dead. Ford gave me his command codes and the Code Bravo. I was able to put them into the system. The MOS is currently locked down with my command codes. We're probably looking at a hostile force of at least thirty? But I can't be sure. I have a list so far of first names and video of my interactions with some." She grimaced. "I apologize. They're not a pleasant watch."

"It's fine," he said, even as his heart twisted at the implications and the grief he could see in her eyes.

"I'll send it now. The strikeouts are no longer a threat. One person I tied up and left so they've likely been found by the others and released. Probably a poor choice on my part but they were unconscious, I couldn't—" Max cut off and dragged in a breath. "Sorry."

"You're good. Take another breath." Nika wanted nothing more than to put his arms around her. "We haven't been able to establish contact with the hijackers. The one message they've sent was claiming Free Mars. Analysis showed it was a cobbled-together fake of Sylvia's speeches. Sylvia has put out a denial of their involvement."

"That tracks." Max shook her head. "There's been no

mention of them from the chatter I've picked up on their coms, and Saqib said he doubted it was the case based on some things he'd overheard. One of them said something to me directly about 'justice for the orphans of war' right before they took their own life. I don't know what that means, though."

Nika heard D'Arcy hiss behind him. Max flicked her gaze past his shoulder to look at the other Neo, but she didn't comment.

"There was a jammer in Main Coms I took out, but I think there's another in Secondary. I haven't been able to get over there to check yet. They took people hostage in the Docking Bay, I couldn't do anything about it. I . . . uh— shit." Max rubbed the back of a hand over her forehead, and Nika heard Jenks's indrawn breath at the dried blood they all could see on her hands. "Nika, there are Neos involved, or one was at least."

"You said as much. We'll go over the lists for you and vet everyone as fast as we can."

"Okay. I don't know who to trust at the moment. I've rescued a few people, if my sis—" She cut herself off with a grimace.

"You're clear, Max; we spoke to her. They're still on station. Safe."

"Oh. Since the shuttle is still on board I'm going to try to get these people on it and out of here before the defenses come back online."

"You said you locked everything down."

"I did, but—" She shook her head. "There's someone named Castle on their side who's almost as good as Sapphi. Saqib mentioned them also, sounds like they're hacking the system, though I don't know why or what they really want. It's pretty clear they're trying to get around my command codes where they can. The door controls are out of my hands now, and I'm sure they're trying to get back the station defenses and coms. Some of it I know they can't. Engineering is a hard lock, but I don't have time to fight them even if I could. Honestly, I'm surprised I was able to get through at all."

"That's us," Sapphi said. "I've got things routed through the FRC *Omar Tazi*, so you're technically using the ship coms, not the station. Don't worry about dealing with them, Max—Lupe and I will get in there and sort it."

"That makes sense about the coms and thanks. I'll see what I can do about that jammer at Secondary after I get these people off the station. I—" Max stopped talking and looked to her left for a long moment. "I have to go. I'll try to touch base again with you when I can; it seemed to work with the tablet if I can't get to a console. I just can't guarantee I'll keep a hold of it or that we'll be able to get through."

"It's fine, Max," Nika whispered.

"Max, wait!" Sapphi said. "Here, I'm sending you something that might help. It should allow you to turn your DD back on safely. You'll know what to do with it. There."

"Got it." Max nodded, looked at Nika, and her attempt at a smile tore at his heart.

There were a thousand things he wanted to say in that moment and no time for any of them, so he lifted his hand to his mouth, pressing his fingertips against his lips. Max echoed the gesture and the coms went black. Then Captain Nier reappeared.

"Did you hear all of that?" Nika asked.

"We did." She nodded once. "We'll hold here, wait for your orders."

"Okay." Nika leaned down and tapped the console.

"She's taken out eight of them already," Jenks whispered. The sharp edge of grief in her voice was almost Nika's undoing and made the hollow look in Max's brown eyes and her unusually scattered responses viciously clear. Only slightly physically injured then, but worse would be the mental side of it.

"Nika, you've got to get me on that station somehow. She shouldn't have to do this alone."

The last thing he wanted was to throw his sister into this meat grinder also. Nika held up his hand. "One thing at a time. D'Arcy, what was the noise for?"

"The people who attacked Sylvia said the same thing about orphans," he replied. "I don't have anything more than that, but maybe these lists they gave us will lead somewhere." D'Arcy tapped his head. "You want me to pass them along?"

"No, I want you to start the op there and with the list Max gave us. I'll have Captain Clark find you a conference room to set up in. You're on planetside detail. I want a rundown on every single person of interest. I also want security checks on all the personnel on the MOS within the hour. If anyone else is a danger, we need to know about it now." He gestured to Drani and Kenta who'd been silent during the exchange with Max. "Captain Jaishankar, Captain Hosaka. Commander Montaglione, Drani is head of Mars Intel. Kenta's running the negotiations."

"D'Arcy, I'll get you Intel's files ASAP," Drani replied. "Let me know what else you need."

"I will," he replied. "I've got something to talk to you about if you can walk with me?"

"Jenks, you're with D'Arcy. Your priority is clearing the people on the station, make sure they're safe." Nika knew she needed to be moving, and until he knew if it was safe to send someone to the actual station, that was the best thing to keep her occupied.

"Do you need Chae?" she asked as she pulled away from Tamago.

"Not at the moment. Captain Clark is wrangling Grady."

"Chae, we'll start pulling names off the NeoG roster for the station and civilians. We'll want the ship manifests from the last twenty-four hours from Ground Control as well. We can use that to cross-reference names," Jenks said, and dragged a hand through her hair as they headed for the door. "This is obviously a wide net but it's a start. We'll do a cross-check as we go."

"You want me to set up a program to look for references to 'orphans of war' also?" Chae asked, and she nodded, patting them on the shoulder.

"Good idea. Do it. Anything and everything that looks relevant."

Nika turned back to the console. "Sapphi, start figuring out if there's a way for you to get into the MOS system from here and give Max a hand against that hacker of theirs."

"Should be able to. Hey, D'Arcy, uh, can I steal Lupe?"

"You basically already did." He waved at the petty officer, then activated his com. "Chaske, I'll send you a location in a minute; you and Aki meet us there. Heli, Emel, you're with me."

Nika brought up the com on his DD. "Captain, you and your people can come back in. I need a conference room for my people to work in. We made contact with Max."

MAX HAD NO CHOICE BUT TO SHOVE ASIDE ALL THE FEELINGS that seeing her crew had dragged up and squeeze herself into a dark corner of the freighter's cargo bay. The tablet she'd wired into the airlock console was in full view as the voices stopped right outside the open door.

Please don't look. Please don't look.

"No, we've got control of the doors again. Orders are to move the hostages to the Cargo Bay. We'll come back and sweep for stragglers later, but Castle has all the active DDs tagged. No sign of Carmichael." There was a pause and then the voice continued. "Copy that, we've got forty-eight. Collins has seventeen down in Cargo already."

"Is it just me or has this already turned into a clusterfuck?" another voice muttered.

"Keep your mouth shut. Simon, we're moving out, get everyone on their feet."

Max stayed where she was as the sounds of people filtered past the freighter. Then she waited another minute, slowly counting out the seconds in her head. She eased from the corner, heard the unmistakable sound of boots scraping on the deck, and froze.

"They're gone," a voice said, and a rising murmur of more voices answered them. "Shh. Stay quiet, everyone. Move slow. Stick together."

Max crept into view on the ramp as the group of people came around the back of the freighter. The person in the lead was in a bloody CHN Marine uniform and had a sword much like Max's own in their hand. Their DDs were off.

Max tapped the hilt of her sword softly against the bulkhead in a pattern that said "friend" in the old Morse code and the whole group froze. The Marine whipped around, sword at the ready and dropped it when they spotted Max. Max gestured with her free hand, and the Marine rushed the six others with them up the ramp into the freighter.

"Gunnery Sergeant Ebony Ranta, she/her." She exhaled, relief glittering in her dark eyes. "I am really glad to see you, Commander. Little surprised you know Morse code, but glad to see you."

"Long story. Are you hurt, Gunny?"

"It's all theirs," she replied with vicious satisfaction. "Took two of these bastards out in the initial chaos. I was on journo escort duty for the handover." The smile faded. "They killed two of my Marines, forced the others to surrender. I was able to duck into cover and they missed me in the chaos. Overheard them talking about using the DD to tag people so I shut it down. I've been collecting other hiders."

Max nodded, looking over the civilians huddled together in the dim light of the Cargo Bay. She recognized a few of the faces from the crowd at her shuttle, but none of the journalists she'd developed a rapport with were among them.

"They're moving everyone down to the Cargo Bay, though I don't know why." Max unplugged the tablet as she spoke, tucking it into the sling bag she'd liberated from a locker on the ship. "I was in the middle of something. Keep a lookout and give me a minute?"

"Yes, ma'am."

Max spun up the program Sapphi had sent her. It was a

beta version of Lupe's stealth programs for the Interceptor ships, but it looked like it had been configured for use with DD chips.

She didn't want to test it with a handful of civilians around, though, and Max went through her options as fast as she could.

All the way back up to the second level was too dangerous. Bringing them with her to the Cargo Bay to try to liberate the other hostages was only less so.

"Hey, Ranta, you know how to fly a shuttle?"

"Not well, but needs must. I can land it without wrecking something if I have enough space. Why?"

"You might not have to, but I figured I'd check. I've got a plan. Come on." She looked at the civilians with a reassuring smile. "Everyone stay quiet and follow me. Gunny, you've got the rear."

Max led them carefully across the dock toward the shuttle area. There would be a few other ships available, and she could give Ranta clearance.

She spotted her shuttle, still in dock. There had been a wistful hope that they'd have gotten away after she spoke with Nika, but a hope nonetheless. Her heart slammed hard against her ribs at the fear that followed, but the door was still closed and locked. With a quick prayer that Sapphi's program worked, she flipped her DD back on and hit the com for the shuttle. "Aggy, I thought I told you to get out of here."

"Working on it," they replied cheerfully. "Just trying to get a game plan together with Captain Nier for when things inevitably go sideways. Commander Vagin didn't want us to risk the defenses coming back on without backup."

Max exhaled. "Open the door, then. I've got some extra passengers for you."

There was a moment's pause, and Max lifted a hand, assuming that Aggy was double-checking to make sure she wasn't doing this under duress. Then the airlock for the shuttle opened and Max ushered the civilians in.

"You too, Gunny," she said when Ranta hesitated.

"I could stay and help."

"I know." Max shook her head. "But helping right now is you getting your ass on that shuttle. I'll manage."

"Carmichael!" The gleeful voice echoed through the air, and Ranta's eyes snapped wide at whoever had appeared behind Max.

"Aggy, go! Go now!" Max shoved the gunnery sergeant into the airlock and hit the outside door panel. A spatter of razor-sharp fléchettes slammed into the side of the shuttle as it pulled away from the dock, and Max felt the impact hit the sling bag on her back as she threw herself to the side. She landed hard behind a rack of maintenance equipment and spat out a vicious curse.

Well, that tablet is toast. Better it than my spine, I guess.

"Come on, Carmichael. Will wants you alive, but I don't have to be gentle if you choose not to cooperate."

The way the voice said "don't have to be gentle" sent shivers down her spine.

Max kept her DD on. It didn't matter if Sapphi's program wasn't working now; she wanted their attention on her and not the shuttle. Plus, it meant she could listen in to their com chatter.

"Anton, Vres and I will circle around behind her. Keep her distracted."

"I lost her on the cameras when she ducked behind the carts. Don't have a lock on her DD, must be off." Another voice chimed in. "I'll keep watch from here and let you know when she appears again."

That's how they'd found her. They had access to the security cameras again and someone to track her position. But at least it sounded like Sapphi's program was working. Max looked up, trying to figure out where the surveillance equipment would be able to catch sight of her if she moved.

And she had to move. She heard the footsteps, the attempt at silence that would have made Chae snort one of their quiet little laughs.

Don't be where they expect you.

Max took a deep breath and darted from her cover, straight back and slid under the shuttle behind her. There was no sign on the coms that they'd seen her.

Three of them?

She eased the sling bag and the ruined tablet over her head, holding her breath, listening for sounds of movement. They'd get frustrated when they couldn't find her. Give away positions. All she had to do was be patient.

"Damn it, did we lose her?" The voice was an echo on the coms and just above her. Max watched the booted feet pace a few steps forward, stealth forgotten all too quickly, and stop a meter away.

"Charlie, you got anything on the video for us?"

"Negative. She's there somewhere, though. Has to be."

"Everyone be quiet."

Max scooted to the edge of the shadow the shuttle threw on the deck. The booted feet hadn't moved; they were facing away from her and the others were farther away. At least that was her guess based on not being able to hear their voices.

She carefully laid her sword down on the ground and rolled out into the open and onto her feet in one movement. The hijacker was smaller than she, and Max broke their neck before they even knew she was there.

She lowered the corpse to the floor, grabbed her sword and their gun, and cut behind the tail of the shuttle into the deeper shadows at the back of the dock.

The shouting followed just a moment later.

"Fuck, she got Vres. Broke her neck. I didn't hear anything. Charlie, give me something."

"I don't have full sensors back yet; Castle is still working on it and Carmichael's DD isn't showing on what I do have. I don't know why. If I were her, I'd have headed for the shadows. I don't have good camera coverage there."

Max expected the hard voice to cut in again, but it was silent. She pulled up the camera positions on her DD using her command access and lined up a shot.

She already had a second line of fire before the exclamations filled both the air and the com.

"What the fuck is she shooting at?"

"Panic fire."

"She's shooting cameras!"

Max fired again, moving into the safe spot she'd created. The other camera she wanted was too far away.

She heard only one pair of boots on the deck as they headed in her direction, and she eased away from the shadows, sticking close to the pile of replacement parts and trying to keep her breathing even as she listened.

Her pursuer blew by her, missing her completely in their

haste. She held her breath, waited a beat, and then rushed them.

"Shit, Ranza, she's behind you!"

The warning came too late. Even though Ranza tried to turn on her, Max was already thrusting her sword forward and it bit into their back.

And got hung up on a rib.

"Damn it," she hissed.

Blood poured out of Ranza's mouth, and they crumpled to the ground, dragging Max with them until she was forced to let go of her sword.

"Drop it." The cool metal of a gun barrel pressed to her cheek, and she froze.

Her own stolen gun clattered to the deck.

"Stabbed him in the back. Rules only apply to everyone else, huh, NeoG?" The one she assumed was Anton pushed their gun against her skin until she stood.

"You started this fight."

Stars exploded in her vision when they hit her with the butt of the gun, and Max dropped to a knee.

"We did *not* start it but we're going to finish it," Anton hissed, grabbing her by the arm and jerking her back to her feet.

Max used the momentum and their distraction to her advantage. Her left hook caught them in the jaw, knocking them back and dislodging their grip on her arm. She kicked out, and the sharp snap of her boot connecting with the gun filled the air a split second before their howl of pain. It spun away from Anton, flying lazily through the air until it crashed to the deck.

Ten years ago, Max would have been frozen in fear. Now

she lifted her hands and gestured, channeling every scrap of Jenks's bravado she could and trusting in her own abilities to win this fight. "Come on then, if you think you can take me."

Anton snarled and rushed her. Max evaded the punch easily, shifting to the side and bringing her left fist down on their back, knocking the air from their lungs. She grabbed Anton by their black hair, bringing their face down into her knee twice until they managed to land a flailing punch to her side and break free.

Ignoring the screaming pain in her ribs, Max gave them no chance to gain their bearings, kicking a knee and hearing the crunch as the joint gave. Anton's shout of pain was cut off by her second kick that snapped their neck.

"Holy shit, she just killed Anton." Charlie's startled exclamation filtered back in over the com, and Max turned until she found an undamaged camera.

She looked straight at it and smiled coldly as she keyed herself into the com channel. "Unless you want this to be you, I suggest you lay down your weapons and surrender. This is your one and only chance."

Silence met her challenge and Max didn't wait around for the reinforcements she knew were on their way. She turned the channel down so it was little more than background static and bent to the corpse at her feet. She quickly and efficiently divested Anton of their bag, slinging it over her shoulder as she moved to retrieve her sword.

The echoing of shouting filtered into the bay and Max scooped up one of the guns; then she sprinted for the shadows, haste taking precedence over silence, and slid under a shuttle over the edge of the drop-off. She dropped the last three meters in a poorly controlled slide that landed her in the maintenance walkway by the shimmering containment field. The impact of razor-sharp fléchettes passed through the field with nothing more than a ripple of their impact and sped away on their lonely journey out into the black.

Max sprinted down and around the curve, pulling up the station schematics in her head. She slid to a stop two strides later, jerking open a maintenance hatch. Max crawled inside, grabbing the cover and closing it. Heart hammering, she left her DD on and hoped that Sapphi's program was working. Less than a minute later the sounds of booted feet hammered past.

"I've got nothing. Where the fuck did she go?"

"They don't call her a ghost for nothing."

"Fuck you, Tony. Do you have any idea what kind of fire Ralka is going to rain down on this place with her brother dead?"

"Will can keep her under control."

A snorting laugh followed the declaration. "If you think he—or anyone—will be able to stop her, I've got a bridge on Uranus to sell you."

Max held her breath until they passed and then shimmied her way through the maintenance tunnel, adding names to her list as she went.

WILLIS WAS MORE THAN A LITTLE GRATEFUL RALKA HAD BEEN off the coms when her brother died, occupied with the puzzle of how to access Engineering now that Carmichael had issued the Code Bravo and locked everything down.

He'd expected Vice Admiral Ford to do it, so the lockdown itself wasn't as much of an issue as one might think.

They had time. Jarvis would continue with the mission on the ground regardless. His instructions were to proceed even after loss of contact.

Ralka would go ballistic when she found out about her brother. It was tempting to exact retribution himself. Kill either of the Neos sitting against the far wall for what she'd done or one of the civilians. Will knew they'd heard Charlie's exclamation.

Three more people down, a shuttle escaped from the dock, and Carmichael nowhere to be found was a problem, though. He'd underestimated her; that much was clear now. Even so, any trouble she caused was a drop of water in the ocean. It would be lost to the waves of change he was enacting today, a futile gesture like so many the NeoG had made over the years.

You should have taken peace when you had a chance.

Even if he didn't get the codes from her, he had a way to make this all work in the end. The codes were the easier route, surprising as it may be, and Will had always been good at getting people to talk.

"We have coms back."

Will cleared his throat at Castle's call and stood. "Good. Marshall, come here. Let's get this party started."

EIGHT

"GROUND CONTROL, DO YOU COPY?"

The incoming call was not only audio but video. The face on the screen too young and too scared. Tamago, along with everyone else in the room, stilled.

Nika put up a hand and all eyes snapped to him. "Sapphi, tight frame on the video on our end, focused on Captain Hosaka. Everyone, you will be quiet."

"Tama, next to me," Kenta murmured, and they moved over to the blank area they'd cleared out for contact. Nothing to give away their location or who else was with them.

Tamago's heart tapped steadily against their rib cage. Jun was just out of frame, eyes focused on the screen that would provide her with a text translation of whatever was said.

More eyes, more ears, more chances to catch something that would save everyone's lives.

"This is Captain Kenta Hosaka of the NeoG. May I ask who I'm speaking with?"

The person on the screen swallowed nervously. "I am Marshall Voss, he/him, with Free Mars. We have taken control of the MOS. Attempts to board the station will result in hostages being ejected. If you do not comply with our demands, hostages will be ejected."

"We'd like to resolve this, Marshall," Kenta replied easily. "Are you speaking on behalf of Free Mars?" he asked. "This seems counter to the work that's being done to achieve the independence they want."

"I am in charge." Marshall's glance to the side lasted only a fraction of a second, but Tamago saw it nonetheless. "Mars has suffered for too long under the tyranny of the CHN. We will be free. I am sending you a list of names. Release our compatriots within the hour or hostages will be ejected."

"We don't want anyone ejected," Kenta replied softly. "The people on the station haven't done anything to you. How can I resolve this?"

There was a long pause. Marshall shook his head. "You have one hour."

The com went black.

Tamago started the timer on their DD.

"Captain, you are not seriously considering letting anyone go?" Grady's voice was the first into the air, and Tamago exchanged a look with Nika. His face was pulled into an expression they knew all too well from the rare moments when someone actually crossed his impressive patience.

Kenta was unruffled. "I am doing my job, Mr. Grady. Tama, what did you get?"

"Not in charge," they replied with a shake of their head. "Did you catch the look?"

"No."

"Off camera, just for an instant. They're too nervous. Whoever pulled this off is a professional, not some child. Marshall isn't more than twenty-five. I'd put feds on it."

"Captain Hosaka, I have the file. Headed your way."

"Thank you, Lieutenant Zika." Kenta tapped Tamago on the arm. "Take a clip of Marshall to Commander Montaglione, have him pull a file if he can."

Tamago nodded and headed for the door, sliding a glance at Nika, where their former commander was speaking in a low, clipped voice at Grady.

"I would appreciate some cooperation, Mr. Grady. Captain Hosaka is one of the best negotiators in the system. *We* are not here to negotiate, *he* is."

"He shouldn't be negotiating at all," Grady hissed back, and Tamago bit their own tongue against the surprising desire to snap at the man.

"Mr. Grady, we had this conversation. I am not sending a force to assault the station without any idea of what is going on up there. Negotiating with these people is Captain Hosaka's *job*, as dictated by the SSOP-47. People's lives are at stake. Or did you not hear the part about spacing hostages?"

Grady's reply was lost as Tamago hit the corridor, though they hoped for his sake he didn't say anything but "Yes, Commander." Nika had a very even temper, unlike Jenks, but push him too hard, and well, it was sort of difficult to remember the pair of them weren't actually related.

Tamago easily found the conference room D'Arcy and

the others had set up in and exchanged a smile with Master Chief Emel Shevreaux as they passed.

"You look good, Tama," the older woman said, her regulation blue hijab framing her round face.

"You do, too. I need to interrupt D'Arcy."

"Over there." Emel pointed behind a portable screen.

Tamago nodded their thanks and crossed the room. D'Arcy was leaning against a table, arms crossed over his chest and a frown on his darkly handsome face. The frown vanished when he spotted them.

"Tama." He spread his arms wide, and they stepped happily into the embrace. "Terrible circumstances," he murmured. "Still very happy to see you. We miss you."

"That's always nice to hear. The move has been good for me, though."

"I don't doubt it. That's me being selfish more than anything. What can I do for you?"

"We officially made contact with the attackers on the MOS. Can I get a workup on this opponent?" They sent the image over. "The name he gave us was Marshall Voss."

"Sounds familiar. Let's see what pulls up on a quick search. I can get you more once we get settled into the more in-depth searches, but we've been getting a lot of easy hits on most of the names, at least with public records."

"That's good, right?"

"Too easy," he replied as he uploaded the information. "Or rather sloppy on their part? I would have expected them to go to greater lengths to hide their identities since they've gone to the trouble of blocking their DD signals." D'Arcy nodded at Tamago's grimace. "Yeah. You and I both know what happens when hostage takers don't try to hide their identity."

It usually meant they didn't care about surviving and also didn't care who they took with them in the process.

"What I don't have is a match for this Will person Saqib thinks is in charge. This image of him is what Max got." He waved his hand and another image, of an older man with a close-cropped beard, appeared. "He looks vaguely familiar, but I can't tell you why."

Tamago frowned at it. "Is he on your list?"

"No. Neither name nor an image that I've seen so far from our databases. I'm trying to get these pulled as fast as possible. Anyway, according to Saqib, this Marshall kid isn't in charge. Shit, he's barely old enough to shave. I am getting old."

Tamago couldn't stop the chuckle at the disgust in D'Arcy's voice. "How's Boston?"

"He's good." He shot them a look as he bumped his shoulder into theirs. "Don't change the subject."

"Your analysis fits with ours."

"Great, so why would this Will put someone else up there instead of talking to you himself?" Before they could answer D'Arcy the screen in front of them lit up. "Here we go—Marshall Voss, twenty-four Earth years old. Graduated on an accelerated program with CHN University, North American campus network, when he was only eighteen. Degree in biosecurity." D'Arcy muttered a curse. "One of our hackers?"

"Maybe." They studied the screen. "Does he have a Soc-Med account?"

"Probably. Yeah, here. Oh, don't like that."

It was Tamago's turn to frown. Marshall's last post on SocMed was a black square with white text reading:

Going to right a wrong today. Love you, Mom.

"Where's his mom?"

"Dead for six years." The silence was heavy as D'Arcy read through the file. "She lived here. Moved here at the same time Marshall went to school, looks like she was an engineer with the CHN and took a private job with a firm designing newer energy-efficient habitats." He sighed. "Looks like she and a coworker were killed when one of Sylvia's splinter groups attacked a habitat they were visiting. Everything on this planet is blood soaked." He muttered the last bit and Tamago reached out to lay a hand on his arm.

"We're trying to make it better. Thanks, and send me anything else you find on Marshall."

"Of course." He mustered up a smile, but Tamago could tell his heart wasn't in it. They squeezed his arm once and then headed for the door.

"Hey, D'Arcy, incoming call from Sylvia Moroz," Emel called from across the room as Tamago headed for the door.

Grady was in the corner, a smug smile on his face, and Nika was nowhere to be found when they came back into the main room.

"COMMANDER VAGIN, I HAVE ADMIRAL CHEN ON THE LINE FOR you."

Nika headed for the captain's office. The sense of unease that had gripped him during Kenta's strange interaction with the kid on the MOS only grew when he spotted the small smile Grady wasn't able to hide behind his coffee fast enough.

What now?

Nika waited for the door to close before he answered Chen's com on the screen. The image spilt, revealing not only the head of the NeoG but a person with perfectly styled brown hair.

Nika straightened almost imperceptibly as he nodded to Chen. "Admiral."

"Nika, this is—"

"Senator Sienna Johnson, Commander, she/her. I am head of the Appropriations Committee." The woman's smile was cool as she interrupted Chen, and Nika immediately took a dislike to her for the insult.

At the same time the alarm bells went off in his head. Appropriations meant military budget, which meant he needed to tread very, very carefully here.

"Senator, what can I do for you?"

"I have obviously been briefed on the situation happening on the Mars Orbital Station, and I'm sure you realize the seriousness of this incident, given your association with Maxine Carmichael. I have some concerns about the handling of the situation, Commander."

Nika clamped his jaw down, glad his hands were behind him so the senator couldn't see him tighten them into fists. This wasn't the first time over the years that someone had tried to imply that his relationship with Max impacted his ability to do his job, but it still infuriated him nonetheless.

Experience had taught him that there was nothing he could say in response, so he waited for the senator to get to the point.

"Not only are there lives on the line here, but there are political factors you may not be aware of since you have spent the majority of your career in the Trappist system." Her smile was condescending. "As such, I feel it would be in everyone's best interest if you would avail yourself of the expertise that is available—namely Mr. Grady."

There it is.

"Of course, Senator," he replied. "Can you tell me what kind of experience Mr. Grady has that will help us resolve this without casualties? His last suggestion involved a full assault, which is against the current operational procedure we're working with."

"Watch your tone, Commander." Green eyes flashed with anger and Nika kept his face expressionless.

"No tone, ma'am. We have an extremely competent team of people here who are doing their jobs. At this time, I would hope you could see how inadvisable an assault would be. Our negotiators need a chance to—"

"This situation is a political time bomb, Commander. If Free Mars is allowed to—"

"This is not Free Mars." He knew the interruption could cost him, but it was obvious that Senator Johnson wasn't nearly as well-informed as she claimed if she believed Free Mars to be responsible. "The original message from the station was a fake, cobbled together from previous broadcasts." He wasn't about to tell her that they'd also gotten an assurance from Sylvia herself that Free Mars wasn't involved, for whatever that was worth. Nika suspected that would go over like opening an airlock without checking the door seal.

"Public perception—"

"With all due respect, Senator, I don't care about what the public thinks right this second. That's not my job. My job is to bring our people home alive. The public is not informed, we are. I am fully aware of the political nature of this, but the priority here is keeping people alive."

"Senator Johnson," Admiral Chen cut in before the woman could open her mouth. "I will remind you that the NeoG has jurisdiction on this, as authorized by the CHN. I have put Commander Vagin in charge because I trust his judgment. He can take helpful suggestions from Mr. Grady, but the final call is his to make."

The senator nodded sharply and disconnected without a word. Admiral Chen sighed and then shot Nika a wry smile. "Apologies for that, I hadn't anticipated that there might be a fuss about putting you in charge."

"Is that really what it's about?"

"Partially." Chen lifted a shoulder. "Sienna's not wrong about the political side of this. The last thing the NeoG, or the CHN for that matter, needs is another major incident involving Mars."

"I know." Nika rubbed both hands over his face. "Admiral, you should know Patricia Carmichael was also on board."

Chen's curse blistered the air, surprising in its ferocity.

"She's safely on a NeoG shuttle," he said, holding up a hand. "With any luck she'll be headed this way shortly."

"Luck is in short supply for us right now."

"Tell me about it."

"Nika, I do not want to have to tell the Carmichaels that two of their daughters . . ."

"They will both come home, alive, Admiral." He couldn't believe anything else.

Chen nodded sharply. "Listen to Grady, but feel free to

disregard his suggestions if they continue to be unhelpful."
She cleared her throat. "I will admit for all his abrasiveness,
the man knows the situation on the ground of Mars. He's
been around a long time. Tried to broker a peace deal with
Free Mars back in 2415 but it went sour. It's possible he'll
have something to contribute. If he steps out of line and puts
people at risk, feel free to eject him. I'll manage things here
on Earth; don't worry about that side of it. Senator Johnson
might have her hands on our budget numbers, but I have
friends of my own in the Senate."

"I appreciate the support, Admiral."

D'ARCY: Got Sylvia on the com. You free?

NIKA: Give me a minute.

D'ARCY: Can do.

"Admiral, I need to go," Nika said.
"I'll talk to you later."

Nika disconnected and did a quick search for Parson
Grady as a plan started to coalesce in his head. He scanned
through the information as he headed back into the main
room. This he could work with. He spotted Grady, now
wearing a wider smirk, and met the man's expression with
an easy smile of his own. Grady's smugness faded into uncertainty, and he looked away.

Don't think I don't know how to play this game.

"Hey, Nika," Sapphi called. "I've got an all clear on the
shuttle. Captain Nier said no shots fired from the MOS. You
want them to come here?"

"Do it. Tell Nier to keep two ships pacing the MOS. I want them to escort the shuttle to base and then head back. Mr. Grady, you are with me." He headed out the door, not waiting as the man scrambled to catch up to him. Jenks was leaning against the wall of the conference room. She glanced briefly at Grady, then met Nika's gaze, gesturing at the screen with the smallest tip of her chin.

D'Arcy looked away from the com screen on the wall. His expression didn't shift, but Nika could feel the burning question in the air. Sylvia's mouth tightened when she caught sight of Grady. She also remained silent.

"What is going on?" Grady demanded.

"You wanted to be involved, now you are." Nika nodded sharply at Sylvia. "Moroz, D'Arcy said you were willing to work with us?"

"Commander Vagin." She dipped her head at him. "It's in both our best interests, I would think. Parson, it's been a while."

"Sylvia." Grady was uncharacteristically quiet, and Nika shared a look with D'Arcy behind the man's back. "I am told you're not responsible for what's happening up there."

"Not directly." She made a face. "I suspect that a number of the people involved may have once been part of Free Mars, the ones who didn't think we should make any compromises." A wry smile curved her mouth. "I do occasionally learn from my mistakes."

"A skill all of us could stand to have," Grady murmured. Then he glanced over his shoulder at Nika with a sheepish smile. "Commander, you are in charge, I believe?"

"I've got a list of names of hostiles on the MOS, all of them so far have been associated with Free Mars in some capacity. We've also spoken to the ones on board, and they're still claiming that they're Free Mars. Tell me why I should believe otherwise."

Sylvia eyed him. "You spoke to someone? Who?"

NIKA: Show her the one of Marshall.

D'ARCY: What about the one of Will from Max?

NIKA: I want to wait on that until we know who he is.

D'ARCY: All right.

D'Arcy shared out the image of Marshall so it was visible to everyone, and Nika tipped his head at it. "Who is this man?"

"I don't know." Sylvia shared a look with people off-screen before shaking her head. "I'm sorry. He doesn't look familiar."

"He's demanding a free Mars. But he's not one of yours? He was on the list you gave D'Arcy."

"I'm not going to recognize every face, Commander. I've already told you this isn't us. The names I gave you are splinter groups for a reason. Some of them a decade old. We—"

"Don't have control, I know. I suspect we wouldn't be in this mess if you did," Nika cut her off, earning a flat stare.

"Might I remind you we also wouldn't be in this mess if your people had done their jobs."

"Sylvia, come on," Grady protested.

"Tell me I'm wrong," she snapped. "I accept my people's failure for missing the attack on me in our own compound.

You all have far more resources than we do, and yet you still allowed someone to waltz onto the MOS and take over."

The tension in the room tightened like a choke hold and Nika grappled with his temper. Even as part of him recognized that she was right—Intel, CHN, the NeoG—they'd all dropped the ball on this.

And Max was going to pay the price.

Sylvia looked away, sighed, and turned back to him. "I am also extremely aware that if this goes badly, it will not be the NeoG who gets eviscerated in the press and in the overall public opinion. It is not the first time it's happened. If Maxine Carmichael dies, our lives are done." A weary smile pulled at her lips. "Some lives are worth more, whatever the government tries to claim."

Nika couldn't stop himself from rising to the bait. "Watch your fucking mouth."

"Damn it, Syl," D'Arcy muttered, and shook his head.

"I am merely stating facts, Commander. We all know it. Surely you've all realized the timing of this isn't coincidental. While it's possible whoever this is would have chosen to hit the MOS during the handover regardless, the fact that someone like the commander was on board has to be a major factor in why they've chosen to do it at all."

"You think they're after Max," Nika said quietly as he wrestled his temper back into submission. The thought had occurred to him also; he'd have been a fool to think otherwise, but when Marshall hadn't mentioned her, there'd been hope he was wrong.

"Possibly. Though I think it makes more sense to say they're after as big a scene as they can make. Targeting one of the more powerful families and the darling of the NeoG is precisely the way to do that. Even in my younger days, I wouldn't have started a fight like this."

"She's telling the truth about that at least," D'Arcy said under his breath.

"Max hates it when people call her that," Nika said to Sylvia. "But you're right about us letting these people take over the station. It was something we should have prevented. Now we could sit here and continue to point fingers about who's at fault, or we can figure out how to fix this."

Sylvia studied him for a long moment before she nodded. "I am willing to help. Not only because I am aware of the politics of this, Commander, but because I don't want to see anyone else die, either. The independence of Mars has been my priority for closing in on half a century. Whatever you think of me, I want peace for the people of this planet and freedom. I am not willing to let anyone stand in the way of it. The only way you're willing to believe my sincerity is to offer myself up. To offer our help. And we can help. We have contacts here on the ground who will not work with you, no matter what is at stake. We can help figure out who these people are."

"And the NeoG being willing to work with you conveniently gives you more legitimacy with the CHN as a whole," Grady said.

Sylvia dipped her head in his direction. "It does. I'll admit that. I'll also admit you're right, you all could do this alone. However, we want the same thing, don't we? For our people to be safe and for there to be peace on Mars."

Nika didn't reply but flicked his gaze toward the image still up on the screen.

"Nika," Fábia said over the com. "Captain Nier reports the shuttle has landed. They're headed our way."

He was unprepared for the relief that flooded him and fought to keep his expression blank as he refocused on whatever Sylvia was saying to D'Arcy.

"We'll head into Serrano," she replied. "I'll speak with you again shortly. I am willing to come to the base, if that will help."

The screen went dark and Nika shared a look with D'Arcy. "Her people aren't going to be happy about that."

"Ours might not be, either." He didn't look at Grady when he said it, but the man huffed a laugh.

"I'll see if I can help with that on the civilian side of things." He nodded to both men and left the room.

"That's unexpected."

Nika rubbed his face. "Tell me about it. Ten minutes ago, I was fending off the senator in charge of appropriations because Grady was mad at me. Now he's wanting to help?" The more paranoid part of him wondered what the man was up to. "Do me a favor, D'Arcy? Run a thorough background on him for me?"

"Sure. You want to tell me why you didn't show Sylvia the image of Will?"

"I don't trust her to give me a straight answer." Nika held his hand up before D'Arcy could protest. "Look, she's right that this blows back more on Free Mars than it does on us, but it will spatter on us regardless. I'm willing to work with her to a point. Right now, we don't know who he is, but we can find out. We ask Sylvia—maybe she tells us the truth, or maybe she lies to us. Which one puts Max in more danger?"

D'Arcy nodded reluctantly. "Point taken. I'll speak to Captain Clark. If anyone has issues about working with Free Mars, they can leave the base," D'Arcy replied.

"That works. I won't tolerate anyone interfering with this situation. For now, let Sylvia know it's probably best to wait for the all clear from me before they show up here. Fábia said that Pax's shuttle landed; they're en route to us now."

"Small miracles," D'Arcy replied. "I'll make Will the priority. Let me know what else you need."

"I will. Keep me in the loop."

"Nika," D'Arcy said, catching him by the arm. Nika froze and shook his head. Everyone was watching and he was barely hanging on to his emotions as it was. D'Arcy squeezed his bicep hard.

D'ARCY: You let me know what you personally need. I'm here for you, don't forget that.

All Nika could do was drop his chin in acknowledgment.

Jenks fell into step with him as he headed out of the room, and he stopped just outside the door, but she gestured across the hall and gave him a little shove into an empty office.

"Luis is on his way to London and said to tell you he's talked to Stephan and is mostly up to speed. They're all-hands-on-deck back at Trappist; whatever we need we've got, and I've already sent them some files to run. Luis will coordinate with Intel at HQ, and they'll do a deep dive into all the station personnel, see if they can tag anyone else who might be sour."

"Okay." He nodded. "The kids?"

"Tivo took them to his parents and will stay with them." She tapped the door closed. "Talk to me. You almost lost it in there."

"I can't."

"Yeah, you can." She grabbed him and dragged him into a hug. "I know you and I'm feeling the same fucking terror right now. So here's me, as your senior chief and as your sister, giving you five minutes to fall apart so you can go back out there and do your job."

Nika collapsed against her, Jenks easily taking his weight as he let the tears spill over. She didn't say any useless words of comfort, instead just held him, standing as solidly as always.

"What am I going to do if she—" He couldn't make himself finish the sentence.

"The same thing I did. Figure out a way to keep going because you know that's what Max would want. But it's her and she won't give up. So we'll do whatever we can down here to make it easier for her to come home."

Nika straightened and wiped his cheeks clean. Jenks reached up and cupped his face for a moment, her mismatched eyes locked on his. Whatever she saw in his gaze was enough and she squeezed gently, then let him go.

He caught her hand as she opened the door, holding it tight for a moment before she could head back to the conference room. "I love you. I'm glad you're here. And I am really sorry about the ruined vacation."

"You can make it up to me by doubling it." She grinned over her shoulder and Nika, despite himself, laughed.

"I'm not that sorry."

SAQIB LIKED WATCHING PEOPLE OUT OF HABIT, BUT IT WAS ALSO something both teaching at the academy and his Interceptor job had trained into him. There was a range, of course, from people like Jenks whose thoughts and actions almost always lined up in perfect synchronicity to people who were deliberately and maliciously duplicitous about their words and actions.

He suspected Will fell firmly into the latter category. He also suspected Will was very good at what he did. While Saqib hadn't been able to see the conversation taking place in the other room, he'd heard someone from the NeoG on the com and the careful replies of someone who was definitely not Will.

Why have someone else negotiate?

He was glad he'd been able to send information to Max and could only hope that she'd be able to do something with it.

The com was over almost before it had begun, and silence fell once more, broken only by murmured conversations in the rooms adjoining Ford's office. Will had returned and settled into the chair behind the desk, ignoring the two Neos on the floor as he flipped through something on his DD.

Despite Ford's protests, Will had sent the civilians off under guard, supposedly to the Cargo Bay with the other prisoners. None of the guards who came and went engaged with Saqib or Jackson at all, so there was no chance to recruit an ally or garner sympathy. But they weren't forgotten.

Every shift or whispered exchange was met by a look from Will or Charlie, who was posted by the door of Jackson's office, gun held loosely in their hands.

There'd been no more communication with Ground Control, at least not in their hearing, but Saqib suspected not at all as the minutes ticked away. It didn't seem to bother Will in the slightest, which wasn't typical hijacker behavior. Most people would be nervous about the lack of official response, escalating to threats and wanting to talk to someone in charge.

Will, by contrast, was perfectly happy just waiting. He walked a regular pattern—Saqib wasn't sure how conscious he was of it—from Jackson's desk to the front room where Castle was occupied, hacking into the systems with several others, out into the hallway, and back through. However, it wasn't restlessness or nerves. It had all the hallmarks of a long-standing routine.

"What do you suppose he's up to?" Jackson kept his voice low, barely above a whisper, and had waited until Will was passing out the door.

"Nothing good. He's clearly in charge but he didn't talk to the NeoG on the ground."

Jackson didn't reply. Charlie had a clear line of sight on them again. They'd lost the ability to use their DDs to chat shortly after returning from medical. Saqib didn't know if it was because of the message he'd sent Max or to keep him from talking with Jackson without their captors knowing. He wasn't sure how they'd known they were on and in use, but the threat from Will, the same one he'd had Marshall issue, was enough.

Saqib didn't understand the demand to release members of Free Mars. These people didn't behave like the people he'd known before his parents had moved them back to Earth. Granted at the time he'd been only a teen, but the Free Mars members who were known around their neighborhood were warm and cared about the kids playing in the streets. They helped their neighbors, kept the streets safe from outsiders who encroached in the hopes of taking advantage.

And also none of these people bore the usual markers of someone involved in the independence movement. While Free Mars drew its share of Earth-born supporters, very few of them actually made the leap from financial and vocal support to actively fighting for the cause on Mars itself.

Will's guards—the ones who had rotated through so far—were a mix of Mars and Earth accents, and he was even sure he'd heard a Trappist accent from a slender person with long, dark hair.

Saqib had studied the briefings for the handover, which had included a warning file on potential disruption from Free Mars, but Will's name and face hadn't been among any of the possible suspects.

It was a hard thing to put into words. Quite simply, these people didn't *feel* like Free Mars, but Saqib couldn't explain it to the vice admiral even if he'd had the time to.

Yet here they were, pretending to be Free Mars.

Will had to know they couldn't keep up the act. Sylvia Moroz wasn't going to sit still and let someone else ruin decades of her work, and the NeoG wasn't going to let a challenge like this go unanswered.

Unless that's what he is counting on.

Saqib filed this into the new list he'd started. Even

though he couldn't get in touch with Max right now, he wanted to be ready if the opportunity presented itself.

And the key to all of it was that something about Will was off—Saquib could feel it in his gut. He hadn't run more than a handful of negotiations since his arrival in Trappist, and all of them were much lower stakes than what they were facing now. Most of those had been talking down anxious freighter captains, who'd made spectacularly terrible choices about what to carry in their cargo holds when they weren't nearly good enough at lying to get away with it.

But he'd run plenty of simulations, both in official negotiation training and practice with Max and Jenks—who was surprisingly diplomatic when she chose to be—and in the vast majority of those scenarios, hostage takers were often people driven to the brink, those with no option left besides violence or the promise of such. They were usually more agitated and frantic, hard to pin down on decisions, and harder still to calm down to rational discussion once they got angry.

Then there was a small subset of those who operated on a rage that burned cold rather than hot, and with every minute that passed, Saqib was more and more sure Will fit there.

He was also sure that Will hadn't done all this for a free Mars—he would bet Jenks a full month of head cleaning on that.

That was even more apparent because it was hard to believe that Mars Intel would have missed something this big. That said, the specter of the attack on Jupiter Station still haunted all of them, and it wasn't completely out of the question, no matter how much Saqib may wish otherwise.

"I want to talk to our people in the Cargo Bay," Jackson

murmured even though Will had returned to his desk. "How do we convince him to let me do that?"

"He's probably going to want something in exchange," he replied, keeping one eye on Will, whose hard blue gaze had flicked in their direction when Jackson had spoken.

"You have nothing I want," the man said, pushing out of the chair and coming around Jackson's desk. He leaned against it with a calculating look, arms clasped loosely in front of him. "But please make an attempt; it will be amusing if nothing else."

"We could speak on your behalf with our people on the ground," Saqib said. "It would go a long way to know that you're allowing the vice admiral to take care of his people and the civilians you have."

Will hummed. "Is this before or after I chuck someone out an airlock? Seems like that's going to sour relations pretty quickly."

"You don't have to kill anyone."

"I already told the ground what needed to happen to prevent it. What they do is up to them."

"I think goodwill is goodwill," he replied carefully. "We can have a peaceful resolution to this, and one of the ways to assure that is letting Vice Admiral Ford speak with his people. He can make sure they cooperate."

He didn't like the way Will studied him or the intelligence lurking in the icy depths of his eyes. "Cooperate . . . You mean like how Commander Carmichael is cooperating? I believe I was told no such orders would be given." Will smiled slowly. "You—"

"Will," Charlie called from the door before Will could say whatever it was he was thinking, and Saqib watched as he strode away from them. Another guard was standing there, out of breath as if they'd been running.

He heard the whisper, and even though he didn't understand the meaning, all he really needed was to see the way Will's shoulders went still to know it was bad.

"Carmichael took Anton's bag."

"JESUS, MAX. WHAT HAPPENED?"

"Ah, I made some people mad." Max had never understood Jenks's constant deflection and humor in tense situations better than in that moment as she sank down into a chair in the relative safety of the second-level break room.

Seo-Yoon gave her a hard stare in response before relenting. "You won at least."

"Oh yeah, couple of times. Got some people off the station, too. We'll call it a success across the board. They've moved everyone else down to the Cargo Bay, but I don't know why."

"Away from available transport, I'd say. The access is harder, though I suppose they're not using the normal security options."

"They've got door access and coms back. Cameras also, which makes moving difficult," Max replied. "Still locked out of life support, Engineering, and the station defenses. If I had a way to wreck that entirely, I would."

Seo-Yoon shrugged. "You could. It would just require getting into the Command Deck or outside."

"Neither of which are good options at the moment," Max replied. She shifted in her seat with a groan, all too aware she couldn't afford to sit still for long. "Can you move?"

"Well enough. Why?"

"I could get you all back down to the shuttles. Lia should have had basic flight training and could manage to get you all clear at the very least so a ship could pick you up. Though we'd have to crawl through the maintenance tunnels."

"Of course we would. Probably a fan or two that we'd have to bypass as well."

Max laughed, and regretted it instantly as the pain burst, sharp and bright, across her side. "Thankfully I haven't had to go into the vents. What do you say? Should we get the five of you out of here?"

"You're trying to ditch me, aren't you, Carmichael? Was it something I said?"

"Stop making me laugh, will you? I'm pretty sure Anton cracked a rib or two." Max glanced over her shoulder at the three civilians and the young Neo huddled around the table in the corner. "We need to get them out of here, and you need a doctor."

"You should go look in the mirror," Seo-Yoon countered, but then she sighed. "I know. I know. I just would feel better if you had a friendly face to keep an eye on you."

"Well, the good news is that with the coms up I should be able to get in touch with the people on the ground when I need to. I just need to find another tablet." Max made a face.

"Mine's probably still in Flight Control. I'll even give you the passcode."

"All right." Max pushed to her feet. "Get the others ready to head out, and I'll go see if I can find it."

Moving out in the open was a risk. She'd been able to slip into the break room with a careful removal of a single camera that covered the door around the corner from where the maintenance hatch opened. But the problem of how to get the two between the break room and Flight Control without being spotted was trickier. Max turned up the coms channel and listened.

"Strike Teams Delta and Echo, start sweep of second level. Check all offices. Captives are to be taken to the Cargo Bay. If they resist, shoot them. Strike Teams Foxtrot through Juliet, you have the Main Docking Bay and Shuttle Docking Bay. Search all ships, trash all the flight computers and consoles."

Max muttered a curse. Could they still get to the shuttles before the strike teams?

Only if you move.

She took the chance that whoever was watching the cameras before couldn't keep eyes on everything all at once and picked off the ones in the hallway with quick, precise shots. Darting out of cover, Max sprinted down the hall to Flight Control.

There was a tablet on the floor in the corner, the screen undamaged, and Max snatched it up, hoping it was the right one.

"Come on, we have to move," she said as she skidded through the door of the break room. "They're sweeping this level and the Docking Bay, trashing the ships. We might be able to get you all out of here before they get to the shuttles but only if we go now."

Max got them all out the door and into the maintenance tunnel. She put Lia in the lead, coaxing the civilians in after her and then crawling in after Seo-Yoon to pull the hatch quietly shut just as the sounds of booted feet echoed in the hallway behind them.

"First left and the ladder down," she whispered the instructions up the tunnel to Lia. "Move fast but quiet. Stay ready, there might be hostiles."

When they emerged from the tunnel into a shadowed corner of the Shuttle Docking Bay, Max could hear the sounds of the strike teams. "Stay here. If I tell you to go, you get back in that tunnel, understood?" she ordered, and Lia nodded sharply.

Max slung the gun off her back and passed it to Seo-Yoon. The woman took it with a wince. She was sweating and had her free hand pressed to the wound at her side as she dragged in deep breaths.

No one was near them, at least as far as the DD scan was concerned, but Max slid warily from the shadows, keeping out of the camera sight lines as she made her way to the nearest shuttle. She slipped through the open airlock and muttered a curse.

The scant hope that they hadn't started the sweep on this end of the Docking Bay died the same cruel death as the sparking console in front of her.

The escape pods were a death trap if—or rather when—they regained control of the station defenses. Though she had to hope that there were already a number of CHNN and NeoG vessels sitting at a minimum safe distance who could scoop up an escape pod easily.

Think, Max. Think!

If she could manually lock down the Cargo Bay, that would keep everyone safe until they could get them off the station.

All I have to do is figure out how to take out the guards down there. Right.

Max shook her head and left the shuttle, heading back through the shadows to deliver the bad news to the others.

She was halfway there when the internal coms of the station blared an attention tone and that same cold voice she'd heard on the coms during the fight with Anton echoed through the air, and several screens lit up.

"Commander Carmichael, you have something of mine. Surrender and turn it over."

H3nergy Break-In Work of Teens
DECEMBER 31, 2445 (ESD)

A break-in late last week at the H3nergy facility at Melas Basin turned out to be the work of bored teens from the nearby habitat. The break-in occurred at approximately 03:37 a.m. local time and the security on duty responded immediately. Mars PeaceKeepers were not called until the facility supervisor arrived, as the teens were not apprehended but had fled upon discovery.

Video surveillance at the facility and DD chip scanners easily tagged the offenders; however, the energy firm's public relations department issued a statement saying that no charges would be pressed and that the break-in was largely "kids looking to blow off steam on a weekend night." According to the spokesperson, nothing was taken, and other than some minor graffiti, there were no damages.

This is the fourth such break-in over the last eighteen months for H3nergy. A warehouse in Serrano was tagged at the beginning of the year, and two others on Earth have suffered break-ins. In those three cases the offenders were not caught due to malfunctions in the security equipment. [*Read More*]

NINE

D'ARCY WENT BACK TO THE SOOTHING IF SOMEWHAT TEDIOUS process of putting together the boards they needed for the investigation. At the top of one projected screen that stretched along the wall of the conference room was the image of Marshall with a huge question mark next to the word "leader." Next to that was Will's photo, which was still missing a file, and D'Arcy couldn't shake the feeling that the face was very familiar. Their early searches had netted nothing, no connection with Free Mars or any of the splintered factions.

He hoped Nika was making the right call not telling Sylvia.

Arrayed below the photo was Max's list: some names only, other names had images from Max's recordings, and still others with additional photos they'd collected from files. Enough of them had red Xs through them that it made D'Arcy's heart hurt.

Not that he wanted them alive where they could do more damage. The ache was for Max. He knew that she had taken almost all of them out herself and that sort of carnage left a mark on a person.

"Found another. Edwina Bolton." Emel joined him, and the image of a smiling woman appeared under the name Max had given them: Eddie.

It was a punch in the gut.

"Fuck," D'Arcy muttered.

"You knew her?" Emel's voice was quiet, pitched low to keep from carrying to the rest of the room even though it was only the Interceptor crews.

"She was definitely Free Mars," D'Arcy replied, the memory as bitter as bile in his mouth. "Or at least had been. Probably going to be a lot of that."

"Is this why you don't believe Sylvia when she says they're not involved?"

D'Arcy dragged in a breath. "It's not that—I believe her. I just have a feeling I'm going to recognize a lot of these names. That a lot of them maybe aren't Free Mars now, but they were back in the day. Even if Sylvia's telling the truth personally, the fact is she's lost her grip on the organization over the last year or more." He scanned the lists off to the side that Sylvia had given him. "There's Eddie's name." He tapped it twice to connect it to her photo. "Splinter group by the name of Live Free or Die." He snorted. "I'd say 'fucking children,' but she was old enough to know better."

"It's interesting," Emel murmured. "It says here her family was killed during a standoff between Free Mars and Mars PeaceKeepers in '23. Final report was that it was the

Free Mars explosion that brought the building down. You think that's what pushed her to the splinter group?"

D'Arcy glanced at the file, surprised by the pinch of grief. He'd been long gone by that point, but recognized Eddie's wife in the news article. Their two children had been born after he'd joined the NeoG, the oldest ten, the youngest four.

This fucking war claims us all in the end.

"Got another," Jenks said as she joined them. "Possible match for Levi Han based on the image Max got. Popped up on my list of civilian personnel from the MOS. They have no ties to Free Mars, though, but they were a student at Mars University. Their parents were caught in the cross fire when a splinter group fired on a group of Neos out to dinner in Serrano last year. Both pronounced dead on scene. Levi vanished off the grid about a month after."

D'Arcy hummed. "Flag it and keep looking."

Both women nodded and went back to work, leaving D'Arcy to frown at the screen.

Three different hijackers losing their family to this conflict wasn't a pattern, not with as much death as there had been over the years; but thanks to Stephan's influence, it was enough to make his brain twitch.

D'Arcy's DD pinged with the warning of an incoming com.

"Commander Montaglione? Chief Tangeu. I've got an incoming call for you from Trappist, Captain Yevchenko. Connection's pretty stable through Jupiter."

Like I summoned him. D'Arcy huffed out a laugh. "Put it on through," he said, moving to the tablet on the nearby table. "Stephan."

"D'Arcy. Sending some files your way." The head of Trappist Intel's brown hair was disheveled, a departure from his normally tidy self. "Three of your hijackers lived here on Trappist-1d in the last five years, all born on Mars. Only one was actively involved with Free Mars, but it was way back in 2421. I don't have anything recent."

"Families?"

Stephan tipped his head at the question. "None living, why?"

"Interesting link. Could be nothing." D'Arcy waited for the files to finish downloading and then flipped through them. "Does the phrase 'justice for the orphans of war' mean anything to you?"

"Nothing I've heard lately," Stephan replied. "Back on Mars, though, several years after things had cooled down, we'd hear that occasionally. I'm surprised you didn't."

"We weren't particularly concerned with justice," D'Arcy said with a wry smile. "Revenge, sure. Justice in a system ruled by the CHN seemed out of reach."

"Fair enough." Stephan nodded. "Let me do some digging. Also, mention that phrase to Drani; she's been on Mars longer. She might have heard something more recent."

"Will do."

"How's everyone holding up?"

D'Arcy glanced sideways at Jenks, who was leaning over Chae's shoulder reading something off their console screen. He'd watched her follow Nika out into the hallway earlier, seen the tear tracks on her tan skin when she'd come back in. "Mostly okay since we saw Max. Though, I won't lie, everyone's worried."

"You're not alone on that front. This was entirely too well planned. Drani's not the type to miss something, so whoever you're up against is good. And you don't need me to tell you this isn't about independence, at least not in total. Don't drop your guard."

"I won't. Thanks for the help."

"Of course." Stephan gave a final nod and then the screen went black.

"Hey, Heli, come here."

His newly promoted lieutenant joined him; without taking out any furniture along the way, he noticed. They'd been a hazard to themself and anyone around when they'd first joined his team, but thankfully the passage of years and a whole lot of practice had smoothed out the awkward clumsiness.

Their past spatial troubles aside, Heli had an eye for picking out patterns that was unmatched by anyone D'Arcy knew.

"What's up?" they asked as they joined him.

"As we start matching names to files here, I want you to go through the files with a sharp eye and start looking for any links, patterns, anything you find odd." He very deliberately didn't tell them what he'd noticed, wanting to see if they'd spot it on their own.

"Can do. Do you want me to include just hostiles or everyone on the station?"

"Do both," D'Arcy said after a moment. "Keep them separated, though."

He hoped that Lieutenant Ruiz had been an anomaly and there weren't more traitors working with Will among the NeoG. Or hiding among the hostages. But if there were, figuring out if anyone else was working against Max and Saqib could save their lives.

SYLVIA COULD PRACTICALLY FEEL CLAIR'S SEETHING GLARE, somehow bouncing off the front window of the shuttle and shooting back to where she was sitting with Maria. The expected argument over this trip into Serrano had been vicious, but as with most things, Sylvia had won in the end.

"They're not wrong, you know," Maria murmured. "Clair and I could go, but you shouldn't."

"I know, but needs must," she replied. "I'll apologize for my recklessness when this is all over."

"If we're all still alive."

Sylvia laughed softly. "Ever the pessimist. As strange as it sounds, I trust D'Arcy to do what's right."

"Do you? Even though he walked away from us to join the enemy?"

Sylvia knew the bitterness in Maria's voice wasn't just about D'Arcy turning his back on the cause, it was about him turning his back on her, but now wasn't the time to point that out. Sylvia had found her peace with D'Arcy's choice—the right one for him at the time, and probably, from what she'd seen, the right one for him overall—but it was unsurprising Maria was still holding a grudge.

Broken hearts had a tendency to heal poorly.

"Maybe he's right where he needs to be."

Clair's snort from the front of the shuttle was loud. "Only fools and children think fate is on their side."

"Not a word." Sylvia pointed at Maria, who held up her hands with a poorly concealed look of amusement. "D'Arcy aside, I will not let whoever has done this monumentally terrible thing ruin our best chance at peace on Mars."

"I know that much," Maria said, the amusement sliding

off her face. "But why do you think we need to risk your life going into Serrano?"

"You all know that we have to be involved or we risk getting left behind. That I have to be involved, specifically. I have not spent my whole life in pursuit of a free Mars to sit back and let that happen without me."

"You don't have to use your speech voice on me," Maria said. She dodged Sylvia's poke, catching her hand and squeezing it. "I know. I even agree with you. But I also agree with Clair. We can't trust the NeoG. I'd feel better if you didn't go to Serrano Base at all. Coming into town is bad enough."

"I'd feel better if this whole thing wasn't happening. But we don't get that grace. And you know what I said to Commander Vagin is the truth. We will be eviscerated by the press if Maxine Carmichael dies. We will lose everything, and the CHN will take that opportunity to tighten their grip on Mars and we will never be free.

"So I will be a fool and choose to believe that D'Arcy being here now is a good sign, maybe the best sign."

"Forget being ridiculous," Maria muttered. "Now I'm worried you hit your head earlier. How many fingers am I holding up?"

"You are a brat. I'll do what I need to, including going to the base if necessary." Sylvia laughed as she leaned back in her seat. Maria wouldn't admit it even if someone stuck her feet in a fire, but grudges aside, Sylvia had seen the emotions she couldn't quite hide when looking in D'Arcy's direction.

Sylvia was too old to believe in the ridiculousness of love enduring and knew that whatever lights were still in Maria's eyes, because of the damage of D'Arcy's betrayal—as far as she was concerned anyway—the woman wouldn't forgive nearly as easily as Sylvia herself had. But maybe there was some peace to be found on that front also.

Maybe I did hit my head, worrying about love and forgiveness instead of the trouble on the MOS.

That shook her a bit. So with the same ruthlessness that had garnered her the leadership of Free Mars so many decades ago, Sylvia turned her attention back to the email she'd been trying to compose to former Senator Patricia Carmichael.

Carmichael was one of the few allies she had. A woman who believed in peace on Mars and was willing to do the work for it. But if her sister was hurt or killed by whoever had control of the MOS . . .

Sylvia knew it would be all over for them, and any friendly faces would look the other way as the CHN regained control firmly and finally on the Martian people.

And they would react with more bloodshed.

"I'M READING A LARGE CLUSTER OF DDS IN THE CARGO BAY," Sapphi said, pointing to the map of the station that hung in the air on one side of the control room. "Jenks and Chae have identified most of them as station personnel—both civilian and military. But I'm getting weird DD tags for the others."

"Define 'weird,'" Nika said.

"Scrambled? Can't get a hard lock on them to get any kind of info. I had Captain Nier sneak as close as possible and do a heat scan just for some numbers."

"So guards, then? But they're doing something to their DDs to keep us from reading them."

"Most likely." She nodded, then pointed up to the top level. "Another handful of heat sigs up here. The vice admiral and Saqib's DDs were easy to pick out, but then they vanished. I'm hoping that means the bad guys made them shut their DDs down and not, you know."

She grimaced and tapped a bright dot down by the shuttles, hustling along. "Max. At least, her last location when we spoke to her. The downside of the program I gave her is that it hides her from our scans, too. She could be anywhere now."

"That's fine." Nika rubbed at his chin. The synthetic skin of his right hand always felt just a few degrees cooler than his left. "Even if we can track her in real time, I don't want to risk her location being public knowledge."

Sapphi glanced behind him at the rest of the room. "You think we should be worried about someone in here working for them?"

"I think the fact that Ruiz tried to kill Max is more than a little concerning, but I also don't want to believe that we somehow let a number of our own people betray us the same way they did on Jupiter."

"True."

Nika patted her shoulder. "Luis is working on that back on Earth with Intel there; we should have a green light within an hour."

The noise at the door drew his attention, and Nika looked around to see Max's sister stride into the control room, the murmurs of surprise following her like a wave. He recognized her partner Kavan, but had to pull handshakes for the other two people on her heels.

He sent their information to D'Arcy.

NIKA: Max's shuttle pilot and a Marine just got here with Pax and Kavan. Give me a fast-tracked background on both of them.

D'ARCY: On it, I'll have something for you as soon as I can. Also, here's your background on Grady, nothing strange or setting off warning bells. He was born here, and from the looks of it has been trying to work for Martian independence for a long time. He wrote the original Independence Declaration that went to referendum in '09.

NIKA: Seriously?

D'ARCY: As this whole situation. Explains how he and Sylvia knew each other.

NIKA: Interesting. Thanks for that, I'll read it when I have a minute.

D'ARCY: When you have a minute, you should get some sleep.

NIKA: I'm sending these two military people your way after debrief. If they clear, find something for them to do. If not, let me know.

D'ARCY: I will and I'll put Jenks in charge of them; it'll give her something to do.

NIKA: Good call.

D'ARCY: I'm serious about the rest, Nika.

NIKA: When Max is home.

"Pax."

He was always startled when anyone from Max's family greeted him with enthusiasm, but this time the hug she pulled him into was less surprising and very tight. "Have you talked to her again?" she asked as she stepped back.

"No, not since the com with you. Have you spoken to your family?"

"Not yet. Though I did send Scott a quick message. He's at Jupiter and will likely show up." She smiled. "It's on the list to speak with our parents, and soon probably. They're out a ways past the belt, and the news may not have reached them. If either of them coms you before I get to them, just shuffle them over. At the very least I can run interference for you on that front."

He looked her over, even though he suspected her partner had already checked Pax for injuries. Seeing nothing obvious, he offered his hand to her partner. "Kavan, good to see you."

"Nika." They gripped his forearm hard for a moment in silent sympathy.

"Do you need a medic?"

"No. Gunny here double-checked me on the flight down. Heal patch did its job." They gestured at the Marine next to them.

"Commander. Gunnery Sergeant Ebony Ranta, she/her." She nodded briskly to Nika.

"Are you hurt, Gunny?"

"No, sir. None of this is mine. I was leading a group of civilians through the bay when we ran into Commander Carmichael. She helped me get them onto the senator's shuttle." She glanced over her shoulder. "You probably want details on what I saw before the airlock closed."

"I do. In a minute." Nika looked past her to the NeoG petty officer standing quietly at the rear. "Petty Officer Bennet. Thank you."

"Doing my job. How can I help, Commander?"

"Report in to your commanding officer first. Tell them I'm going to put you to use," Nika replied. "Then go find Commander Montaglione. I'll send you his location—he'll likely put you with Senior Chief Khan if you see her first. She'll find something for you to do. Main Coms is two doors on your left."

"Sir." Aggy nodded and took off out of the control room at an easy lope.

"Good kid," Ebony said with a tight smile. "Nerves of steel handling the flight off the station."

Nika nodded but didn't respond. Instead he said, "Come with us, Gunny." Nika gestured for Pax and Kavan to follow him as he headed for Fábia's office. He hitched a hip onto the desk. "Talk."

"Someone shot at Max while we were loading into the shuttle. I caught a glimpse before she shoved me inside. I was trying to talk her into letting me stay." Ebony shrugged a shoulder at Nika's raised eyebrow. "It's my job, Commander. No shade to you, but I'd rather be up there than down here."

"I know the feeling, believe me."

"I suppose you do. Anyway, I've got video of the person who shot at her. Tall one. Black hair. Black fatigues. He was carrying an Aegis46; those are CHN-only fléchette guns. He could have gotten it off a captured Marine. But—"

"But you think otherwise?" Nika's DD pinged with the file request, and he accepted it.

"Whoever this is, they trained together. A lot. I'm not making excuses here, believe me. Just stating the facts. We were hampered by the civilians, but they moved in on my team *fast*. It looked like something you all would have pulled off in the Boarding Games."

Nika nodded. Training together implied there was a base somewhere. He held up his hand as he keyed his com. "Sapphi?"

"Yeah?"

"Can you have the *Omar Tazi* scan for outgoing signals from the station?"

"Sure, anything in particular I'm looking for?"

"I'll let you know when I see it."

Sapphi laughed over the com before she disconnected.

"Nika, it wasn't just the one. Aggy spotted three people with the shuttle's outside camera before we took off," Pax said. "There might have been more. If they—"

"They would have taken her captive," he said softly. It wasn't much of a reassurance, but it was the best one he could give. "If they caught her. She's too valuable a hostage."

"That's what she said about me." Pax pressed fingers to her lips as the emotions welled up. Then with the same sort of self-control he'd seen time and again from Max, she sniffed away the tears and forced a smile worthy of a politician. "Apologies. Are you finished debriefing the gunny? I have something important for you."

"I am, unless you have more for me?" He glanced at Ebony, who shook her head. "All right, same as Aggy. Coms and check in, then head for the conference room. Find someone to get you some clean gear." He sent her the location and waited for the door to close behind her before he looked back at Pax.

She rubbed her hands over her arms and paced the length of the office. "Over a year ago I managed to talk Sylvia Moroz into meeting with me, unofficially. My hope was that I could start up some line of communication between Free Mars and the CHN again. Make a second attempt at peace."

"Based on the success with Trappist?"

"Yes. I still have a lot of pull among the sitting senators. Things have improved so much with Trappist; a number of them—myself included—had hopes we could translate that into something similar here on Mars. I knew with the plans already in the works to turn the station over to civilian control it was the best time to retry something, anything to get Free Mars to the table."

It was habit, more than anything, that had Nika not telling Pax he knew about the meetings until she'd finished with the whole story. The look he got from her in return was enough like Max's that he couldn't stop himself from smiling even though it hurt.

"D'Arcy said Sylvia had mentioned it when they met. I appreciate the details, though."

"She met with D'Arcy? When?"

"A little while ago. Thankfully Sylvia seems to be levelheaded. Our adversaries tried to pin her attempted assassination on us."

"What?"

"Between that and the fake messaging from the MOS attackers, it feels very much like someone was trying to set the NeoG and Free Mars at each other's throats—or *more* at each other's throats. I'd like to avoid that. Sylvia is headed into town, for obvious reasons not here just yet. Are you familiar with Parson Grady?"

"Yes, we've worked together." She frowned. "He was supposed to be on the station for the handoff."

"He had a shuttle issue and got stuck down here. We didn't exactly hit it off." Nika tipped his head at her when she laughed. "I know; however, he seems to have come around and I'm aware he's got experience we can use. If it's helpful, I can have him join you."

"Absolutely. I know a lot of people find him . . . difficult to work with, but the same can be said about me," she said wryly. "Anyway, we've always gotten along well."

"I appreciate it." Grady hadn't spoken up since the meeting with Sylvia, except to offer a few pieces of commentary on the situation when Nika had asked directly.

"Nika, about Max . . ." Pax paused mid-thought, absently chewing on a knuckle for a moment until Kavan reached out and gently tapped her hand. She laughed and dropped it. "Sorry, old nervous habit."

"You're worried, it's fine," they replied, and Nika's heart ached at the exchange.

"You're not going to tell me Max is tough, and she'll be just fine?" she asked Nika.

He shook his head, grateful Jenks had given him the space to get some of his feelings out of his chest so he could handle all this with a clearer head. "She's trapped on a space station with a bunch of people who probably aren't afraid to use her to get what they want—up to and including killing her. I trust Max with my life, but I also know that pretending like she's not in danger doesn't do any of us any good."

He also knew the longer this went on the more danger she was in. She'd get tired, injured more than she already was, and eventually make a mistake.

"I understand more and more every time we talk why she loves you," Pax said, her voice pitched for his ears only.

That hurt, reminding him of saying goodbye to Max, but he didn't let it show as he gestured for the door. "Let's get to work. We'll see if Captain Clark can find you an empty office."

"WE'VE GOT TEN MINUTES," TAMAGO SAID WHEN THE WARNING flashed on their DD. "How are we doing?"

"I just heard from the Southern Pointe rehab facility; they've got their three ready to go out the door, just need the word. That was the last on the list." Jun sent the file over to Tamago without their prompting.

"Kenta, we've got them all."

"All right, let's com the MOS and let them know."

Tamago watched him cross the room and speak with Nika. There'd been a lot of movement in the background as their team had worked on getting the Free Mars people released. They'd seen Pax come in; the former senator had given them a nod of greeting before disappearing into Captain Clark's office with Nika. She'd left shortly after with her shadow of a partner following, and Grady had apparently gone to join her. Tamago wasn't sure what had gone down with the man, but he appeared to be cooperating.

They wondered if the people on the MOS would be equally cooperative now that they were getting what they'd asked for.

"Why you frowning?" Jun asked softly.

"I don't know," Tamago replied. "This felt too easy. All these people they wanted released are low-level Free Mars doing a year, maybe two of rehab and community service. Nothing that would have made the CHN balk about releasing them. For the threat, it feels . . ." They grappled for a word that fit.

"Underplayed?" Jun supplied, and Tamago nodded.

"Sort of. Stalling? It feels like they're just stalling, but I don't know why." Tamago rubbed their hands against their pant legs and made a face. "This whole thing feels weird."

"Nika, they're moving Ford," Sapphi said. "I think."

"You think?"

"I caught a blip of his DD just now in the elevator, then it vanished again."

"Where would they be moving him?"

"Down to the Cargo Bay? That's where they seem to be putting everyone. Hold on—I'm getting an incoming com. It's Marshall."

"Tamago." Kenta waved them over as he moved back to their station. "Sapphi, put him on-screen."

Marshall appeared, looking more pale and worried than previously. He was chewing on his bottom lip and his eyes darted around him in a restless pattern before they settled on Kenta.

"Marshall, we have your people ready to be released." Kenta's smile was easy and there was no trace of the tension that had been in his shoulders just a moment before.

"Good, uh, we'll be in touch again."

"Wait!" Kenta tried, but the screen had already gone black and Tamago's unease grew.

They shared a frown with Kenta. "What is going on?"

"Oh Hades."

Tamago heard Sapphi's curse and crossed to her before they even fully realized their legs were moving. "What is it?"

Sapphi had a hand pressed to her mouth in shock that she removed only to point a shaking hand at a blinking DD marker just before it changed to a dull red. "That was Vice Admiral Ford."

"We gave them what they wanted," Kenta protested. "What are they doing?"

"Sapphi, get the MOS back on the coms now," Nika ordered, and Sapphi's fingers flew over the light keys.

"No response," she said. "Wait, I'm getting something. It's a broadcast, not live."

"Do not play it, Sapphi. Clear this room now." Nika's voice rang in the air, and everyone jumped into motion. "Kenta, you and your people stay. Captain Clark?"

"I'm right here," Fábia replied. "Rog, get on the door, don't let anyone in."

Tamago reached down and felt Sapphi link her fingers through theirs.

There was no sound on the vid. The angle of Vice Admiral Ford's face meant it was probably from the airlock camera. The man stared into it for a moment; he was saying something and then a surprisingly serene smile appeared on his face.

Captain Clark's choked sob was loud in the room when

the camera cut to an outside view, and they watched as Ford floated away from the station.

"Send Captain Nier in," Nika said softly. "They'll be able to tag his DD and retrieve his body as soon as the station moves out of range. I don't want a word of this to leave this room. Kenta, figure out why the fuck they did that when we gave them what they asked for."

MAX STARED FOR A LONGER MOMENT THAN SHE SHOULD HAVE before she ducked for cover. But no attack came. She recognized Will from the image Saqib had sent her. The man smiled and jerked Ford into the frame, and Max inhaled sharply. The vice admiral was sporting a large bruise on the side of his face.

"Commander Carmichael, you will return my property. Or the vice admiral here is going for a walk. You have a minute to respond."

Max's breath went viscous in her lungs when he shoved Ford toward the airlock. She didn't even know what she had, which meant the only way to stop this was to turn herself over.

There were no airlocks like that on the first or second levels of the station, which meant they were actually down here at the Docking Bay. But where?

She keyed on her com. "I don't know what you want, but let him go. I'll meet you."

"Max, do not comply! That's a direct order."

Will punched Ford in the side, causing the Neo to fold over with a groan. Will shoved him into the airlock. "Forty-five seconds."

She'd heard the faint echo of Ford's shout before it was

cut off and Max took off at a sprint toward the nearest air-lock. She wove through the ships and racks of maintenance tools, every screen around her lit up with Ford's face.

"I'm on my way," she said, sending the desperate com directly to him as she ran.

"No."

"Ford."

"I'm serious. The man you saw is named Will. He's in charge, no matter who he's been putting in front of the camera to talk to the people on the ground. If I know you, you've figured out how to talk to them so make sure they know."

"I did already," she whispered. "Ford—"

"I don't know what his end game is. But he's waiting—for something. Find out what it is and figure out what you have that he wants. Whatever it is, he needs it for what he's planning. You can't save me."

"I can't let you die."

"Max, while I understand you're iffy on following orders, I need you to obey this one for me. They want your command codes, and whatever is in that bag you've taken from them. Both of them are important enough to die for. I know the cost of keeping people safe. I've always known it."

"Don't. Please."

He smiled, and Max skidded to a stop as the airlock opened and Ford was sucked out into the black. She barely bit back the wail as she sank to her knees.

You can't fall apart right now, Max. I know, I'm sorry. Get up. Back to what you were doing.

She staggered to her feet, swallowing back her tears, letting the rage burn them away as she made her way back to where Seo-Yoon and the others were waiting.

SAQIB GROANED AS HE REGAINED CONSCIOUSNESS. HE REACHED up and touched his temple, fingers coming away sticky with blood.

The last thing he remembered was the butt of a gun in his vision because Ford— Saqib jerked upright. "Vice Admiral?"

"He wakes." Will's dry voice cut through the misery and Saqib lifted his head. The room spun dangerously, but he pushed himself to sitting and glared at the man who dropped into a crouch in front of him.

"Where's Ford?"

It was the smile that had Saqib deciding Will was missing something important inside him—*no one* took that much joy in the words that followed. "No longer with us, I'm afraid. He took a walk. Commander Carmichael refused to play nicely, and there has to be consequences for that."

"You bastard."

Will tutted. "Now, Lieutenant Commander, such language out of an officer of the NeoG. I laid out the terms, Ford ordered her to ignore me, and she obeyed like a good little Neo."

"What do you want?" Saqib snarled the words. He was done playing whatever game Will wanted to play.

"Too soon for that. You'd maybe ignore my warning about contacting Max to spill the secret. All things considered I am right on schedule." Will tapped a hand on his thigh and stood. "Don't worry, we'll do a few more spins around the planet as things fall into place like tumblers in a lock and then you'll see. There's a med kit for you to patch yourself up, but I think a trip to medical would be too risky."

Saqib bit his tongue and reached for the kit, even though

his hands itched to wrap themselves around Will's neck. He knew he'd be lucky to get on his feet at this point, let alone take this man down.

As he pulled out the supplies, he let his mind wander through various options of escape or contacting Max again that wouldn't end in his death, or worse, someone else's.

Nothing immediately came to mind, but Will wasn't the only person who could be patient.

TEN

NIKA LEANED AGAINST THE BACK WALL OF THE CONFERENCE room, out of the way of D'Arcy's team, and stared, unseeing, at the images scrolling on the screen across the room.

The loop of Ford's death played relentlessly in his head.

He hadn't spoken to his old academy instructor for years, but he'd never forgotten him. Ford had taught Nika so much—not just about strategy but how to be a leader. The first person who'd seen something in him and took the time to nudge him down the path that had led him here.

And he'd failed him.

"Sometimes all the strategy planning in the world isn't going to save you." Ford's words from long ago suddenly echoed in his head. *"I need you all to remember this. Plans fall apart. Shit happens that you cannot and will not anticipate. You learn how to deal with the unexpected and make decisions with the information you have available. Our goal is to save lives, but*

you have to be aware that you won't save everyone. Sometimes people die regardless of everything we do to try to save them."

"Commander?"

Nika blinked at Grady and then rubbed a hand over his face. "Sorry, I was—"

"No apology needed." Grady sighed. "Did you know the vice admiral well?"

"I knew him from my academy days. You?"

"Our paths crossed obviously, but no. He seemed like a good man. Always very levelheaded and focused on the task at hand." Grady cleared his throat. "You have my condolences, and my apologies for how things started off between us, Commander. I have been in this a very long time and something Sylvia said reminded me—well, we all make mistakes. Learning from them is the important part, and I shamefully haven't done that."

Nika stayed quiet as the man rubbed his hands together before he continued. "I was one of the original architects of the Independence referendum, you know? I'd only just moved to Mars in 2407 with my wife and my teenaged son. Both of them took to this planet as if they'd been born here. In some ways it was hard to blame them; I was working long hours and in the office more often than not.

"But when we did spend time together, I could see the beauty of it through their eyes, and since it was beneficial to my career, I made it a point to get to know our neighbors and the people of Mars. We were all very excited when Senator Hale approached me to help him draft the referendum, and so hopeful that it would pass."

"I can't imagine how heartbreaking it must have been," Nika murmured.

"In so many ways and we all of us expressed it differently. Ilyia retreated. Our son, Cale, got angry. I threw myself back into my work and missed all the signs that my family was falling apart until it was too late." Grady shrugged as he wandered closer to the opposite wall where the images shifted and changed on the screen.

Nika had read all this in the file D'Arcy had given him on Grady, but the man seemed to need to tell the story so he didn't interrupt.

"Cale joined Free Mars. I disowned him, for the sake of my career. And my wife left me for the betrayal." Grady's smile was tight with pain. "I thought we could do this the right way—bring independence through the Senate. Part of me still wants to believe that. But Cale, he . . . well, he remains as impulsive as his mother. I suppose I am luckier than most in this conflict; they are both still alive. But still, 'Grief turns a garden into unchecked, angry weeds.' One of my wife's favorite poets, Kadra Shavi. She's written a lot about the conflict here."

"Am I interrupting?"

Nika looked away from Grady and smiled at Pax. "No, did you need me?"

"I was looking for Parson, actually. Huh, why is Senator Hale on your board?"

"Who?" Nika glanced back at the screen and Grady frowned.

"Willis Hale, I don't understand why he would be on here; he dropped off the grid in 2414 about six months after his husband was killed at Hellas," Patricia said, gesturing. "How do you stop the playback?"

Nika reached out and touched the screen. He tapped it twice and swiped back until Pax said, "Stop. That one."

The photo from Max stared back at them and Nika swore. "I'm sorry, that's Willis Hale?" Even as he asked the question, he pulled a file on the former senator and dropped a firestorm of curses that would have impressed Jenks when the photos gave him a face match of a reasonable percentage with the age difference. "D'Arcy!"

The big man joined them in two short strides. "What's going on?"

"Patricia is saying this is Willis Hale."

"She's right," Grady said. "Older but I know that face."

"Why didn't we find it in the initial search?" D'Arcy muttered. He knew Heli wouldn't have missed it.

"He went off-grid after his husband died," Pax said. "That would have wiped his file from the database."

"For public searches, yes," D'Arcy replied. "But it would have still been in official records and should have come up. That's not right. The files are still there, but they don't pop up unless I access them directly. I need Sapphi to look at this."

Will was definitely older in the photo from Saqib, and Nika didn't like the hard look in his eyes. "What happened to his husband?" Nika asked.

"Hellas," Grady whispered, and judging from the way D'Arcy froze, it wasn't good. Nika pulled up a file as the CHN man continued, still staring at the photo of Hale as if he couldn't quite believe what he was looking at. "A transport freighter was shot down by the NeoG; there was intel failure. They thought that Sylvia would be on board, but it was members of Hope for Mars on their way to deliver supplies to the habitat."

"If he blamed the NeoG, why try to implicate Free Mars?" Nika asked.

"He blamed *everyone*," Grady replied with a shake of his head. "Everything changed that day. He said if all these fools were intent on rejecting peace, there was no point in continuing to try. The deal we'd been trying to do died the following year."

"This was all before my time in the Senate," Patricia replied. "The only reason I recognized him at all was because I'd watched his earlier speeches extensively. But yes, I believe he resigned from his seat the next day. Six months later he sent a letter to several news outlets and the president of the Senate at the time, announcing his intent to drop off the grid. It was all very by the book, down to him giving away most of his assets to a charity organization on Mars."

"An organization that vanished about a year later," D'Arcy murmured. "He orchestrated a disappearing act in full view of everyone, all to plot this attack more than thirty years later?"

"It certainly looks like it," Nika replied grimly.

MAX HAD DONE HER BEST TO PACK THE FEELINGS AWAY BEFORE she'd gotten back to the others. She'd told them in a low, even voice what had happened, keeping it as formal as a report so her emotions didn't bubble up again. Only Seo-Yoon seemed to understand; the sympathy in her dark eyes was almost more than Max could bear.

After leading them down from the Docking Bay to the

fourth level, Max found a supply closet to hide in that had a maintenance hatch leading directly to the Cargo Bay.

She followed it down and then eased out of the maintenance hatch hidden behind some cargo crates, one eye on the group of hostages, the other on the two guards she could see by the airlock. They were deep in conversation, uncaring of the scattered Neos and civilians sitting closer to her in tight clusters. Everyone was quiet, but she had no way of knowing if they were at all aware of what had happened to Vice Admiral Ford.

Now she spotted the handshake she wanted, sitting off to the side, and crept around the wide pallet, keeping it between her and the guards.

"Bruce," she whispered.

The journo stiffened, then stretched and glanced her way. After a quick look at the guards, he slowly brought a hand up to his mouth. "Carmichael, am I fucking glad to see you."

"Likewise." She smiled. "You okay?"

"I mean—I'm a hostage. But yeah, better than some. We've got a few military people injured from the fight, but nothing major, thankfully."

"How many bad guys?"

"They've been rotating. Right now, there's four at the door. Two by the airlock. Three more just went out into the hallway. Did something happen? They all got really tense there for a few minutes."

"You could say that." Max scanned the group. She could easily pick out the Neos and Marines, plus there was one Navy pilot closest to the door.

She dragged in a breath and hoped she wasn't making a mistake trusting them.

> *CARMICHAEL, M:* Do Not React. This is Commander Max Carmichael. Vice Admiral Ford is dead; I am the ranking officer on board. I'm going to come up with a plan to take down these guards. Weapons will be incoming.
>
> Wait for my signal. Semper Protegens.

Max sent the message, praying that all the military people had enough self-control to follow the order to not react.

A few shoulders stiffened and then relaxed. She saw one person bow their head and mouth a silent prayer. No one looked around, though, and for that she was grateful.

"Spread the word you saw me, quietly. Tell them I'll be in touch and don't make a move until they hear from me. I want to do this bloodless if we can. But things may go south. If the shooting starts, you get everyone you can behind cover and stay down," she ordered, keeping her voice low.

Bruce swallowed again but nodded his head once. Several other hostages had noticed her, and despite Bruce's gesture, the murmur rose enough to get the attention of the guards.

"Hey! Pipe down over there."

Go, Bruce mouthed.

Max flattened herself against the pallet as the shouting rose in volume and drew closer. The open maintenance hatch was two steps away, but it was visible now if either of those guards looked over in her direction.

Bruce's voice rose over the din. "All I'm saying is that we could use a bathroom trip. It's going to get messy otherwise." Max winced at the sound of a fist hitting flesh and then there was more shouting.

It was the distraction she needed, though, and she slipped back into the tunnel pulling the hatch closed behind her. She moved backward from the opening as quickly and quietly as she could until she reached the juncture and hauled herself back up the ladder to the storage closet where she'd left the others.

"Did you talk to someone?" Seo-Yoon asked as Max took Lia's hand and let the younger Neo help her out of the tunnel.

"Yeah, got a look at the opposition, too, but I want to circle around and check out a few other things. You all stay here."

"Carmichael, take Lia with you."

Max chewed on the inside of her cheek as she stared at the woman. "I'd feel better if she were here."

I can't get anyone else killed.

"We're snug as can be in a closet," Seo-Yoon said. Then softer. "Look, I know you're trying to keep her out of the line of fire, but you need the backup. She's a Neo, she knows the risks. Same as Ford. Take her. Please."

"All right." Max rubbed a hand on her pants and looked at the ceiling. She suddenly, desperately wanted a shower and a drink.

Long way to go for that, Max. Stay focused.

"All right," she repeated. "Lia, how much did you train with that gun?"

"Just basic, but I can shoot it."

"I'm sure you can. Leave it, though; the sword is quieter and probably more what you're used to." She waited a moment by the door, listening for noise in the hallway, and cracked it when she didn't hear anything.

She wondered how much more adrenaline she could burn before it tapped out and left her on the floor as she led Lia down the hallway.

There was a weeklong session in Interceptor training: SERE—Survival, Evasion, Resistance, and Escape—that involved a lot of sleeping on the floor of a ship, your crewmate's hip as a pillow, and trying to solve problems that came at you at almost the speed of light.

At the time it had been exhilarating, even as she dragged her weary ass from one day to the next. But it had also been safe, the knowledge that if something actually happened, the exercise would be called off. That wasn't the case here. The slightest misstep could result in her injury or death—or worse, someone else's.

"Max?" Lia's hand on her arm dragged her back to the present. The squeeze was reassuring, though her voice was concerned.

"I'm all right. This way." She shoved away from the wall and cut across the hallway to the dubious safety of an open doorway.

There were fire suppression systems in the Cargo Bay, accessed via the control room just outside the main doors. Max and Lia played a careful game of hide-and-seek with the cameras and the few guards traversing back and forth from the bay as they made their way around the level to their target.

Unfortunately, when they reached it, the room was occupied by four more guards—two standing out in the hallway and two more just inside the door.

She backed up, motioning for Lia to try the door behind them. It slid open, and Max ushered her into the tiny office, closing the door.

"I could get them to chase me?" the Neo offered.

Max shook her head. "I thought of that, but they'd alert the other guards inside the bay, and more people out here isn't what we want. Find me a hardline, there's probably one over there?" She slipped Anton's bag over her head and dug out Seo-Yoon's tablet. It was tempting to empty the whole thing onto the desk and see what she had that Will so desperately wanted, but she had priorities. Max keyed in the passcode as Lia moved to the corner desk. The young Neo scooted underneath and emerged a moment later with a cable in her fist.

"What are you going to do?" she asked.

"Call in some help," Max said. "Hopefully. I'm counting on them not having turned the jammer back on. Keep an eye on the door for me." After Lia had moved away, Max held her breath and brought the coms up on audio only. "Sapphi, you there?"

"I am. I'll get Nik, hang on."

"Actually, I need you."

"You got me," she replied, and the cautious note in her voice pinged Max's attention. "How are you?"

"Tell someone over there that I will have a host of suggestions for the Interceptor SERE course when I get out of here," she replied as lightly as she could.

"Will do. New classes are going to hate you for it." There was laughter in Sapphi's voice, but it was tinged with worry. "Gunny Ranta said you were in a fight when they pulled out. I take it you won?"

"I walked away; that's a win in Jenks's book, right?" The relief from Sapphi's unspoken news that her sister had arrived safely on the surface surged through her, battering at her carefully constructed walls, but Max swallowed it down.

"So she says. What do you need, Max?"

"First off, can you do something about the cameras from your end? We've gotten lucky so far because I think they've only got one pair of eyes and it's hard to keep track of everything, but they were tracking me with the surveillance feed earlier and I'd rather avoid that going forward."

"Sure, I'll see what I can do about it. Shouldn't be too hard, actually; Lupe almost has an in on some secondary power access consoles, and we can maybe route something through there. What else?"

"It looks like they've put all the hostages, except for Saqib—" Her voice caught on the emotions, and she cleared her throat. "Put them in the Cargo Bay. I figured I can cause havoc with the guards using the fire suppression system, give the military folks inside a chance to take them by surprise; but getting to the control room as it stands is a bit difficult."

"I can get into the suppression system easy," Sapphi replied. "Gonna have to talk to someone about that, now that I think about it. Hey, Lupe, we can just make fog happen, right?"

Max heard a bit more faintly, "We can. It's not great to breathe in, but it's not going to cause any long-term lung problems."

"Give us a few minutes, Max; we'll have something for you." Sapphi paused. "How do you want to take out the guards in the hallway?"

"I don't know yet," she admitted. "There's four of them. If you have ideas, I'd love to hear it."

"Sure thing, though now I am going to get Nika. He'll want to talk to you."

For a moment Max was tempted to turn the video on, even knowing it was a risk. She wanted to see his face.

"Lia come here," Max said, and the Neo turned from the door. "What's your DD model?"

"Alter774. Dad had it upgraded last year."

"When I tell you, turn it on, download this file I just sent you, and turn it off immediately." She pulled her sword free and moved to the door. If someone came to investigate, she was going to have to deal with them quickly, but there would be more.

"Done," Lia said a few tense heartbeats later.

"Good. Run it and turn your DD back on."

"Can I ask what it is?"

"Something that should make you invisible. Swap places with me at the door again." Max moved back and picked up the tablet. "Hey, Sapphi. Hypothetically, if I gave someone else our equally hypothetical stealth program, how would I see them?"

"Hypothetically, there's a setting for crew members where you can add handshakes," Sapphi replied, and Max could hear the amusement in her voice. "In the menu."

"Found it, thanks. Will keep the secret as best as we can."

"Hey, if it gets you and everyone else out alive, I'll go stand on the street corner and shout about it until you come home."

Max swallowed hard. She couldn't afford to have such dreams yet, so she didn't answer Sapphi. "Lia, I need you to go back to Seo-Yoon, take the guns, and then follow the maintenance tunnel to the Cargo Bay. Make contact with Bruce Eamin and tell him you have weapons from me. Get them in the hands of the Neos and Marines, carefully but quickly, then wait for my signal."

Lia nodded in acknowledgment and slipped back out into the hallway as silently as a ghost.

"Hey, Max." Nika's voice on the line was a balm, easing over the ache in her chest. "Holding in there?"

"I am."

NIKA: Talk to me. Are you injured?

MAX: You asking as my commander or my boyfriend?

NIKA: Asking as someone who cares about you, so both.

MAX: Couple of cracked ribs, some bruises that will take longer to heal than a week. I've got a heal patch on the one fléchette wound in my shoulder. Overall, I've been pretty lucky. Little worried about adrenaline dump here in an hour or so, but I'll deal with it when it happens.

NIKA: If you can get to medical or find an emergency kit, you could circumvent that for a while, but the backlash will be hell.

NIKA: I'm worried about you.

MAX: Yeah, I don't blame you. I'm the one who's here, though, and you'd tell me the same thing, wouldn't you? I'll see it through to the end.

NIKA: I know. I just want you to come home to me after.

She wanted so desperately to promise she would. That everything would work out and things would be okay. But they both knew she'd be lying, and they'd sworn to each other to never do that—not after it had almost destroyed them before.

MAX: Nika, Vice Admiral Ford's dead. I . . . I took a bag from one of the bad guys. They were trying to force me to give it up. He ordered me to stay away. I was lying, but I . . .

NIKA: I know. We saw it happen.

MAX: Will is definitely in charge. Ford said it seemed like he was waiting for something.

NIKA: You did everything you could. Everything you should have done. Okay?

MAX: It doesn't feel like it. I just let him die.

"Max," Nika said out loud and she jerked when the video kicked on. "Sapphi's done something 'extra' to this connection, so we're not at risk of getting overheard. We're running a secondary security sweep on the NeoG personnel and civilians still on the station. I want you to wait on this plan until we know for sure all those hostages are actually hostages. And we know who Will is."

"Who?"

"Former Senator Willis Hale."

She dragged in a deep breath. *"What?"*

"Grady and Pax both think that his husband's death in the Hellas incident back in 2414 is the reason for the attack; though if that's true, he's been planning this for a long time. I'm telling you so you have all the information, okay? I don't want you to confront him, I want you to focus on getting everyone out of there alive."

Max nodded as the words spun around, jangling in her brain. She knew of Hale; the Hellas disaster had been required material in more than one class at the academy. As much as she wanted to deny it, Nika was right. Her priority was getting everyone to safety.

"How long on the hostage vetting?" Pushing her wariness out of the way had been a thing of necessity in the moment, but Nika was right there also. If there were any more traitors buried with the hostages, she'd be putting them all in jeopardy by attempting to rescue them.

"Hard to say, but Jenks will have answers for me shortly. Trappist and Earth are also running names. You keep doing what you can up there; we'll get you the information you need."

"Have I mentioned lately I appreciate all of you?"

"Pretty sure you have. We appreciate you, too." Nika's voice was light, and Max told herself that she'd imagined the hitch in his reply. "As far as we can tell Saqib is still up on the Command Deck. His DD's been off."

"I know, I've tried to get in touch a few times. Both his and Ford's were off until—" She broke off and looked away.

"Max, listen to me. You've done what you had to do." His voice was firm, assured, and commanding, and it was exactly what she needed in that moment.

She looked back at him, trying to remember how his hands felt when he touched her face and looked at her with his beautiful blue eyes. She'd fallen so hard for him without any prompting all those years ago. Max had been half-convinced she would just spend her life alone when she'd arrived at Jupiter Station, hoping that it would be doing a job she loved. Instead she'd found a whole new family.

"I know. I'm okay," she whispered.

"Don't lie to me," he murmured back.

"Tell me what you know about this?" *I need the distraction.*

"As far as we can tell, Hale was trying to put the NeoG and Free Mars at each other's throats," he replied, allowing her the deflection. He broke down all the info they had so far.

Max rolled the news over in her head several times. The implications were terrifying, and she was grateful it seemed like cooler, more rational heads had prevailed. "Do you think that's all he was trying to do? Does he know that Sylvia is still alive?"

"That I don't know." Nika shook his head. "I think there's probably more to this than just an attempt to set us both off, especially if Ford said he was waiting for something. I've got Sapphi looking for any outgoing com signals from the MOS that might be directed here."

"That would make sense if they have people on the ground," Max replied. "All of this speaks of a lot of training and preparation. I think I'll let you all handle that. I have enough on my plate."

"That's advisable. Sapphi said you needed help with a distraction? Let's get something planned while we're waiting for them to clear names."

JENKS TOSSED THE FILE UP ONTO THE SCREEN WITH THE OTHERS. "That's the last of them. As far as I can tell, everyone else who's on the MOS is clean. Ruiz was the only one on the military side and Marshall on the civilian side. If anyone else is a traitor, they're hiding it better than I can find." She glanced up at the image of the smiling lieutenant and made a face. "What a fucking waste. Who gives an oath and doesn't keep it?"

"Who indeed," D'Arcy agreed, putting a hand on her shoulder. "Go tell Nika; he's on the coms with Max right now."

Jenks nodded and headed out of the conference room. The hallways were bustling with activity, and she wove her way through the crowd with ease.

She spotted Kavan leaning against the wall outside an office. They were watching the passing crowd with dark eyes, missing nothing, assessing everything.

"Senior Chief," they said with a nod.

"How's the arm? Don't bullshit me."

"Fine, thank you."

"Bullshit."

They cracked a rare smile. "It's not the worst injury I've had, but if it makes you happy, I'll tell you it hurts."

Jenks smiled back. "How's Pax holding up?"

"Keeping herself busy; she just got off the com with her parents."

Jenks made a face. "Please tell me they're not going to come in here and cause a scene."

"Thankfully they're too far out to get back here quickly. Pax assured them everything is under control. That seemed to be enough."

"Well, thank God for small miracles, I guess," she replied. "Let me know if you need a break, I'll send Chae over to stand guard."

"I will, and thanks, I appreciate it."

She continued down the hallway to the control room, spotted Nika leaning on the console near Sapphi, and headed over.

"I think that's the best you're going to get," Nika said. "So keep your eyes open. And Max? You do what you have to in order to stay alive."

"I know." Max's voice wavered a little, and Jenks knew her sister was going to need a shit-ton of therapy when this was over. Therapy, hugs, sparring, and anything else she wanted. Jenks would make it happen when Max came back.

Because she *was* coming back. Jenks refused to entertain the notion that Max wouldn't survive.

"Can I talk to her, or does she need to go?" she asked.

Nika glanced over his shoulder at her, and Jenks didn't miss that he muted the audio. "She's safe for the moment. She watched them kill Vice Admiral Ford, though, Jenks. They were trying to get her to give herself up. He ordered her not to."

"Fuck," she muttered, shaking her head. "Okay."

Nika turned the audio back on. "Max, Jenks is here. She wants to talk to you."

"Hey, Jenks."

"This is a hell of a thing after you harassed me so much about taking a vacation," she replied.

There was a moment of startled silence on the other end of the line and then Max laughed. A real laugh. The sick knot in Jenks's chest eased up just a bit.

"I'll make it up to you when we get out of here."

"Eh, no worries. Nika already promised me double vacation."

"I did not!"

More laughter.

"Okay, maybe not. But *you'd* better. We finished running security checks on all our people on the MOS, and Ruiz and Marshall are the only ones working for the other side. You should be good trusting anyone else up there."

"I'm really glad to hear that. It means a lot coming from you."

Jenks had never hoped so much in her life not to let someone down.

"Hey, will you do me a favor?" Max's request knocked her brain away from the fear-induced spiral it wanted to dive into, and Jenks cleared her throat.

"Anything."

"Anything? Shit, I should—"

"Almost anything, you brat. You can't have my dog."

Max laughed again, the sound coming even easier this time, and Jenks caught Nika watching her. He mouthed *Good job* at her and then went back to talking to Sapphi.

"I don't know if Command Master Chief Galen Rost has been shaking trees around there or not, but if you'd let him know I've got his daughter with me and I'll keep her safe, I'd appreciate it."

Jenks had cursed pretty wildly when she'd spotted his name in Lia's file and immediately sent it off to D'Arcy to deal with. It was unlikely he'd do anything until they had more information, though; no matter what position the man held within the NeoG, it wasn't enough to get answers they didn't have.

"You're lucky I love you. Making me talk to the CMC."

"I know. I love you, too."

The wounded look in her sister's brown eyes was almost her undoing, and Jenks gritted her teeth against the echoing pain in her own chest. *Damn it, Max, don't do this,* she thought. *Don't treat this like it's the last time you'll ever talk to me.*

Before Jenks could say anything else, Max cleared her throat. "I'd better get off the com. I don't think they have a clue where I am, but if they're searching for signals, it could get traced back here. I'll talk to you again soon."

"You'd better," she said once more. "I should be drunk right now, Carmichael. Or getting la—"

"Oh god. Do not. Bye." Max was laughing as she hung up.

Jenks bit down hard on the inside of her cheek, the coppery tang of blood flowing over her tongue as she wrestled her slippery emotions back under control.

"It's just me," Nika said, and a second later his arm was around her shoulders. "Thanks for getting her spirits back up."

"Least I could do. But I'm serious: you need to get me up there. It sounds like she's got some backup, but—" The rest of it, the truth of it, stuck in her throat.

I'm her crew. I should be up there.

"I'm working on it."

Jenks nodded. "Did you know about the daughter of the command master chief of the NeoG being on station?"

"Yeah, but not that she was with Max."

"Safest place on the station. Do we have anything from Saqib?"

Nika shook his head, squeezed her, and then let her go. "No. I just told Max we think he's still up on the Command Deck. I think the only reason we saw Ford's DD was because he was talking to Max in the airlock." Nika sighed and rubbed at his face. "Captain Hosaka is going to reach out to the MOS again here in a few. They haven't responded to any of our other com requests since the message."

"He should let Tama talk to them, they'd probably have everyone home for dinner."

Nika laughed softly. "Don't I know it. I sent Aggy and the gunny to debrief first, and then they were supposed to come to you. I figured you could find something for them to do."

"Haven't seen either of them, but debrief probably lasted that long," Jenks said after checking her DD for the time. "I'll head back." She heaved a sigh. "And I guess I'll be responsible and com the CMC about his daughter. Have I mentioned I'm supposed to be on vacation?"

"Couple of times. Get to work."

Jenks danced away from her brother with a grin. This was an easy game to play and one she hoped helped.

Didn't mean she was looking forward to telling the highest-ranking NCO in the NeoG that his daughter was trapped on the MOS, though. Even if being with Max meant she really was in the safest place she could currently be.

RALKA WAS AWARE OF THE TERRIFIED SILENCE AROUND HER, BUT she ignored it as she went to her knees next to her brother's body.

A thousand images of his face, various ages and expressions, moments forever lost in time flashed through her head as she leaned forward and pressed a kiss to his cold forehead. "For the fallen and the forgotten," she murmured, rocking back onto her feet and standing. She keyed open the com. "Will, where is she?"

"Ralka, we have a plan here. I need you to remember that."

"My focus has not shifted in the slightest. She has Anton's bag, and we need that, right? Where is she?"

"We don't know."

"Your plan obviously didn't work. We do mine." She bared her teeth, heard people shuffle nervously around her. "Find her, Castle."

"I'm working on it, Ralka, believe me. Someone on the ground is fighting me over cameras, though, and I've lost access to them. Trying to get it back now," she replied.

"Ralka," Will said before she could snap at Castle. "You can track Carmichael down. You may *not* kill her. Get the bag and bring her to me. We need her alive for the codes."

You need her alive, Ralka thought. *It doesn't matter to me if she dies now or later. But she put her hands on my little brother and that means her life is mine.*

She started putting the pieces of the puzzle together. Carmichael would head for where her people were. She'd try to save them. Ralka knew that much to be true, and she could respect the Neo for her devotion, even as she respected the cold-bloodedness that had allowed Carmichael to stand by while her fellow Neo was ejected into the black. She snapped her fingers at the three people hovering nearby. "We're headed for the Cargo Bay. Everyone else keep your eyes open," she said over the main com. "I'll start the sweep from the bottom. Castle, get control of those cameras again and get me some eyes. She's only one fucking person. We'll corner her and finish this."

"*Alive*, Ralka," Will called out.

We'll see.

With that, Ralka walked away from Anton's corpse, the last of her family. The last of her past. All that was left to her was the path she'd chosen and the fiery death at the end of it.

Eighteen Arrested in NeoG Operation
NOVEMBER 4, 2413 (ESD)

The Near-Earth Orbital Guard, in conjunction with Mars PeaceKeepers, stopped a Free Mars plot to demolish a construction project on the northern side of the former EM housing section. Much of the section was burned during the early days of the 2409 riots and has languished in the intervening years. This spring the CHN had approved new construction in the hopes of improving the community and drawing new occupants to the area.

Free Mars has repeatedly insisted the sections that were destroyed should remain as is, an unofficial memorial to those who lost their lives in the violence that happened in the weeks following the rejection of the referendum for Martian Independence by the CHN. But people who live in the area wanted to see it restored, and Phil Glick of the EM Community Council said that's exactly what they petitioned the CHN to do. "The people who live here, who work here, want to move on. We deserve safe and warm places to stay, and those remnants of the violence of our past don't serve anyone except the ghosts."

Last Tuesday, the NeoG and the PeaceKeepers closed out a three-year-long operation against the radical Free Mars group, resulting in the arrests of eighteen people. Many of those arrested are purported to have close ties with the leadership of Free Mars and have been involved in a number of attacks on personnel and property. No names have been released.

Free Mars leader Sylvia Moroz issued a brief statement on the arrests. "The unlawful detainment of Mars citizens by the occupational forces of the CHN continues to prove why Mars deserves to have jurisdiction over their own people." [*Read More*]

ELEVEN

"COMMANDER MONTAGLIONE?"

D'Arcy looked over at the petty officer and the gunnery sergeant behind them, tagging their handshakes with a nod. It was the pair Nika had told him about. "That's me."

"Looking for Senior Chief Khan. Commander Vagin said she'd be here. Would find something for us to do to help," Aggy said.

"She actually went to talk to Nika." D'Arcy's DD pinged and he caught Drani's eye from across the room. She mouthed *Clear* at him, and he opened the files on the pair that she'd sent over. "Let's put you two over here until she gets back. Hey, Emel?"

"Yeah?" She looked away from her conversation with Heli.

D'Arcy passed them off to the master chief and his DD pinged again. "Montaglione."

"Commander, Chief Tangeu again. Incoming com for you from Sylvia Moroz."

"Put her through, Chief." He kept it on his DD rather than putting her on a screen and waved a hand at Chaske as he stepped into the adjacent office and closed the door. "Sylvia. Thanks for the lists, we've matched a few names." He didn't add that the majority of them had tied back to Free Mars rather than the NeoG or the CHN. He also didn't tell her about Willis Hale. Or that her asset on the station was actually a double agent for Intel according to Drani. That was information that probably needed to be delivered in person, if Nika cleared it at all.

"Good," she replied, glancing off-camera for a moment. "I have something else for you. Can you meet me?"

"Where?" Even as he asked the question, the location appeared on his DD. D'Arcy refocused on Sylvia. "That's an interesting choice." It was a building smack in the middle of one of the worst areas of the Am-zed Projects.

"It's a safe house. Which we're clearly willing to burn for this meeting. Can you do it?"

"Give me half an hour."

"Done. And D'Arcy?"

He waited patiently while Sylvia chewed over whatever she wanted to say to him.

"Plainclothes but come armed. And don't bring Jenks, she's too recognizable."

The com disconnected, leaving him frowning at the empty air.

"Nika, I just heard from Sylvia." He sent the coordinates over. "I'm taking Emel. If you don't hear from us in forty-five, come rescue our asses."

"I've got my hands full already, D'Arcy," Nika replied, his voice dry. "Don't get in trouble."

D'Arcy laughed sharply. "Don't I know it. Send Jenks; it'll give her somewhere to burn off her frustration at being underutilized. I'd take her, but Sylvia said no and something tells me it would be a bad idea."

"Noted. Seriously, don't get in trouble. I don't have time to save your ass."

"You'd come. You love me."

Nika hissed a curse, and D'Arcy muffled the urge to ask if he was okay as the line went quiet and Nika spoke again. "Be careful, please."

"We will." He disconnected and strode back into the conference room. Jenks was back, talking animatedly with Emel, and he crossed to them.

"Chaske, you're in charge until we get back." He pointed at Emel. "You're with me. Petty Officer Bennet, I hear you fly shuttles?"

"I do," they replied.

"You're with us, too." D'Arcy shook his head at Jenks's hopeful look. "Sorry, not this time."

"Figures," she muttered, but flashed him a smile right after. "Come on, Gunny, no one loves us, so we'll find our own party."

Emel and Aggy followed him from the room and out into the bright sunshine of the late spring day. He'd long ago stopped trying to make sense of the difference between seasons and time zones—the early days of Interceptor training on Earth had thrown those things into sharp relief. It was far easier to let the DD chips do the work.

Some part of his brain remembered, though, and tried

to reconcile it with the cooler weather they'd left on Earth not a full day earlier.

"You have civilian clothes on board?" he asked Emel, who hid her surprise at the question with ease.

"I do."

"Aggy, we'll meet you at your shuttle."

The petty officer threw a salute and peeled off, heading across the base to the landing pads, as D'Arcy and Emel continued toward *Dread*.

"You going to tell me what's going on?" Emel asked, pulling herself up the stairs and through the airlock.

"I don't know. Sylvia just said plainclothes and weapons, and gave me a location." He sent it over, watched her shoulders stiffen, and braced himself.

"Bringing Jenks actually would have been a good idea," she said instead, surprising him. "Would be a hell of a distraction."

"I hadn't thought of it that way." He raised his voice so she could still hear him as he crossed into his quarters and unlaced his boots, kicking them off and stripping out of his duty blues. He pulled the civilian clothes out of his locker. They were more Trappist than Mars, but would pass enough even where they were headed.

"She's going to need something to do beyond culling names."

"I know," he replied, shoving his feet into a pair of worn brown boots. "That's Nika's problem, though, at least at the moment."

"Do you trust her?"

He didn't have to ask to know she was talking about Sylvia. D'Arcy sighed. "Once upon a time, with my life. Now? I think her priority is the cause, which at the moment means she's aligned with us. She worked with Hale before '09, and after?" He rubbed both hands over his face as he stood. "We shed a lot of blood here, Emel, but I don't think she wants that now. Feel free to tell me I'm being a sentimental idiot."

"I won't," Emel said, meeting him in the corridor. "I understand the feelings you're wrestling with better than anyone probably. And I'd like to think I can read people well enough; she seems genuine." She passed over a fléchette gun and a sword that was distinctly not NeoG with a wink. "Don't ask."

"I absolutely don't want to know." He hooked the pirate sword onto his belt as he headed for the door. "Willis Hale wanted us to think Free Mars is responsible for the MOS and wanted them to think we were responsible for killing Sylvia. That's easy. It's what else he has planned that I haven't figured out yet and that makes me nervous."

He didn't say out loud that it also made him very nervous that the man had so casually ejected Vice Admiral Ford off the station. A person like that had zero care for life and it made them doubly dangerous.

Emel nodded with a grim smile, and the pair headed off *Dread*, crossing the yard to where Aggy waited with the shuttle. It was a short hop to a nearby drop point, the shuttle traffic busy enough to hide their presence, and soon D'Arcy was standing on a busy street corner with Emel at his side.

"Who says you can't go home again," he muttered, and headed for the coordinates Sylvia had passed him. The sights and smells of home enveloped them, Martians rushing by on their business without so much as a glance in their direction.

EMEL: Handshakes?

D'ARCY: Leave it on. We're not really trying to hide, just be unobtrusive. Maybe it'll stop someone from picking a fight.

EMEL: Or start one.

She wasn't wrong on that point. It was a fifty-fifty split in this area but dressed as they were meant people wouldn't pay much attention to their handshakes unless they were really looking.

They fell into step with the ease of several years together. Emel's arrival to *Dread* had been like two cargo freighters running headlong at each other, and there had been more than a few moments where D'Arcy hadn't been sure they would survive the inevitable impact.

Somehow they did. Somehow they'd untangled a past born on these very streets and reforged a friendship he valued deeply.

The safe house was nestled among several other crushed-together buildings, their brownish-red brick stretching up toward the blue sky and their front porches occupied by people ostensibly lazing around in the midday warmth.

A young person with skin as dark as his and no handshake stood when D'Arcy came to a stop at the foot of the stairs. "Keep on walking, NeoG," they said, crossing bare muscled arms.

"But I was invited," he replied. The easy grin slipped onto his face along with the memory of being that young once, that full of confidence. That full of anger.

The anger, thankfully, had faded with his youth.

A person behind their challenger leaned down and whispered in their ear. There was a moment of stunned silence; then they eyed D'Arcy closely as the murmured sound of his name rippled through the group.

"Prodigal son and all that, huh?" They tapped their hip. "Weapons stay outside."

"I'm sorry. Weapons stay with us," he replied with a shake of his head. He already knew Sylvia wouldn't have told him to bring them if she hadn't intended for them to stay armed.

They glared, dark brown eyes too hard for a face that couldn't have been more than eighteen, and this time D'Arcy felt a pang of weariness.

Would this ever get better? Or are we always going to have children growing up too fast?

The door cracked open. "Josiah, what part of 'get them inside quickly' was confusing?" Clair hissed, and the teens all snapped to attention like a crew of new Neos fresh from basic.

Emel only barely covered her laugh with a cough, and D'Arcy kept his eyes on Clair rather than risk a smile breaking out on his own face. "We were having an arms negotiation. Permission to come inside?"

"What are you? A fucking vampire? Get in here." Clair pushed the door open as D'Arcy headed up the stairs through the crowd.

"Just being polite."

"Sylvia's in there." Clair stepped back out onto the porch, closing the door behind them, and D'Arcy didn't have to hear anything through the thick wood to know that someone was getting a dressing down.

"Almost like being on base," Emel murmured.

"Don't say that too loud; someone will take offense."

It was true, though. Even if Sylvia wouldn't admit it. She ran Free Mars as much like the military as the NeoG did, and it was one of the reasons they'd lasted so long against the might of the CHN.

D'Arcy nodded at Mikhail as they passed through the doorway into the living room. The big man gave him a flat look in response, and D'Arcy tried hard not to sigh. It was clear that while Sylvia and even Maria were willing to work with him, some of the people from his past still thought him a traitor to the cause.

He told himself it was fine, that he'd made his choices and wasn't disappointed with where they'd led him. D'Arcy headed across the room to where Sylvia sat on a narrow, worn couch in deep green. The girl next to her couldn't have been more than sixteen, and her hair was as pale blond as Heli's; her handshake read *Mila Johansson, she/her.*

Maria was suspiciously absent.

The girl's face was tear streaked, and her blue eyes snapped open in fear at the sight of D'Arcy and Emel. Sylvia locked a hand down on her arm before the girl could scramble away, and D'Arcy put his hands up as he lowered himself into the chair opposite them.

"Not here for a fight," he said.

"Mila, it's all right. They're here to help."

"They're *NeoG*. I don't understand."

"Do you trust me?" Sylvia asked, and the question was enough to drag the girl's gaze away from D'Arcy and back to her. Mila nodded and Sylvia slid her hand down to link her fingers through the girl's. "Then tell them what you told me."

"My sister, Wilke, and I joined Free Mars three years ago. Our parents were—" She hesitated, glanced in Sylvia's direction.

"They were killed," Sylvia said. "By the NeoG."

He'd been expecting it, but it didn't make it any easier to hear. "Where?"

"Outside of Roswell. If I am being honest with myself, D'Arcy, Free Mars was just as culpable in their deaths. The NeoG bombed a small outpost of ours, based on intel that I was going to be there. Mila and Wilke's parents were delivering supplies at the time. They were just farmers, not involved in the cause."

"I'm not entirely sure how that makes you culpable," D'Arcy replied, feeling Emel stiffen in shock next to him. It was the truth, though. His loyalty to the NeoG aside, he knew they'd fucked up on Mars and continued to do so even as they all stumbled their way toward peace.

"They weren't supposed to be there. The outpost was a decoy; we'd cleared it the week before. No one told them the delivery location had changed."

D'Arcy saw the fury in Mila's expression flashing quickly across her face and felt an answering swell of sympathy. He'd spent so many years so angry at everything before it had finally settled into a manageable seething bed of coals.

"My parents died," she whispered, looking down at her hands. "Wilke is all I have left. No one cares about the orphans except us. We bounced around with friends of the family for a while; some of them were very vocal about Free Mars, and we were interested. Ralka took us in, got Wilke a job at a local warehouse."

EMEL: Ralka, huh?

D'ARCY: Yeah, isn't that interesting.

"A few months ago she started going to meetings at night. I tagged along the first few times." Mila shrugged a thin shoulder, unaware of their conversation as she continued. "But everyone was so angry, you know? I just want to try to live my life. I think my parents would have wanted that."

"They would have." Sylvia squeezed Mila's hand and the girl smiled. "Tell D'Arcy the rest of it."

"This morning, I heard Wilke at the doorway with someone. I only caught pieces of the conversation, but I heard her say MOS and an address. When I heard the news about the station, I came straight to my squad leader. They contacted Sylvia." She looked up at D'Arcy again. "I don't know what she's going to do, but it's something bad. Please stop her, but . . . she's all I have left. If she dies, I'll be all alone."

"I can't make you any promises," he replied, and extended his hand. "A lot depends on her, too. But I'll try, okay?"

Mila took it, her fingers small and pale in his grip, and D'Arcy forced out a smile, hoping he wasn't about to make yet another enemy of the NeoG.

"The address?" he asked Sylvia as he released Mila and got to his feet.

"Clair's got it. Maria is there already, watching the building."

"Emel, stay here," D'Arcy said, following up the order immediately with a chat message.

D'ARCY: I know, but something's off here. I want you with Sylvia.

EMEL: Something's "off"? Can you give me more?

D'ARCY: Max isn't the only one whose gut gets twitchy. There's something I don't like about this. If I'm wrong, no harm. If I'm not, I want you here to keep Sylvia alive.

EMEL: I should be keeping you alive.

D'ARCY: So you do love me.

EMEL: My wife loves you. I tolerate you.

He flashed her a grin and headed for the door. Clair met him with a piece of paper, and D'Arcy laughed before he could stop himself.

Clair glared. "Not all of us have chips in our brains, space cop."

He took the address with a wink. "That insult's too old to hurt much, kiddo. Try harder."

They hissed at him and shoved him toward the door. D'Arcy headed down the stairs through the crowd of teens and said without looking back, "Stay back a ways when you shadow me; I don't know what's going to go down, and I'd rather you all not get caught in the cross fire if it happens."

When it happens.

D'Arcy then muttered a curse under his breath and headed down the street at a run.

SLOW YOUR BREATHING, MAX. IN THROUGH YOUR NOSE, OUT through your mouth.

The problem was that in through the nose meant the sharp smell of hot blood drove itself into her brain with every breath and that was the very thing Max was trying to calm down from.

Sapphi's distraction setting off a few alarms in the control room had worked perfectly. The four hijackers now lay sprawled on the floor where they'd fallen, one after another. Each one dying too fast for the others to really process what was happening before Max's next shot picked them off.

And while she was glad for a quick resolution of this confrontation, she was sure she'd let her anger carry her into the room, even knowing she shouldn't. There was just something disturbingly soothing about making *someone* pay for Jackson's death.

Even knowing that none of these people were the ones she really wanted on the end of her sword.

Max found the console she needed, ignoring the squelching of her boots in the blood on the floor. Sapphi and Lupe were hard at work on getting control of the airlocks, especially in the Cargo Bay, but without any way to stay in contact Max had to trust they were going to do it.

She found the fire suppression system and took a deep breath.

"Lia, are you ready?"

"We are," the Neo replied. "I've tagged five hostiles inside the bay."

"Outside hostiles have been neutralized. I'm sending the message to the others now." Max sent the signal as she hit the button for the suppressant and then bolted through the doorway.

Straight into a forearm that hit her right in the diaphragm and knocked the wind out of her lungs.

The punch that followed drove into her left eye, pain exploding outward, before she could even think about getting her hands up to protect her face.

Reflexes alone still saved her, as her right hand came up of its own accord, slapping the flat of the blade against her attacker's side and buying her just enough time to roll into a clear space in the hallway. Max grinned viciously at the hiss of pain, and she kicked out hard, catching her opponent in the thigh and sending them staggering back a step.

"No! Hold your fire! She's mine!"

Max wasn't about to question whose she was and caught a glimpse of vicious green eyes as she stumbled to her feet and skidded around the corner. She heard the impact of fléchettes hitting the bulkhead behind her.

"Hold your fucking fire!"

"Lia, hostiles outside. Get the doors locked down any way you can!" Max gasped out the order, dragging air into protesting lungs as she got her feet under her and sprinted down the corridor away from the Cargo Bay.

The first access hatch wasn't maintenance, but actual ventilation; Max jerked it open anyway and dove into it without hesitation as the sounds of shouting followed her down the hallway.

Unfortunately, there was no time to pull it shut behind her. Fléchettes slammed into the metal near her a second time as she wormed her way through the shaft, praying silently she hadn't just backed herself into a corner.

She had.

"Fuck."

The fan in the open space ahead was spinning swiftly, too fast to stop with her bare hands. It would likely even rip her sword out of her grip. Once again, though, Max didn't hesitate, grabbing for her boot and ripping the laces free.

A second prayer, this one a little more desperate, before she thrust her boot into the fan. With a whining protest, the blade ground to a halt. Max threw her sword and bag into the gap and wiggled through after them.

The lethal whine of fléchettes filled the tunnel as she reached for her boot, impacting both the rubber sole and the fan blade, dislodging one and setting the other spinning again. More pain spiked in her face. Max swore and rolled, sliding down a secondary access port a meter away.

She landed hard, a hot stab that felt entirely too much like a rib streaked through her left side and Max lay for a moment, gasping and sobbing before she dragged herself upright.

I'm running out of ribs.

Then,

Keep moving. Max, you have to keep moving.

She took a deep breath, the agony swirling so wildly it was impossible to tell the source, and then another until it subsided enough for her to crawl forward the last few meters to the maintenance hatch opening.

"Max? Max, where are you?"

Breath was still hard to come by, but Max did her best to keep her voice level as she responded to Lia. "I don't know. There was an unexpected complication. Give me a minute. Are you all safe?"

"For the moment," she replied. "There's a pack of angry hostiles outside the doors, but unless they have access to a laser cutter, they're not getting through. No one's getting through. I, uh, I maybe shot up the door controls."

"Good job," Max said with a laugh she immediately regretted. "Check your map of the station and put people on the maintenance hatches that lead into the bay. I wouldn't put it past these bastards to try to get at you that way. I'm going to try to get somewhere I can hook up and talk to Ground Control again, see if we can't send a rescue for you all."

"Let me know when you figure out where you are," Lia replied. "I'll come to you."

"No, your job is to get everyone to safety, Spacer Thorn. I'll be fine."

"Max—"

"That's an order." Having just had to endure brutal orders from Ford, Max knew how it must feel to be on the receiving end. She softened her tone. "I'll check back in when I know more. You stay put and stay alert. Lia—these people need you. *I* need you to do this. Clear?"

"Yes, ma'am."

There was blood on her hand and the sudden sting when she touched her cheek pointed her at the source. Either a piece of debris or a fléchette had gotten too close for comfort. Max leaned her head back against the wall with a sigh, trying to ignore the way it felt like she could sense the rotation of the station itself when she closed her eyes.

As she caught her breath and listened for any sign of

pursuit, Max replayed the fight in her head. Whoever her opponent was they were fast, almost faster than Jenks.

"Hits as hard, too," she muttered with a wince.

They also hadn't wanted the others to intervene in the fight but hadn't seemed on the fence about shooting at her to slow her down.

And that had been pure hatred on their face, born of something more than the reason they were all on the MOS in the first place.

It was a puzzle Max was going to have to put away for now. She rolled toward the hatch with a soft groan and cracked it open, waiting for any sign of the enemy.

The corridor was silent, so Max slipped out into it and limped her way down to the nearest open door. She was down on the Engineering level, but only in the office section. The access to the station engine itself was locked down, not even her codes would gain her entry.

She hit the panel and slumped to the floor as the door slid closed, hot tears sliding free before she could stop them. "It's fine. You bought them time. That's what you're here to do." She let the tears flow for a minute more, then swiped them away and got to her feet to look for an emergency medical kit.

This time her luck held and even more there was an adrenaline inhaler in the cheery yellow box. Max stared at it for a long moment before picking it up. She exhaled and put it in her mouth, pressing the button. The effect was immediate and rushed through her, clearing her head even as it made her hands shake.

She took a few more deep breaths and then set about

smoothing a heal patch to the cut on her cheek using a tiny mirror she scavenged from someone's desk drawer.

In the same drawer she found a pack of protein gels and ate them with a grimace, choking a little on the sticky contents and wishing for water.

The pain in her left leg wasn't her ankle but above her knee in the muscle. Max stretched, hoping it would help as she hunted for a cable under a desk in the back to connect to her tablet.

The door slid open, and Max froze as a voice echoed through the air.

"No, that's what I'm saying. Ralka's not going to stop hunting Carmichael until she finds her. And frankly, even if Will wants her alive, I'm not sure that matters enough to stay Ralka's hand. Anton was all she had left." The person who'd come into the room sighed heavily. "I *know* Carmichael has Anton's bag. She can't run forever, though. We'll get it back. You just focus on figuring out how to get through this fucking lock."

Max slowly and carefully pulled her legs under the desk with her as the voice got closer.

There was rustling as if they were going through a desk near her. "Here we go, found it. Captain R. Harmony, right?"

The response appeared to be in the affirmative as her unwanted visitor hummed and the footsteps headed back to the door. A loud crunch was followed by a curse and Max held her breath.

"I'm fine, just stepped on something. Huh, that's weird. What? No, someone used the e-kit before they bugged out."

Max's sword was on the floor by the desk she was hiding under, in full view if they looked in her direction.

Please just go.

She resisted the urge to reach for it and rush them, dragging her frayed patience back under control. Getting in touch with Ground Control was the priority and killing this person was going to do nothing but alert the hijackers to her location.

"No, I'm coming, calm down." More footsteps and the sound of the door opening and closing again.

Max counted to a hundred before she moved, her ears straining for any sound beyond her own breathing. Silence surrounded her as she carefully crawled free and peeked out into the room.

Empty.

She knew she couldn't stay here long, not if what she'd overheard was correct. Anton had meant something to Ralka, and it sounded like she would be looking for Max. But not just for payback, she—

"The bag."

Anton's bag.

What did she have that they wanted so desperately?

Max grabbed for the bag lying near her sword and dug out the tablet. She hooked it up quickly and sent Sapphi a quick message. Then dumped the contents onto the floor.

"Fuck," she breathed.

The gleaming metal cylinders, each no longer than her handspan and about four centimeters in diameter, rolled across the floor into her sock-covered foot. Max grabbed her tablet and took a photo, sending it to Sapphi with a tag of:

MAX: Please tell me these aren't what I think they are.

A moment later the incoming com buzzed on the tablet and Max reluctantly hit the video as she grabbed a nearby toolbox and started rummaging through it.

Sapphi's eyes snapped wide, echoed by Tamago's, as the two lieutenants had their heads pressed together. "Zeus's unfaithful ass, Max. You look terrible," Sapphi said.

"I'm fine."

"You're a liar," her lieutenant replied, glancing to the side and dropping her voice. "I'm gonna let it slide if you tell me why the fuck you have a pair of what Tamago tells me look disturbingly like detonator keys for fusion bombs?"

"I didn't make them if that's what you're wondering."

"I should hope not. They're highly illegal. Sorry." Tama waved a hand at Max's flat look.

"Can I just toss them out an airlock?"

"Absolutely not," Tama hissed, eyes going wide in a panic. "That tech is old and highly unstable. There's no way of knowing how good the builders were. A weird bump or anything could set them off."

And by extension whatever bomb they were attached to.

"I was afraid of that." Max exhaled. "Can you scan for the bombs? I have a guess where they might be, but I'd rather have some confirmation."

"Let me get with Captain Nier," Sapphi replied. "I'll let you know what we find."

"Okay, tell Nika to get a ship in here to get those hostages out of the Cargo Bay. We've locked it down. They're safe for the moment. Do you have control of the airlocks?"

"Not yet but I'll make it a priority. Hey, Lupe!" She turned slightly and started talking to him off-screen.

"Max," Tamago said softly. Just her name, just enough to chip again at the tight grip she had on her emotions. "You hang in there, okay?"

"I'm trying." She offered up a weak smile. "It's good to see you."

"We're trying to get them to talk to us again, but there hasn't been a response since, well, you know." They lifted a shoulder. "Kenta sent another message asking to speak with Will directly but seeing those detonators makes me doubt our ability to negotiate with them at all."

That was Max's thought as well and it fueled her next words. "I'm going to find someplace safe to stash these and then go see if I can rescue Saqib."

"Max, be careful." Tamago swallowed. "And I know you have a lot going on up there, but if you find these bombs before us, I need you to try to get a good look at them; let me know as soon as you can."

A lot going on was quite the understatement. Yet the request was already on her mind.

"I'll do what I can," she replied, and disconnected. The toolbox had yielded a wrench, a spool of wire, and best of all, a smaller, flameless welding torch. She pulled off her other boot with a sigh. Then scooping everything back into the bag and slinging it over her back, Max got to her feet and grabbed her sword.

There was a locker room on this level, and that was her first stop. With any luck she'd find some new boots and maybe a locker to hide these keys in.

Yes, because luck has been very kind to you so far.

Max ignored the entirely too correct voice in her head and limped for the door.

EVERYONE WANTS SOMETHING. THE TRICK IS FIGURING OUT WHAT *it is and what they're willing to give up for it.*

The words of Tamago's negotiation instructor rang in their head as they watched the flow of activity in the room. They were glad they'd been over talking to Sapphi when Max's com came through. Even more so that they'd been able to help at least a little, but they'd seen the shadows in Max's brown eyes she tried so hard to hide from them. Being alone up there. Being hunted. Ford's death. The deaths she'd caused.

All of it was taking a toll on her.

The compounded problem of something like a homemade fusion bomb only made the muscles of Tamago's shoulders tighten all the more. They wished they could be up there with Max, watch her back, and at the very least, be able to tell what kind of explosives they were facing.

"Tama, I'm getting a com from the MOS," Sapphi said. "Do you want to take it?"

TAMAGO: Com from MOS.

KENTA: We're on our way back. Answer it. You know what you're doing.

It both filled them with pride to have him say that, but also put a cramp in Tama's stomach. The responsibility was now squarely on their shoulders, and it was weighty.

"Chae, can I grab you?" they asked, spotting the petty officer across the room.

"Sure, what do you need?"

"Just stand next to me and watch whoever I'm talking to. It's good to have a second pair of eyes. Jun, you ready?"

She nodded. "Yeah, go ahead."

Tamago gestured at Sapphi and waited for the com to come through.

"Your girl's good." It wasn't Marshall or Will on the screen, but a familiar face with bright green eyes and a frame of pink curls.

Tamago's brain skidded to a stop in shock. "I know you."

"Castle." She grinned, crossing her arms over her chest. "Hi again."

Tamago locked their surprise down. Gone was the overexcited young woman from three years ago wishing them good luck just before their championship sword match with Nika. In her place was a sharp-eyed hijacker.

"Sucks we're on opposite sides here. Hey, good fight, though, back at the Games. I really enjoyed it. Seems like a long time ago." She smiled wistfully. "I thought about joining the NeoG. Folks wanted me to go to the university instead. Would have been far harder to get out of that when they died than school, huh?"

"I'm sorry about your parents. That sounds like it's been rough."

"You know, yeah," Castle said with a sigh. "It is."

"I wish you had joined; we could have been there for you. Helped you carry this grief."

"Yeah, well, that's life, isn't it? One second you're on top of the world meeting your heroes. The next it kicks you when you're down and you find yourself staring at a blank com screen after some stranger tells you your parents have been disintegrated."

Tamago's heart broke at the grief and pain that shattered across Castle's face before she sniffed and forced out a wholly fake smile. "Anyway, here we are."

"What did you mean?" Tamago asked, trying to steer the conversation back to something less painful. "Who's good?"

"Max." Castle shrugged a thin shoulder. "Though I'm assuming Sapphi's the one on the ground who's been kicking my ass out of station programs left and right?"

"Possible," Tamago replied, allowing a hint of a smile through. "What about Max?"

"Wreaking havoc. She locked Ralka and the others out of the Cargo Bay where the hostages are. Whatever she did to the airlock doors toasted them. I can't get them open." Castle sucked air through the gap in her teeth. "And she killed Ralka's brother. Man, was *that* a bad idea."

"Max is doing her job, Castle," Tamago said as gently as they could. It was a risk. They could set Castle off with something so challenging, but they were hoping the young woman would respond and give them a chance to build some kind of rapport with her.

"Fair point. Still—Ralka's, whew, she's bad news on a good day, and this, as they say, is not a good day."

"Castle, we could make it a better day. What do you want?"

"Man, you know my father used to say that to me when I got in trouble?"

"Castle, let's talk about this. We can come to a resolution. No one else has to die."

"Try telling Ralka that." Castle whistled low. "Also, let's be honest; as far as body counts go, Free Mars is still in the lead."

It was the bitterness that caught Tamago's attention. "It seems like you're really angry at Free Mars."

"You know, I was at first, right after my parents, but life moves on. Like, relentlessly. It's wild. Everyone around me just sort of forgot they'd existed at all. Sometimes I do, too. Willis was the first person I met who really understood that."

"He understood it?"

"Yeah. You know that thing—uh, connection, I guess—where other people who've been through the same shit you have are really the only ones who get it. Like *you* wouldn't, your parents are alive."

"They are."

"Yeah. Well, we'll make people remember."

"Castle—" Tamago's next question was cut off by a sudden spike of noise that was loud enough to be heard on the com, and Castle's eyes went wide as she muttered a quiet "Oh fuck. I've gotta go."

"Castle, wait!" But it was too late, and the screen had already gone black.

"That was interesting," Chae said.

"Strange," Tamago murmured back. "It was like she just called to chat. But it was clearly planned, not something she was sneaking."

"Agreed, even that sign-off didn't feel like it was from being afraid of getting caught. More like something unexpected was going on." Chae tapped Tamago on the arm. "You did good, LT. Got her talking. I'll see what we can pull on Castle. Sapphi gave me Ralka's image from Max already; it matches the one we have in Anton's file. They were siblings."

"Max killed Anton, and now Ralka's after Max."

"No false hope from me, but I'd put feds down on Max any day of the week." Chae seemed to think about it, then nodded once as if agreeing with themself and headed for the door.

Tamago really hoped they were right about that bet.

SAQIB WASN'T SURE WHAT WILL WAS UP TO LETTING CASTLE make the com to Ground Control, or why the man was letting him overhear the conversation between the young hacker and Lieutenant Uchida.

It was like staring at pieces of a puzzle that were so clearly not meant to fit together. They'd killed Ford to try to force Max to give herself and whatever she'd taken up, but that hadn't worked. Now it sounded like Max had managed to safeguard the other hostages right out from under Will's nose.

Saqib had braced himself for violence about that, but Will seemed only slightly annoyed by the development.

He really is waiting for something. Why can't I figure out what?

Saqib didn't have a chance to contemplate that any further before angry shouting filled the air and Castle hastily signed off. The person who shoved past Will with a raised hand and headed straight for him could only be Ralka, and Saqib didn't have time to do anything before she grabbed him by the throat and yanked him to his feet.

"I am going to drag you out there and make you scream until she comes out of hiding," she screamed, pure fury on her face.

Saqib knew it was a bad idea, but he sort of wanted to

bite her. He could hear Jenks in the back of his head about picking fights you couldn't win, though, so he kept his mouth shut.

"You're going to let him go, Ralka. Now."

There was a long pause. The space between breaths. Everything hung still for a moment. Saqib concentrated on his full lungs, the rapid decrease in oxygen and increase in carbon dioxide. He could hold his breath for a good while, but eventually things would shift for the worse.

Ralka hissed a furious curse and shoved him away. Saqib caught himself on the edge of the desk and felt the press of the scalpel still hidden in his cargo pocket. He dragged in a breath as Ralka snarled something at Will and flipped his DD on for just a moment.

SAQIB: Max, if you're out there. Watch out. Ralka's gunning for you.

MAX: Saqib! Are you okay?

SAQIB: Good enough, I guess. Heard you locked off the others so figured I'd take a chance with the DD. They made us turn it off. Ford's gone. They killed him.

MAX: I know, I saw.

SAQIB: How can I help you?

MAX: You hang tight, I'm going to come get you.

SAQIB: Okay. Shutting back down.

MAX: Wait, download this; it might work to hide your signal and they'll think your DD is off.

He accepted the file and shut his chip down as Ralka's parting shot at Will filled the air.

"I'm not waiting for the end of this, Will. I want blood *now*."

"And I keep telling you that you can't have it yet! You hunt her down, get the bag, and bring her back here *alive*, or I will cut your throat and leave you to choke on your revenge. She'll be yours when I have what I need, but until then, *follow the plan*. Is that understood?"

Ralka's reply was the heavy tread of boots back out of the office.

"My apologies for that," Will said, leaning against the desk next to Saqib. "Though had Max just cooperated, we wouldn't be in this mess."

"If you hadn't hijacked the station, we wouldn't be in this mess," he replied evenly.

Will laughed. "Fair enough, Lieutenant Commander. We could likely throw blame all day back to the beginning of time. Are you injured?"

"No."

"Excellent." His smile was cold. "Wouldn't want you to get hurt."

TWELVE

D'ARCY SLOWED TO A WALK AS HE NEARED THE ADDRESS CLAIR had given him and ducked into the alleyway to circle around the back.

"Nice try. You still look like a fucking fed when you walk."

He stopped and turned to face Maria. "Not really trying to fool anyone beyond the first glance," he replied as he slipped through the door she was holding open. She didn't step back and the move put them toe-to-toe.

"Rude as a fed, too. Why'd you ask Clair for permission and not me?"

"I can't win for losing around here. How'd you know about Clair if they don't have a DD?"

Maria looked up at him and the slow smile that curved over her mouth still did things to him after all these years. "I'd be a fool to just offer up all our secrets."

All the responses that crowded his brain were inappropriate, so he slipped by Maria and looked around the tiny room. The worn furnishings and the meticulously polished floor. The portraits on the walls. All of it reminded him entirely too much of his childhood home. "Wilke's next door?"

"As far as we know," Maria replied, moving past him, her shoulders stiff. "Mouse saw her go into the home, though the family that lives there has no ties to Free Mars or any other faction. No one else has gone in or out for an hour. What do you want to do?"

"Take her alive if we can." He told himself her surprised look didn't hurt. "Her sister asked." The words slipped out before he could stop them, and he muttered a curse. "Besides, we need someone who can tell us what they're plotting, and it sounds like Wilke's possibly had direct contact with the people who are on the MOS."

"All right," she said, reaching for the gun on the table. "Let's go."

"Just the two of us?"

"I told my people to stay back. Problem?"

D'Arcy sighed. "Beyond Emel kicking my ass? No."

Maria grinned, then sobered. "Hadi would both cheer and be beyond disappointed in the pair of you."

"Me, maybe." D'Arcy shook his head. "But you won't ever convince me that he was anything but proud of his sister for what she accomplished."

"Fair enough," she said, surprising him again. "Shall we go?"

For a second D'Arcy was tempted to say no, to call in

help and do a more thorough survey from the air before sending anyone into the building. But the clock was ticking, and he knew that Max could only avoid her pursuers for so long before she slipped up and got caught.

Or worse.

He pulled his sword free and crossed the street quickly. The back door was unlocked, swinging open under his hand. "I don't like this," he muttered as Maria crowded against his back.

"Me either, but as Sylvia likes to say, 'Needs must.'"

"Sweep to the left?"

"Sure."

It was like old times, he thought. How easily they slipped into the same pattern as in their youth, except now both of them had some actual experience and weren't just playing at soldier.

He took in his surroundings in an instant. All these houses were stacked. The second level only accessible from the outside as a separated home rather than connected inside. Some enterprising souls had fixed that problem with built-in stairs cutting through the floor into the above home so that several families could share the space.

In this case, the ceiling above was pristine, so D'Arcy moved to his left, Maria on his six like she'd never left, and they cleared through the rooms one by one.

"It's empty. How?" she whispered as he eased the last door open.

"Not empty," D'Arcy said. He backed up a step from the large pile of explosives in the center of the room and the ominous flashing light of the detonator. "Fuck. Maria, run!"

THIS TIME SYLVIA WAS SLIGHTLY MORE PREPARED FOR THE AT-
tempt on her life. Though judging by the speed of Emel's
reaction, the Neo was even more ready for things to go to
shit.

The master chief went from lounging in the chair opposite them to flinging the heavy book from the table next
to her straight at Mila's head. It connected with impressive
accuracy and the girl went limp, the jet injector in her hand
dropping to the couch between her and Sylvia.

Emel had moved at the same time she'd thrown the book,
grabbing Mila by the jaw. Mikhail grabbed Sylvia around
the waist and hauled her backward, shouting for backup.

"I need pliers!" Emel shouted as Clair and several others
flooded into the room.

"Pliers?" Sylvia watched in confusion as Clair didn't even
hesitate but pulled the pliers from the pocket of their cargos
and slapped them into Emel's hand.

"Hold her down."

"Bennie, grab her head," Clair ordered the smaller girl.

Mila's brief period of unconsciousness came to a stop
as Emel jerked a tooth free. She shrieked and thrashed in
Clair's grip before she collapsed in a sobbing heap against
the couch.

"Do you have something to tie her up with?" Emel asked,
and Clair nodded.

"Left leg pocket."

Sylvia patted Mikhail's arm until he released her, and
she bent to carefully pick up the jet injector from the floor
as the others bound Mila hand and foot. "What's in this?"

"What you deserve." Mila spat the words. "You *all* deserve it."

Sylvia held back her response, morbid fascination dragging her eyes to the bloody tooth in Emel's hand. "How did you know?"

Emel shrugged. "Long story. Short version is we've seen it once already. Probably the same poison that's in the injector," she replied, flipping the pliers over and holding them back out to Clair. "Aggy, we've got a suspect. Get Captain Jaishankar on the com; I need some backup and—"

The heavy boom shook the walls of the house, sending Sylvia staggering into Mikhail and books tumbling from the shelves.

Her eyes met Emel's, and the fear echoed between them.

"D'Arcy," the Neo breathed.

"Maria! Do you copy?" Sylvia had never queued up her com so fast in her life, nor been quite so panicked at the silence that answered her.

There was a moment of static where all she could do was pray and then the com crackled to life. "Sylvia?"

Her breath rushed out. "Maria, where are you? Are you hurt?"

"I don't know," she replied. "Underground, maybe. The whole place went up. D'Arcy shoved me, he—"

Sylvia saw Emel wave a hand at her. The Neo mouthed D'Arcy's name and gave her a thumbs-up after tapping at her temple and a second wave of relief swept over her. "Emel's got D'Arcy on her com, I think he's okay. See if you can find him. We're on our way."

"Okay."

She waited a beat and queued up Josiah on the com. "Status."

"There was an explosion. The house Maria and D'Arcy

went into. He'd warned us to stay back just in case." He coughed. "Can't see anything."

He saved your life, Sylvia thought. "We're headed to you. Sit tight." She could hear Emel on her own com, lightning-fast orders flying from her mouth even as she made eye contact and held up a hand with fingers spread.

"D'Arcy's banged up, not quite sure how bad because he lied and said he was fine," Emel said as she wrapped up her conversation and crossed to Sylvia. "Help is incoming in five minutes. I need to get down there. Clair, can you handle this?"

"Maria sounded okay, but she might be hurt. I told her to find D'Arcy if she can. I'm coming with you." Sylvia was surprised her security chief wasn't going to protest her leaving the house, but Clair just waved a hand, their focus entirely on Mila, now bound but still spitting curses into the air.

The three of them ran from the house and out into the chaos of the street. Smoke and the haze of rubble pumped into the sky from the collapsing buildings, filling the air, and Sylvia covered her face with her sleeve as best she could.

"This is a bad idea, Sylvia," Mikhail said in a low voice. His hand was warm and solid on her back, and she could see Emel ahead of her through the grit hanging in the air.

"Tell me something my eyes can't clearly see. Holy Mary," Sylvia murmured when they rounded a corner and came upon the location where Maria and D'Arcy should have been. The building was gone, and the surrounding ones were heavily damaged in a several-block radius from the force.

A sick feeling of despair choked her. Everything was

crashing down around them—some of it literally—and there was nothing she could do to prevent it.

He let loose the groan he'd been hiding from Emel, even though he was pretty sure his master chief knew his assurances were half-bullshit. "Yeah?"

"Thank God. You stupid bastard." Maria's voice was thready with pain and tangled with relief.

D'Arcy cracked an eye open, though it made no difference in the pitch-black. "How is this *my* fault?"

"Everything's your fault. Where are you?"

"Fuck if I know. Trapped under something." He wiggled his feet and hands, pain flaring with the movement, but at least he had movement and that was better than the alternative. He wasn't pinned and very carefully he eased to his left out from under the wide beam that had stopped the building from coming down on his head.

I owe you thanks at some point, I guess. He directed the thought upward with a weary sigh and the "Allahu Akbar," he muttered felt strange on his tongue, yet also the most natural thing in the world.

"You praying again?" Maria's voice echoed out of the dark. "Wonders never cease."

"Least I can do, given the circumstances. When the universe drops a building on my head and it doesn't kill me, I tend to pay attention. Give me a minute. I can't see shit." He checked his DD, flipping the vision over to night mode, and made a face. It was better, but not by much given how little light they had to work with.

D'Arcy shifted around more rubble, wincing at the pain in his side and the uncomfortable warm wetness of blood seeping into his shirt. "Talk to me, Maria. I'll work my way to you."

"I could but I'm right behind you." There was laughter in her voice when he jerked.

"How can you see?" He turned, his hand landing on her arm and closing around it for a moment before he released her.

She laughed. "I can't, but I'm used to it. We practice this rather than relying on fancy technology."

"Hush," he muttered, knowing she was right. "You talk to Sylvia?"

"Yeah, they're headed our way. We're not that far underground. Work our way up through the rubble or go forward?"

"Forward is safer, I think. There might be light ahead," he said. "Do you want to go first?"

"Always such a gentleman." She slipped around him with another soft laugh. "How do you manage that?"

"Are you *flirting* with me?"

Silence met his shocked question, and D'Arcy bit his tongue against the curse he wanted to utter, willing his focus back to the task at hand.

Maria moved away and he followed.

They picked their way free of the rubble, but not, D'Arcy realized, to the surface. Instead their path led them into a wide tunnel, the bricked-up walls curving up over his head high enough that D'Arcy could reach up and still not touch.

"Hold up a second." Now that there was a little more light, he shrugged out of his coat and hiked up his shirt. The cut on his side was as long across as his hand and still ooz-ing blood, though judging from the stain spreading down the side of his pants, it had slowed considerably.

"Why didn't you say you were hurt?" Maria demanded, reaching for him.

He hissed, partly in pain, partly in shock when her hands touched bare skin. "It's a scratch, give me a second and I'll—"

"I've got it." She tugged her long-sleeved shirt over her head, leaving her in a deep green tank. Maria shook it to get the worst of the dirt out and then flipped it inside out. "Here." She pressed the fabric to his side, clicking her tongue at him when he cursed. "Baby."

"Bully."

She leaned in, wrapping the arms of the shirt around his waist. "I'm sorry about earlier. I could say it was old habit, but I don't know. It's entirely too easy to forget who you are. I never did have very good self-control where you were concerned."

"I'm still me, Maria. Not some weird manifestation of the whole NeoG. Still, you don't owe me an explanation." He rubbed his hand over his face. "This is either the best time or the worst to tell you I have a boyfriend."

"Is that so?" She looked up at him, her fingers still busy tying the ends of her shirt over the wound.

"Couple of years now. His name's Boston." He smiled softly, thinking of Boston Hasbrook. He'd met the head of security for Trappist Minerals when they'd been working the missing ships case, and while nothing had happened then, more than a year later D'Arcy had run into him in Amanave on a bright spring day. One thing had led to another, and before he'd known it, their lives were wrapped around one another's.

"It's nice." Stable. Easy. "We've been talking about moving in together."

"You really did go and grow up, didn't you?" Maria asked softly.

"I guess so." He stopped himself from reaching for her. "I thought about you a lot over the years, for what that's worth."

"Oh, don't do that." She pulled away, eyes shining in the dim light. "I cried enough tears for you, D'Arcy. You make me cry more and I will punch you."

"I'm sorry, Maria."

"Don't apologize, either." She sniffed. "Sylvia was right, you'd have died if you'd stayed with us. So many of us did. You did what you had to do when you got out."

It was so much more complicated than she knew, but not only did he not know where to start, this wasn't the place to have that conversation. "Can I give you a hug?"

"Yes." She turned back around and stepped into his embrace, arms going high to avoid his wounds, and D'Arcy held her tight for several heartbeats, pressing his head to hers.

"I've missed you," he whispered. "Don't punch me, I'm injured."

"I'm letting you get away with that only because if I did punch you it would mess up my bandage job."

He let her go with a laugh. "Should we figure out how to get out of here before people start getting really worried we're dead?"

"Probably a good idea." She tilted her head. "I'm admittedly also very curious about this tunnel. Must have run under the house."

"If Wilke exists, I'd put feds on this being how she left without you noticing," D'Arcy replied. "And how they got the explosives in."

"If she exists? What makes you say that?"

He shrugged. "You do this long enough it starts becoming a little easier to tell when people are lying to you. I hate that I was right about Mila."

"I can't believe you just left Sylvia there with her."

D'Arcy answered Maria's glare with a flat look. "I left Emel with both of them. She handled Mila and can handle whatever else happens."

"You'd better hope so."

"Come on, let's see where this leads."

JENKS HOPPED OUT OF THE SHUTTLE, THE DUST OF THE RUBBLE puffing up around her boots, sticking to the black surface. Chae and Gunnery Sergeant Ebony Ranta were on her heels, the pair quietly waiting for orders as she surveyed the damage from the bomb. "Good job not dying, D'Arcy." When she'd been desperate for something to do, this had not been what she meant, and she pushed away the memories of smoke and rubble on Jupiter Station with ruthless efficiency.

"Jenks!" Emel waved at her from across the crowd of rescuers crawling carefully over the rubble. "Over here."

"Come on." She tapped Chae on the shoulder and the trio worked their way over to the master chief. Jenks spotted Sylvia; the Free Mars leader was in the thick of it, directing rescue efforts as Mikhail kept watch behind her left shoulder. Even the Neos who were working were apparently taking direction from her. The older woman caught her gaze, and a flicker of a smile appeared when Jenks threw her a salute.

"You responsible for that, Master Chief?" she asked Emel.

Emel smiled. "Only partly. I may have told any Neos who arrived to follow her orders. She knows the area better anyway. We've only got a few people injured, nothing major. Gonna need a shitload of paint and some screen doors, though."

Jenks snorted. "I'm legitimately surprised there isn't more damage."

"Me too. D'Arcy's got some minor injuries, but otherwise he and Maria are okay."

Relief rushed through Jenks at the update, hot and fierce as she stared at the demolished building. "How the hell did they survive that dropping on their heads?"

"That is what takes this story to the next level. Like I said, things could have been worse." Emel gestured. "Blast leveled the house it was planted in, and the buildings around it in a block radius will probably have to be demolished, but there's minimal damage past that. However, here's what's interesting."

Jenks followed her finger down and to the left. "Okay, gaping hole in the ground not all that interesting." She lifted her hands at the master chief's flat look. "Kidding."

"This way." Emel headed around the pit toward one of the homes across the street. She exchanged a nod with the Marine sergeant standing guard at the door, and they stepped aside to let them all in.

"Ooo, secret tunnel," Jenks said, whistling when she

caught sight of the lifted hatch in the floor of the small closet. "Now that *is* interesting. We going down?"

"We are. D'Arcy thinks our targets are using the tunnels to move through the city undetected. I kept one of them from killing Sylvia and then herself. Drani collected her ten minutes ago and took her back to base."

"Why would they try to kill Sylvia again? They'd have to know by now we haven't bought the ruse. It's all over the news that NeoG and Free Mars are working together on the MOS situation."

"It still benefits them if she's dead." Chae was the one to answer Jenks's question.

"Or they just want revenge," Ebony added. "No logic needed. Just emotion."

"'Justice for the orphans of war.' Mila claimed her parents were killed by a NeoG drop," Emel murmured, and Jenks frowned as she followed the master chief down the stairs into the tunnel.

"You know, several of the people on Max's list had lost family to the conflict. It wasn't always the NeoG who was responsible. Sometimes it was Free Mars."

"Tamago just talked to someone named Castle up there whose parents had also died," Chae said.

"At some point that's not a coincidence," Jenks replied.

"Quiet," Emel said softly, lifting a hand, and Jenks froze as the sound of raised voices filtered through the air of the tunnel. She shared a look with Chae and they both eased their swords free. "D'Arcy and Maria are up ahead. He said they can hear the people talking but can't get around to them."

"Gunny, stay with Emel," Jenks whispered. "We'll go

take a look?" At Emel's nod, she slipped down the side tunnel, Chae on her heels.

Whoever was up ahead of them was in a full-blown argument. Sloppy, given the situation. She couldn't tell how far away they were from the blast site, but you'd think these people would be a little more cautious.

Unless they were deliberately trying to lure them into a trap.

A glance at Chae told her the petty officer was thinking the same thing. They shook their head.

CHAE: Trap?

JENKS: Maybe? I'll take the distraction, though, if that's what it is. You hang back a step in case it is a trap. I'm going to ease forward here and get a head count.

CHAE: Don't kick anything over.

Jenks blinked at them for a long moment, fighting the urge to smile at the sass from her normally quiet Neo, and settled for poking them in the ribs with her free hand.

JENKS: I've been a terrible influence on you.

Chae grinned brightly at her. Jenks eased around the corner, watching her feet, because yes, one time she'd kicked over a bucket during a boarding and alerted the pirates they were there.

One time.

"They've got my sister!"

"Your sister knew what she was volunteering for, Wilke. If she'd done her job right, Sylvia would be dead and so would she."

"But she's not, is she? The NeoG have her and we have to get her out. She's all I have left."

"Welcome to the fucking club." The answering laughter from the person with their back to Jenks was harsh. "Yeah, sorry. Will doesn't have it on the list for me to mount a fucking incursion onto a NeoG base. We stick to the plan and get to the next target. You don't like it, take a bite and find a tunnel to die in. Pascal, you and Tru and Hannah take the north path and watch for hostiles. The rest of you with me. We're moving out in five." They spun their hand in the air and the other seven people got to their feet to gather their gear.

Wilke angrily swiped the tears from her cheeks, but the hesitation on her face was clear before she grabbed her bag and gun and headed after the others.

JENKS: Got nine targets. Armed with late-model CHN fléchette guns. Two have swords. They split—three by six. Three taking the north path—their words, not mine. The others are headed . . . How can a person tell which direction is which down here?

CHAE: East, Chief. The others headed down the east tunnel.

JENKS: How do you know that?

CHAE: It's the tunnel next to the north one?

D'ARCY: Focus.

JENKS: Right. Sorry. They're talking about heading to the next target, suggest we follow. They might be headed your direction so be careful. Also, Wilke might not be as on board with this whole thing as her sister suggested. Can I do something—eh, call it ill-advised?

D'ARCY: Am I going to regret it?

JENKS: Maybe, but I suddenly don't want this kid to die and that's the direction she's headed.

D'ARCY: Granted then. Just be careful.

JENKS: Hey, I'm not the one who got blown up today, just saying.

She waited for Chae to join her, and then together they eased into the open area and followed the group down the eastern tunnel.

"What are we doing, Chief?" Chae whispered.

Jenks didn't poke them for falling back into the verbal habit as they hung back at a corner and watched the group head up a long stretch of straight tunnel with nowhere to hide. They were far enough away the voices wouldn't carry.

"Hopefully saving someone's life." Jenks watched as Wilke slowed even more, the space between her and the others widening in a physical manifestation of her hesitation. "Be ready for this to go to shit, though, just in case."

"Got your back, Senior Chief," they replied.

"Damn right." She leaned her forehead against theirs for a moment and then eased ahead as Wilke finally disappeared after the others.

Jenks moved as fast as stealth would allow for, nodding her head in approval when they reached the end of the stretch, and the direction Wilke had followed her companions in turned into a twisting narrow passage.

"What are you doing?" The low curse was filled with pain as Wilke threw the question into the quiet. Jenks tapped Chae and set down her sword, then held up three fingers, counting down and slipping into the space behind the young woman.

A boot as gently as she could apply to the back of the knee forced Wilke to the ground. Jenks slipped an arm across her throat. The other hand over Wilke's mouth, fingers digging into the girl's cheeks at her jaw.

"I am really hoping you don't want to die today, so don't bite down, okay? I wanna talk."

The sudden tears were unexpected as Wilke sagged in her grip.

Jenks was pretty sure that was a surrender; still she hoped she wasn't making a mistake when she released the young woman's mouth and moved around to face her. Chae was hanging back in the shadows, sword at the ready.

"I took the poison out the same day they put it in. I never wanted any of this," Wilke whispered, the sob catching in her throat. "Mila used to be so happy. Our parents' death hit her hard, but I thought we were going to be okay, just the two of us. Then these people showed up and everything fell apart. All she talked about was revenge, justice for the fallen. I just wanted us to be a family again and I thought maybe I could convince her to leave."

"Instead you blew up a building."

Wilke nodded miserably, her eyes big in her pale face. "I tried to clear the area, packed the explosive so that most of the blast would angle down instead of out—"

Jenks held up her hand to cut Wilke off. "We're gonna debrief on this in a little bit. The question here is, can I trust you to follow behind us and stay out of trouble? I can't promise you anything, Wilke, but I'll try to get you out of here and back with your sister."

"Yes, whatever you want. She's all I have left."

"All right. How many more targets does this group of yours have left? And are they all explosives?"

"We've got three more, and yes."

Jenks heaved a sigh. "Of course, it's yes. Okay. Chae, come here." She gestured at her Neo over Wilke's shoulder, and the young woman stiffened. "It's all right. Hey, D'Arcy," she said into the com, keeping her voice low and one eye on the tunnel in case one of Wilke's friends doubled back to check on her.

"Yeah?"

"Three more targets, all explosives. I don't have sizes."

"I have the sizes and locations," Wilke offered.

Jenks grinned. "Scratch that. I do apparently have those and the locations, according to my new friend. Give me a minute and I'll send them along. We're probably going to want to get some backup."

"Maria and I will continue to follow since it sounds like our two groups are meeting ahead. I want you and Chae to take your *friend* back to base. Get with Drani when you're topside and have her send teams to the other two locations to sweep for explosives."

Jenks made a face but didn't argue. "All right, I guess."

D'Arcy chuckled. "We'll be fine."

"Blown up once today, remember. Don't do it again." She clicked off and looked at Chae, taking her sword back when they handed it over. "We're headed up top, let's go." She patted Wilke's back with her free hand. "Give me those locations, Wilke; let's see if we can save some lives today, okay?"

The Case for Reconciliation
JULY 22, 2439 (ESD)

The conflict on Mars has existed for most of our lifetimes. An endless-seeming maelstrom of anger and violence—some warranted, to be sure. At what point do we admit that this fight for independence from our neighboring planet, our original home, is doing more harm than good?

I know people will argue that independence is worth dying for and that we should never give up this fight, all the while gesturing at our collective past. A past that nearly resulted in the death of humanity itself. I'm sorry, but that's not a great basis for an argument.

As we stand here on the precipice of a new decade, I would hope that we are willing to admit our wrongs, lay aside our differences as they have done in Trappist, and look to a future with Earth rather than against her. [*Read More*]

THIRTEEN

D'ARCY HAD TRIED NOT TO THINK TOO HARD ABOUT WHAT KIND of trouble Jenks could get herself into with an "ill-advised" decision as he and Maria followed the small group of hostiles. Still his shoulders were tight until she'd contacted them with the news of Wilke's somewhat willing capture.

"So two against eight?" Maria asked after he finished explaining what had happened.

"That's not bad odds." He shrugged.

"It's not *good* odds," she replied, then grinned. "But what the hell. I guess you're only young once. Come on. If we take out these three on the way, it'll make life easier."

Are we young? he thought. But his blood was already pumping at the promise of the imminent action, and so maybe he wasn't quite at the "getting too old for this shit" mindset just yet. D'Arcy bumped her lightly in the shoulder as they started off down the tunnel again. This wasn't what he'd expected when he came home, far from it, but a part of him was glad to be working with Maria again.

He just hoped they really could stop these people and get to the bottom of whatever this plot truly was.

Both Gunny Ranta and Max had said the people on the station moved like they'd trained together, almost as well as the CHN military. But these people were clearly not of the same caliber. They weren't quiet enough, and the assumption that they were alone down in the tunnels had relaxed them too much even as they headed for their next target.

It was almost too easy, even with the unfamiliar sword in his hand. The first person never saw Maria coming, sinking to the ground with a quiet gasp before D'Arcy could get his mouth open to demand a surrender. He muttered a curse and drove his sword through the second person before their shout of alarm truly broke the air.

Maria grabbed the third target and D'Arcy's hissed "Wait!" was too slow. She drove the knife into their throat and twisted.

"What?"

D'Arcy rubbed a hand over his face. "I have rules of engagement, Maria. I can't just go around killing people."

She blinked at him and the amused surprise on her face pissed him off even before she spoke. "Really?"

"Oh, *fuck you*," he muttered and spun on his heel.

"D'Arcy, wait. Look, I'm not sorry for it. They deserved what they got. They're blowing up my home, my people. They tried to kill Sylvia *and* me. I am sorry that I forgot you have different rules." She offered up a small smile. "Ones that you actually follow, I see. It's too easy to think of you as the D'Arcy I knew."

"Yeah, he died a long time ago." Pain and frustration made his voice sharper than she really deserved, and he felt worse when Maria flinched.

"That's on me, I suppose. I'm sorry, D'Arcy. For a lot of things, especially for not coming to save your ass like I promised I always would."

"Apology accepted." He studied her for a long moment before he sighed and shook his head. "Look, this conversation is longer and more complicated than the other one, but it's also not suited for a tunnel with people who want us dead. Can you just let me at least try to get them to surrender first?"

"Fine. It makes things more difficult, but you're in charge, Commander."

D'Arcy snorted at the complete lack of respect she'd managed to load in his rank and tagged the location on his DD before he continued on the path Jenks's message had given him.

She's not wrong about the difficulty, a bloodthirsty voice whispered in his head, and D'Arcy batted it away. Whatever Maria thought, and D'Arcy could admit some of it was deserved given how badly the NeoG had mangled things on Mars over the years, he had always tried to do things the right way and this was the absolute last place where he should change that.

"Commander, you copy?" Chaske said over the com, pulling D'Arcy back to the present and the mission at hand.

"Copy. Little busy, though. What's up?"

"I know. Emel, Aki, and I are working our way around to you from topside. Just wanted to give you a heads-up and see how you want to handle this assault. Drani said to let you know she's got strike teams and explosives experts headed for the other two locations."

D'Arcy shook his head. "I suppose Jenks called you?"

"Maybe." There was laughter in Chaske's dry voice. "Not going to leave you hanging, man, come on."

"All right. Maria and I took down three; I want to try to bring these other five in alive if we can. I'll let you know when we're close. You wait if you beat us there unless it looks like they're going to move. We don't want to give them a chance to detonate anything."

"Roger that. We'll hold until we hear from you unless needed."

D'Arcy signed off and continued on through the dimly lit tunnel. "Backup," he said over his shoulder.

"Good," she replied and lapsed back into silence. Unlike their previous comfortable quiet, this one felt laden with too many things unsaid and D'Arcy did his best to push it aside as he followed the trail through the dark.

"FIGURES." MAX KICKED OFF THE LAST PAIR OF BOOTS WITH A sigh, the third pair that didn't fit. Too big, too small, she felt like some fairy-tale princess.

Do they get trapped on space stations these days?

She choked down the laughter and bent to strip off her socks, stuffing them into the bag at her back. The floor was cold under her bare feet, but trying to run in those was asking to get killed.

Pulling the detonator keys free, Max shoved them into her boot. She paired it with one of the too large ones and set them both back into the locker, tossing a hoodie on top for good measure. The other boot she tossed into the recycler with an apology to its owner.

Then for far longer than she should have, she agonized over her decision. She didn't want to carry the keys around, better that they were hidden in case something happened to her, but now she was worried it was too obvious.

Still safer than keeping them on you. At least this way, they have to tear the station apart to find them.

Max dragged in a breath and crept back over to the door, listening for a long moment before she slipped into the hallway. She followed the sound of voices to an office up ahead and paused in a nearby doorway, sword in hand, to listen.

"So Ralka confirmed there's no access through the maintenance tunnels. All those hatches locked down when Carmichael tripped the warning. Will seems convinced he can get the codes out of her once Ralka brings her in." The speaker chuckled. "I love that he thinks she's not going to just kill Carmichael first chance she gets."

"Will's in charge for a reason, Brant."

"Sure. I'm just saying that no one has control of a tiger, even if you raised it from a cub. And Ralka was well beyond feral by the time Will got to her. Anton could talk sense into her. Now it's just stay out of the way and hope for the best."

"That's not really any different from before, let's be honest. Anton didn't bother to talk her down all that much," the other person replied, and blew out a noisy breath. "I don't understand how some of these bastards are perfectly cool with riding this station down to the planet. No thank you."

"Keep your mouth shut about that," they snapped and there was a moment of silence. "I am seriously not interesting in losing my spot on the shuttle, and you know we will if word gets out about Will's limited seating situation."

"Fine. Whatever. So according to the schematics on Captain Harmony's tablet, if we laser through the floor here, it'll put us directly into the main control room for the station engine. After he does his thing, we lower the bombs and kaboom. Get on the coms and tell Will I'll have an estimate for how long it'll take us to get through once we start cutting."

Ride the station to the planet?

Kaboom?

Her heart was pounding in her ears. Drowning out everything else as she grappled with the information even as her brain started spinning the actual mechanics required to knock the MOS out of orbit and crash it into Mars. That's why they needed control of Engineering: not just for the bombs, but if they changed the course of the station, the planet's gravity would do the bulk of the work.

If they wanted this to hit planetside, not just blow up in the black.

Max eased away from the door, fully intent on removing these two hijackers from the equation, when a commotion at the other end of the hall echoed through the air. She muttered a curse and slipped into the dark office behind her. There weren't a whole lot of options for cover, so Max crouched behind a desk in the far corner, making herself as small as possible in the shadows.

The whining hiss of fléchettes slicing through the air was followed by the impact in both metal and flesh. A gasp of pain and the stumbling of boots drew closer as well as the sound of pursuit.

Max dared a peek and shocked gray eyes met hers for

just a moment. Before she could wave them over, the Neo shook their head, mouthed *Stay down*, and pushed away from the doorframe of the office. She could hear the rhythmic pounding of their sprint down the hallway until it was drowned out by the shouts of their pursuers passing the door.

Then she could do nothing but listen, hand clamped over her mouth to keep the grief and horror inside, as the unknown Neo was overtaken. Their shouted words of defiance cut off by the sharp fléchettes and the ugly sound of laughter.

"Poor little rabbit, not fast enough." This voice she recognized and something inside her snarled in fury.

Thomas, the one who'd almost caught her just outside the Docking Bay. "Once we get the Cargo Bay doors open again, Will should let us just release them one at a time into the station for a hunt."

Every cell in her body was screaming at her to get up, to exact revenge for this stranger—this fellow Neo—who had just saved her life; but Max stayed where she was, crouched in the dark with tears streaming down her face.

Again.

"I can't. Not this time," she whispered fiercely as the voices faded down the corridor. Even as part of her brain was screaming at her about the foolishness of wasting their sacrifice, a bigger part insisted she get up and follow. That she exact some kind of revenge for this, no matter the cost.

She stopped only briefly at the body, left where they had sprawled in the middle of the hallway, to scan their DD chip and gather their info. Then she continued around the curve after the hijackers.

They'd stopped at the elevator. Still laughing and joking with each other, fueling the rage in her chest even more until the more logical part of her was forced into silence. Max struck hard and fast, taking off the head of the person closest to her and dropping into a swing that sheared through the second one's leg, separating it at the knee.

They went down screaming, and Max could only hope the sound of the laser would drown them out.

Not that it mattered. Thomas barely had a chance to recognize her before Max jammed her sword up under his ribs and into his heart.

"It's less fun when the rabbits fight back, isn't it?"

His mouth opened to reply, but it was too late for him, and Max watched the light fade from his eyes with a shameful satisfaction. She pulled her sword free as the elevator dinged open, but it was thankfully empty, and she let Thomas's body fall inside.

"Jesus Christ."

Max turned to the last of the hijackers. They were clutching uselessly at their injured leg, blood pooling on the floor around them at an alarming rate.

"Please don't kill me."

She glanced over her shoulder, but there were still no signs that the others down the hall had heard anything. "You're already dead," she said, tilting her head to the side and watching them. "Two minutes, five if you're lucky. How long does the elevator take to get up to the Command Deck, do you think?" She kicked the fléchette gun on the floor away from them. "I'll give you a fair shot. If you survive on the way up, tell them they're next."

Max kept one eye on the sobbing hijacker as they crawled toward the elevator. Then she turned and dragged the headless corpse into the elevator with them. She bent down, swiping her hand through the blood trail, and wrote her message quickly on the wall. "Just in case you don't make it," she said with a cold smile as she hit the button for the top floor and stepped back.

She considered, briefly, heading back to take care of the pair trying to tunnel into the station engine core, but the sound of voices echoing down the corridor shut down that line of thought. Max grabbed the guns and headed for the nearest maintenance hatch. There wasn't anything to be done about the trail of blood she was leaving, but once she crawled in and pulled it shut behind her, she fired up the welding torch and melted the hatch in place.

The climb back up to the Cargo Bay was slow, and Max had to stop twice, clinging to the ladder with an arm hooked over the rung, to catch her breath.

To see if she could catch a bit of her humanity.

With a deep, shuddering breath, she approached one of the maintenance hatches into the Cargo Bay. "Is someone on guard out there? It's Commander Carmichael. I'd rather not get shot."

"Carmichael! Hey, Cho! It's the commander."

Max spotted the shocked look from the Neo that morphed into a concerned frown as she crawled from the hatch. "I'm fine."

"Holy shit, no you're not, Carmichael." That was Seo-Yoon, who caught her by the arm when Max wobbled unsteadily. "How much of this blood is yours?"

"None of it." The shame surged again, and Max squeezed her eyes shut, trying to keep the confession in her throat even though it burned.

"Everyone, get back." Seo-Yoon snapped the order. "Bennie, get people back. Where's Lia?" Her voice softened as she slipped an arm around Max's waist and led her back to a secluded corner. "Why don't we have a seat, Carmichael? It's all right, you're all right." She lowered Max to the floor, going to a knee at her side.

Max felt Seo-Yoon's hands on her as the woman gently divested her of the weapons and her bag, murmuring words of comfort as she did so. "Gonna wipe your face off here, okay?"

Max nodded, eyes locked on her still bloody hands, barely registering when Seo-Yoon reached down and wiped those off also.

"Max, drink this." She dimly recognized Lia's voice and took the bottle that was pressed into her grip. The water had that familiar recycled tang, but once she started, she didn't stop until it was empty.

"Good job, here you go, Max. Why don't you lie down for a minute?"

"No time, I need to talk to Nika."

"There's time. Rest." Seo-Yoon pressed her down onto a folded blanket, draping another over her. Someone else elevated her feet—*like you'd do for someone in shock*, she realized—and Max let the encroaching exhaustion drag her down into the dark.

NIKA STUDIED THE MAP OF THE STATION, HIS HANDS CLASPED loosely behind his back as the room swirled with activity behind him. Their attempts to com the station continued to be ignored, and with every failed request, Nika's gut cramped all the more.

Captain Hosaka leaned against the console next to him. The negotiator from Earth was an old friend of Stephan's, and even though he and Nika hadn't met until now, they were getting along just fine. "You doing okay?" He kept his voice low enough that no one around could hear.

"I don't like this silence, Kenta. What is going on up there?"

"I know. It's the worst part. They'll talk, though; they always do."

"Before or after someone else gets killed?"

"Max is smart, Nika."

"I know." He allowed himself a smile. "It's one of the many reasons I fell in love with her."

Smart wasn't going to keep her safe forever, and Nika already knew that the aftermath of surviving something like this was just as difficult as the event itself. He'd coached Jenks through enough panic attacks and flashbacks over the years. He didn't want that for his little sister and certainly not for Max.

The explosion in Serrano had only complicated matters, and though he'd been able to keep the news of Vice Admiral Ford's death in a tightly controlled group, it would get out eventually.

Kenta hummed. "I've been thinking, if we get Hale on the line, it might be worth having Grady try to talk to him? They have a history, a good one from the sounds of it."

"You think he could talk Hale down?"

"Maybe? Since Max locked down the bulk of the hostages,

we have a little room to breathe. Obviously, Lieutenant Commander Vahid's life is important, but . . ." Kenta trailed off; both men knew that sometimes the math didn't shake out the way you wanted it to.

Which didn't stop Nika from feeling guilty about putting Saqib in harm's way, even though the man would tell him it was part of the job. He spotted Chae, and gestured to get their attention. They crossed the room to him, greeting Kenta with a nod. "Captain. Commander, Jenks and I brought back someone we think is part of the hijackers. She surrendered to us. Captain Jaishankar brought her sister in a little earlier."

Nika nodded. "The one who tried to kill Sylvia. They're across the yard in the brig; Drani's interrogating her. How's D'Arcy?"

"A little dusty is my understanding but okay. He and one of the Free Mars people are tracking the other group to their next target. Chaske and the others are circling around to flank them. There's more explosives apparently, but we got the locations from Wilke."

"Wilke?" Nika frowned as he tried to make the connection.

"Sorry, she's sister to the one Drani brought in, but it seems like she's not as on board with the whole plan. Jenks talked to Captain Jaishankar, and other teams were headed for the other two bomb sites. We think they're going for as much general destruction and chaos as possible. We didn't get a why out of Wilke, but I think Jenks wants to sit down and talk to her when she has a moment."

"Did she go with your prisoner?"

"No. Aki asked for a second pair of eyes on what she's

been working on, so she peeled off. She'll be in shortly unless you want me to go get her?"

Nika shook his head. "It's fine. Sapphi's been tracking the signals from the MOS and there's something I want you two to go check out, but it can wait."

The com buzzed suddenly, and the entire room froze.

"It's the MOS, Nik," Sapphi said. "Official channel."

Nika put up his hand. "All right, people, you know the drill. Everyone, and I mean everyone, will be quiet. Captain Hosaka and Lieutenant Uchida are the only voices I want to hear."

"Nika, stand in on this one," Kenta said. "I want to see if there's a reaction. Tamago, you'll take the lead. Grady, over here."

Nika swapped places with the negotiator lead. He'd had the same basic training as all the Interceptors, but he was thankful for all the time he'd spent helping Tamago with their studies for the extra training they'd done.

"Sapphi, tight focus on the visual."

"Got it, Commander. Give me a go."

Nika glanced around and was satisfied with what he saw, so he pointed at Sapphi when Kenta nodded. "Bring it up."

The screen lit up, and the man Max had identified as Will studied them both before he smiled a predatory smile. "Ah, what a pleasant surprise. Commander Vagin. Lieutenant Uchida."

Nika spotted the flicker of a frown that danced over Kenta's face out of the corner of his eye. He nodded to Will, but allowed the silence to stretch out, waiting for the other man to make the first move.

"You did quite good with Castle earlier, Lieutenant. Very empathetic, got them talking. Though admittedly with Castle that's not difficult. She'll talk your fucking ear off if you give her half a chance."

"We'd like to talk to Lieutenant Commander Vahid," Tamago replied.

"Are you in charge here, Lieutenant? Where did Captain Hosaka go?" Will shifted his gaze to Nika. "Commander Vagin, I am curious if Maxine was this much trouble for you? Or is this your sister's undue influence on the youngest daughter of such a notable family?"

"Commander Carmichael is doing her job, Senator Hale."

A slow smile spread across Hale's face, and he clapped his hands slowly. "Oh, well done, Commander. Well done. I maybe should have made an effort to take you out of this equation."

Nika heard a few sharp inhales, thankfully too far away for the microphones to catch with their filters, and kept his own face blank of expression.

"It wasn't my doing," he replied.

"Is that so? Interesting." Hale's eyes flicked to Tamago.

"We've been more than willing to work with you," Tamago replied, the barest hint of a sympathetic smile on their face. "While you have killed people. I would like assurances that Saqib is unhurt before we go any further." As Kenta had said, they had more room to negotiate right now, thanks to Max getting the Cargo Bay locked down.

"Or I could just tell you that he is hurt, though that was his own fault for interfering. He's still alive. Vice Admiral Ford was a regrettable sacrifice for the greater good. You know how that goes."

Nika watched the cold amusement spread across the former senator's face and struggled to keep his own anger under control.

"You've been in touch with Maxine, I'm sure. Next time you talk, you should tell her that it's best if she turns herself in to me. She's made a rather nasty enemy and the clock is running out for her."

"The clock is running out?"

Willis tutted. "Come now, Lieutenant. All this is hard enough on the commander there; I'm not going to go into detail of what will happen. I will give you a piece of advice, though, Commander: Keep that sister of yours on the ground. Don't do something hasty like sending her up here during the next phase."

"What is it you want?" Tamago asked.

"This is not about what I want, it is about justice, about what is right."

Nika glanced at Kenta and then at Grady. The negotiator nodded and nudged the man into the frame as Nika shifted away.

Grady cleared his throat. "Willis."

Hale's smile was genuine. "Parson. I'd have thought you'd gone back to your office. I could apologize for the shuttle malfunction, but you wouldn't want to be up here."

"Willis, what are you doing? The station was about to be handed over to Mars, something we'd wanted all those years ago."

"Parson, I don't expect you to understand. You have spent the last few decades still lost in the mire of this situation. While I have found clarity."

"Clarity? Willis, you've murdered people. Innocent people—"

"None of us are innocent." Hale swept a hand through the air. "We brought this on ourselves. I recommend you go back to your office and leave this to these fine NeoG folks. They're going to be busy for a while."

The screen flickered and cut out. Nika barely had time to open his mouth before Sapphi swore loudly. "Lupe, shut it down. Shut everything down!" There was a scramble as the two hackers reacted to a threat only they were aware of and the main consoles in the room went dark.

Nika was aware of the shocked silence in the room, the confused noises coming from Grady, and the way his own pulse was slamming in his ears.

Everything about Hale's demeanor had been terrifying, crawling along Nika's spine like a bad omen.

With careful precision born of years of practice, he took the emotions circling in his chest and examined them carefully. His worry and fear for Max and Saqib as well as all the other people trapped on the station was of little help. Sapphi would tell him what was going on with the computers when she had the answers. All that mattered right this moment was getting a handle on what Hale's plan was.

"I didn't—"

"That wasn't you, Parson," Kenta reassured the man. "You did a good job, possibly got Hale to talk a little more than he would have otherwise."

Tamago's hand touched Nika's back, warm through his shirt.

"You did really good holding your temper there," they said in a low voice. "He was deliberately trying to antagonize you."

"I know." Nika dragged a hand through his hair. "Can you tell me that he's not going to blow up the station, Tama?"

"I wish I could," they whispered back. "But I think it's likely."

"We need to get in touch with Max." Nika spotted Jenks coming in the doorway with her eyebrows raised in silent question. He waved her over and then a thought struck him. "Tama, what kind of damage are we looking at if the MOS blows?"

"If we have warning, the ships pacing will be fine. They can get away and the shielding will help. The atmosphere would take care of some of the debris, depending on what's left." Tamago swallowed and looked up at him. "I don't know how big this is. Max hasn't given me eyes on the bombs yet, and Sapphi's scan only gave us a vague location in Engineering because of all the shielding on the tanks and reactor. I can't even tell you where any of the debris will hit on the ground until I have a trajectory to go off of for calculations. All I can tell you is that if Hale's waiting for something, Max taking the detonators is going to play hell with his timetable."

"Max is good at that," Nika said as Jenks joined them. "She learned it from this one."

"Learned what?"

"Ruining people's days."

"You know it. I should be on vacation." Jenks's tease wasn't as easy as it normally was. "Chae catch you up?"

"They did. I need to talk with Admiral Chen. Come on. Kenta, you and Grady also."

Kenta rubbed a hand over his face with a sigh as he fell into step next to Nika. "This is going to get ugly, Nika."

"It *is* ugly." Nika had to swallow down the sick feeling rising in his throat as he said the next words. "Best-case scenario is making sure the station is in small enough pieces it doesn't survive reentry."

"Commander," Grady whispered. "You can't be—" The man cut the words off, his own face pale as they filed into Captain Clark's office and didn't speak again until the doors were closed behind them. "You can't be seriously considering blowing up the station."

Nika heard the noise Jenks tried to suppress and kept his eyes on Grady. Looking at her would break him open and right now he couldn't afford it. "Captain Hosaka, your professional opinion on this?"

"Our interaction with Senator Hale was too brief, but given the fact that he's proven willing to kill hostages and seems unwilling to even entertain the notion of compromise with us, I think it's not unreasonable to assume that he's planning on killing not only himself but the hostages as well and possibly people on the ground. I don't like it, Commander, but I think we need to move to the next phase of Stolen Sun Protocol. Negotiation phase is unsuccessful."

Nika swallowed and nodded as he opened the door. "Sapphi."

She pushed away from her console and crossed to him. "We're back up. Those Hades damned fuck—" She cleared her throat and smiled brightly at Kenta. "Captain."

"Continue, Lieutenant," he replied with a grim smile. "It's nothing I haven't heard before."

"They dropped a ping plague on us of all things. Or tried

to. Thankfully Lupe shut the incoming down the second he saw the first wave, or we'd still be melting off the com requests. Still, some got through."

"We saw it."

"Castle's good. I wish we'd have gotten her on our side." She shook her head. "Anyway, what do you need?"

"Get Admiral Chen on the com for me."

"Okay." She glanced between him and Jenks, and he could tell she wanted to ask but was thankful for once she held the question in. "Give me a minute, I'll patch her through."

"Thanks." He closed the door again and pinched at the bridge of his nose, dragging in a long breath before he straightened.

The screen flickered to life and Admiral Chen appeared. "Commander."

"Admiral, I am sorry to report that the negotiation phase of SSOP-47 has failed. Captain Hosaka and I both feel that our hostiles on the station are not willing to listen to reason. We are moving to phase two."

"Understood."

"Commander Carmichael has been successful in separating the majority of the hostages. I recommend we send a small force to rescue them if possible before we proceed with disintegration of the MOS." Nika forced himself to meet Chen's gaze. "We have not yet made contact with Max, but that will be my next task so we can coordinate rescue of the hostages."

"I will coordinate with Admiral Lidon on getting naval vessels in there. We've had several carriers on standby. They will be under orders to check in with you, Nika, before any action is taken. Are you sending Commander Montaglione up?"

Nika saw Jenks straighten up out of the corner of his eye and shook his head. "I need him here on the ground, Admiral." As much he wanted to send D'Arcy, there wasn't anyone else Free Mars would trust.

"Give me a few minutes, I'll figure out who's in the area," Chen replied. "I'll get you someone."

"Thank you, Admiral."

"We'll talk soon, Commander."

The screen went dark. Nika stayed where he was as Kenta ushered Grady from the room.

"Nika." Jenks's voice was low. "Whoever Admiral Chen sends up there . . ."

He knew what she was going to ask. Wanted desperately to tell her no.

He also knew he wouldn't. His job was down here. Jenks's was up there.

Nika crossed to his sister, gripped her by the back of the neck, and pressed his forehead to hers. "Bring them and you home. No matter what."

There was no question who "them" meant.

Her mismatched eyes locked on his and her voice was steady. "Yes, Commander."

FOURTEEN

THERE WAS NO COMPARISON TO THE BURST OF RELIEF IN JENKS'S chest when Nika gave her the order. He had every right, both personally and professionally, to tell her to shut up and sit down. But he hadn't. Instead he was going to allow her to throw herself into danger, knowing what it might cost all of them.

Interceptor crews were trained on the Stolen Sun operational plans, since they were most likely going to be the first ones through the airlock in a situation just like this. She couldn't imagine what was going on in Nika's head, having to officially declare a move to phase two with Max still on board. One step closer to phase three, which involved total destruction of the station by any means necessary.

I need you to think of anything else, she told herself.

"I'm going to go talk to this kid we brought in," she said

to Nika. He'd let her go, but hadn't moved away and was staring at the wall, eyes unfocused. "Nik?"

"What? Sorry."

"It's fine." She reached out and squeezed his forearm. "I'm going to security. You want to take a walk with me? At the very least get some fresh air for a minute."

"I—yeah, why don't I?"

Jenks kept ahold of him as they left the office and waved a hand at Tamago. "I'm stealing the commander for a minute," she called. "He'll be right back." She didn't quite drag him down the hallway and out the door, but it was close.

She didn't look at him as they hit the outside, instead squinting up into the bright sunlight as she let her feet carry her across the yard to the security building. "This is the job we do," she said softly. "Max knows it. I know it."

"Your kids don't."

"Yeah, they do," she shot back, amusement curling through her because once upon a time she'd have reacted to that sort of challenge with a fist. "Shit, all those kids know better than most how sometimes people don't come home. So I'll tell you this and I suspect Max would back me on it: if we die and you wallow around in guilt, I'm going to come back and kick your ass. Understood?"

Nika's laugh was jagged with pain, but it was still a laugh. "God, I hate you."

"Nah, you love me to the end of it and beyond." Jenks yelped when Nika dragged her into a tight hug, and she wrapped her arms around his waist as he shook in her embrace. "I warned you that you were stuck with me when this started, and you said okay."

"I did. That goes both ways, you know?" Nika cleared

his throat and straightened. "Admiral Chen just messaged me. There's a SEAL team on planet and they're headed our way. We'll start planning a boarding action as soon as they get here."

Jenks heaved a dramatic sigh because she knew it would make him laugh for real this time. "Ugh, fine, I guess they can tag along while I go save Max and the others." She patted his arm. "D'Arcy's here. Chae's waiting inside for me. I'll go see what we can get out of Wilke and her sister."

Jenks flipped a salute at D'Arcy and then headed for the building.

D'ARCY SLOWED HIS STRIDE WHEN HE SPOTTED NIKA AND JENKS in an embrace in the yard near the security building. There was a muttered protest behind him, followed by a yelp of pain; but when he glanced back, Maria wore her most innocent look and Chaske's face was expressionless, not releasing his grip on the man between them.

When he looked back, the pair had separated so D'Arcy continued on at his normal pace, lifting a hand in greeting as he neared them.

"Couple more who decided that dying today wasn't really what they wanted," he said, ignoring the shine of tears in the siblings' eyes. He knew they didn't want attention drawn to whatever had just passed between them and especially not in front of strangers.

"Good to hear." Nika glanced past him and dipped his head. "Sylvia, I'm afraid I can't allow you and the others inside the security building, but someone will be out here in a minute to collect your charges. We appreciate your help."

Sylvia nodded back and then with a perfectly straight face said, "That's all right, Commander. I have a feeling Clair would rather I not go in there anyway."

D'Arcy swallowed down his laugh, but Maria didn't, the sound ringing through the air, and Clair sighed very heavily.

"I'd rather you take this somewhat fucking seriously," Clair muttered, "but I'm apparently not going to get even that."

A pair of security officers emerged, and D'Arcy stepped to the side as they took custody of the prisoners.

"We're moving to phase two of SSOP-47," Nika murmured. "I've got a SEAL team en route to the base; we'll start planning the evac for the hostages."

"Any word from Max?" D'Arcy slipped his hand around Nika's and squeezed. "You all right?"

"No." Nika's voice was barely a whisper, and he gripped D'Arcy's hand tightly for a moment before letting go. "I'm scared, D'Arcy."

"I know." Sapphi had messaged to catch him up on what had happened with Ford and their discovery of who Willis Hale was. He should have recognized the man, but it had been so long since he'd seen him. D'Arcy's own heart was in his throat with worry for Max and Saqib and all the others trapped on the station; he couldn't imagine how much worse it had to be for Nika. "All we can do is work to finish this and hope they come home."

"Jenks said the same thing." Nika dragged in a breath and then let it go. "Is it enough?"

"It *is*," he said with conviction. Softer, "It has to be. We'll get through this, Nik. We know our jobs. *Max* knows her job. Hold on to that faith of yours."

An unwilling smile twitched at the corner of the man's mouth as he started across the base. "The irony of you saying that to me."

"I know," D'Arcy answered with a wry grin. "For what it's worth I *was* praying earlier."

"No lie, I'm pretty sure that's a sign of the end times." But Nika smiled as he tapped him twice on the chest before heading through the door. "I need to get back to it. Pax is in conference room B. I'll send a medic your way and have them bandage up that wound properly." He shook his head. "One day us Neos are going to actually acknowledge when we're hurt."

"One day, but not today."

"Why do I put up with any of you?"

D'Arcy chuckled and waved the group forward as he started down the hallway. Sylvia matched his stride, and though there were a few double takes as they headed through the building, no one said anything or stopped them.

"Better reception than I expected," she murmured.

"They'll follow orders," he replied, exchanging a nod with the guard on duty outside the conference room. D'Arcy knocked on the doorframe and Pax looked away from the screen hanging in midair.

The smile that lit Max's sister's face was genuine and surprisingly warm. "D'Arcy. Sylvia. Come in."

"Kavan." D'Arcy exchanged a quick greeting with her partner, their own eyes flicking away from him to scan the Free Mars trio behind him. "Nika's orders."

"I know, he gave me a warning." Their mouth tipped up on one corner. "Mikhail, good to see you again."

"Been a while," the big man replied.

"Yup." Kavan offered no explanation for the exchange as they shoved their hands into their pockets. "I'm good if they are."

"You all can stand around and glare at each other if it makes you feel better," Pax said. "Sylvia and I can get to work." She gestured for the older woman to follow her back across the room.

"Commander Montaglione?"

D'Arcy turned back at the call and gestured for the med tech to come in. Her handshake read *Chief Jenn Powell, she/her.* "Where do you want me, Chief?"

"Over there will be easiest." She pointed to the chairs in the corner. "Let's get that shirt off. I brought you a new one."

To his surprise, Maria followed them, leaning against the wall with her arms crossed.

"You just going to stand there and ogle?"

Chief Powell choked down a laugh as D'Arcy pulled his ruined shirt off over his head. Maria didn't bother to hide her amusement.

"It was dark down there, D'Arcy. I want to see how much you were lying to me about it being a little scratch. Sorry about the poor patch job, Chief. We were low on supplies."

"No worries. I know how that is. I'd classify it as a laceration, medium leaning into large," Powell said after cutting away Maria's impromptu bandage, "if you want my professional assessment. Looks about two centimeters deep, a little over that wide, and eighteen long. Not a scratch—sorry, Commander."

"Oh sure, agree with her." D'Arcy leaned his head back against the wall and closed his eyes. Powell snorted and bent to her task of cleaning out the wound. The disinfection stung briefly, but he held in the reflexive hiss that tried to escape. Soon after, the soothing coolness of a heal patch covered it all and even the pain of the injury faded into a dull ache. He sat up with a slow exhale and took the offered shirt.

"There you go, Commander. Almost good as new. Your crew medic can put a new one on if needed once that one's used up. Try not to move around too much for the next few hours. I know, I know," she said with a raised hand before he could say anything sarcastic. "When you mess it up, just make sure to see an actual medic again. No offense, that was good work," she said to Maria, who grinned.

"None taken."

"Thanks, Chief."

Powell patted his shoulder after she got to her feet. "Anytime. I'll put these in the disposal." She gathered up the ruined shirts, nodded to Maria, and then left with a little wave over her head.

"All right, out with it," D'Arcy said as he stood and tucked the shirt in. The black looked strange with the tan habitat pants rather than his normal NeoG uniform. If he had a minute to breathe, he'd run back to *Dread* and change. It wasn't vanity. There was a sense of completeness that being in uniform granted him, and—perhaps especially—now, with everything going on, he needed that, almost like it was armor.

Or maybe it's just the comradeship, of knowing all us Neos are in it together.

"I'm sorry for putting you in a shit position down in the tunnel," Maria was saying. "It was your operation, and I should have remembered that."

"We doing this now, then?"

She glanced around the room. "May as well take advantage of the downtime while we have it, though if you really don't want to, I understand. I just—a large part of me wishes I'd not obeyed Sylvia and tried to rescue you. I didn't want to leave you there." She glanced across the room. "Neither did she. But in the end . . . we knew any rescue would get more people killed, you included."

"I know." He sat and Maria took the other chair, her knees bumping his. "I forgave you both a long time ago. And to be clear: I'm not mad about where I ended up, Maria. It was better than where I was headed."

She cracked a smile at him. "You and Sylvia still sound so much alike even after all these years. I forgave you about half an hour ago. Honestly, not sure I'll ever forgive myself, though."

He held his hand out, palm up, and curled his fingers around hers when she took it. "You should try at least. There wasn't anything you could have done. Any rescue operation would have been a disaster, and you know it. They were waiting for it. Once they realized who I was they were hoping that Sylvia would show."

"Do I even want to know how you know that?"

"Probably not. I'm certainly not going to say it out loud with a former CHN senator in the room. Even if she does like me."

"Everyone likes you."

"Eh, not everyone. I'm okay with that." He squeezed her hand and let her pull away.

"So . . . Boston, huh? Is he cute?"

"Oh, shut up." He was laughing when he said it.

JENKS STOPPED AT THE DOOR AND RUBBED BOTH HANDS through her hair as she looked up at the sky. It was so blue, the sun shining, entirely too bright and cheerful a day for everything that was happening.

The perfect day for camping. Not for this.

Especially knowing the sky for Max right now is nothing but black.

She shook away those dark thoughts. There was no time for it.

Chae was waiting for her at the main desk. Her petty officer had grown up so much since they'd first arrived. Their initial entry into *Zuma* had nearly destroyed the team as Chae had grappled with the safety of their fathers. She figured they would possibly be helpful in getting Mila to flip.

If that's what they were dealing with.

"Senior Chief?"

Jenks realized she'd sighed out loud. "Who do we believe here, Chae?"

They were quiet for a moment. "Honestly, Wilke. When she was talking about Ralka and the others, she called them 'these people.' But Master Chief sent me the recording of Mila talking to them and she said 'no one cares about the orphans except us.' Wilke claimed to have removed the suicide tooth the same day they put it in. Intake scans say she's not lying, at least about the removed tooth. I know it isn't hard proof about her not wanting this, but it was in the same spot as the one Emel removed from her sister by force."

Jenks rubbed at the back of her neck, nodding at her petty officer's reasoning. "Wilke also told me she tried to get people clear of the explosion site and that she angled the explosion downward to minimize the outward damage. I saw the initial report on the bomb, and it seems legit. If she's the reason for it, she saved D'Arcy's life."

Chae nodded. "At the very least. There were a lot of people in the area. I ran the background on her—Wilke was an honors student at Mars University, on her way to finishing a degree in engineering when their parents were killed. She dropped out to take care of her sister. Buzz on campus was she was an easy in for a highly coveted PhD program that leads to a doctorate of engineering degree."

"She's smart."

"Yeah." Jenks was an expert at keeping her emotions locked down, but the pressure in her chest right now felt like one of those bombs about to go off. "And all of this is just so stupid. I don't want this to fuck her life up. The more I look at everything people have lost with this mess . . . Chae, maybe there's no happy ending here, but if we can save one life?"

"You saved mine, whatever you want to do I'm all in."

Jenks felt her heart clench and reached out, dragging them into a hug. "I am on a hair trigger, Petty Officer, don't make me cry." She felt their arms close around her and squeeze her back.

"I'll follow your lead. Just let me know what's going on in your head."

She released them. "Shit, even I don't know what's going on up there half the time."

"That's all right, I trust you anyway."

She knew they trusted her—they'd proven that the very first time she'd demanded the truth from them just after Chae had miraculously kept *Zuma's Ghost* from disintegrating into the dirt of Trappist-1d. They'd been responsible for sabotaging the ship in the first place, but she'd understood at the time why they'd done it.

To keep their family safe.

She let Chae go, reaching for the humor that always saved her in moments like this, when the feelings were too big and it felt like she would crack into a million pieces. "It's a terrible idea, really. Come on, let's get this done."

Jenks had been in her share of security buildings—on both sides of the table—and they always made her more than a little uneasy. She'd done so much reading on the pre-Collapse prison systems, the absolutely inhumane conditions, the injustice of it all. And though they'd improved things in some ways, part of her worried how easy it would be to slip back into it. To give up on the idea that rehabilitation saved people's lives and go back to the way it had been.

To remember how easily it could have been her going down this path if she hadn't found Nika and his grandmother.

"You okay?"

Jenks jolted at Chae's question and realized she'd shuddered. "Long story."

"Have I heard it?"

She shrugged and grinned. "Parts of it. Mostly just my brain ranting about pre-Collapse disturbia."

Chae chuckled. "That just made me more curious. I'll try to remember to pin you down for a conversation after this is finished."

"You are not Max's caliber in the cage just yet. I'll happily kick your ass, though, and then tell you," she replied, and then opened the door.

Wilke's head snapped up at the sound, eyes flaring wide

for a moment in panic before she recognized Jenks. "Senior Chief."

Jenks lifted a curious eyebrow; she hadn't told the kid her rank, but her DD had been on and the handshake visible when they'd taken Wilke into custody. "Wilke. This is Petty Officer Second Class Chae Ho-ki, they/them. We've got some questions for you."

"Can I see my sister?"

"I'll see what we can do about that," Jenks replied as she slid into the chair opposite the woman. "You don't have to talk to me, Wilke. I can call a rep for you, and we'll do this the proper way."

"That means rehab for me, doesn't it? What about Mila?"

"Most likely for both of you, though it's hard to say. Mila's got an attempted murder charge and was far less inclined to cooperate than you've been."

"I want to help. If I help, does it help her?"

Jenks really hoped the desperation in Wilke's voice wasn't feigned. If it was, she was a hell of an actor. To be fair, Mila had apparently been quite the actor, according to Emel. She was trusting her gut here and Chae's. Especially since Wilke was willing to waive her right to have a rep present in front of two witnesses. "I don't know. Maybe?" she replied honestly. "What can you tell us about these people you were working with?"

"They call themselves the Orphans of War," Wilke whispered. "It started out as a support group thing. Because so many of our parents had died? I thought initially they'd been sent by some CHN social org, but looking back on it, I never got a good answer on that. Mila and I went to a few meetings, someone brought us dinners. I'd just made the decision to leave school and they were able to help me get a job at a ship design firm in Serrano."

"What's the name of the shop?"

"Above and Beyond. It wasn't a bad place. I don't mind the design work, but I missed getting my hands dirty." Wilke offered up a shy smile. "At school they let us work on repairs, try out new builds in our spare time."

"A woman after my own heart. You mentioned down in the tunnels that it felt like these people encouraged your sister? How?"

"They had weekly meetings. Never in the same place. I made some of them, but between work and trying to stay in touch with school friends, it was hard. You know? But Mila went to all of them, and it seemed like she just got angrier every time. I mentioned once it didn't seem like it was helping with her grief, and she lost it." Wilke lifted her hands. "I tried to go with her more after that, just to keep an eye out. But instead of being able to pry Mila away from them, I got wrapped up in it."

"Why didn't you report what they were planning?" Chae asked.

Wilke looked away from Jenks to them at the question. "I tried! I sent three anonymous messages to the local Peace-Keeper station. Ask them what they did with it."

"Do you have copies of them?" Jenks asked.

"Yeah, I thought keeping them would be dangerous, so I hid them in a purge file on my DD."

A moment later Jenks's DD pinged with a sent file request, and she pulled the files into quarantine with a glance in Chae's direction and then sent Captain Jaishankar a message. The Intel head would be able to verify the information.

Though Jenks would put feds down that the PeaceKeepers just sat on the anonymous tips rather than doing the extra work of passing them along to Mars Intel. That was going to come back and bite someone in the ass.

"I'll tell you everything else I know," Wilke said. "But I want to talk to my sister first."

Jenks tilted her head and worked to keep her smile at bay. There was some steel in her voice, and whatever doubts Jenks had, the one thing she didn't doubt was how much Wilke cared about her sister.

"Okay," she said after a moment and got to her feet. "Let's go."

Jenks called to the guard on her DD and got the room, leading Wilke through the corridor with Chae following behind.

"Careful, Senior Chief. She's hostile," the petty officer at the door warned them as he opened it.

"Mila!" Wilke darted around Jenks, who held out a hand to stop the guard from intervening, and the woman embraced her sister. "Are you hurt?"

"I'm fine." Mila shrugged away, eyeing her sister and then Jenks. "Why aren't you cuffed? What's going on?"

"Mila, they can help us."

Jenks moved before Mila did. The girl was cuffed, but her sister was close enough that her swing would have hit her if Jenks hadn't interceded. She jerked Wilke back toward Chae and put her hands up. "Sit down. We don't want to fight with you, Mila. Your sister is trying to help. There's a better direction for this than the path you're currently on. But if you insist on this course, we will follow protocol."

"So, what, you're going to kill us, too?" Mila spat, fists raised. "It's your fault our parents are dead!"

"How does more death fix that?" Jenks asked gently.

"It's justice."

She said the word with such vehemence it was clear she had a very different definition of the word than most people. Jenks moved a step closer, her own hands up but open. "Revenge and justice aren't the same thing, Mila. It's not right your parents died. It's also not right to kill more innocent people."

"We're not killing innocents. Sylvia Moroz deserves to die for everything she's done."

"There were kids younger than you at that blast site. If your sister hadn't done what she did to mitigate the explosion, they'd be dead."

"Traitor." Mila snarled the word, and Jenks knew the sharp edge of it would cut deep into Wilke. It also sliced through her own frayed temper, and she grabbed Mila by the shirtfront, propelling the girl back into the hard wall behind her.

"Your sister is a hero who saved lives. And *my* sister is on the MOS. If she dies, does that mean I can kill you for your part in it? Is that how your justice works?" Jenks ignored Wilke's choked protest from behind her. She caught Mila by the cuffs when the girl tried to hit her, jerking her arms down between them.

"Jenks." Chae's call was soft, but it was enough to drag her back into some semblance of sanity.

She let Mila go and stepped back, her heart hammering in her chest as she wrestled her anger back under control. "Where does it end, Mila? Humanity brought Earth to her knees with this kind of thinking. Almost wiped ourselves out in round after endless round of payback and revenge. Are we ever going to learn that some things are more important?"

Mila stared at her, hands pressed up under her chin, and Jenks forced herself to watch the fear that skated over the girl's face. "My parents are gone," she whispered, tears gathering in her eyes.

"They are, and I'm so sorry for it." She pointed behind her. "Your sister is still alive and she loves you desperately. She *needs* you. You've got an entire life ahead of you. Are you going to stay for her? Or let this war leave her all alone?"

Mila's gaze flicked to Wilke and Jenks saw the indecision slide across her face.

"I want to help you break out of this cycle, but I can't do it if you don't make the first move." Jenks held her hand out. "Help me save some lives, yours included."

Come on, kid, give me at least one happy ending here.

She hated that the thought was in her head, but it was too late to scrub it.

"I'll get to stay with my sister?" Mila whispered.

"I'm not going to make you any promises I can't keep. I'll do what I can, though," Jenks said.

"I'll go to rehab with her," Wilke said hastily. "Anything if it means we stay together."

Mila's face crumpled then, the tears coming fast, and Jenks let Wilke by so she could wrap her arms around her younger sister.

"You can't go to rehab, Wilke! Not for me."

"Not for you. For us. We're all we have left, right?"

The sobs racked the younger sister's body, Wilke's crying a muted harmony.

"Good job," Chae said softly by her ear. "You okay?"

"Yeah, and thanks." She didn't look away as she reached back and squeezed their hand hard, then let them go.

"Hey, got your back always."

That's two lives saved today, Jenks thought. *I'm coming your way, Max, just hang on.*

"REAR ADMIRAL. IT'S GOOD TO SEE YOU." NIKA EXTENDED HIS hand with a smile as Scott stepped off the shuttle.

"I caught a ride over from Jupiter as soon as Pax messaged me," Max's brother said warmly, gripping him by the forearm and pulling him into a hug. "How are you doing? How's she doing?" He kept the question low, out of earshot of the people behind him, but it was the one he clearly wanted answered.

Nika hugged the man back. The semi-polite camaraderie he'd had with Alexander Scott Carmichael III as a result of their numerous matches in the sword competition of the Boarding Games had developed into a steady friendship once Max's own strained relationship with her once-adored older brother had been repaired.

"Holding on by our fingernails," he replied as he stepped back. "Max is physically banged up, Scott. But nothing life-threatening."

"And mentally?"

Nika didn't want to have this conversation standing out in the bright sunshine, but Scott was too perceptive. He shook his head. "She's taken down a lot of hostiles; at the moment she's also holding on by her fingernails. I—"

"Commander Vagin?"

Nika turned to meet the SEAL captain who'd approached. "Captain Giroux?"

"Yes. Rear Admiral, didn't know you were here." She snapped into a salute, the rest of her team echoing the gesture.

"At ease, all of you," Scott said.

"Thank you for coming." Nika offered a smile in the captain's direction.

"No trouble at all. We happened to be in the area when the call went out. Leave doesn't matter much when our own are in trouble, right?" Her answering smile was wide. "It's a nasty business. Do we have an infiltration plan?"

"We'll get one spun up. I'm hoping to get some more intel from the MOS. Let's head inside." He pointed off to his left.

"Nika," Sapphi said over the team com. "I've got a com from the MOS. Not our bad guys, but not Max, either."

"We're on our way," Nika said, and tapped Scott on the arm. "Com coming in from the MOS."

"Max?" Scott fell into step beside him, the SEALs trailing behind.

"No." Nika didn't want to run, but he also wanted to know who was on the com and where Max was.

Thankfully it didn't take them long to cross the yard and duck into Ground Control. He spotted Drani standing next to Sapphi, talking to a dark-haired person on the screen. He heard Scott murmur to the SEAL captain for her team to hang back, and then the naval officer followed him across the room.

"Commander, Rear Admiral, this is Cho Seo-Yoon. She was the new civilian commander in charge of traffic on the MOS." Drani's voice dipped. "She's also one of mine, if Commander Montaglione didn't have a chance to pass that along."

"Where's Max?"

Seo-Yoon smiled at him. "Sleeping, Commander Vagin. She looks like she'd been in a hell of a fight, but she's okay, considering."

He didn't like the pause before she said that word, as if she were searching for the best way to give him bad news.

"I had one of the Marine corporals check her over. I'll send you the report. Max mentioned wanting to speak to you, but I'd like to let her rest a while longer if that's all right?"

The clock was ticking, but he could give her a little more time. "It's fine. What's your status?"

"Currently holding the Cargo Bay. Though to be honest, the bad guys don't seem to be putting that much effort into getting in here. There's a few guards outside the main door, which isn't going to open without some heavy-duty maintenance." She grinned sharply and then her amusement faded. "We are ready to ship out of here whenever you can get a transport to us. I've done a personnel count thanks to the info from your lieutenant there, and everyone is accounted for as either here in the Cargo Bay or KIA. Lieutenant Commander Vahid is the only one still in the hands of the hijackers."

Nika heard the murmuring at the same time Seo-Yoon's gaze flicked past him and he watched the line of her shoulders tense for just a moment.

"Is there anything else you need, Commander?"

"Not at the moment. We'll get a rescue up to you shortly. Please advise Max we are in phase two of SSOP-47 and have her com me when she wakes up?"

"I will." She smiled and the screen went blank.

Nika glanced over his shoulder. He'd been right to suspect the noise was from Sylvia's appearance. Pax was at her side, and she crossed to them quickly, embracing Scott when she reached her older brother.

"Hey, Jenks," Nika murmured over the com. "Are you finished in the brig?"

"Yup, just wrapped. They had some decent information, I think. I'm on my way back in to talk with D'Arcy about it. What do you need?"

"Nothing immediately. SEALs are here and we're going to start the operational plan. I want your input. It sounds like I'll have a chance to talk to Max again, but you know her best." He looked around the room; there were frowns on some of the SEALs as they clocked who Sylvia was, and Mikhail was glaring back. "Sylvia and her people are also in the control room. One would hope everyone will behave themselves like professionals, but tensions are high. We may need some crowd control before too long, though."

Jenks laughed low in his ear. "You want *me* to be crowd control?"

"I know, but I trust you. You have a good eye for judging if a fight is going to start. Just get over here when you can."

"Sure thing."

Nika took a deep breath and turned back to his task of keeping the peace between all these long-standing enemies.

Ten-Hour Standoff Ends Peacefully
OCTOBER 5, 2441 (ESD)

A ten-hour standoff between pirates who'd boarded an E-class freighter belonging to Off-Earth Enterprises and the Near-Earth Orbital Guard ended early Tuesday morning, Trappist Standard Time, thanks to the tireless efforts of the Interceptor crews *Zuma's Ghost* and *Dread Treasure.*

The freighter was attacked and taken over shortly after exiting into Trappist space from the Jupiter Station wormhole, highlighting once again a need for more patrols to cover the security gaps as more and more traffic between Earth and Trappist strains the resources of the NeoG in the area.

Petty Officer First Class Uchida Tamashini was responsible for talking the pirates down to a peaceful surrender. This isn't the first successful hostage negotiation the Neo has been involved in, and according to their commanding officer, it won't be the last.

"We had every confidence that Tama would be able to convince those on the freighter that a peaceful surrender was the best option for everyone involved," Commander Nika Vagin said. "The NeoG doesn't shy away from a fight, but we also understand that sometimes people make poor decisions born of desperation and going into a situation looking for a fight is the best way to get a whole lot of people killed. Petty Officer Uchida did their job perfectly and because of that we were able to keep everyone safe." [*Read More*]

FIFTEEN

D'ARCY LEANED BACK AGAINST THE CONFERENCE TABLE, ARMS crossed, and stared at the images of the man up on the screen. He hadn't gone to the academy—his entry to the officer corps had been OCS by way of his arrest—so his only knowledge of Vice Admiral Ford was when other officers had spoken of the man. He had been a fixture at the NeoG Academy before he'd taken over the running of the MOS almost a decade ago. In fact, D'Arcy was pretty sure Max's class had been close to the last the man had shepherded from gawky teenagers into something worthy of representing the Near-Earth Orbital Guard.

Even not knowing the man, it had been hard to watch him face his death. But Ford had done it with a consummate grace that was apparently indicative of how he'd faced life in general.

For sure, it was a loss that the NeoG would feel for years

to come. The old but still painful ache surfaced with memories of Admiral Lee Hoboins, lost to sabotage on Jupiter Station close to a decade ago.

What made this so hard was knowing how brilliant a commander Ford was. The vice admiral had the clarity of mind to observe his murderer and send that information on to Max before the end, adding to what she'd gotten from Saqib. Ford had somehow managed to get several dozen photos and two recordings on their way to the airlock, expertly goading Willis Hale into speaking at length. It was clear Hale was intent on revenge, and now they had verbal confirmation that the man seemed to think everyone was responsible for what had happened at Hellas.

The fucked-up part is he isn't wrong. We had so many chances to turn away from the slaughter and time and again chose not to.

D'Arcy rubbed a hand over his face. He'd already been through basic and hip-deep in officer training when that transport had been shot out of a clear morning sky. Part of his sentence had included not speaking of his past and none of his fellow candidates had seemed to know who he was.

In fact, if his instructors had known, none of them had treated him any differently for it.

It had been weeks after the incident when he'd first heard of it, thanks to the lack of free time and the news screening. The report itself had been so heavily biased against Free Mars that he'd initially thought they were responsible for shooting down the transport until the reporter mentioned the NeoG almost as an afterthought.

"D'Arcy?" Emel waited a beat for him to blink dry eyes at

her before she wrapped her hand around his forearm. "You good?"

"Not really," he admitted. "Is this mess ever going to change?"

She took a deep breath and then let it out. "I'd like to say yes, but I know how hard it is to have any hope after everything we've seen. You saved people today, that counts for something."

"I hope so. Did you need something?"

"Just a thought. I know we've written Hale off as far as negotiations go, but Tamago mentioned that one person she'd talked to, Castle? Actually watched us compete three years ago. Her parents were killed in an attack after that Free Mars was blamed for, though Sylvia denied responsibility for it. I pulled everything I could on her. I'm wondering if you think it would be helpful?"

"It might," he replied. "Let me take it to Tama and see what they think."

"I'll send it to you." She patted his arm and headed back across the room.

D'Arcy frowned at the images of Willis for a minute longer before he straightened and headed down the corridor to the main office. Jenks was leaning against the wall next to the doorway and stuck her fist out as he passed. He tapped it with his own.

"You come for the show?" She tipped her head at the SEALs on one side of the room and Free Mars on the other.

"We expecting trouble?"

"It's Navy," she said in such a dismissive tone that D'Arcy couldn't stop his laugh. Jenks didn't join in. "This situation is a hot box. Nika said watch, so I'm watching."

"Holler if you need backup."

"You know it."

D'Arcy pinged Tamago with the information he'd gotten from Emel, and the lieutenant looked up from where they'd had their head pressed with the other two negotiators, staring at something on one of their screens. They waved a hand in acknowledgment, said something to Captain Hosaka, and D'Arcy moved over to join them.

"What's all this?" Tamago asked.

"Emel dug up everything she could find on Dri Castle. She thought it might be helpful. Maybe you could try to contact her again, get her to help."

Tamago frowned, eyes flicking back and forth as they scanned the file. "It might. Thanks. Did she include— Oh, here it is. I don't know much about the history of the conflict here, D'Arcy. Was there really still fighting only a few years ago?"

"Fighting? No." He shook his head. "Bloodshed? That's a different story. There's been a host of splinter groups who feel like Sylvia sold the cause out to the CHN by making concessions. So there have been bombings and attacks on civilians, though not nearly as often as even ten years ago. I keep thinking we'll sort ourselves out, and then we don't."

Tamago reached out and squeezed his arm with a smile. "This has all been difficult for you, hasn't it? Coming home to this?"

"Not nearly as difficult as Max up there on the station."

"It's not a contest, D'Arcy."

He sighed. "I know, but I'd trade places with her in a heartbeat if I could."

"You're not the only one."

JENKS WOULD HAVE KEPT AN EYE ON THE SEAL TEAM WHO'D AC-companied Scott purely out of habit even if Nika hadn't told her to do it. These days it was easier to get along with most Navy personnel, but the tension of the situation put everyone into a weird mood. As far as Jenks was concerned, Max's brother was trustworthy, but she didn't know these SEALs at all.

Scott's promotion to rear admiral had pushed him out of normal SEAL duties and into command of the SEALs on Earth. Jenks suspected he disliked it as much as she would if it ever happened to her.

They ever try to put me behind a desk, I'm starting every bar fight I can until I get busted back down to spacer, she thought.

The tension in the room had multiple layers. Nika and Grady were in quiet conversation with Captain Giroux. D'Arcy had moved over to where the negotiators were. The silence from the MOS had people on edge all on its own, but a good chunk of the tension kept circling back to the four members of Free Mars now standing near Captain Clark's office.

Sylvia and the others had followed Pax into main Ground Control not long after Scott's arrival. So far they'd done a good job of keeping their heads down and not starting any arguments. But between Clair and Mikhail, she couldn't count on everyone keeping their mouths shut.

Jenks scanned everything, looking for any signs this might explode.

Then she'd kick whoever's ass needed kicking and remind them about the task at hand, not their petty squabbles.

For once, she truly wished it wouldn't come to that.

Not today.

Kavan stood in a relaxed parade rest next to Pax, but they would probably be able to tell her the exact location of every person in the room and what weapons they were carrying.

Mikhail's back was as tight as a wire, his face etched into lines of deep disapproval, and Jenks knew even though the two older women were presenting as relaxed, they were also aware of the fact that they were surrounded by the very same military they'd been fighting for years, no matter how unofficially. Clair didn't quite shift nervously, but Jenks could see the urge in every line of their body.

She was pleased that the Neos, at least, had gone back to work without much more than curious glances. Evidence, most likely, of how well Captain Clark ran her show down here. Though also possibly it was because there were more than a few native-born Martians among the crew.

Navy, as per usual, was being less casual about it. Especially the redhead whose handshake read *Lieutenant Ewan Ryan, he/him* and who kept throwing glares in Sylvia's direction.

JENKS: This SEAL is eyeballing Free Mars like they stole his lunch money. Twenty feds we're gonna have an issue at some point.

NIKA: No thank you on the bet. That's sucker money.

JENKS: Haha. Do I get a free pass for this inevitable fight?

NIKA: Just keep an eye on them, Jenks. And keep the peace if you have to. Giroux seems like a decent sort but she's occupied with what we're doing. Message Scott directly if you think you need help.

JENKS: Have I mentioned I should be on vacation where I could be a not responsible adult?

NIKA: You were in the wilderness with children. I should hope you were going to be responsible.

JENKS: That was Luis's job.

She shot Nika a grin when he leveled a look in her direction and then turned her attention back to the slowly developing situation across from her.

Jenks's experience reading people and predicting fights had started long before the NeoG. Her years living on the streets of Krasnodar, dodging—sometimes running with—the various gangs who occupied the ruins of the pre-Collapse city, had taught her that most people couldn't be trusted.

She'd learned differently over the last decade plus, mostly thanks to her brother and Luis. Though there was a host of other people who'd taken a chance on her and showed her what trust looked like—one of whom was currently trapped up in space with a bunch of hostiles.

What remained from her years on the streets was hypervigilance of people's behavior and an innate sense of when the shit was going to hit the fan.

Like now.

If you'd asked her, she couldn't have told you what

tipped her off. The flex of his hand near his sword, the way he shifted on the balls of his feet, the look that crossed his face. Maybe all of it.

KHAN, A: Rear Admiral, you should see to your boy there.

CARMICHAEL, S: Who? Oh, well, not mine . . . you've got my permission, Senior Chief, keep the peace however you need to.

Strange as it was that he wanted her to handle it, that was all she needed. Jenks moved as the lieutenant did, sliding easily into the space in front of the Free Mars contingent and blocking him with a wide smile on her face. She didn't have to look to know that Kavan had likely stepped in front of their partner.

"Turn yourself around, Lieutenant, and go on back to your team." Jenks kept her voice calm, her hands open and empty at her sides, as the whole room slowed to the held breath of potential violence.

"They shouldn't be here." The SEAL was a solid two dozen centimeters taller than her but that had never stopped her before and wasn't much of a consideration now.

She spotted the SEAL captain, Ella Giroux, start to open her mouth to call her lieutenant back, but Scott put a hand on her arm and shook his head.

Interesting. He wasn't going to intervene at all.

"They were invited here by former Senator Carmichael and they're not your concern," she said, waving her hand. "Go on back with your team."

"They're *terrorists*." Ryan put his hand on his sword and Jenks sighed.

"I didn't realize you were an expert on solar politics," she said.

"I don't need to be—"

"If you pull that sword, Lieutenant, I hope you're prepared to use it on me," she said softly.

Blue eyes flicked in her direction, clearly shocked by the ultimatum and the ease with which she issued it. "Why are you defending them?"

"Duty. My commander said to keep the peace. That's what I'm doing. Pretty sure you got a similar order before you all walked in here, but if you didn't, I'm telling you now—don't start anything. My crewmates are up on that station and I'm not going to let anyone put them in any more danger than they're already in. Which is what you are doing with whatever bullshit is cooking in your lieutenant-sized brain."

Jenks wiggled a hand at him. "Now I know that you didn't volunteer to help just to start a fight instead, so I suggest you take a step back."

He didn't move.

Jenks sighed more heavily this time and saw Sapphi bite her lip to hold back a laugh. "Are you going to listen, Lieutenant, or am I going to break several of your bones?"

"This isn't your cage, NeoG."

What a tired old insult, she thought. Laughing at him would make him have to take a swing at her, and for all her joking about getting to fight, Jenks really didn't want to. Not with people who were supposed to be on her side. Still, her response was as sharp as the edge of her sword still safely covered by its microsheath.

"Don't I know it. But it's not every day I have full fucking approval to beat down a Navy highbrow. I'll let you choose which arm I snap if you want." She smiled up at him then, a bright, dangerous smile, and she knew the look on her face had made plenty of opponents nervous both in the cage and out of it.

Fucking lieutenants, though, they never knew when to back off.

Ryan's fingers tightened on his sword, though he didn't seem to realize with as close as Jenks was standing, he wouldn't even get it clear before she took him to the ground.

She supposed she should be nice and not break his sword arm. Being responsible still sucked.

"All right, Ryan. That's enough. You get on my nerves sometimes, but it would be embarrassing to watch you get your ass kicked by Jenks." Captain Giroux finally cut in between them and gave her lieutenant a little shove backward. "Hand off your weapon—that's an order."

Jenks schooled her expression into something more neutral but didn't relax her muscles just in case Ryan had a case of really shitty lieutenant decision-making and ignored a direct order from his captain.

Thankfully his brain seemed to finally engage, and he nodded once, then stalked back to the other SEALs.

"Sorry about that, Senior Chief."

"About what I expect from Navy." Her reply slipped out before she could stop it, and Jenks muttered a curse but Ella just laughed.

"Fair enough." She patted Jenks on the shoulder. "I was going to step in, but the rear admiral didn't want me to intervene unless absolutely necessary. Said it would be good for Ryan."

Jenks swallowed the surprised laugh that threatened. Either Ryan had crossed Scott at some point in his young career or she was apparently now considered a character-building exercise by the Navy.

She was admittedly super curious which it was.

NIKA TURNED BACK TO SCOTT ONCE THE LAST OF THE TENSION ebbed from the room and he was sure that the lieutenant wasn't going to make a mistake and go after Jenks. "Interesting choice," he murmured to Max's brother.

Scott chuckled softly as he turned back to the map of the MOS. "I know Ryan's previous CO. According to them, he's a good kid, but he could stand to learn the kind of humility that would come with a beatdown from Jenks. You know the sort of person who always thinks he's right? He got transferred over to Ella's team when her guy broke his leg. I suspect command was hoping it would help ground him a little since she's rumored to not put up with that sort of behavior."

"Doesn't look like it's helped so far. You know Jenks's lessons usually require a month to heal from. We don't have that kind of time."

"True." The humor bled from Scott's face. "Commander Paulit just sent over the final salvage list. They'd towed the three ships away from the planet's gravity well and found eight more escape pods. Your people retrieved thirty-three escape pods, but we won't have a full count until the dust settles since people were just scrambling for available ships. She's sent along a full list for me with the names of the dead who were collected." He frowned at the map in front of them. "Max said several dozen people are still on station?"

"Close to fifty between the NeoG, Marines, a few scattered Navy, and the civilians is what we have on the roster. We're still trying to match the IDs Sapphi scraped up with what's on the duty rosters. They're locked in the Cargo Bay, and the access is going to be tricky: both the airlock and the doors into the station have been disabled."

"We can't load people straight from the Cargo Bay anyway." D'Arcy shook his head. "That's designed for the small haulers that move things from the ships in the dock down to Cargo."

"He's right, even the SEAL shuttle won't be able to get all the way inside the field. We can fit everyone on the shuttle and the *Omar Tazi*, but we'll have to load them at the Docking Bay." Scott tapped the map. "The shuttle can dock at an airlock and off-load the SEALs, then move to pick people up. If we get in there quietly, it should work."

"Providing the station defenses aren't active and they don't realize you're there." Nika rubbed a hand over his eyes.

"It's risky, but we've got the maneuverability that the fixed defenses would have a harder time countering, especially once we get in close. They're honestly more designed for big ships or asteroids. And our shields can take more damage than those freighters that tried to escape. We should be able to at least get in and get people to safety," Scott replied.

"There's a lot of 'maybe' in that plan, Scott," Nika said.

"What about Lieutenant Commander Vahid?" Captain Giroux asked as she rejoined them.

The two men shared a look and Nika shrugged a shoulder. "Max will go after him if he's still alive. I'm hoping she'll take a few of the Neos from the bay with her, but it's equally likely she won't want to risk any of them."

"You could order her," Scott said softly, lifting a hand at Nika's sharp look. "I'm saying it's an option. Chain of command and all that."

"You know as well as I do that *she* knows I can't make her do shit, especially from down here."

"Unlikely you could make her do it if you were up there," Scott murmured. "That said, I think it's worth it to at least remind her that her duty is to save as many people as possible—including herself. And that might mean leaving people behind. Once the SEALs hit the station the clock starts for real."

Nika knew Scott was right, even as his gut twisted at the thought of abandoning anyone up there. SOP was an hour out from landing. That was all they had before the Navy ships opened fire on the station.

He also knew Max better than her brother, and order or advice, it wouldn't override her sense of duty. What he could do, though, was send her help.

"I'm sending Jenks with the SEALs—she can help with evac and back Max up." He glanced Ella's way. "Any objection?"

"Nah, the senior chief knows her shit," Giroux replied. "We'd be happy for the assistance."

"All right, let's figure out where in the Docking Bay we need everyone to go and how best to make it happen," Nika said, pulling up the station layout. "Jenks, get over here. Hey, D'Arcy?" Nika called to the big man.

"Yeah?"

"Hang around, I want to talk to you about some signals

Sapphi has been tracking on the ground. I want you to go check them out."

D'Arcy tossed him a quick salute. "Can do. Good luck."

Nika resisted the urge to reply that they were rapidly running out of luck.

MAX WOKE WITH A GROAN AND THEN BOLTED UPRIGHT. SHE RE-gretted that choice immediately and fell back with a curse.

"Easy, Commander." The voice at her side was unfamiliar. "Corporal Shez Oluo, she/her. You're pretty banged up, staying down is—" She broke off when Max pushed herself to a sitting position. "A good idea."

Max patted the Marine with one hand while she rubbed at her face with the other. "A good idea would have been to turn down the suggestion to oversee the handoff, but we're past that. You a medic?"

"Field training only, ma'am."

Max checked her DD—she'd been out for almost an hour—and reached for the med kit sitting between them. "Good, you can't yell at me too much then when I do something that's definitely a bad idea."

"She won't but I will, Carmichael."

Max grinned up at Seo-Yoon. "You know it's not going to stop me, right? I need to get back out there and figure out how to get to the Command Deck."

"I know *you* think you have to, but get your hand off that adrenaline injector and let me catch you up first. Corporal, you got some pain meds for her?"

"They're combat, ma'am," Shez said, pushing them at her when Max tried to refuse them. "Won't mess with your head, but remember they also don't actually fix anything. You've still got a pair of cracked ribs, a strained hamstring, and four million bruises and cuts in varying degrees of severity."

"Four million, huh?"

"Give or take," Shez replied.

"Duly noted, Corporal, and thanks." Max took the water bottle and tossed the capsules back with a swallow.

"Take that with you." Seo-Yoon snatched the med kit away before Max could go back into it and handed it to the Marine as she took the woman's place next to Max. "I spoke with a certain Commander Vagin a bit ago, who said to tell you to com him when you are awake."

Max blinked at Seo-Yoon for several seconds as the words circled in her brain. "You talked to Nika?"

"Seemed like checking in was a good plan after you passed out on me. I wasn't sure how long you'd be unconscious. Your brother was there also."

"Scott? Why?"

"Well, for one, I suspect because you're *here*. Kinda surprised your whole family hasn't stormed the station, to be honest."

Max laughed and regretted it. No amount of pain meds was going to stop her ribs from protesting that movement, and they'd apparently not quite kicked in yet. "Some, maybe. Actually, if Scott was there, it's probably because there's a SEAL team close behind."

"Only a few meters behind, give or take," Seo-Yoon replied. "They were standing by the door, but still in camera frame."

"You're awfully observant."

"Part of the job." She smiled and lifted a shoulder. "Speaking of—I wasn't entirely honest with you when we first met, Max, and I understand if that pisses you off now."

Max forcibly let go of the bottle in her hand and dragged in a breath. "I'm going to assume since you're not trying to kill me that it's not too terrible?"

"True enough. I'm Mars Intel. I've been working undercover in Free Mars for the last two years. They think I've been sending them information on NeoG movements between Earth and Mars. It's relatively complex, but I guess you could call me a double agent." Seo-Yoon looked down at her hands. "I am so sorry for not stopping this before it started."

It took a minute for the apology to make sense, for any of it to make sense. Then Max reached out and laid her hand over Seo-Yoon's. "Pretty sure when I asked you, you said you were on my side. That's all that matters. It's too late to flay ourselves for not stopping this sooner. Free Mars obviously isn't responsible anyway, so I don't know how you could have known. Let's just concentrate on how we get everyone out of here in one piece."

"Roger that. The good news is that almost everyone who needs off this station is in the Cargo Bay."

Max looked at the ceiling. "The bad news is Saqib is not."

"Yup, and I can't order you to not go back for him. Hell, Commander Vagin didn't order it, though he might when you com him."

"Maybe, but he also can't stop me from down on the ground."

"Maybe you should let him. Max . . . you're hurt, and honestly as ideas go, this one is not great."

"I will not sit here and let him die!" Max knew her voice was too loud. She didn't even have to look around to know everyone was probably staring. "I can't do it," she said, softer. "I can't leave him."

"I know." The other woman forced a smile. "At least talk to Commander Vagin, get an ETA on when the rescue is coming and what the plan is, okay? I'll even let Corporal Oluo back into the med kit for that adrenaline once you're done."

"All right." Max got to her feet; the aches were starting to ease as the pain meds went to work, accompanied by that very strange euphoria she'd only experienced twice in her career.

The first time had been during Interceptor training so that all the Neos could get a sense of what combat meds felt like.

The other had been the end of a wild and terrifying fight with her and Jenks against a band of well-equipped mercenaries in the ruins of a pre-Collapse city on the eastern coast of North America. What had started out as a weird but routine stalking case involving a friend of Jenks's, the famous holo-vid actress Asabi Han, had exploded into a twisting mission with said mercenaries, a massive arms theft, and a previously thought-to-be-extinct cephalopod.

"Max?"

Max realized Seo-Yoon was looking at her and that she'd been laughing. "It's a long story. I was just remembering the last time I had to take combat meds."

"It worries me a little that you find it funny, but I suppose I shouldn't be surprised. Here, we used the coms in the office." She pointed across the bay.

Max exchanged greetings with a few of the Neos and tried to ignore the fact that most of the eyes in the vicinity followed her as she crossed the wide room to the office tucked into a corner.

She caught sight of her reflection in the window and winced. The heal patch on her cheek was still working on the cut, and her face was bruised. There were streaks of dried blood on her cheek and neck and in her hair. Max looked around, spotting a towel slung over a nearby chair, and made an effort to clean herself up some before nodding to Seo-Yoon to put the com through.

Nika appeared on the screen, Scott and Pax on his left. The unknown woman on the right had a Navy handshake: *Captain Ella Giroux, SEAL, she/her.* Max bit the inside of her lip before forcing out a smile she hoped looked somewhat natural.

And that Nika wouldn't call her bluff in front of her siblings.

"I hear we'll have visitors coming," she said.

Nika nodded. "We'll launch soon. Sapphi's confident that the station defenses are still offline, but even if they aren't, the ships can take some fire. Captain Nier will follow the SEALs in with the FRC. Between those two ships there will be plenty of space to load everyone. Jenks is coming up with them to give you a hand."

Max's breath caught. Relief and terror at the news. She didn't want Jenks up here. She wanted her safe on the ground.

It's not your call, she thought, and shoved it all away as she refocused on Nika's voice.

"We've been trying to nail down where we should load

and thought you'd want to hear the options. You'll have the best idea of what's safer."

"We can't get either of the ships into the Cargo Bay, and I understand the airlocks and main door there are out of commission," Scott said.

Max brought the station layout up on-screen and stared at it. "The Docking Bay is the most logical choice, but it's exposed."

"Agreed, on both counts. We've figured out the best defensible spot that shouldn't be occupied. I'm sending that info now." The worry in Nika's blue eyes made it hard for her to keep her face neutral.

"We've got enough people and weapons to handle it," Seo-Yoon said. "It's the fastest route, too. You're thinking the way you came in through the closet, right?"

"Furthermore, my team can play decoy, Commander," Ella offered, and highlighted an airlock on the opposite side of the Docking Bay from where Nika had highlighted. "If we dock here, go up a level, and cause enough noise, will it make these bastards come to us?"

"Maybe?" Max frowned. "They're not the most predictable, and they're pretty well trained. Regardless, I need to get to the Command Deck and rescue my lieutenant commander first, though. I don't want to put him at risk."

"Fair enough," Ella agreed. "We can wait for your signal. I'd suggest moving everyone to the Docking Bay in the meantime, though; maybe hide them in one of the disabled freighters. Then they can move for the ships as soon as you give the word."

"That should work. Once you're closer, we'll be able to talk on coms, but I'm not sure how secure they are."

"We'll work on that and let you know," Nika replied. "Max, about Saqib—"

"Please don't give me an order you know I can't follow," she whispered and saw the pain flash in his eyes. He'd had to have thought about it, she knew, and she didn't want to spend what little time they had left fighting.

"I was going to say, please be careful, and I love you. I'm going to give you a minute with your siblings." He started to move aside.

"Nika?" He paused. "I love you, too."

He smiled. "I'll see you when you get down here." And then he moved off-screen, Ella following him.

"I'll give you an order," Scott said, and Max's choked laugh tasted like ash in her mouth.

"Nice try. You're not in my chain of command."

"Way I hear it, wouldn't matter much if I were," he teased gently and she bit the inside of her cheek to keep the tears at bay. "I am your brother, though, which I figure is all the authority I need for this. You come home to us, you hear me?"

"That goes for me, too," Pax said.

"I will. I promise. I love you both. Make sure you tell the others." As soon as they echoed the words, Max hit the disconnect and sank down into the chair, the tears falling free at last.

She felt Seo-Yoon's arms wrap around her, the older woman hugging her gently. "Let it out, Max. It's all right. We're getting out of here. There's no way I'm dying without telling my wife I got to flirt with a Carmichael."

"Don't make me laugh," Max begged. "These pain meds haven't fully kicked in yet." She dragged in a breath and wiped her face with the heels of her hands. "Don't take this the wrong way, but I'm glad you're here."

"I cannot say 'me too,' but you are someone I would happily go to war with, Max."

"I supposed that's good, because that's where we're headed."

"Damn right. Picking a fight with the NeoG is asking for an ass-kicking."

"Now you sound like Jenks," Max replied.

Jenks, who was about to willingly walk into the line of fire simply because Max was up here.

She rested her head against Seo-Yoon's shoulder for a moment. "Let's go talk to everyone else and get a plan together."

"First, we get you some boots. Someone here should be wearing your size."

Max looked down, and remembered she was barefoot.

What the hell am I doing?

SIXTEEN

HIS BUSINESS WITH TAMAGO DONE, D'ARCY DRIFTED OVER TO Sylvia as Nika and the others talked with Max. As much as he wanted to see her, to say something to bolster her spirits, he knew it was more important to give her family the chance to talk with her.

He didn't want to think about the possibility it could be the last time as the com ended.

He spotted Maria watching him when he turned his attention back to the room at large. The look of concern on her face was both achingly familiar and surprising. It was also surprising to realize just how much he'd missed having her around.

Sylvia and Pax were now in deep discussion in the middle of the room, Mikhail and Kavan standing guard like a pair of mismatched bookends.

"Did they get something hammered out?" he asked Maria, leaning against the desk where she and Clair stood.

"The start of something anyway," she replied. "Of course, we'll see if it survives contact with the real world."

"That's the best test. Most stuff doesn't, but it just means you go back to the table and try again."

"Easy to say when you own the table," Clair muttered. "Ow."

D'Arcy was easily as surprised as they were by the smack Maria delivered to the back of their head.

"Don't be rude in someone else's kitchen," she said, and then looked at D'Arcy. "I'll smack you, too, if you've got something smart to say."

He lifted his hands with a grin. "Everything I say is smart, but I'm good. It's been a while and I don't miss it." He paused when Nika crossed over to them.

"Sapphi and Lupe narrowed these outgoing signals from the MOS to this location. Go check it out," he ordered in a low voice.

D'Arcy pulled the file after his DD pinged and frowned, the warehouse was on the southeast side of the city. "You think heavy presence?"

"Possibly. Can you go in quiet?"

"Yeah." He glanced at Maria. "You and Clair want to go for a ride?"

"What?"

"You want to come with me and Emel to check this out?" He waited with more patience than he actually felt as first Maria then Clair looked at Sylvia, who'd turned to see what was happening. "Can I steal your people, Sylvia?"

"I'll be fine, go," the older woman said, and tipped her head at the door. She met D'Arcy's gaze. "Bring them back in one piece."

He threw a salute—to which she returned a rude gesture—as he headed down the corridor. Emel was on his right as normal and a few seconds later he heard Clair's light footsteps catch up to them. Maria's steps were almost silent; she'd always been good at moving like a ghost.

"Where are we going?" she asked.

"Signal," he replied, turning right and avoiding a harried-looking lieutenant rushing down the corridor.

"What?" Clair asked.

"The hijackers on the station are talking to someone else on the ground. The group we caught had also received orders," Emel explained as D'Arcy pushed through the door and headed across the tarmac to the motor pool. "Lupe isolated the location and it's nearby."

"And we're only taking four people?"

D'Arcy said, "I'm hurt you have so little faith in me."

"I—"

"I'm teasing. We're scouting, Free Mars—that's all. See what's going on and then we'll figure out from there what needs to happen." D'Arcy exchanged a nod with a senior chief. "You got a ride for us, Guffin?"

"Who's driving?" he asked, and D'Arcy glanced over his shoulder at Clair and Maria.

"You know these streets better than we do probably." He ignored their twin looks of shock and turned to meet the spacer who ran up with a set of fléchette guns in their arms. He pressed his thumb to each of them and then to the tablet and grabbed the straps on all three, slinging them over his shoulder, and headed for the vehicle. Emel and Maria were walking side by side, but Clair hadn't followed.

"Come on, Free Mars," he said.

"It's *Clair*." The correction was soft enough that D'Arcy almost didn't hear it as he opened the back door and laid the weapons on the seat.

"We starting over, then?" he asked and held out his fist. "Hi, Clair, I'm D'Arcy. Nice to meet you—better circumstances and all that."

"How are you so calm about this? Someone tried to blow you up just a few hours ago."

"Practice." D'Arcy said. "And training, I guess, if we're being serious. My friends and a whole lot of other people are in danger, so panicking doesn't help them. You haven't panicked when someone keeps trying to kill Sylvia, you just do your job. Keep her alive. This is my job."

Clair nodded in understanding, then offered up a shy smile. "I figured all you Neos would hate us."

"You should know, unofficially, I always root for the underdog," D'Arcy replied, and tapped Clair on the shoulder again with a smile. "Get in, time's wasting."

They climbed in the back seat with Emel as D'Arcy got into the passenger seat.

"Where are we going?" Maria asked, starting the vehicle.

D'Arcy sent her the location and settled back into his seat.

TAMAGO HAD WALKED BETWEEN GROUND CONTROL AND THE conference room so much that they were surprised a groove hadn't appeared in the floor. D'Arcy's suggestion to try to contact Castle, to see if they could convince her to change sides, had been met with a surprising amount of enthusiasm from Kenta, who'd given them the go-ahead.

They wanted to be doing something, so despite the doubts that anything they said could flip Castle, here they were staring at the screen with practically every detail about her life. It was better than standing around, worrying about Max. And now also Jenks, who'd departed with the SEALs with a grin and a wink and a promise to behave herself that Tamago actually believed.

Mostly.

"What are you looking for?" Chae asked, joining them.

Tamago paused the recording of Castle's presentation for her Earth History in the Post-Collapse Years class. "Honestly? I don't know. I keep hoping something will jump out at me, anything to give me an in with her." Tamago spun their hand in the air. "What are your thoughts on this?"

"Can I say 'goat fuck'?"

Tamago laughed softly. Chae had been so soft-spoken when they'd first joined *Zuma*. But the years had seen them settle in and bloom into an even better version of themself— one that swore a little more like Jenks with every day that passed.

"You wouldn't be wrong. I'm mostly tired of the sound of my own voice in my head, so give me something else to listen to? Thoughts on Castle."

"I think to understand the people involved, we need to understand the situation in total." Chae whistled low. "It feels like Trappist, but amped up to well above the max, which I get, given the history here. But none of this acted like a typical hostage situation from the very beginning. Right?"

"Right," Tamago agreed.

Chae gestured at the board. "All these people lost someone, multiple someones in so many cases." They sobered and rubbed at their nose. "I can't imagine what it would feel like if I'd lost my dads. Castle wants her grief acknowledged. It happened so recently, I'm sure the pain is unbelievable."

Tamago couldn't imagine it, either, especially if it had happened before they'd found their family in the NeoG. They reached for Chae's other hand to give it a squeeze as they remembered the fight they'd tried to pick with Chae when Sapphi had been hurt and all Tamago wanted was to make someone else pay for their best friend ending up in the hospital. It was a fury they weren't proud of, but now they could see how it could eat someone alive.

"Chae . . . if I'd come to you before we crashed on One-d and said I knew what you were trapped in and offered to help. What would you have done?"

Chae was silent for so long that an apology formed on the tip of Tamago's tongue, but then the petty officer rested their head on Tamago's shoulder. "I was so scared, Tama. And I felt so alone. Didn't know who to trust, honestly didn't think I could trust anyone. I'm not sure what I would have done, but knowing you now, I think you would have found a way to get through to me. To make me feel seen."

Tamago wrapped their arms around Chae, and they stood in silence for a long while before they both straightened and wiped the tears from their cheeks.

"I admit that I feel better now that we know the hostages will be okay." Chae dragged in a deep breath. "And Max will be okay."

Tamago appreciated Chae's confidence in the team.

Tamago had it, too, and yet had a lot more experience than the younger Neo. So while they weren't the praying type, Tamago hoped that something in the universe was listening and would bring their friends safely home to them.

Because all the skill and experience in the solar system meant nothing if you didn't also have a little luck on your side.

THE END RESULT OF THIS AGREEMENT IS THE EXPECTATION THAT Mars will receive the ability to have full representation within the CHN Senate and all final say via popular vote in matters that directly impact the citizens of Mars and their planet.

"Sylvia?"

She pulled her attention away from the document scrolling across her DD, looked up at Mikhail, and smiled. "I think we've actually done it."

He returned the smile, unease still flickering in the depths of his gaze. "What does this Faustian bargain net us?"

She laughed and then rubbed a hand over her neck with a sigh. "Hopefully peace and hopefully we have cheated the devil out of more dead."

"Maria's waiting out front with the others, says they have something to show us."

"That was fast. They're back already?" She waved a hand at Patricia who was talking to Kavan on the far side of the room. "We're going with Maria, I'll be back."

Patricia nodded and gave a little wave goodbye.

"Did Maria say what it was?" She remembered they were going to scout a signal, but she wasn't sure what that exactly entailed.

"She didn't elaborate," he replied, ushering her down the corridor and out the side door of the building. "Said they were moving in to investigate and would be off the coms, but sent me a location."

Sylvia nodded, striding for the main gate of the base. The guards there didn't do much more than wave them through.

"Never thought it would be that easy to get off a NeoG base," she commented to Mikhail with a grin. Then she frowned. "Wait—I thought you said Maria was waiting for us?"

"No, Clair is," he replied, and pointed to the vehicle across the street. "There. Let's move, I don't want you exposed for too long."

Sylvia could have sworn he'd said Maria, but her head had been whirling all day, and she thought she could be mistaken or exhausted or both. She crossed to the vehicle and reached for the door, yelping at the hot sting that lanced through the side of her neck.

"Easy," Mikhail murmured as he caught her. "It's going to be okay."

Sylvia desperately tried to call for help on her DD but was met with only silence. "Mikhail, what have you done?" She had no feeling, no movement in her limbs, and couldn't stop him from loading her into the back seat.

"I'm making things right. Bringing justice for the orphans of war," he replied as he pulled the door closed behind him.

IT DIDN'T TAKE THEM LONG TO GET TO THE LOCATION ON HIS DD. Maria knew the streets well enough to avoid the more trafficked areas of Serrano. D'Arcy straightened in his seat as she pulled into a crowded parking lot and tucked them into the back.

"We'll want to walk from here. I doubt pulling a fed-registered vehicle right up to the warehouse would be a good idea."

"You're not wrong," D'Arcy said.

"How much attention are we going to get with the weapons?" Emel asked.

"No more than your uniforms bring in anyway," Maria replied.

D'Arcy and Emel had both found the time to change back into their ODUs. The operational duty uniforms were dark NeoG blue with a black shirt and boots. Emel's hijab was also blue.

By contrast, Maria and Clair were in tan cargos and darker brown shirts. D'Arcy wondered idly where Maria had gotten a replacement for the shirt she'd bandaged him up with before he shook his head clear and refocused on the mission.

"You want me to go up over there?" Emel asked, and after a moment of deliberation he nodded.

"Maria, you and Clair with me." He gestured and started walking. Emel took off in the opposite direction, disappearing down a side street.

"Up?"

He grinned at Maria's question. "Emel's one of the best snipers in the NeoG despite not having a lot of opportunity to use that skill in space. She'll be able to cover us from on high and hopefully be able to see a lot more than we will."

D'Arcy could practically see Maria's estimation of his master chief shift as he spoke, but he continued on, weaving

his way through the buildings and warehouses that domi-
nated this section of Serrano.

"In position," Emel said in his ear. "So far, I've seen a
dozen people. Four very obvious lookouts at the major inter-
sections, three on the roof who are armed, and five inside."

"I think we're coming up on one of the lookouts," D'Arcy
replied, and slowed to a stop. He glanced over his shoulder
and held a finger up to his lips, then gestured for Maria and
Clair to follow him through the open gate on his right.

"What is it?" Maria asked.

"Emel thinks lookouts are on the main streets. One of
them is ahead of us on the right."

"Do you want them alive?"

"What are you thinking?"

"Clair." Maria made a complex series of hand gestures.
The younger person nodded and slipped back into the alley
before D'Arcy could stop them.

Despite the fact that he was listening for it, all D'Arcy
heard was the normal sounds of the city. Then the sounds of
Clair's footsteps slightly heavier than normal. The reason for
it was apparent when they came through the gate with the
lookout slung over their shoulders.

It was D'Arcy's turn to be impressed. The person they'd
knocked out without effort was twice their size. He grabbed
for the lookout, taking some of the weight as Clair tipped them
off toward the ground.

"No suicide tooth on the scan," D'Arcy murmured. "Interesting."

Their handshake read *Leza Hernadez, she/her,* and D'Arcy
tapped the woman's cheek a few times until her eyes fluttered
and then snapped wide.

"Ah, ah." D'Arcy held a hand up. "No yelling."

"Who are—" She cut off, no doubt at the sight of his handshake, and glared. It had little effect on him; she wasn't any older than Clair, practically a child.

D'Arcy felt unreasonably weary again. "What's in the warehouse, Leza?"

"How am I supposed to know? I was just minding my own damn business and got yanked off the street by the feds."

"Technically you got yanked by Free Mars," Clair said dryly.

D'Arcy cleared his throat of the laugh that threatened with the look of absolute shock on Leza's face. "You're working together?"

"Enemy of my enemy," D'Arcy replied, deliberately not looking at Maria when he said it. "What's in the warehouse, Leza, and what does Willis have planned for the MOS?"

"Boxes and shit. Second question, I don't know. I'm just a lookout. They don't tell me shit. Jarvis is the one who'd know."

"That was extremely unhelpful and also suspiciously easy," Maria muttered and Leza flushed.

"Look, I was just here because my boyfriend asked me if I wanted to stick it to the feds and make some money for a few days. Seemed like a good way to pick up a few extra. Honest truth, those people in there give me the weebles. I overheard some of them talking about reuniting with their dead families and shit. I got a family. Granted they suck a bit, drive me to the street more often than not, but I don't want to go out in some flaming glory. I like my life."

"You got an image of this Jarvis?"

"Sure. Be careful with him, fed; he's a mean one."

D'Arcy's DD pinged and he ran the file through quarantine before opening it. The man in the image was built for heavy lifting. Dark eyes and hair, and he knew immediately what Leza meant by "mean." Jarvis had the look of someone who'd sooner kill a person than talk.

"Can I go?"

"Will you cross me if I say yes?"

Leza shook her head. "I'm out. The sex was mediocre anyway."

Maria actually giggled, the noise slipping out before she muffled it. D'Arcy sighed and shook his head. "Make better choices, kiddo," he said, then nodded his head at the gate. "We're good. If I walk into a trap, we're going to have an issue. Understood?"

"Believe me. I am gone like liquor store inventory on basic day." Leza saluted him with her thumb and first two fingers, then vanished through the gate.

"Emel, sending a file your way. Target by the name of Jarvis. You have a visual?"

"Give me a minute," she replied. "He wasn't one of the five inside originally, but a group just rolled up to the ramps in a cargo truck. Did you run a search?"

"How long have I been doing this?" His DD pinged again, and D'Arcy swore. "Ah fuck, former Neo, Emel. Petty Officer First Class Jarvis Boehm. Dishonorable discharge in '27. His squad tangled with one of the splinter groups, everyone but him seriously injured or killed. He apparently went on a revenge spin through every bar in a fifteen-kilometer radius, put a bunch of people in the hospital. Did ten years in rehab, been driving trucks for H3nergy since then."

"Sounds like rehab didn't stick. Speaking of trucks, your guy just climbed out of the driver's seat. Should I kill him?"

D'Arcy knew he shouldn't be surprised by Emel's matter-of-fact question. She was much like Jenks in that respect, preferring the peaceful solution but willing to do what was necessary when it came down to it.

"No," he replied. "I want that one alive if we can manage it. What's on the truck?"

"Crates." Emel snorted. "Something important in there, they're lined. I can't see anything with the scope."

"I kind of wish Jenks hadn't left Doge on Trappist," D'Arcy mused. "He'd be super helpful right about now. Okay, we're going to try to get closer, see if we can get a look at what's inside."

"Wise thing to do would be call in some backup."

"I know, but if whatever is going on down here is connected to the MOS—and we both know it is—then we need to find out what it is."

Emel sighed heavily. "All right, you just watch your ass, please? I don't want to have to explain to Boston that I let you die on Mars."

"I'm sure he wouldn't blame you." He looked at Maria. "Okay, let's see if we can get into this warehouse without kicking up a fuss?"

"What happened to just scouting?" Clair demanded.

"It's technically still scouting." He grinned. "Just more fun."

NIKA STARED AT THE MAP IN FRONT OF HIM AND TRIED TO FIGURE out if the unease seething in his chest was because of Max or something new.

Jenks had left with the SEALs, carrying Max's space suit in a pack and looking decidedly relieved to finally be moving.

"Do I need to be concerned about the look on your face?" Scott asked softly.

"I don't know," Nika replied. "I've felt like this since Admiral Chen commed me. The problem is I can't untangle if this is just worry for Max or something else. Nothing about this fucking mission makes sense. Why involve yourself in an elaborate negotiation charade just for revenge? Why didn't they just blow the station when they had control? What are they waiting for?"

"Jenks to go back on vacation," Scott murmured with a half laugh that Nika echoed.

"You have no idea how long I'm going to hear about—" He broke off.

"I will give you a piece of advice, though; keep that sister of yours on the ground." Willis's words suddenly rang in Nika's head.

"Fuck," he muttered.

"What?"

"Willis knew Jenks was back. In the information from Saqib that Max passed to us, Willis mentioned her being on vacation. But when he was talking to me and Tamago, he said I needed to keep Jenks on the ground for the second phase. How did he know?"

"Reasonable guess? She did go out into the city. Anyone could have seen her."

"I told her to keep a hat on, and the area was roped off from journalists and civilians. It's possible someone from the ground op was watching, I suppose, I just—"

"Nika?" Pax joined them, her face filled with worry. "I'm sorry to interrupt. Do you know where Sylvia went?"

"She left?"

"She said she was going to meet Maria. I can't raise her on the coms."

"Maria went with D'Arcy to find the people on the ground that the MOS has been in contact with," Nika replied. "I don't know why she would have wanted Sylvia in a dangerous area." He queued up his com. "D'Arcy?"

There was no answer and Nika swore. "Master Chief Shevreaux, do you copy?"

No response.

"Lieutenant Commander Landon, get in here."

A moment later Chaske jogged into the room. "Commander?"

"I can't raise D'Arcy or Emel on the com. Take your crew, Chae and Rona. And Gunny Ranta. Find D'Arcy."

"I'm going with them," Scott said, a smile tugging his face when Nika shook his head. "You technically can't order me not to."

Nika sighed. "Fine. Don't get killed and make me regret it." He waved a hand and turned to Sapphi.

"I don't like this," she said.

"Join the club," Nika replied. "Figure out what the fuck is going on. I want to know yesterday. Why can't we make contact?"

"I'm assuming you don't want the first options that popped into my head." Sapphi winced at his flat look. "Fine, it's fine. Look, if we're talking coms? A jammer is the most likely thing. Something big enough to cover a wide area like a warehouse but not interfere in the . . . Wait, hang on."

He waited, long years of experience teaching him that no matter what was going on, leaving Sapphi alone to do whatever it was that had derailed her was usually a good idea.

Usually.

"Sapphi, time is important."

"I know, I know. Hang on." Her hands flew across the light keys in front of her. "There're reports of com issues in the area around where the signal was bouncing. Supposedly a relay station caught fire."

"Convenient. Forward that information to Lieutenant Commander Landon."

"Already done. I'm also going to—" She glanced around, made a face at all the people watching them. "Do something to fix this. Don't you all have jobs?"

"Back to work, people!" Nika ordered and several people jumped before obeying. "Whatever you're going to do is fine, Sapphi, just get me coms back."

"DOWN, GET DOWN." D'ARCY CROUCHED BEHIND A LOW WALL AS the vehicle passed them. They'd spent longer than he'd wanted watching the guards outside until they could slip through the opening the now long-gone Leza had left.

"Car's here. I'm sending them around to the back. Roger that. I'll follow." The voice came from somewhere behind the wall, and D'Arcy shook his head slightly at Maria's questioning look.

They're headed this way, she mouthed.

No, they're headed to the back.

The back is this way.

"For fuck's sake," Clair muttered, and launched themself over the wall. There was a brief sound of a scuffle, but by the time D'Arcy was on his feet, the person was unconscious on the ground.

Clair waved her finger between him and Maria several times with a hard look and took off for the back without saying a word.

D'Arcy cleared his throat and followed. He swore he could feel Maria shaking with suppressed laughter behind him, but he wasn't going to give her the satisfaction of acknowledging it.

They caught up with Clair. The Free Mars soldier held up a finger to their lips and then a spread hand. D'Arcy dared a peek around the corner of the building. He counted the five people Clair had spotted. The driver of the vehicle and four others who'd converged from the warehouse.

The back door of the vehicle opened, and D'Arcy heard Clair's sharp intake of breath when Mikhail emerged. The big man ducked back in, and it was D'Arcy's turn to curse when he pulled Sylvia's limp form free.

He locked his hand on Clair's wrist, reaching back to grab Maria as he backpedaled into her. "We can't rush in," he hissed.

"What is it?" Maria demanded.

"Let me go." Clair's free hand flashed out, and D'Arcy barely dodged the likely illegal taser she thrust at him.

"Clair, please. If you run in there, you'll just get killed." He caught their other hand, hoping that Maria's confusion would last long enough for him to get Clair to stand down.

"They have Sylvia!"

Well so much for that, he thought.

"They *what*?"

"Maria." It had been a long time since he'd said her name with so much frustrated desperation, but it apparently was enough.

"Clair, stop." Her order was low and enough to get Clair to freeze. Maria rubbed both hands over her face, and when she dropped them, the tears in her brown eyes were worse than if he'd gotten zapped. "D'Arcy, please."

"We'll get her, I promise. Just give me a minute to think. Keep watch." He turned away from the back of the warehouse. "Emel, we have a situation."

More than one, apparently.

There was nothing but dead air on the coms.

CHN Navy Officer Honored for Mission
MAY 30, 2414 (ESD)

CHN Navy SEAL Ensign Ella Giroux was honored today in London for her and her team's quick response that helped save lives during the Pluto Outpost #43 incident. The ensign, who is the newest member of SEAL Team Twenty-Five, was part of the rescue effort staged from the nearby destroyer *Valentina Tereshkova* when the CO_2 processing unit in the outpost failed.

Giroux and the rest of her team were responsible for saving more than two dozen civilians during the evacuation. Giroux herself had been instrumental in constructing a temporary repair for the outpost that bought the rest of her team time to evac that section of the base. When asked about her contributions, she had this to say: "I know how difficult it is to lose people you love, and my heart and apologies go out to the families of those lost. I don't think I deserve anything special here. I was just doing my job, which is to save lives, and if we're being honest, I failed at that."

Among those present for the ceremony were former Senator Willis Hale, whose own husband tragically perished in the Hellas accident. Hale has not been seen in public since the accident, which happened back at the end of March, and declined to make any comments to the media after the ceremony. The funeral service for his husband was held over a month ago in a small, private ceremony. [*Read More*]

SEVENTEEN

IT WAS WEIRD TO BE ON A SHIP WITH A BUNCH OF PEOPLE JENKS didn't know. Rather than the normal pre-mission banter, she was stuck in the silence of a SEAL ship with a bunch of space squids.

If she believed in hell, this would probably qualify.

The guilt was immediate. These people were risking their lives to rescue people off the MOS, she should probably be a little more charitable.

Right. I love the Navy. They're great.

The snort of laughter slipped out into the air before she could stop it. Lieutenant Ryan eyed her but didn't say anything. He'd avoided her since the confrontation in Ground Control, while the others had been surprisingly friendly as they'd gotten ready to leave.

"Something funny, Senior Chief?" Lieutenant Commander

Jordan Cerlio, they/them, asked. The lieutenant commander was as tall as her brother but broader across the shoulders and had an easy grin that reminded her of Tivo.

"Long story," she replied with a shrug. "We'll just say a decade ago this would have been a recipe for disaster."

Jordan chuckled at that, and Ella joined in from her spot next to him. "Most of these kids are too young, Jenks. We haven't told them the scary stories about you yet."

"I've heard a few," Chief Petty Officer Sy West, she/her, said. The black-haired woman's smile held a familiar hint of challenge. "Is it true you broke Rear Admiral Connell's nose?"

Jenks frowned. "Connell? Connell . . . Oh! No. I didn't break his nose." She laughed at the memory and then stifled it with a cough. "He was a captain at the time and too drunk to be starting fights. All I did was get out of the way when he fell. The bar broke his nose."

"We saw your championship fight with Commander Carmichael." Petty Officer Second Class Steven Lynn, he/they, had blond hair as pale as Heli's and a surprisingly sweet smile. "I won fifty feds off Mak." They gestured up at Petty Officer First Class Mak Lee, he/him, with a wink.

"Ah, well, sorry and congratulations I suppose. Betting against Max is always a risky proposition."

"I'm surprised it doesn't bother you to lose, Senior Chief," Mak replied over his shoulder from the pilot's seat.

"Sure, it does, who likes losing? At the same time, I trained Max with the idea that she'd be good enough to beat me someday. Why would I be mad when she did it? Either way, we came out on top." A part of her brain reminded her that talking shit about beating Navy while in a ship surrounded by them was probably not the brightest of ideas, but all the SEALs—except Ryan—laughed.

"So you've all been together a while?" Jenks asked. It was probably a good idea to take the focus off herself for the duration of the flight.

"Seven years, except for Ryan," Ella replied. "Lieutenant Naf broke his leg a few weeks ago in a training accident. He doesn't respond well to the bone regrowth treatments so Command stuck us with Ryan." She patted the lieutenant with a grin. "I kid, you're doing fine. Lucky Jenks didn't turn you into paste, but doing fine."

Jenks felt an unexpected swell of sympathy for him. She knew how hard it had to be to come into a tight-knit crew. It had felt like that when she'd first joined *Zuma*—all the history and stories and inside jokes that left you feeling lost.

"I'm sure you'll settle in, Lieutenant," she said, and watched the startled look slide over his face.

"Captain Giroux, we're coming up on the station. Everything is quiet," Mak said.

"Roger that. Ground Control, this is Captain Ella Giroux. We are making our approach, going radio silent."

Nothing actually changed, but Jenks felt the very real weight of not being able to talk to Sapphi, or anyone else, settle down around her. She caught Ryan's worried blue gaze. He had to be nervous about what she assumed was his first real mission, so Jenks offered up a smile she hoped he took as reassuring and not condescending.

I have gone so soft, she thought.

"*Omar Tazi* just peeled off for the Docking Bay," Mak said. "We're five minutes out, people, get yourselves ready."

The time passed simultaneously at a slow crawl and faster than the blink of an eye. There wasn't a peep from the station defenses, and Mak docked them at the airlock without so much as a whisper. Jenks shook out her limbs as she followed Ella and the lieutenant commander off the ship. The chief and the petty officer were behind her with Ryan bringing up the rear. It made for tight quarters in the airlock, but the door slid shut behind them.

"Separated. Heading to rendezvous point," Mak said over the com.

"Roger." Ella keyed open the interior door and stepped through, Jordan on her heels. "Moving to phase two. Clock starting."

"Aren't we waiting for Max?" Jenks brought up her own coms, cursing at the static in her ear. "The fuck?"

"Watch out, Senior Chief!" Ryan's shout was all the warning she got before things predictably went to shit.

MAX WAS LACING UP THE SECOND DONATED BOOT, COURTESY of Corporal Oluo, when the internal coms buzzed to life. The conversation in the bay fell silent and everyone looked her way.

"Commander Carmichael, if I could have your attention please." Willis's voice echoed through the air.

She glanced at the clock on her DD. Captain Giroux and the SEALs should almost be to the station by now, but she was out of time.

"Seo-Yoon, after I go, you take everyone to the Docking Bay. Find a freighter to hide in. Lia, you send me the location. As soon as the ships are ready to load, I'll let you know." She grabbed for her bag, shoving the tablet into it, and sprinted for the maintenance hatch.

"Carmichael, you be careful!" Seo-Yoon yelled at her, and she threw the woman a quick salute.

"What do you want, Willis?" she asked as she crawled her way toward the ladder leading upward. She didn't turn at the exit for the closet, but continued up toward the third level.

"I want my detonators," he replied. "And I'm reasonably sure your lieutenant commander wants to live. Not take the same cold walk as Ford."

Don't let your opponents in your head. She could hear Jenks's advice even as the fury sprang to life in her chest.

"Saqib knows what's at stake here. I'm not letting you detonate those bombs."

"Come now, Max. You really value this station over the life of your crew?"

"Willis, it doesn't have to be like this. What you're doing isn't going to bring anyone back, it only brings more destruction. Blowing up this station won't get you anything."

Willis chuckled. "Poor NeoG, so certain that you know everything."

At the second-level landing Max dragged in a breath as she leaned against the ladder. "You know, I don't have a lot of patience for riddles right now," she said once she could talk without sounding winded. "You want to share what's on your mind, Willis? I'm listening."

"Max! He's trying to track you through the com, Ralka's—" Saqib's sudden warning broke off into a grunt of pain and then silence.

Max couldn't say for sure what tipped her off the rest

of the way or why the shock of Saqib's interruption didn't fatally distract her. Instinct told her to move so she moved. She grabbed for the ladder, planting both feet on the outside edge, and jumped.

The gloves that the Navy pilot, Lieutenant Ramos, had pushed on her saved her hands on the poorly controlled descent back down to the third level. Fléchette rounds shook the ladder, slamming into the bulkhead behind it, and shouted outrage echoed from above.

Max landed hard but upright and felt the protest of her leg even through the combat meds as she threw herself into a side tunnel. She scrambled away from the shouting, turning quickly and finding the first exit she could back into the station interior.

The corridor she kicked her way into was blessedly silent; Max raced for the elevator stairs and had just passed the second level again when she heard noise above. She silently backtracked, slipping through the door back on the third and out into the hallway.

"Max!"

"Saqib? Where are you?" She heard a grunt and the slight echo of his voice. "I'm coming for you."

"No need. I got loose. Elevator stairwell three. Hijackers in pursuit."

"I'm on the opposite side from you. Make for the Docking Bay, I'll come that way. Spacer Lia Thorn and Cho Seo-Yoon are leading the others there to meet up with the extraction ships."

"Will do. Hey, Max?"

"Yeah?"

"Thanks for sticking around for me."

"You saved yourself." She laughed. "And there's no way I want to have to wrangle Jenks alone, so you not dying is definitely in my best interest."

"See you soon, Commander."

She queued up the com again. "Lia, Lieutenant Commander Vahid got free, he's headed your way via elevator stairwell three. I'm on the opposite side and have to work my way around."

Possibly farther around than she wanted to. If they were still tracking her, Max didn't want to lead them straight into the bay filled with people.

"Roger, Commander. I just made contact with Captain Nier of the *Omar Tazi*; they're only a few minutes out. The SEAL ship hasn't responded to their com, not sure what's going on there. We're almost to the Docking Bay. It's really quiet out here. Makes me nervous. Sorry."

"You're fine. Keep your eyes open and trust your gut. I'm going to shut down for a few minutes; don't panic if you can't get me." Max signed off and shut her DD all the way down. "Track that," she muttered.

THE SHAPE OF THE SCALPEL IN HIS CARGO POCKET WAS ODDLY comforting under his hand as Saqib watched the steady increase of activity in the vice admiral's offices. Castle and team frequently dissolved into curses, which could only indicate that somewhere in cyberspace Sapphi and whoever else the NeoG had brought in were kicking their asses out of system after system.

At one point the lights had gone out and Saqib wasn't

entirely sure that them coming back on meant Castle's crew
had control again.

"Up," Willis said, without any of his previous charm.

"What's going on?"

"We're going to have a little talk with your commander."
Willis's smile was tight and Saqib wondered again what Max
had taken that seemed to have thrown the man's plans into
a spiral. "I tried to do this the civilized way, but it seems she
insists on the alternative."

Saqib kept his mouth shut this time. Willis would learn
soon enough that there was no convincing Max now. He'd
lost that chance when he'd sent Vice Admiral Ford to his
death.

"Ralka, are you ready?" Whatever response Willis received made him smile. "Castle?"

"We're up, just get her talking. I should be able to iso-
late the signal once I find it. Though again, needle in a goddamned haystack."

"Unless you'd like to give up your seat and stay for the
party, I suggest you make it happen," Willis snarled, and
Castle swallowed.

"Fine, yeesh. I'll find her. You gotta keep her on the com,
though."

Saqib wasn't prepared for the sudden hand across his
mouth or the gun pressed behind his ear.

Willis smiled at him and his captor—Charlie, he assumed. "I don't like interruptions, so just to make sure you
stay quiet," he said. "Commander Carmichael, if I could
have your attention, please."

"What do you want, Willis?" One of the many things

Saqib admired about Max was how calm she was all the damn time, and this was no different.

"I want my detonators," he replied. "And I'm reasonably sure your lieutenant commander wants to live. Not take the same cold walk as Ford."

That was unwise, Saqib thought. Max had the patience of his own mothers, and he'd never seen them get truly angry. But everyone had a breaking point, and both his mothers had gotten close more than a few times during his difficult teenage years.

Saqib listened to the back-and-forth between the two, waiting, hoping for a moment where he could shake Charlie free and warn Max. He'd already made peace with the fact that he might die, but if he could save her in the process, it was worth it. Castle flashed a thumbs-up sign in Willis's direction, indicating she had a lock on Max's position, and Saqib knew he had to move. He rammed his elbow hard into the guard's diaphragm and Charlie doubled over with a gasp of pain. "Max! He's trying to track you, Ralka's—"

Willis's fist was like a hammer. The punch caught him in the jaw and sent Saqib flying backward into Charlie. They both crashed to the ground, and Saqib shook off the pain, already pulling the scalpel from his cargo pocket and stripping off the protective paper to reveal the lethal edge.

The scalpel sliced all too easily through the side of Charlie's throat, and Saqib was back on his feet, sprinting down the hallway before he saw the carnage. He heard the shouting and the slam of booted feet racing after him, but he passed the open elevator and ducked into the stairs instead.

He leaped easily over the railing, sticking the landing on the stairs below as he flipped his DD back on.

"Max!"

"Saqib? Where are you? I'm coming for you."

He grabbed the railing again as the door above him slammed open and vaulted over it. "No need. I got loose. Elevator stairwell three. Hijackers in pursuit."

"I'm on the opposite side from you. Make for the Docking Bay, I'll come to you. Spacer Lia Thorn and Cho Seo-Yoon are leading the others there to meet up with the extraction ships."

"Will do. Hey, Max?"

"Yeah?"

"Thanks for sticking around for me."

"You saved yourself." She laughed. "And there's no way I want to have to wrangle Jenks alone, so you not dying is definitely in my best interest."

"See you soon, Commander." He slipped out into the Docking Bay level and ducked into the shadows along the nearby wall.

"WATCH OUT, SENIOR CHIEF!"

The warning from Ryan was the last thing Jenks expected, but it was enough to save her life. Jenks twisted to the side, the knife that Petty Officer Lynn had thrust at her sliding harmlessly through the air instead of into her kidney.

The lieutenant hit Lynn, knocking them both into the bulkhead with a bone-crunching thud. Jenks spun, grabbing for the roll bar above the airlock, and kicked Ella in the chest before she could pull her sword free. The SEAL captain staggered back into the hallway, and Jenks darted forward, slapping a hand against the airlock panel. The door closed between them, and when Jordan grabbed her from behind, she used their body to brace herself and shattered the door controls with her bootheel.

She kicked again, swinging her leg down and back to catch Chief West when she joined the fray. This time her heel connected with a knee joint, but the effect was the same. West dropped like a rock, a cry of pain filling the air.

Jordan rushed forward, and Jenks couldn't get her leg up in time to keep them from crushing her against the airlock door. However, their move had dropped their shoulders below hers and she snapped her head back.

The crack of her skull versus their nose was followed by the warm gush of blood down the back of her neck. Jordan squawked in pain and their hold loosened. Jenks heard another grunt and then a gasping choke but didn't have time to look and see if it was Ryan.

She really hoped not. Wasn't this the weirdest fucking day?

Jenks spun, grabbing Jordan by the shoulders and driving her knee into their groin. They dropped to the deck next to West as Ryan shoved away from Lynn, who slumped sideways, a knife buried in his chest.

Ryan dropped to a knee, clutching the bloody wound in his side with one hand. Jenks swore.

The shrill warning tone of the outer airlock hatch sounded, and Jenks rushed for the lieutenant. "Helmet up, Ryan!" She hit her own, glad the fools hadn't let her get out of her suit before they attacked.

Jenks managed to snag Ryan by the belt, grabbing for the static line just before the door snapped open and they were sucked outside. The line brought them up short, swinging them into the side of the station, and Jenks grunted when she was crushed a second time.

Jordan and West, plus Lynn's body, spun past them out into the black with nothing to slow the speed of the decompression. Even if they got their helmets up in time, the options were a whole lot of black or the planet's gravity dragging them into a burnup.

Fucking bastards, she thought. Followed quickly by *No one deserves to go out that way.*

Jenks dragged her eyes away when the lieutenant groaned.

"Ryan, hey, look at me," she snapped. "Keep your hand pressed to that wound. Hang tight."

He nodded sharply, grabbing on to her with his free hand while she dug in the leg pocket of her suit, pulling free a patch.

"Too much goddamned experience with this bullshit. On three," she said when she'd finally unwrapped it. "Hold on tight because your suit's going to try to push you away. Ready? One, two, three." Jenks lunged forward with the patch, slapping it in place the moment his hand moved.

It wouldn't help the wound, but it would keep the air in his suit. Hopefully long enough for her to find a way into the station.

"This is not how I thought my first mission would go," Ryan murmured, and she didn't like the way his voice was slurring.

"Pretty close to how my first one went, actually. Less betrayal, though. Okay, LT, I am not going to die wearing my favorite dinosaur underwear." She tapped him on the helmet. "And I haven't had a lieutenant die on my watch yet, you don't get to be the first."

"Please don't make me laugh, Senior Chief, it hurts."

"Shouldn't have gotten stabbed."

"I figured it was me or you and I owed you one."

"That's the spirit." She did her best to keep her voice calm even as she hid away her own worry while she clung to the outside of a damn station filled with a bunch of people who wanted to kill her.

I should be drinking a beer and playing with my kids.

"All right, there's a maintenance hatch about four meters up and to our right. Sort of a secret airlock. Let's get to that and then we can figure out how to patch that hole in your side." She tapped him on the arm. "Start climbing. Slow and easy, get a grip with one hand before you let go with the other. I don't want to have to go get you."

"Yes, ma'am."

"Don't 'ma'am' me, I work for a living."

And my first job is saving our asses.

MAX HEARD THE VOICE BEFORE SHE CAME AROUND THE CORNER and relief rushed through her when she recognized Captain Ella Giroux. As she stepped into view with a raised hand, the woman's words hit her in the chest.

"Khan took out my entire team. I should have cut her throat on the fucking ship instead of listening to you and trying to take her alive. No, she's breathing vacuum now. Mak's headed to the designated airlock. I suggest you get what's left of your people down to the Docking Bay, and— Carmichael!"

Max stalked forward, sword in hand. "Where is my sister?"

"Out in the fucking black," Ella spat, pulling her own sword free.

"Wrong answer."

Jenks wasn't dead. She *couldn't* be dead. Max refused to believe it, so the fury she channeled into her attack was as cold as the blackness of space.

Captain Giroux backpedaled, blocking Max's swings with expert skill. But Max had spent the better part of the last six years training with the best sword fighter in the known systems. She executed an empty fade that Ella bought, and deflected the woman's thrust, slicing deep along her right side as she passed her.

The SEAL staggered away, sword still raised and a snarl on her face. "You have been the biggest pain in the ass, Carmichael."

"So I hear." Max wiggled her free hand. "Come on."

Shouting filled the corridor and Captain Giroux smiled coldly. "I think not. Sounds like my backup is here."

Max swore, spun on her heel, and ran in the other direction. She ducked into the stairwell and took the stairs two at a time upward to the second level. Exiting and finding the first open room she could, Max slid down the wall gasping for air.

She flipped her DD back on with the intent of calling Lia to warn her they had incoming when Jenks's voice filled her head.

"Hey, Max? You copy?"

"I'm here." She couldn't stop the sob that escaped with the words. "You're not dead."

"Pffft. Of course I'm not dead. You think some renegade

SEALs can take me out? Where are you? Never mind, I see you on the map. We're close."

Max's laugh was sharp edged and brittle. "I had a run-in with Captain Giroux. She said she spaced you."

"Eh, fair, she did. Not my first airlock incident, though. All in all, it was a mediocre effort. Like not even top ten of people who've tried to kill me. She really just ended up killing two of her own instead, unless someone manages to pick them up. Lieutenant Ryan and I are currently working our way through a fucking maintenance tunnel."

"Ryan?"

"Despite being a space squid, he's a decent sort—especially since he's not a traitor."

"That sounds like a good companion to have."

"I'm not going to marry him, if that's what you mean."

Max never thought she'd be so happy to hear Jenks's rambling, jokey responses in her entire life, and she choked down the rush of emotion that threatened to overwhelm her.

"Are you hurt?"

"A little banged up. LT here is worse—could use a patch once we get somewhere that doesn't resemble an MRE tin."

"LT, huh? That was quick," Max teased. Jenks wasn't known for automatic affection, especially for naval officers, but her easy use of the phrase for her companion hinted at a heck of a story.

"He saved my life. Those are the rules. Even if he is Navy."

"I am also on the com, Senior Chief," Ryan broke in. "Commander Carmichael, what's the best way to get to you?"

Max bit her lip at Jenks's sputtered protest about knowing her directions on a damned station as she pulled up the map and rattled off a route for them, sending along a visual to their DDs. According to what she could see, it would only take them a few minutes to reach her.

She commed a warning to Lia as she kept watch at the doorway, heart hammering in her chest until the hatch eased open and Jenks wriggled free, followed by a lanky redhead who stumbled a little and went to a knee. Max gave a little whistle and Jenks's head snapped in her direction.

"In here," Max said with a wave.

Jenks helped Ryan to his feet and into the room, where he sank down onto the couch with a groan. "You still don't get to die, Ryan, come on. Let's get you out of this suit."

"Don't you have to buy me dinner first?"

"He's funny," Jenks said to Max. "First he's picking fights with me and now he's flirting."

"Seems about standard for you," Max replied, digging through her bag for the medical supplies Seo-Yoon had pushed on her. The relief of familiar banter wrapped around her as they got the lieutenant patched up.

"Here, swallow those," Max ordered, pressing two combat pain meds into his hand. She turned back to Jenks, met her sister's worried blue and brown eyes, and fell into her outstretched arms.

"I'm so glad to see you."

"Sorry it took me so long to get up here," Jenks whispered.

Max hiccupped on a sob that lodged itself somewhere in her throat. "Sorry again about your vacation."

There was a beat and then a snort. "You can't apologize before I bitch about it, that ruins the fun. I'd hug you tighter, but I know you got cracked ribs."

"I can't feel them."

"Doesn't mean they won't puncture a lung. Straighten up and let me see this wrap job. Oh, I brought you your suit." She shucked the bag off her back, and Max didn't protest as Jenks fussed over her.

"Saqib got free," she said, and caught Jenks up on what had happened.

"Of course he did, good man. He's at the dock?"

"Yeah, Lia said he arrived when I called to warn her about possible incoming." She glanced over at the couch. "How are you doing, Ryan?" she asked.

"Fine, ma—uh, Commander."

"You already yelled at him for saying 'ma'am,' didn't you?" Max murmured.

"It's good for him. Okay, you look like shit, but you'll survive. Let's get to the Docking Bay and get you two on the FRC. I've been here all of fifteen minutes and I hate this station."

"Probably going to have to fight our way out of here," Max said.

"That's fine. I need to kick someone's ass for fucking up my vacation, and I don't think I'm allowed to fight Admiral Chen."

EIGHTEEN

"COMMANDER CARMICHAEL, CAPTAIN NIER WITH THE FRC *OMAR Tazi*. We are almost to the Docking Bay location, what's your situation?"

"Good to hear from you, Captain. We ran into a bit of trouble. Be advised that SEAL Team Seven, with the exception of Lieutenant Ewan Ryan, is hostile. Three of them are dead outside the station somewhere. Captain Giroux is on station, and location of Petty Officer Lee is unknown but suspected with the shuttle."

"Explains why we lost contact," Nier replied. "Thanks, Commander, I'm passing it along to Ground Control. Is Senior Chief Khan with you?"

"She is and uninjured. Can you take all our passengers?"

"It'll be a squeeze, but we'll make it work."

"All right, we're headed to the Docking Bay now. Expecting resistance."

"Noted, we may be able to help with that. It'll make a mess, though."

"At this point, I think we've got bigger things to worry about," Max replied. She was still worrying the issue of the bombs over in her head, trying to figure out why Willis hadn't just detonated them shortly after taking over the MOS.

"Hey, Jenks, what happens if you blow up Engineering?"

Jenks glanced across Ryan. Despite his protests that he was fine, he was leaning on both of them as they made their way down the stairs to the third level.

Well, he was leaning on Max. Jenks had her arm around his waist and was holding him up.

"Large boom at the base if we're talking about a reasonable amount of explosives. Really would depend on what you were trying to do," she replied after a moment's thought. "Station would lose power, life support, the works. It wouldn't really disintegrate, though the structural integrity would be toasted. Possibly snapped in half? Eventually it would get sucked out of orbit by Mars's gravity without the thrusters making adjustments." She made a face. "It would probably break up in the atmosphere, but there'd still be some chunks big enough to cause some damage, depending on where they landed. The engine core with all the reinforcements would likely survive, even if the explosion was nearby. Do I even ask why you want to know?"

"They were lasering a hole down into Engineering."

"Because you locked it down with the command codes," Jenks said, and Max nodded. "It makes sense, that's the fastest way to get to it when you don't have access."

"Would you really have to laser down, though? The bombs they had were not small. Couldn't they just detonate them above the engine and get the same result?"

"That's more of a Tamago question, to be honest, but maybe?"

"What if they wanted your codes for a different reason?" Ryan asked suddenly.

"Like what?" Max asked.

"If they had your codes, they would be able to change the station's trajectory, fire thrusters, all sorts of things."

"You can't fly a station like a ship, LT."

"No, but you could crash it somewhere specific," he replied to Jenks's protest.

"What, like the construction yard? Or on the ground, I guess, though that's like slingshotting a ball at someone on the other side of a city—you could hit them if you did enough math ahead of time, but why make all the effort?"

Max frowned, then she stopped and held up a hand. "Table that. You two stay here." She eased open the door and slipped into the hallway.

She heard the sounds of combat before she reached the Docking Bay. "Captain Nier?"

"Right here, Commander."

"Evacuees are under fire at bay forty-three. Once you get docked can you bring your rail gun around and point it at these coordinates?"

"Can do, give us a minute."

It was hard to tell from the sounds of the fighting, but Max thought Saqib and the others were holding their own. She sprinted back to the stairwell. "Combat ahead; let's get the LT here under some cover, Jenks, and then you and I can make poor life choices."

Jenks laughed at her while Ryan looked vaguely horrified.

They found a spot for him to tuck his lanky frame behind and Max queued up her com.

"SAQIB, YOU COPY?"

He took a shot at a hijacker and ducked back down behind cover. "Yup. We're a little occupied here."

"So we see."

"We?"

"'Sup, Lieutenant Commander. Heard you got yourself free, though it looks like you landed right back in trouble again," Jenks said.

"You bring me some backup, Senior Chief?"

"I brought me, that counts."

"I thought you were bringing SEALs. I'd ask how you pissed them off before you even got here, but we all know the answer."

"In my defense they tried to kill me first. That's what happens when you trust Navy. Have everyone cover their heads, Saqib." Jenks's voice rose. "Hey, Ella, try harder next time!"

"Everyone down!" Saqib had learned quickly that while Jenks often seemed to be a chaotic entity, she rarely did things without a good reason. And this was no different.

Her challenge distracted the force assaulting them, turning their focus to the pair of Neos standing out in the open on the far side of the Docking Bay. Saqib heard a garbled response as a number of them rushed toward the senior chief.

Unfortunately for the hijackers, Max and Jenks were standing in front of the Fast Response Cutter *Omar Tazi*, and several well-placed rail gun slugs slammed into the very space the hijackers were running toward.

Saqib grabbed for Lia, ducking even lower as the debris flew overhead, some of it slamming into their cover with enough force to send them sliding several meters back.

"Talk to me, people!" he yelled. "Everyone okay?"

A chorus of affirmatives echoed back.

"Saqib, you're clear. They're retreating," Max said. "Stay low and behind cover."

"Copy that, Commander. We're moving now." He spun his hand in the air. "Move for the ship. Stay low, people; keep your eyes peeled."

Saqib had realized upon his arrival to the Docking Bay that he was the ranking officer, and had broken their group up into smaller units. He'd placed the military people who had weapons in the groups, and now they were able to herd their civilian charges toward the rescue ship with relatively seamless precision.

"How are you doing?" he asked Seo-Yoon as Lia helped the woman to her feet, and the three of them started for the ship. Saqib kept his eyes and the fléchette gun in his hands pointed toward the still smoking area that was currently being sprayed by the station's fire system.

"I've had better days," she replied, waving a hand at Max.

He spotted Jenks ushering a SEAL onto the FRC, despite the man's protests. "You hush, LT, and sit your ass down. Stab wound—we slapped a heal patch on it and he's had pain meds. Probably bleeding internally, but I didn't have the time to do a good check," she said to a nearby medic.

"This one, too," Saqib said as he helped Seo-Yoon sit down next to Lieutenant Ryan. "Jenks."

She slipped an arm around his waist in a quick hug. "I'd say it's good to see you, but I should be on vacation."

"I'll make it up to you."

"So everyone keeps telling me. At this rate you all are going to have to survive without me for six months, and I'll be honest, I don't think you can."

"Jenks, get them out of here!" Max's sudden cry was punctured by the sound of fléchette rounds slamming into the side of the ship, followed by a second, larger explosion. More cries erupted into the air as the last of the civilians scrambled for the ship.

"Found the SEAL ship," Captain Nier deadpanned. "We need to launch now. We're too exposed here."

Saqib was right behind Jenks, headed for the exit, but she caught him in the chest with the palm of her hand and shoved him back onto the ship. "Get the rest of these civvies on board, then close the goddamned door and go now!" Jenks ordered, and even though he wanted to point out she couldn't order him to do anything, Saqib didn't argue. He hustled the remaining people onto the FRC then boarded himself.

The door slid shut, and he watched helplessly as Jenks ran toward the fight, sword in hand.

RALKA CRASHED INTO MAX LIKE AN ASTEROID HITTING A PLANET, knocking her gun out of her hands and driving Max backward into a storage container.

"Jenks, get them out of here!"

Fléchettes whirred through the air, and the screams of civilians followed after. Max punched Ralka twice in the head, knocking the woman aside enough to give her the space to wiggle free.

"Commander, we have to go. The SEAL shuttle is firing on us." Nier's voice was cool over the com.

"Do it," she grunted, blocking one of Ralka's wild swings but missing the other as it drove into her stomach. "Get out of here."

Max turned just enough, dodging so that Ralka's next punch hit the pack with her suit that Jenks had given her, and she heard the woman swear viciously.

I hope you broke your hand on that, she thought with grim satisfaction as she shook free of the pack and tossed it to the side. "Come on then, if you're set on doing this."

Max backed up, hands raised, as Ralka circled. This wasn't the cage; it wasn't even the semi-amusing bar fights that happened at the Boarding Games, and while she'd had her share of fights with people who were well and truly trying to kill her over the years, she already knew this was a different level.

It was personal and there was no room for error.

Ralka moved in again, and Max blocked the flurry of punches the shorter woman threw at her, feeling the jarring impact of each as the analytical part of her brain calmly cataloged it all.

Her ability to observe people, size them up within moments, and predict their moves and choices with a frightening accuracy had garnered her the reputation of being a ghost in the ring and out in the black, and was now at the forefront of a fight for her life.

372 K. B. WAGERS

Ralka could throw hits quick, but she dropped her guard entirely too much when she did. Max slapped the next punch away almost contemptuously and back-fisted Ralka with her right hand in the side of the head, sending the woman staggering.

Max ignored the sound of fléchette fire off to the side—either it would hit them or it wouldn't, and she couldn't afford to take her eyes off Ralka for a second.

The woman rushed forward, fists raised, and this time Max didn't dodge. Instead, she braced herself and kicked, hitting Ralka square in the chest. The hijacker flew back, crashing into a rack with enough force to domino it into several others.

"Max, drop!"

She obeyed Jenks's call without question and Captain Giroux's sword sliced harmlessly through the air where she'd been standing. Max rolled away and bounced to her feet. "I gave you an order!"

"I'll apologize later if you want," Jenks shouted back, tossing her sword at Max. Then she tackled Ella, the force of the impact sending the SEAL's sword spinning across the deck.

JENKS RACED AWAY FROM THE FRC, SWORD IN HAND, STOPPING only to scoop up the fléchette gun lying on the deck. She dropped her sword as she went to a knee behind a stack of boxes, sighting and picking off the targets one at a time.

She could hear the sounds of Max fighting someone and spotted Captain Giroux working her way around to the noise. Jenks fired her last few fléchettes at the SEAL, forcing Ella behind cover.

"You know, we could talk about this," Jenks called. "Seems like a shit way to end a career. Sure you don't want to surrender?"

"Fuck you," Ella snarled back. "What the fuck do you know?"

"I know you swore an oath, same as me." Jenks threw the gun to the side and scrambled to her feet, sword in hand. She tapped it on the box as she stepped into the open. "Look me in the face and tell me what's worth breaking your word, Captain."

Ella stood. "I'd rather put my sword through your throat."

Jenks rolled her shoulders with a sigh. "All right, give it a try, then."

She deflected Ella's first thrust, dancing back from the taller woman with Nika's words about getting to know your opponent ringing in her ears.

"Watch them the same as the cage. The difference is there's a weapon in one hand, but don't get distracted by that. Use it to your advantage."

She'd gotten better over the years, but still preferred her fists to the sharp-edged sword. More, Captain Giroux was good and fucking fast.

And Jenks was stuck fighting in her space suit.

Good news was, so was the captain.

Debris and disrupted cargo, along with maintenance racks, littered the bay around them, providing a deadly field of battle. It was one Jenks was used to from her early days and one she'd insisted all of *Zuma* and the other Interceptors continue to train in.

So she was able to watch the flare of shock on Ella's face as she chucked a piece of bent pipe in the woman's direction.

Her opponent ducked to avoid it, which put her at a disadvantage when Jenks moved in.

Apparently, SEALs didn't adhere to the same vigorous standards NeoG did.

Ella barely blocked Jenks's sword, grunting with the effort as Jenks put all her weight to bear on her. But the captain wasn't some untried lieutenant—she had the experience of years and shifted to the side just enough to let both swords come slamming down.

Jenks managed to lean out of the way, avoiding the worst of the headbutt that followed, and Ella's head struck her shoulder instead, throwing her off-balance.

Jenks rolled, kicking a mobile rack and sending it sliding into the SEAL with enough force to knock Ella backward. It bought her the time to get to her feet.

Ella stumbled back a few steps before she caught herself and thrust the rack back in Jenks's direction, forcing her to scramble over a nearby box. She landed on her feet, backing into the more open area of the Docking Bay with a slow smile. "I bet Lieutenant Ryan fights better than this."

"You should have tested it on the ground. I was really hoping you hit him a time or six."

"You stopped me. Besides, he's not a bad sort—for either an LT or Navy. At least he's not a traitor."

Ella's eyes narrowed. "Lie to yourself all you want. We both know you'd burn the world down if something happened to your family."

"Maybe or maybe I'd just get some fucking therapy so I didn't hurt innocent people."

Ella barked a laugh. "There's no such thing."

"Therapy?"

"Innocent people."

Jenks ducked under Ella's rushing attack, sidestepping and slicing her sword across the woman's side. The white fabric of her suit separated under the matte black edge and blood bloomed in its wake.

Jenks kicked her in the back of the knee, sending Ella stumbling forward with a curse of pain on her lips. She knew she should attack, press her advantage, but Jenks couldn't bring herself to stab the woman in the back.

"The irony that you're the honorable one," Ella said with a laugh, pressing her left hand to the wound as she straightened.

There was a loud crash. Ella looked to her right. Jenks's view was blocked by a rack, and she had to dodge to the side when the SEAL pushed it in her direction and ran. Jenks raced across the deck after her. Max was several meters ahead, watching Ralka struggle out from the rubble, unaware of the hostile bearing down on her.

"Max, drop!"

Years of long practice had her commander, her friend, her sister moving instinctively, and Giroux's strike whistled harmlessly over her head.

"I gave you an order!" Max shouted as she leaped back onto her feet.

"I'll apologize later if you want!" Jenks flipped her sword to her fellow Neo as she passed, then crashed into Ella.

Jenks rolled free with a groan, pleased that it took Ella longer to get to her feet. As weird as it might have sounded, it immediately felt like she was fighting in the cage once the sword was gone. Everything was clear as the lake she'd been looking forward to swimming in with the kids.

She also wasn't distracted by anger. Instead she had the razor-sharp focus of a fight she wasn't going to lose. Couldn't afford to lose because she'd promised to come home—to Luis, to Tivo, to her kids. Probably to Nika, too, if she thought about it. She didn't have time for that now, though, as Jenks blocked Ella's wild punch, hooking her arm around the hijacker's neck and bringing her down into her knee hard.

Ella got two punches with her free hand to Jenks's kidney, the force enough to make her let go and spin to the side to reassess the situation. She barely had time to block the back kick, muttering a curse as the force of it rocked through her own leg.

A glance over told her Max and Ralka had collided again in the background, the hijacker kicking Max's sword from her hand before she could get a good swing in and following up with a punch to her ribs that had Jenks wincing.

Focus, you need to focus.

The warning came just in time, fueled by instinct or self-preservation. Either way it was enough for Jenks to catch Ella's fist before it made contact with her head and direct it past her. She stepped into her opponent as she moved, bringing her left hand up hard into the woman's throat. In the cage it would have been a light tap.

This wasn't the cage.

She felt the trachea give under the force of her strike, and Ella dropped, both hands grasping at her ruined throat.

Jenks backed up a step, hands loose, as the woman pitched forward onto the deck. Her own breath was loud in her ears and regret rolled in her stomach.

"Fucking waste," she muttered and turned to Max.

THERE WAS NO TIME FOR MAX TO HELP JENKS. RALKA HAD GOT-
ten to her feet and kicked Jenks's sword from her hand before she'd even fully contemplated her next move, and Max
was forced to stagger backward out of range of the spinning
second kick that followed.

"You think you're so smart, NeoG," she spat. "I'm going
to kill you and then your friend there, and your corpses can
join me when we slam into Serrano and show everyone the
real meaning of war."

"If you're as good a fighter as your brother, I have nothing to worry about. I've had better fights from brand-new
Neos," she snarled.

Whatever sanity might have been left in the woman disappeared, and Ralka charged, all fury and no strategy.

Max, though, was calm as she grabbed Ralka, using her
momentum to throw her into the bulkhead. The woman's
head connected but she didn't go down, and so Max kneed
her in the face hard enough that the crunch of her broken
nose echoed in the bay.

"And now it fucking ends," she said—unsure if it was
a mutter, a whisper, a shout, or just something in her own
head—as she slammed Ralka's head into the wall a second
time. And then a third. She felt the woman go limp, but
didn't stop.

Someone grabbed her from behind, and Max swung
without looking. Jenks's startled "Damn it, Max, it's me!"
was barely enough to get through the haze of fury wrapped
around her.

She shook herself free and started forward again, only
to be blocked by Jenks's upraised hand.

"You back off, she's down."

"She's not dead!"

"Max, *back off.*" Jenks's voice was soft, but the order was clear, even though she had no right to give it and Max had no reason to obey.

No reason beyond that this was her friend, her sister, and they both knew she was right. Max staggered back a step, struggling to get air into her lungs as she went to her knees.

Jenks moved to Ralka's unconscious form, cuffing the woman's hands behind her back before returning to Max. "You okay?" she murmured.

"No." Max couldn't have stopped the tears even if she'd wanted. "I'm sorry."

"Don't worry about it," Jenks said, even though the tone of her voice clearly said she was worrying. "Get your feet under you, okay? I'll grab our stuff."

Max couldn't look away from Ralka as she dragged in one painful breath after another. She heard Jenks collecting their swords and the pack with her suit, the metallic creak of rubble settling in the bay, and her own heart beating out a rapid pace.

Suddenly she felt very empty, and Max sagged back on her heels with a sob.

"Max, hey, look at me. Look at me."

Jenks's face was blurred by tears, and Max had to blink several times before they scattered free. "I—"

"You saved a whole bunch of people," Jenks said softly as if she knew exactly what was rolling around in Max's head. "I want you to repeat it."

"I saved a whole bunch of people," Max whispered. That felt like a lie, or rather she couldn't stop seeing all the faces of the people she'd killed in the process. She must have made some kind of noise because Jenks tightened her arm around her waist and urged her to her feet.

"I know, Max, believe me. But I need you to get up. I promised my kids I'd come home and I'm not leaving without you. Keep moving for me, okay? We need to figure out how to get off this station because I am not riding it to the ground."

I don't understand how some of these bastards are perfectly cool with riding this station down to the planet.

. . . you could crash it somewhere specific.

. . . when we slam into Serrano . . .

"Saint Ivan protect us," Max murmured as she staggered to a stop, her previous thoughts about the station crashing collided with everything else.

"What? What is it?"

"I can't believe I didn't say something before, I was— they're going to crash the MOS into Serrano. That's what Willis was waiting for, the right angle, the right moment. Fire the thrusters. He needs to be in Engineering to access the computers there."

"I thought they were going to blow it up."

"They weren't planning on detonating the bombs until just before the station hit the planet. You said the engine core would probably survive reentry."

Jenks stared at her in horror. "It would obliterate the city."

"It would cover the world in ash."

"Motherf . . . We've got to tell Ground Control."

Max was already digging in her bag. "Please don't be broken." She pulled the tablet out with a triumphant cry and spun on her heel, looking for a nearby connection.

"Over there," Jenks said.

Max slid to a stop at the top of the ramp, whispering a second prayer of thanks that the Docking Bay consoles had been ignored in the sweep by Willis's people—if the coms were up, she didn't even need her tablet. "Sapphi? Anyone copy? They're not blowing up the MOS, they're planning on crashing it into—"

The station suddenly went completely and utterly dark and silent.

Peace Talks Fail as CHN Walks Back Offer

JANUARY 23, 2442 (ESD)

The most recent peace negotiations between the Coalition of Human Nations representatives and Free Mars leader Sylvia Moroz collapsed under their own weight today when it became known that the CHN would not be honoring the previously discussed offer of "governance on the ground" for the people of Mars.

Instead it was revealed today that the CHN is only willing to extend the same offer they have come to with Trappist— that is, the people of Mars would have elected representatives sitting within the Senate. Not true independence as had been previously discussed.

Moroz rejected the offer out of hand, stating, "What Trappist chooses to do is on them. Mars deserves, after all these years, the same benefits accorded to the peoples of her sister planet in the Sol system. The people of Mars should have their own government, not one beholden to Earth, set on Earth's schedule, and ultimately only concerned with the problems of Earth." [Read More]

NINETEEN

NIKA'S HEART STOPPED, THEN RESTARTED WITH A PAINFUL lurch, and he tightened his grip on the back of Sapphi's chair as he stared at the blank screen where just a moment before the MOS readouts had been.

The room around them was so quiet he could hear Sapphi's quiet prayer. "Freya's mercy, please no."

He forced himself to say the words. "Is it gone?"

"I don't know," she replied, and her fingers flew over the light keys. Then she shook her head, shoulders sagging in relief. "It's still there. I'm getting satellite pings. From what I can see, there's no power. Lupe, did the whole station just go down?"

"It did," he replied. "I don't know why."

"Captain Nier, hold on a second," Sapphi said. "Okay, you're live. Nika's here."

She appeared on-screen and Nika spotted Saqib standing next to her. "Commander," Nier said. "I have the hostages on board."

"Where are Commander Carmichael and the senior chief?" The relief he'd felt vanished when Saqib shook his head.

"Still on station," he said softly.

"Do you have eyes on the station, Captain Nier?"

She frowned at the question but nodded. "We do. What do you need?"

"As far as we can tell it went offline." He was pleased he managed to keep his voice level. "Visual confirmation the MOS is still intact is helpful."

"It is, Commander." There was understanding sympathy in her eyes. "I'll see if we can raise anyone on coms from here, give you a moment with the lieutenant commander."

Saqib waited a beat as the woman moved away. "Nika, I've got Lieutenant Ryan with the SEAL team you sent; his team turned on him and Jenks when they hit the station. They attacked us along with the hostiles on board as we were trying to evac." In a smooth voice he filled Nika in on what had happened.

They hadn't gotten on the ship; he was going to— Nika closed his eyes and dragged a breath in through his nose.

"What the fuck?" Sapphi's curse filled the air. "Sorry, Nik, the MOS is back on."

"Hang on." He held up a hand to Saqib and looked at her. "Excuse me?"

"Everything is back." She gestured at the screen. "I'm locked out of coms again. Lupe, what in Zeus's unfaithful ass just happened?" She looked across at him, brown eyes wide. "Did they just turn it off and on again?"

"I didn't realize they could do that, but yeah, I think so?"

"Sapphi, I need to know what's going on," Nika said.

"I don't know," she responded. "Somehow those bastards reset the MOS."

"God help us." That exclamation came from Grady as he crossed to them. "If they did a manual reset, they'll have access to Engineering."

Sapphi snapped her fingers. "Max said they were cutting through the floor. She assumed because of the bombs and maybe that's right, but they were also trying to physically get into Engineering. To get to the reset. So they could regain control of the station?"

Nika tried to follow the rapid-fire conversation, but he felt like he was missing something. "They're locked out, though. Between Max's codes and what these two have done, they don't have access."

Grady shook his head. "No longer applicable. There's a manual reset in Engineering. It's for extreme emergencies because you run the risk of destabilizing the orbit. I can't think of a single time it's been used. Because you also lose everything—power, life support, gravity, the works." His face was pale, and his voice dropped to a whisper. "This is of the highest level of security, Commander. A manual reset would give them control again. It's set up as a fail-safe. It's just dangerous to do, because there's so much risk in not getting everything up in time."

"Before what?"

"Before it all comes tumbling down," Grady replied.

Sapphi turned back to the keys, and Nika knew her brain was already spinning faster than the MOS around the planet as she pieced everything together. It would have been a glorious thing to watch if he wasn't so terrified for the two women up on the station itself. "We wondered what they were waiting for? They were waiting for this."

The image of the planet appeared on the screen in front of them, a blinking green dot that was the MOS traveling in real time around it. A dotted red line appeared on the path ahead, tracking down to the surface.

"They're not just crashing the station into the planet. They're going to try to crash the station into Serrano," Sapphi whispered.

Nika's first impulse was to run for the dock. Not to save himself, but to get out there and get Max and Jenks off the MOS. His second impulse was the cold logic of his duty, and it was the one he had to follow.

Because this news meant that the time they had to shoot the station down had just shrank dramatically.

"I need coms back up, Sapphi. Both for the MOS and for D'Arcy. Whatever you have to do to make it happen, do it. And send a message to Admiral Chen that we're now on phase three, and I need to talk to the ships that are up there ready to fire. Captain Clark?"

"Right here."

"Get your people out of here."

"We can't evac the city, Nika," she replied.

"I know." He clenched his fists. "We can get some people out, so do it."

TAMAGO FROWNED AT THE SCREEN IN FRONT OF THEM. SOME OF the chaos had died down but the room still buzzed with activity. They could hear Nika issuing orders in the background and Sapphi and Grady in a rapid-fire conversation, but they weren't really paying attention to the words until they heard Sapphi say: ". . . crash the station into Serrano."

The whole room froze and Tamago dragged their attention away from the file, heart pounding.

Nika's face was terrifyingly blank, and Tamago could only guess at the pain he must be feeling as he ordered Captain Clark to evac. They turned toward Kenta, the demand to stay put in their mouth, when he shook his head.

"We're not going anywhere, Tamago. Do you have anything we can use to try to talk them out of this?"

"Hale, no." They shook their head. "But . . . look at this? Castle's parents were killed in an explosion not long after she watched us in the Games. I'd asked D'Arcy about it, and he admitted that it was rare but not unheard of for these attacks to happen so recently. What both of us missed, though, was that the explosion didn't happen on Mars. Castle's parents live on Earth; the explosion happened at a restaurant near where they lived on the New East Coast of North America. None of the other dead had ties to the CHN or the NeoG or anything that would make them a target for Free Mars."

Shock slid across Kenta's face. "Are you suggesting that Hale was responsible?"

"Yeah, I am. I have zero proof, but Castle was already making waves at school with her programming skills, even though she was only in her second year. If I wanted to take over a space station, I'd want someone with that kind of ability. I double-checked the files for all the people involved; Castle's parents are the most recent deaths. Everyone else lost someone well before that and here on Mars."

"You're not going to convince her without proof, Tama."

"What if the doubt is enough?" they countered. "What if it's enough to get her to lock down Engineering again? I have to try, my friends are up there." They struggled to keep their voice from breaking, knew they'd failed at the flash of sympathy on Kenta's face, but the man nodded.

"Come on," he said. "We need somewhere more quiet for this. Nika," he called as he strode for Captain Clark's office. "Tamago thinks they might be able to get through to Castle."

Nika's eyes found theirs and he nodded. "All right, whatever you need to do, you'd better make it quick."

They were running out of time.

CASTLE KEPT HER EYES AWAY FROM THE STREAK OF RED FROM where Willis had dragged Charlie's body out of the office, even though the smell of blood and death slithered relentlessly into her nostrils.

"Castle, focus." Willis snapped his fingers in front of her face. "Look at me. Our people on the ground are in position. We're almost done here. What's our trajectory?"

She turned back to the console and swallowed hard. "We're looking good, coming up on the drop point zone. Those guys in Engineering need to get a move on or we'll miss the window."

He smiled and patted her cheek. "We're not going to miss the window. We'll have our justice—for your parents, for my husband. I'm headed for Engineering. You finish up here and get to the shuttle."

"Okay." Castle watched him go. The hard reset of the station had worked exactly as Willis had said it would, undoing all Sapphi's hard work to keep her out of essential systems and obliterating Commander Carmichael's lockdown.

Castle wondered if they'd figured out the plan on the ground. Her stomach twisted a bit. Willis had insisted that crashing the station into Serrano was a necessary message, and at the time she'd agreed to do this, she'd still been so angry at the world.

Now she couldn't help but think about all those people on the ground, just going about their lives, completely unaware that it was the last moments they'd ever have. Just like her parents.

The warning buzz of an incoming com made her jerk in surprise, and Castle hit the button before she realized that was probably a bad idea.

"Castle, don't disconnect," Tamago said, a hand raised. "Are you alone?"

"Yeah, Willis headed for Engineering several minutes ago."

"We need to talk."

"Nothing left to talk about." She started to turn away. She still had to get Willis's message sent to the news lines and scrub the SEAL shuttle from the registry.

"Your parents weren't killed by Free Mars. Willis had them killed so he could recruit you."

Castle's heart stopped beating, then lurched back into motion. "What?"

"He needed someone smart enough to be able to hack into the station systems. He knew he couldn't send just anyone toe-to-toe against people like Sapphi, he needed someone amazing—he found you." Tamago shook their head. "But you had a family and a life. So the only way he could get you to agree to this was to take it all from you."

"You're lying."

"What reason do I have to lie to you? We've got two Navy

carriers with orders to destroy the station. This grand plan of Willis's isn't going to happen, and you're all going to die."

"You won't blow this place up with your people on board."

"They're not on board anymore, Castle. Most of them were evac'd, and the ones who are left . . . well, they know their duty."

"Why are you even telling me this?" Her mind raced, trying to figure out what possible angle Tamago wanted. They'd known the carriers were a possibility; Willis had said as much, but he'd been certain they would be able to crash the station before that happened. That he could stall them just long enough.

"I'm trying to save lives. Yours, the people on the ground, *my friends*. Castle, it doesn't have to end like this. You can help. I know the systems are all back up and I know you can lock them out of Engineering from there. You can also talk to Max and Jenks, tell them where Willis is."

Castle worried at her lower lip with her teeth. "They won't trust me."

Tamago smiled. "Tell Jenks she doesn't get to die without buying me that real chicken dinner she owes me. They'll handle the rest."

The entire station shook and Castle grabbed for the console. "Too late," she whispered. "Feels like they just fired the thrusters and changed course. I'm sorry."

"Castle—"

"I can't do anything from here to fix it. All the controls are in Engineering." She shook her head. "I have to go." Castle disconnected the com. The shuttle would leave without her, and for all that she missed her parents, she wasn't ready to die.

Her parents . . . Had Willis really killed them?

She exhaled sharply, trying to ignore the incredibly foolish part of her that wanted to take the lift down to Engineering and ask him. That wouldn't solve anything and had about a 99.9 percent probability of ending in her death.

"Fuck," she muttered and reached for the com again. It was easy enough to pinpoint the DD of Senior Chief Khan and establish a direct link. "Senior Chief, this is Dri Castle . . ."

SYLVIA'S JAW STILL WORKED AND SHE WAS SUPREMELY TEMPTED to bite Mikhail as he pulled her from the car, but she also didn't want to get dropped on her head so she kept her teeth together as he carried her up a short flight of stairs.

She couldn't see anything but the black material of his shirt until he set her gently on the floor, bracing her up against a stack of boxes. There was sorrow in the big man's dark eyes as he backed away, and she hated that it made her own heart twist.

"Why?" Her limbs wouldn't work, but her voice had never once failed her. "We're so close to peace after all these years. Why are you doing this?"

"This isn't peace." He shook his head. "After everything we've been through, all the people who've died for you. Like Luca did. How am I supposed to watch you betray them all? No. Better to end this now. Start over from the ashes."

Luca. It burned, how many faces she had to shuffle through on her DD until the young woman's smile appeared. Sylvia had long ago given up keeping track of all the people she'd lost over the years, her own memory filled with everything else and her sanity begging for relief from the endless grief of burying friend after friend.

But Mikhail was wrong: None of them had died for her. They'd died for Mars.

"How is peace a betrayal?" she whispered. "How is giving Mars a chance to live without more war worse than adding more dead to the pile? This was never about me, Mikhail, it was always about freedom for all of us. Peace means learning to walk away from the past, not dragging its bloody carcass with us into the new day."

His face twisted in pain.

"Mikhail—"

The blow to the side of her head knocked her to the ground and Sylvia was only dimly aware of Mikhail's shouted protest as someone grabbed her by the back of the neck and hauled her upright.

"The Butcher of Mars." The man who sneered at her had an active handshake that read *Jarvis Boehm, he/him.* She didn't recognize him, but the moniker was all too indicative of the NeoG's attempts to smear her reputation in the years after the protests. "Do you have any idea how many times I dreamed about this?"

"I'm sure you're going to tell me." Weak people always wanted to convince themselves of their own greatness.

As such, the slap was expected and Sylvia spat the blood that welled up in her mouth back at him. Jarvis dropped her with a curse, and Sylvia thankfully landed on her shoulder rather than face-first onto the red concrete floor.

Something told her she would be less pleased once the feeling came back, but as the sounds of fléchette fire and more shouting echoed through the warehouse, she realized that was the least of her problems.

Never mind the fact that her lungs picked *now* to protest,

and she tried to keep her breathing steady through the sharp tightness.

Jarvis lunged for her with a snarl, only to be tackled from behind by Mikhail, the two men crashing over the top of her and into the boxes behind.

D'ARCY'S HEART WAS THUMPING DOUBLE-TIME IN HIS CHEST AS he reached through the lower window into the warehouse and laid the fléchette gun gently on the floor before angling his shoulders and crawling through. No coms meant timing this whole thing was iffy at best, but he couldn't stand by and do nothing with Sylvia's life potentially hanging in the balance.

Clair had wanted to be the one to go in, and although it would have been far easier for them to work their narrow shoulders through the frame, D'Arcy knew they'd work with Maria better on the distraction of an assault without coms.

He stayed low, scooping the fléchette gun off the floor and working his way around to the sound of the voices. He was halfway there when he spotted the towering pile of containers in the center of the warehouse and his breath left his lungs in a rush.

There were at least a dozen containers of liquid metallic hydrogen he could see buried among various other boxes and crates of explosive and flammable materials. "Fuck." If this went up, it would devastate a large chunk of Serrano, kill hundreds of thousands of people.

Except nothing here was big enough to ignite it . . . unless there was something he wasn't seeing buried under all of it.

Or above it.

The horrific thought was interrupted by the shouts and the ensuing firefight. D'Arcy spotted Mikhail on the ground, the ring of people who turned to meet Maria and Clair's assault, and through their legs—Sylvia laying on her side.

He raced across the warehouse as Jarvis turned back to her, but before D'Arcy could reach them, Mikhail launched himself from the ground at the former Neo, sending them both flying into the stack of crates behind Sylvia.

D'Arcy wasted no time now, skidding up next to Sylvia, scooping her over his shoulder, and taking off for the nearest cover. She smacked him weakly as he lowered her to the ground, looking surprised when her hand connected with his chest.

"Drug's wearing off," she murmured, voice thready. "I need . . . my inhaler, left pocket."

"I've got you, hold on." He fished it out and held it up for her as she took a deep inhale. "Good?"

"Yes. Mikhail?"

"He was tangling with Jarvis—I didn't stick around to see who came out on top. What did he shoot you up with?"

"Some sort of limited nerve blocker? I'm starting to get feeling back, and apparently some movement. Sorry, I didn't mean to hit you. Where are Maria and Clair?"

D'Arcy jerked his head back toward the sound of the gunfight. "Causing a distraction so I could find you."

"That's a terrible plan."

"Yeah, well. Better than Clair rushing in and getting their ass killed." D'Arcy rested his gun on the edge of a crate and watched as a hostile dropped to the floor. He couldn't see Clair or Maria, so he hoped it meant Emel had figured out what was going on.

Suddenly his com sprang to life again and Chaske's soothing voice was in his ear. "Commander."

"Talk to me," D'Arcy replied.

"Not even a 'hi, how are you?'"

"Not now—"

"Are you in the middle of this ruckus?" his lieutenant commander asked.

"I don't know where else you'd expect me to be." He took a few shots and sent people scattering.

"You should hear Emel swearing in my other ear," Chaske replied dryly. "I don't know why she didn't just call you directly."

"This wasn't my fault."

"We're almost there."

"Good—hey, no heavy ordnance. There are entirely too many things in this building that go boom." He could hear Sylvia on her com, voice as calm as always, as she assured Maria she was unharmed.

"I've got a lock on your location; I'm sending Scott your way."

It took D'Arcy a long moment, and seeing the figure of Max's brother, before he realized Nika had let the rear admiral participate in the retrieval.

"Your lieutenant commander made me carry the med kit like a new guy," Scott said cheerfully as he slid to a stop near them. "Sylvia, what do you need?"

"You got anything in there that will give me the feeling in my legs back?" she countered.

"Probably, but that's outside of my area of expertise to be honest."

"That figures."

D'Arcy let them banter while he listened to the chatter on the coms and kept an eye out. Part of him wanted to join the assault, go find out what had happened to Mikhail and Jarvis, but he also didn't want to leave Sylvia alone.

"Rona, come here," he called to the petty officer when he spotted her ducking around a low wall. "You stay here, keep an eye on these two. Shoot anyone that moves in on you."

"Will do," she replied, settling easily into his position.

"Where are you going?" Sylvia demanded.

"To find Jarvis, if he's still alive. I want answers." He broke cover, heading back toward where he'd found Sylvia. On the other side of the boxes, he found a pool of blood, but no bodies. D'Arcy stayed low and followed the trail away from the firefight.

He found the pair grappling near an open door. Mikhail was a big man, but Jarvis clearly matched him in strength despite the bloody wound in his shoulder.

"Should have known this was a setup," Jarvis hollered, punching Mikhail twice in the head. "Should have known the NeoG would sink to working with Free Mars, just like Willis said. Neither of you deserve this planet after everything you've done."

D'Arcy couldn't get a clean shot off, not without the possibility of shooting Mikhail—which, for some reason, he wasn't keen to do—so he fired a shot just past Jarvis. Enough to distract him as D'Arcy asked, "So your boss's big plan is to drop the station on Serrano and kill a bunch of innocent people? That's what you call deserving?"

"Boom." Jarvis's eyes were bright with malicious glee. "Wipe out Free Mars and the biggest NeoG presence on the planet in one fell swoop. Gotta sacrifice some of us for the greater good."

"No, no more," Mikhail gritted out and he drove Jarvis backward into the wall. D'Arcy saw the knife in Jarvis's hand as Mikhail twisted it back on the man and used his own bulk to slide it into Jarvis's chest.

D'Arcy muttered a curse as the man dropped to the floor. Mikhail took a step back, turned and dropped to his knees, a hand pressed to his chest high on the left side to the wound D'Arcy hadn't seen. He coughed, blood spattering to the floor.

"Hang on for me," D'Arcy demanded as he went to a knee next to Mikhail. D'Arcy kept one eye on Jarvis, but the man's green eyes were staring sightlessly at the ceiling, so he turned his full attention to Mikhail.

"No good. It's fine." Mikhail coughed and spat blood in Jarvis's direction. "I fucked up."

"Why?"

Mikhail shook his head. "Tell Sylvia . . . I'm sorry, I—" He exhaled and fell forward into D'Arcy.

D'Arcy pressed his forehead to the crown of Mikhail's head with a deep sigh. "Goodbye, my friend," he whispered and lowered the man's body to the floor.

"D'Arcy, warehouse is secure," Chaske said.

"Copy that. I'm headed to you."

Dragging in a breath, D'Arcy strode across the warehouse back to Sylvia. The ping of the incoming call and the sight of Nika's contact information sent a rush of relief through him.

"D'Arcy, do you copy?"

"There you are. What the f— Nika, we're in a bit of a situation here. Mikhail kidnapped Sylvia, and we are currently holed up in a warehouse full of liquid metallic hydrogen. Pretty sure Hale's trying to crash the MOS into it."

"How much?" Nika didn't even pause, didn't sound like he was the least bit surprised.

"More than makes me comfortable," D'Arcy said. "If I were Jenks, I might say 'a shit-ton'?"

"Damn. Do you have Sylvia?"

"I do, she's shaken up but unharmed. Got dosed with some sort of external nerve blocker. It's still wearing off."

"Chaske and several others are headed your way. You should be able to get in touch." He dragged in a breath audible over the com. "You're right. They got into Engineering and reset the station."

"You can do that?"

"Apparently. Sapphi is showing a trajectory that puts the MOS down into Serrano, probably the spot where you're standing. I need you out of there—"

"We need to get this LMH out of here."

"I know, but I need you in the air. Max and Jenks are still on the station and the carriers are almost in range." The agony Nika was barely holding in check cut through D'Arcy. What he didn't say—what didn't need to be said—was that Nika wouldn't be going anywhere. "How much time do I have?"

"Thirty-five minutes."

"All right, tell Lupe to spin up *Dread* and come get us. I'll figure out something here. Nika . . ."

"Yeah?"

There were too many things he wanted to say, none of it on an open com in the middle of a firefight. "I'll see you after."

TWENTY

"WHAT IS GOING ON?" MAX GRABBED FOR JENKS, ANCHORING them both against the console as their feet left the floor.

"Gravity is off," she replied. "Ouch, don't pinch me."

"That is extremely obvious. Give me something better."

"*Everything* is off. We need to get you into your suit."

That time Max knew it wasn't Jenks being sarcastic. If the gravity was off, then life support likely was also. Though with the amount of air on the station, they'd have a little time before it was an issue.

The power kicked back on, and the slight whir of the ventilation system filled the air as they both dropped back down to their feet.

"What the fuck?" Jenks muttered. "Did they just turn this can off and on again?"

"It certainly seems like it. Why?"

"Shit." Jenks's second curse was less confused, and she

tapped Max twice on the side. "Get your suit on, we'll worry about the rest in a minute."

"Should we try the coms again?" Max asked as she started getting into her suit.

Fléchettes slammed into the console next to her, and Max dove for cover one direction, Jenks going the other.

"Get into your suit," Jenks hissed. "I'll deal with this." She rolled behind a pile of scattered debris that had crashed back to the floor.

"You should have killed me when you had the chance, Carmichael." It wasn't Ralka's voice that echoed out into the air, and Max dared a peek in the shooter's direction as she scrambled back, keeping as much cover between them as possible.

It was Harro, the one she'd left alive in Secondary Coms.

"Willis doesn't need you alive anymore, Carmichael, but it would be a delight to strap you to this station and make you have to contemplate your mortality—" Harro broke off with a cry of pain and dropped to his knees.

"Monologuing and not paying attention to the fact that there were two of us. Sloppy." Jenks pulled her sword free of Harro's back and shook her head.

"Is he dead?"

"Probably."

Max wasn't going to take any chances. She kicked Harro over and stuck her sword into his heart.

"Max!"

"No, I left him alive once and he nearly shot you for it," she snarled.

The senior chief stared at her for a long moment, face unreadable, before she lifted her hands and took a step back. "Fine. Grab the gun, and then let me check your suit. I wish the range on these DDs were better," she muttered as she looked away. "This is Senior Chief Altandai Khan, anyone with the CHN read me?"

"Gun's only got a shot left." Max tossed it aside and kept one eye on their six as Jenks checked over her suit to make sure there was no damage. She tested the helmet, breathing a sigh of relief when it came up without an issue and then flowed back down exactly as it was designed to when she retracted it.

Then Jenks pulled something up on her DD, looping Max in so she could see the schematic of the station's orbit and the path toward the planet, a red line breaking off from the steady blue, trailing toward the surface.

"That's what I was afraid of," Jenks muttered. "They're gonna drop this before the time runs out on the SSOP-47. It'll already be on its way to the planet. Too close. We need— shit."

The floor under their feet shuddered, and Jenks let loose another curse, grabbing for Max and the console. "I do not like that," she announced. "What the fuck?"

"They got into Engineering."

Jenks made a face. "Shouldn't matter. They're locked out of the computers . . . unless, no, that can't be possible. How fucking stupid would that be?"

"I'd like you to think out loud all the way here. Still can't read your mind after all these years," Max prompted, and Jenks turned to her, mismatched eyes wide.

"Pretty sure that turning the station on and off again reset everything, even your lockdown. Don't ask me how or why. Though I will say for the record that if that's what happened it's a terrible security risk!" Jenks kicked a bulkhead in frustration.

Max froze. "Okay, so what's the plan?"

"Where'd you hide those detonators?"

"Engineering-level offices, in their changing room. Why?"

"We blow the station up before it reaches Serrano. If we do it before they can steer it into the planet, it's a win, yeah?"

"Okay."

"I'm going to need a little more from you than that, Commander," Jenks said with surprising formality.

"Really?"

"We're not talking about minor property damage here."

"You want me to order you to blow up the station?" Max asked with an incredulous laugh.

Jenks shrugged. "Just to cover my ass, yeah."

"Do you think your ass would need covering after that?"

"I don't want my children to learn their mom was both killed and dishonorably discharged."

And there it was. The admission that this was probably not something the two of them were going to walk away from. It was scary. Knowing she was going to die. Knowing she'd never hold Nika again. That Jenks would be torn from her family forever.

But it was also the only choice. The only thing Neos could possibly do.

We took oaths, Nika.

She hoped he'd understand. She knew, in time, he would. He'd taken the same oath.

"Fine. Turn on your DD to record." She did the same. "Senior Chief, under SSOP-47, I order you to do any and everything required to make sure that this station doesn't reach the ground of the planet below us intact. Understood?"

"Perfectly, Commander."

"COMMANDER, YOU COPY?"

D'Arcy looked up and spotted his ship. "Copy you, Lupe. Where are you thinking for boarding?"

"Not a lot of places to put her down, D'Arcy," Lupe replied. "Can you get on top of the warehouse?"

"Should be. Give me a minute and I'll let you know."

"No problem."

D'Arcy paused and looked around the building as he pinged his crew with a "round up" order.

"What is it?" Sylvia asked. She was sitting upright on a nearby cargo container—one that held only harmless textiles, thankfully—the last of the nerve blocker finally wearing off.

"I need to go." He glanced upward and then back at her. "We still have people on the station. I want you all on the trucks and out of here as fast as you can."

"Evac? What about all these people?" Clair demanded. "You're just going to leave them?"

Sylvia held up her hand and shook her head before D'Arcy could reply. "We can't evac almost four million people, Clair. We can't even announce it because all it will do is cause panic and potentially get more people killed."

"So we're just going to sit here and do nothing?"

Sylvia looked at D'Arcy with a soft smile and her next words were like she'd been in his head. "No, D'Arcy is going to go do what he does best. We are going to get these explosives clear of the city, and we're going to trust that the NeoG will do their jobs up there and keep the MOS from dropping on top of us all." She pointed at Maria. "You go with him. No, don't back talk me."

"I'm going to. My place is with you."

"Your place is somewhere safe, or at least safer than down here on the ground. I'd tell Clair to go too except—"

"You couldn't pry me away," they said.

Sylvia gestured and then held out her hand. "Please, Maria, do this for me."

D'Arcy stayed quiet as Maria embraced Sylvia and then Clair, who released her and leaned over to poke him in the chest. "Don't die up there, NeoG."

"Don't die down here, Free Mars." He pointed at the ceiling as Emel joined them. "Can we get on the roof? Lupe says that's going to be our best option for boarding."

"Access stairs, over there," she replied.

"You all go, I need to talk to Scott."

Emel nodded sharply and took off with the others as D'Arcy headed across the warehouse with Maria on his heels. "*Dread* is headed up to the station."

"Max?"

"And Jenks," D'Arcy said.

The rear admiral swallowed. "I'll stay. We need to get this stuff out of here at bare minimum. I've got two more trucks inbound; there was another warehouse nearby with haulers in the back," Scott said, pointing at the containers of liquid metallic hydrogen the Neos were carefully loading. "I realize in some ways the futility of it, but—"

"It's better than leaving it." D'Arcy lifted his hand. "Sylvia said they would help. Make sure she gets on a truck, Scott."

"I will." Scott caught D'Arcy by the arm as he turned to go. "If you can, Commander, bring my sister home."

D'Arcy bit the inside of his cheek and nodded. Then turned on his heel and sprinted for the stairs; he took them two at a time up to the roof, Maria right behind him.

She caught his hand when they hit the open air, tugging him to a stop. "Thank you, D'Arcy, for everything. I mean it. You saved Sylvia, maybe helped save Mars. It wasn't what I expected, to see you again, but I'm glad I got to before the end."

He dragged her into a hug, murmuring an apology for the overstep even as his arms closed around her. "Stop talking like we're going to die, damn it. Max and Jenks have been in worse than this and they won't leave us hanging. Come on." There was more he wanted to say, dancing on his tongue, but there wasn't time.

They headed across to where *Dread* hovered near the lip of the building with an impressive gap of less than a half a meter. D'Arcy took the jump easily and then reached back across.

"Easier if you just get out of my way," Maria said, and then cleared the jump herself when he did.

"Welcome to my ship," D'Arcy said before he forced himself to turn and head for the bridge. "Emel, get Maria into a seat. Lupe, we're in—let's go." He grabbed for the roll bar as the door closed and they headed for the black.

Just hang on you two. He sent the thought winging out in the stars along with his ship. *We're coming for you.*

THEY RAN DOWN THE CORRIDOR TOWARD THE STAIRS. JENKS LET Max take the lead, though she kept a sharp eye out for hostiles. The station seemed mostly deserted now, even more so than when she'd been crawling through the tunnel with Ryan, or that could have just been her nerves.

She was glad she'd kissed everyone goodbye.

And she hated that the thought was in her brain.

The attack came from an office just before they reached the stairs. A pair of hijackers who barely had time to shout their fury before Max was on them.

The hot ball of worry that had been seething in Jenks's chest exploded outward as she watched Max catch the first person on her sword, the tip sliding easily through their chest and out their back. She actually used it to swing them into the path of the attacker behind them. Max then drove forward, backing the second attacker into the wall until her sword pierced their chest also.

It was over in seconds. Both hijackers dead, now sliding to the floor with looks of shock still on their faces. Jenks couldn't see her friend's face, but the tight set of her shoulders as she efficiently stripped the blood off her sword made her heart break.

"Max—"

"Let's go." Her voice was calm, too calm, and if they'd had any time at all, Jenks would have told her to stop.

But the clock counting steadily down in the corner of her DD made her follow Max down the stairs without another word. Her com buzzed to life in her ear and Jenks skidded to a halt, grabbing Max by the arm.

"Senior Chief, this is Dri Castle."

"What the fuck do you want?" The snarled reply wasn't the least bit diplomatic, but Jenks wasn't going to worry about it now. She was full up between Max's behavior and trying to figure out how they were going to get off this flying scrap of metal before it went kerflooey.

"I . . . Tamago said you can't die before you buy them that real chicken dinner you owe them."

Jenks snorted.

"What is it?" Max whispered.

"Castle," Jenks replied after muting the com. "I don't know what she wants, but she's been talking to Tama and apparently they trust her." She flipped her mic back on. "You've got thirty seconds, Castle."

"Tamago said Willis had my parents killed. All so he could recruit me for this."

Oh son of a bitch.

"I— Look, he's down in Engineering. He's going to crash the station into Serrano. Even though Max stole the detonators, he'll figure out some way to set the bombs off. You have to stop him. There's LMH on the station and on the ground where it's supposed to hit. He changed course before I could lock him out of the computers. I know I fucked up—"

"Yeah, big time." Jenks rolled her eyes. "Is there anything you can do to help? Or are you just clearing your conscience to me?"

"I want to help . . . I just don't know how."

"How many down in Engineering?"

"Five, plus Willis."

Those odds sucked. Jenks made a face and held up fingers to Max, whose face hardened even more into a gut-twisting sheet of ice. "Castle, can you turn the lights off when I say so?"

"Yes. The emergency ones will come on, though."

"That's fine, give us a minute to get into position. I'll

com you back." A thought came to her. "Also, com Ground Control since you have access and we don't. Tell them that the timing is off, but Max and I will take care of it." She hated being this vague, but she also didn't want to risk giving anything away if Castle really was playing her somehow.

All she really wanted was for Nika to know they were trying. It wouldn't make much difference in the end if the message didn't get through.

"I can do that."

"Good. I'll— Hey, Castle? You got a ride off this tin can?"

"I'm supposed to get on the SEAL shuttle. I think the pilot is the only one of them still alive? There were a handful of us Willis wanted to evac so we could tell the story. I don't know how many are left, but I can't fight them all."

An idea she really didn't like was already blooming in Jenks's brain. "You seem smart, Castle, you can figure out a way to take over one little shuttle. After you shut the lights down, get out of here. Head for the construction yard and maybe we'll see you on the back side of this mess."

"Okay."

Jenks kept ahold of Max as she relayed the information, feeling Max's muscles shift under her palm at the instinctive need to bolt for Engineering and finish Willis herself. "Commander, I realize you outrank me, but I need you to listen for a second. You cannot go in there with this red haze over your eyes."

"I am fine."

"Don't fucking lie to me. You think I can't see it?" She released her arm only so she could grab Max by the face and tug her down until they were eye to eye. "I know that look, Max. It's been a long damn time, but I remember seeing it in the shards of a mirror when I was on the streets, my own blank eyes staring back at me. You have done what you had to in order to survive, but I need you to think now and not do anything reckless. You let me deal with Willis, okay?"

"I won't promise you that."

Jenks sighed and pressed her forehead to Max's. "I don't want to die here, and I don't want you to, either. Please, Max."

For a long moment she was sure that her begging had just slid right off her best friend, but then Max's hands closed around hers and she felt the pressure shift as she leaned closer. "I promise to try, okay?"

"Yeah, that's good." Jenks sniffed back the tears that threatened and let her go. "All right. We need to move."

The stairwell was silent, and when they hit the Engineering offices, the noise level remained the same with only the muted sounds of rapid-fire conversion.

"Main entrance," Jenks said in a low voice and pointed off to her left at the opened door. "Castle, you still there?"

"I'm here, I called the MOS, they said to tell you '*Dread*'s coming,' which frankly would be ominous even under good circumstances."

Jenks choked on a laugh. "Hit the lights for us, and get out of here."

"Okay," she replied, her voice tight. "And, Jenks, good luck getting off the station."

"Thanks."

The lights went down, dropping them into pitch-black for a moment before the red wash of emergency lights came up. Both of them were already moving before the hijackers could shake themselves out of their confusion.

THE WAREHOUSE WAS QUIET AS SYLVIA FOLLOWED SCOTT CAR-
michael toward the last truck, Clair at her back. They'd quietly cleared the area as best as they could. Still mindful that
panic of any sort was going to cost lives—lives that could
be saved if the people still up on the station could somehow
stop it from crashing into the red dirt of the planet.

She climbed into the truck on the passenger side, Clair
sliding into the back seat with the other Neos who'd stayed
to help load the LMH.

Sure, just riding in what is essentially a very large bomb.
Sylvia huffed a soft laugh and shook her head as Carmichael
got behind the wheel. "Don't mind me. Once upon a time I
wouldn't have thought twice about riding around with this
much explosive material."

His lips curved, the amusement transforming his darkly
handsome face. "Tell me about it. I suppose getting old does
make us a little wiser?"

"More aware of our mortality," she admitted. "Any news
from D'Arcy?"

"Nothing," he replied, shaking his head and pulling the
truck out onto the street. "But I know my sister, she won't
stop until they've figured out how to save the day."

"For what it's worth, I hope your sister makes it."

He grunted softly. "Me too. She'd say it's her job and that
peace is worth it."

Sylvia hadn't prayed in decades, but as they drove out of
the city, she found herself whispering a quiet hope to anyone
listening that peace would prevail.

TWENTY-ONE

THE SOUNDS OF GROUND CONTROL WERE MUTED NOW, NIKA RE-alized as he glanced around. He'd thought for a moment Kavan was going to have to carry the former Senator Carmichael bodily from the base, but Pax finally agreed, kissing him on the cheek before they left to board Aggy's shuttle. Captain Clark had overseen the evac of the nonessential personnel to a safer location. Though depending on how bad the explosion was if the station hit, he wasn't sure anywhere on Mars was technically safe.

Which had been the low-voiced reason Grady gave him for staying.

Chae and Rona and Gunny Ranta had returned, all three of them giving him determined looks and the same line about duty that Captain Hosaka had told him when he said his team was going to stay and "see it through to the end."

Max would be so proud of them.

He pushed the thought aside, if only because it cracked his composure, and the last thing he could do was break down in front of the three faces on the screen in front of him.

Or all the ones at his side.

"The FRC *Omar Tazi* is aboard. The only other ship we are reading in the area is the *Dread Treasure*," Commodore Sameera Moussa, she/her, of the CHNN *Jicheng* reported. The older cis woman watched Nika with kind dark eyes, almost as if she knew how much self-control it was taking for him not to pace the floor.

"I'm showing T-minus eighteen minutes on the clock. Confirm?" Commodore César Lattes, he/him, of the CHNN *Glorious* was young for his rank, but he held himself with the same kind of poise Nika was used to seeing in Max.

You need to stop thinking of her or you're never going to get through this.

"Confirmed," Nika said, his voice somehow steady. "Sapphi, anything from the MOS?"

"No," she replied. "Not since Tama talked to Castle. I'm still trying to get someone to pick up over there, but I can't patch anything through directly to DDs. Maybe once D'Arcy's closer, I can try the same trick we did with the *Tazi*? But again, that's only if someone is also trying to get in touch with us."

"They will. Keep trying." He had to believe that Max and Jenks were still alive, that they were trying to stop Willis, and that they had a plan to get off the station before time was up.

Until he heard from them, all he could do was stare at the numbers steadily ticking toward zero.

"Nika, Rear Admiral Carmichael on the com. Audio only," Sapphi said.

"Put it through."

"We've got the last of the LMH headed out of the city," Scott said without preamble. "On our way to the rendezvous point."

That was something good at least. "Copy that. Thanks, Scott."

"I'll see you in a little while," the man replied, and the line went quiet.

There was the brief sound of conversation from Moussa's screen before Saqib and Lieutenant Ryan appeared next to the commodore.

"Nika, any word?" Saqib asked.

"No, I—"

"Incoming com from the MOS," Sapphi said, her voice tight with anticipation. "Do I answer it, Nik?"

"Everyone be quiet." Admiral Chen's order was delivered in an even tone. "Let Commander Vagin handle whoever is on the other side."

He hadn't really had a handle on just how badly he'd wanted it to be Max or Jenks or both on the fourth screen that appeared until he saw pink curls and a pair of wide, green eyes, and disappointment crashed down like the station that was headed for them.

"Uh, hi. Is Tamago there?"

They stepped up to Nika's side at his gesture. "Castle, where are you?"

"Still on station. I . . . got in touch with Senior Chief Khan, told her what you said. She and Max were headed for Engineering. Willis is still down there. She wants me to turn the lights off for them as a distraction when she coms again. She also told me to tell you the timing is off, but they'll take care of it."

Nika felt Tamago's fingers tangle with his and squeeze hard.

"Good. Castle you did good. I need you to do something else for me. When you talk to them about the lights, tell them *Dread* is coming."

"I can do that." Castle nodded, her pink curls bouncing. "Khan said I was smart and should figure out how to take over the shuttle. If I . . . manage that somehow, can you all pick us up?"

"Yeah," Tamago said. "We can try."

"Good. We'll be over near the construction yard. The senior chief said it would be safer over there, and I figure I can talk Mak into thinking it will hide us from the carriers." She offered up a tight smile. "I suppose maybe I'll see you again."

The screen went blank before Tamago could answer her.

"Jenks figured out the timing was wrong because of the trajectory change," Nika said. The burst of pride in his chest quickly swallowed by his worry.

"She doesn't know by how much, though," Sapphi replied. "And I don't have any way of getting that to her."

"Try Castle again."

There was no answer to Sapphi's com.

"Nika, I think I know where Max and Jenks will go, though," Sapphi said abruptly. "Look." She pointed at the orbits on the screen. "She told Castle to go to the yard. The MOS is going to pass the construction yard. They could make the jump with some EMUs, and the shielding would provide some protection from the debris wave."

"They don't have EMUs."

"There'd be some in the Docking Bay," she replied.

"That's still a hell of a jump, but I think you're right. It's the only option they have," Tamago said, eyeing the distance. "Can D'Arcy get in there before the boom?" They pointed at the screen. "If he comes in over here, he'd have the yard between them and the station."

"It would also put him on track to disable the shuttle," Nika murmured. He sighed. "I don't like the idea of a dogfight that close to where Jenks and Max might be."

"Honestly, it might be the least of their worries," Sapphi replied; then she shot him an apologetic look. "Sorry, Nik."

"Forgiven. Get D'Arcy on the com. I want him filled in while those two try to . . ." He shot Admiral Chen a look. "Blow up an orbital station."

"They're operating under the SSOP-47, Commander," Chen replied without a hint of a smile. "There won't be any sort of disciplinary action for it."

If they survived.

Saint Ivan, please bring them both back to me.

THE FIGHT WAS OVER IN A MATTER OF MOMENTS. WHATEVER training these people had, it wasn't a match for Max and Jenks. For ten years of watching each other's backs and reading each other's movements.

Or for the hours Max had spent on this station fighting for her life.

She wanted to go home. To Nika. To the rest of her crew and her family.

She knew why Jenks was worried about her. There was nothing but a burning focus as she cut her way through the first hijacker, dropping them to the floor in a spray of blood and kicking the feet out from under the next one before they could cry out in alarm.

Max stabbed down, trying to ignore the voice in her head that was keeping count as she moved farther into Engineering.

Someone rushed her from the side, crashing into her before she could get her sword up.

"I won't let you ruin this!"

Willis.

Max's head cracked on a console, and she slid to the ground in a tangle with the man as she braced herself for the feeling of fléchettes or a sword—something sharp that was going to end this.

It never came.

Instead, Willis squawked as Jenks grabbed him by the back of the collar and hauled him off Max. "I would very much appreciate it if you'd just surrender," she said as she flung him a meter away and leveled her sword at the man. "Max, you good?"

"Yeah." She scrambled to her feet, blinking blurry eyes in the red wash of light. "Any more?"

"Nah, I got them. Put your hands on the floor where I can see them, Willis. You've lost." Jenks shook her head. "This wasn't the way to go about it; losing people hurts, but—"

Willis slumped to the deck and looked up at her. "What do you know of loss?"

"I know I never knew my parents. That I grew up in the streets, and barely had enough to eat. I also know none of that matters. I know that taking my pain out on everyone around me doesn't fix a damn thing. I know that a whole lot has gone wrong with this conflict and there are heroes and villains everywhere we look, but what does more death accomplish?"

"Justice." He lunged at her, but even as Jenks shifted, Max shoved her booted foot between them and she slammed Willis back to the floor.

"There's no justice for the dead if all you do is make more dead," she said softly as she carefully put weight on the man's chest until he stopped struggling. "The only justice comes from staying alive and trying to make things better."

"The war won't ever stop, and someone has to pay."

"Bullshit," Jenks countered. "You could have been working for peace all this time instead of running, instead of plotting mass murder."

"It's finished," Max said, surprised by the surge of sympathy she felt for him as she moved back. "I can't make you take responsibility, but you're going to stay alive and face the consequences of what you've done."

"What about what *you've* done?"

"I'm going to have to face that, too."

Willis's laugh was bitter. "Have fun with that."

The movement startled her, but the training was innate at this point. Max brought her sword up at the flash of silver, but Willis buried the knife in his own heart, and slumped over.

"Well, that's one way to do it," Jenks muttered. "Come on, Max, we need to get this situation sorted and get off this station. The clock is ticking very rapidly, and I really want this place in pieces before Navy tries to blow it out of the black."

Max dragged in a breath, and tried to settle her jangling nerves. Whatever satisfaction she felt over Willis's death was bitter on her tongue. "How are we getting out of here?"

"I have a miniscule percentage of a plan that is frankly the worst idea I've had in my entire life. You're not going to like it." Jenks paused. "Hell, I don't like it."

"Does it give us a shot?"

"You could say that." Jenks pointed at the bombs. "First things first. Tell me again where the detonators are?"

"In the locker room. Do we need them?"

"Can I let you out of my sight?"

"What's that supposed to mean? I'm fine." The sound of her voice was harsh, almost unnatural to her own ears. They'd been friends long enough that even this conversation stripped to the bone was clear as day to Max, and she sighed softly, but Jenks still picked up the sound.

Mismatched eyes pinned her in a flat stare, and Max muttered a curse.

"I can get the detonators."

"Go on, then." Jenks jerked her head at the door. "And be careful."

Max paused near the bodies of the Neos who'd been down here when the attack came and collected their IDs before she went out the door. The hijackers must have slaughtered them once they gained access.

I should have come down here before that. I could have saved them.

Willis was more right than he knew about what she was going to have to live with.

JENKS WATCHED MAX FOR A MOMENT AS SHE LEFT THE ROOM, her friend kneeling by the Neo bodies piled in a corner. She wasn't the praying type, that was Nika's purview. "If there is such a thing as God," she muttered. "A—you shouldn't let shit like this happen to people like Max, and B—will you keep an eye on her when I can't?"

She blew out a breath and turned back to the console.

A couple of minutes later Max returned with the detonators. Jenks took one and slipped it into a leg pocket. "You keep that one."

"So I thought these bombs weren't going to be enough to actually destroy the station. How are you going to do that?" she asked.

"You remember that H3nergy freighter we stopped from exploding when you first joined the Interceptors?"

"The one with the engine failure? Yes."

Jenks had tried to get Max to leave, but she'd flatly refused, standing her ground with nothing more than a faint hope her new crewmate could work a miracle and keep them from dying. Looking back on it, that was when she really had started to respect her new lieutenant. Even though she was stubborn enough that it took Max saving her life to admit to it.

"You can do that the other direction." Jenks mimed an explosion with her hands. "And now we've got the bombs to help it along. I suspect the hijackers were just going to use the bombs to ignite the LMH after they'd cleared the atmosphere, which would have given them a smaller explosion. Enough to keep the bulk of the station intact but also create a pretty big debris cloud and a bigger damage area.

"We're going to use it to make a bigger boom and vaporize this can."

"Using the engine and the bombs," Max clarified.

"Yup." Jenks tapped at the keys on the console. "First, I'm going to adjust the life support and flood this place with oxygen. Give us even more fuel up top so the explosion can crawl that way. We can wait on the lids, though—it'll take a bit for the mix to go lopsided." It was a good plan to wait on the helmets, saving every scrap of air in them for when they really needed it. Plus running with them sealed sucked.

"What kind of time frame are we looking at?" Max asked.

"Fifteen minutes, give or take?"

"I don't like the uncertainty there."

Jenks's laugh was sharp. "Believe me, neither do I. But it's a lot of calculus to try to do in my head, so that's the best we've got. We can control the detonation but not the overload. Basically, I'm going to hit the switch and we're running for the Docking Bay." She shot Max a sidelong glance. "How are you doing?"

A guilty look scuttled across her face. "Jenks, I'm sorry."

"We'll deal with it once we're off the station and safe, okay?" she said firmly. "I've got this set, just need the go-ahead."

"Where are the EMUs?"

Jenks's DD lit up as she called up a map of the station and she sent it to Max. "Locker on that corner. There's an airlock next to it. It's the closest of the trio to where we are now. Run up three flights of stairs, out the door, and ten meters on a slight diagonal." She looked at Max. "We don't know that they're in there, though, or what condition."

"Okay, backup plan?"

"Next closest locker is across the bay and that run will suck, but we can do it and get dressed in under ten minutes."

"What's your worst case?"

Jenks tried not to smile but couldn't help herself. Max knew her too well. "Marine drop ship on the far side. You said they trashed the flight computers, but I'm hoping they'll have missed the shielding. I can hot-wire it, but it'll be close depending on when the station engines decide to blow. And . . ."

"We'll be inside," Max finished quietly.

"Near as, yeah." Jenks made a face. "It's not great odds, but better than just standing out in the open."

Max dragged in a deep breath, and slipped the detonator key in her left leg cargo pocket. "All right. We go closest locker, then second option, then the drop ship in that order, and let's hope we don't have to resort to anything beyond the first choice."

"Give me the order, Max."

"Start the overload sequence, Senior Chief."

Jenks nodded and hit the button. They both turned and ran for the door without another word.

THE STAIRS WERE A BLUR OF MOTION AND THE HARSH SOUND OF her own breath in her ears. Max reached the top first, able to take them two at a time, and she didn't wait for Jenks more than a few pounding heartbeats before racing across the bay toward the locker for the EMUs that was just ahead.

"I need a few more lucky breaks if you could," she said, tossing the prayer out to anyone who might be listening as she jerked the door open to reveal a row of dingy-looking EMUs.

Jenks skidded to a stop next to her and cursed. "When

was the last time they did maintenance on these? Never mind, I don't want to know." She flipped it on and was apparently satisfied with the response she got from the technology. "Turn around, you first." She didn't give Max a chance to argue, already spinning her by the arm and pushing her back until she lined up with the connections on the extravehicular mobility unit that looked to be about as old as she was.

A chime sounded over her DD as the suit and the unit connected, and Max gave a thumbs-up as she straightened and pulled away from the holding rack. "Your turn," she said.

"This one is good. You laugh, I'll smack you," Jenks said as she kicked the step open and hopped onto it, turning around and leaning back slightly until Max saw the connection lights on the EMU flip to green. She stuck her hand out and helped Jenks upright and back down to the floor.

The clock ticked relentlessly in the corner of her vision.

"This really might be the worst idea I have ever had," Jenks muttered as they stepped into the airlock. She grabbed for Max's tether, hooking it on to her suit and repeating the process in reverse with her own tether. "Hooked. Check."

"I don't know, that time you tried to outdrink Candy's squad was pretty terrible." Max hit the door panel and then the button for her helmet. She looked down, tugging on both clips. "Checked on the hooks. We're green."

"True. I'm still impressed you carried my ass home." Jenks laughed as she remembered, then keyed her own helmet.

Max waited for the coms to kick back on before she replied. It was a relief that whatever was going on with the station coms didn't affect their suits. "You were so *wiggly* and you wouldn't stop singing. Grab on, I'm starting the vent sequence."

Jenks grabbed for the bar by the outer door. The extra propulsion from just blowing the airlock would put them on too uncertain a trajectory, so they'd decided to vent first. "I could sing now if it'll help."

"It will not. Be quiet, I'm trying to watch the clock." The vent sequence finished; Max opened the outer airlock door. Her heart rate picked up again as the construction yard for the new station came into view. While they both had EMUs, if they didn't time the exit from the MOS right, it would put them too far behind the yard.

Too far out of the range of their EMUs' limited fuel supply, and the yard would only continue to drift away from them on its slow orbit around Mars. While they would be stuck out in the open when the MOS exploded.

"Now," Max said, and shoved Jenks out the door into the black, stepping out behind her. "Thrusters."

There was enough play in the tethers that the microsecond difference between thrusters didn't matter, and they soared through the black toward the empty, evacuated construction yard that held the almost completed first stalk of the new station.

The shielding was done and that's all they cared about. Enough protection from the debris spray that the counter in the corner of her DD was steadily ticking down toward. Unchecked by friction, it would explode outward and shred anything in its path.

But station shielding was designed to protect against at least some of this, and Max understood Jenks's hope that with the MOS speeding in the other direction, they'd be safe enough to survive.

Her EMU flashed the fuel reserve light, and she knew Jenks's was likely kicking over at the same time. The construction yard loomed in their field of view, growing steadily closer.

"There!" Jenks pointed, and Max spotted an opening several meters wide in the hull of the stalk. They landed; Max stumbled a step before she engaged her boots.

The clock in her vision was almost at zero and she fished the detonator out of her pocket. "Say when."

Jenks had her eyes on the station, watching, Max assumed, for some sign of the engine going critical. The silence stretched as the MOS continued its path away from them, and Max felt like her patience was still attached somehow, straining to the breaking point. Just when she thought she couldn't stand another second, Jenks spoke.

"Do it."

They both flipped the switch on their detonator keys and pushed the button when it lit up. Max's heart thumped hard. Nothing happened.

"Damn it—"

The flames raced from base to top as they ate every scrap of available fuel in a matter of seconds and the Mars Orbital Station exploded in silent fury.

"We do not want to be here," Jenks said, grabbing Max by the arm and tugging her away from the opening. "Come on."

"MAX, JENKS, DO YOU COPY? LUPE, ANY SIGN OF THEM?" D'ARCY asked the petty officer when there was no answer on the com.

"Still working on it," Lupe answered, his eyes focused on the screen in front of him. "I'm getting intermittent pings but nothing strong enough to make a connection. Plus I don't know if the pings are them. I can't get a lock on either of their DDs—there's too much interference."

"Commander, I'm getting a read on that SEAL shuttle," Chaske said, his eyes locked on the console in front of him. "They're coming up on our two o'clock, a little low. I don't think they've seen us yet."

D'Arcy put a hand on Chaske's shoulder. "How many life signs?"

"Five," he replied, dashing what little hope he had that maybe it was Max and Jenks. "And they've spotted us, weapons just went hot."

D'Arcy hit the com. "SEAL Shuttle Seven, this is NeoG Interceptor *Dread Treasure*; shut your weapons down and broadcast a surrender or we will fire." He'd talked to Nika and knew that Castle was likely on board, but unless she could pull off a miracle, he wasn't inclined to cut the SEAL shuttle any slack.

Not when his ship needed to be here for Max and Jenks.

"Fuck you."

"You've got nowhere to go," D'Arcy replied calmly. "Even if you get a miracle and get by us, there are more than a dozen CHN ships out here and all of them will be gunning for you."

"Whatever, we'll—"

Suddenly there were sounds of a scuffle on the com, and a cry of pain that was abruptly cut off before it all went quiet again. D'Arcy shared a look with Emel as the weapons on the shuttle went quiet.

"Hi. Don't shoot. We surrender." Castle's voice was breathless. "Well, I surrender, I guess, and the others get to come along for the ride."

"What just happened?"

"A munity? Overthrow? Though technically Mak wasn't in charge, he just thought he was because he was piloting the ship. Listen, I knocked him out and sealed myself in the cockpit; but there are three angry people with weapons in the back and I . . . can't actually fly this thing."

"D'Arcy, the MOS just blew." Chaske's announcement was clipped.

"Shields up. Castle, brace yourself." D'Arcy hoped that Mak had put the shields up in preparation for a fight with the Interceptor, or the shuttle wasn't likely to survive the debris wave. "The rest of you, brace."

He grabbed for the roll bar, sparing a glance across the bridge to Maria in Emel's chair, her knuckles pale where she was gripping the arms. He tore his gaze back to the console, watching the wave heading toward them on the screen. There was nothing to stop the momentum of the deadly shrapnel besides the construction yard.

Dread at least had shields. Max and Jenks might be in the yard with nothing but suits.

He refused to even entertain the notion that they might have still been on board.

"Ten seconds to impact," Chaske said. "Getting a com from Ground Control."

"Put it through. Nika, give us a second. Riding out the debris wave." D'Arcy tightened his grip as the ship shook, rocking slightly as the debris glanced over the shielding and peppered it with impacts. He waited until the red flashing lights on the console dulled to a sullen orange. "Okay, go."

"Both carriers are reporting MOS is destroyed. We're issuing shelter in place orders here on Mars for possible debris over the next hour." Nika paused, the silence heavy. "Anything?"

"I don't have contact yet, Nika."

"I'm scanning now, D'Arcy," Aki said, her fingers flying over her console.

Come on, you two, give us a happy ending.

WE HAVE COME THIS FAR; DO NOT LET US GET SHREDDED BY *stupid shrapnel*, Jenks thought, pulling Max behind a bunch of cargo crates that were strapped to an exposed beam with bright orange tie-downs

She only had a guess at how far away they were when the station blew, but Jenks counted up over the com anyway because it gave her something to do.

The first pinging impacts made the structure vibrate at the minute mark, and even though they were tethered together, Jenks kept a tight hold on Max. Four heartbeats later the construction yard was battered with debris, whizzing around them and over their heads, slamming into the cargo crates.

A tie-down snapped and the crate slammed into them, knocking Jenks forward onto her hands and knees and sending Max tumbling above her. A piece of shrapnel missed Max by inches but cut through their tether just moments before a second crate broke free and crashed into her.

"Max! The tie-down!" Jenks pushed off from the floor, momentum aided by a piece of debris to the back that was going to leave a bruise and knocked the breath from her lungs.

Thankfully Max had heard her and grabbed for the colored strap as she floated out into space with Jenks not far behind. Jenks fumbled, the fabric sliding through her gloved hands for several terrifying seconds before she could wrap it around her arm and close her fist on it.

"Hold tight." She hauled Max back toward her, hand over hand, until their helmets touched.

"You shouldn't have—"

"Shut up," Jenks said, kicking Max in the shin lightly. "I promised my brother I'd bring us home." She hit the distress beacon on her DD and tried the coms. "Senior Chief Altandai Khan. Is there anyone out there?"

The com crackled to life in her ear, followed immediately by D'Arcy's deep voice. "I thought you two were supposed to be in the yard?"

Jenks choked back the sudden sob that threatened. "Well, you know what they say. No good plan survives contact with physics, or something. Hi, D'Arcy."

"Hi, you two. Coming up on your six."

"It's really—really good to see you," Max managed around a sob.

Jenks thumped her on the side of her helmet. "No crying. You'll aspirate." She turned her head as the Interceptor flew in behind them, D'Arcy's familiar silhouette in the open airlock.

He pushed away from *Dread*, tethered to the ship and

with two other clips in his hand that he hooked into both of their suits. Jenks still kept ahold of Max as D'Arcy pulled them all back to the ship.

The next few moments were a blur. Jenks only realized she was still holding tight to the strap from the construction yard when Emel put both hands over hers. "Jenks? You want to let that go for me?"

She forced her fingers to unclench. "Where's Max?"

"She's okay, D'Arcy's with her. Are you injured?"

"Some bruises." Bravado was always easier. "They were crap fighters." The first breath stuck in her throat, the second sounded like a sob. Her hands were shaking, and she locked her fingers down on Emel's the second the woman took her hand. Her skin was warm, or she was cold. She had no memory of taking off her suit.

She was alive. They were alive.

Everything hit her in a rush, and Jenks gasped but Emel seemed ready for it and caught her in a tight hug. "You're good. Breathe for me. You're safe. You both are."

She spotted Max over Emel's shoulder through the tears. D'Arcy was holding her, his head bent against her curls as her shoulders shook with sobs, and there was little doubt in Jenks's mind that he was telling her the same thing Emel was saying.

It was over. They were alive. And whatever Max had to deal with in the aftermath, she wouldn't do it alone.

Final Four Sentenced in MOS Hearings
PUBLISHED: APRIL 13, 2446 (MARS STANDARD DATE)

The last of the Mars Orbital Station hijackers were sentenced today, wrapping up months of testimonies in the hearings that had most of Mars and a good chunk of Earth's population riveted as they waited for an outcome.

Former Navy Petty Officer First Class Mak Lee was dishonorably discharged and sentenced to ten years in a medium-security military rehab facility on Mars. Twenty-three-year-old hacker prodigy Dri Castle will participate in four years of rehabilitation at the Blue Cedar facility on Earth. Wilke and Mila Johansson were sent to the same facility, but only for eighteen months, thanks in large part to a favorable testimony from Senior Chief Altandai Khan. The NeoG enlisted officer was passionate on the stand about the assistance the sisters had provided and the importance of letting people learn from their mistakes.

Missing from the testimonies, which included civilians and military personnel who had been on the orbital station at the time of the attack, was Commander Maxine Carmichael. She did not make an appearance at any of the trials, as many had thought she would, to speak either for or against clemency in the sentencing.

It was reported in the early days that Carmichael had delivered a statement to the court in writing, the contents of which was not made available to the public. However, the NeoG officer, who was instrumental in preventing more deaths by blowing up the MOS before it could be crashed into Mars, did not leave the Trappist system for the duration of any of the hearings and has continued to refuse any and all requests for interviews.

The NeoG confirmed shortly after the incident that former Senator Willis Hale, whose husband had been lost in the tragic Hellas accident, was responsible for planning the attack. Senator Hale was among those killed when the MOS exploded.

[*Read More*]

TWENTY-TWO

Three Months Later

> The mood here can only be described as celebratory,
> Quentin. We'll have to wait for the actual voting, of
> course; but by all accounts, the special referendum
> that was introduced in the wake of the attack on the
> MOS will not only win the popular vote on Mars, but
> the CHN Senate will issue approval with only a few
> dissenters. In just a few short months Mars will finally
> have full voice in the Coalition of Human Nations.

D'ARCY ROLLED HIS COFFEE MUG BETWEEN HIS PALMS AS HE leaned against the counter and watched the morning news broadcast.

"It's a day few of us thought we'd ever see, Roberto, that's for sure," the newscaster back in the studio said with a bright smile. "That was Roberto Tengu reporting from downtown Serrano. The news tonight on Mars is all about the deal worked out between former CHN Senator Patricia Carmichael and Sylvia Moroz, leader of the independence group Free Mars, during the tragic attack on the Mars Orbital Station three months ago today. Thanks to the heroic efforts of many people, including NeoG Commander Maxine Carmichael, the loss of life was minimal.

"Up next, a new hybrid sunflower in development at Mars Agriculture might change the bioelectric game."

D'Arcy stood and turned the screen off with a tap of a finger. It was surprising how second nature it was now to open his email and send a quick message to Maria.

His com buzzed a moment later and he opened it on the same screen he'd been watching the news on. "Are you drunk yet?"

Maria laughed and lifted the beer in her hand. "Working on it. Clair's actually ahead of me, if you can believe it."

"Are they even old enough to drink?" He heard the protest off-camera and then Clair's face smooshed in next to Maria's.

"Watch yourself, NeoG," they said before Maria pushed them back out of frame with a laugh.

"Congratulations," D'Arcy said, lifting his own coffee. "I mean it."

"We're not done, not by a long shot. But no lie, D'Arcy, this feels good." Maria looked away for a moment and he could see the sheen of tears in her eyes. "I didn't think—"

"I know," he said with a smile.

"Maria!" Boston's voice was bright as he came into the

kitchen. "I was just coming to tell D'Arcy the news, but I should have known that he would have already seen it. Congratulations."

"Thank you."

"You should come visit," Boston said with a devilish look on his face.

D'Arcy elbowed his meddling boyfriend in the ribs and hid his own smile behind his mug. He'd been surprised after coming back to Trappist how often his thoughts had wandered to Maria, even more surprised when she emailed him and they'd continued to keep in touch. The conversation with Boston about their past had been easy enough, and though these new feelings were more difficult, D'Arcy had wanted the man to know what was going on in his head.

"I may do that," Maria replied, her voice almost drowned out by the sudden cheer that went up around her. "I should go."

"Have fun. Make sure you pour some water into the kid."

Maria smiled. "I will. We'll talk later."

D'Arcy let Boston steal the last of his coffee. "You're a menace."

"Maybe." Boston shrugged, an unrepentant grin on his face. "You're both dancing around this, though, have been for months. I get the distance issue, and your past—"

"And the fact that I love you?"

"Of course I get that! But she makes you happy when you talk to her." He reached out and cupped the back of D'Arcy's head, drawing him closer until their mouths almost touched. "And I like seeing you happy."

D'Arcy shifted with a hum, trapping Boston between his

body and the counter as he sank into the kiss. He still wasn't sure how he'd ended up here after everything, but he wasn't going to question it.

"EVENING, LIEUTENANT."

"Waygo, how are you doing?" Tamago smiled at the front desk guard as they stepped through the scanner.

"Can't complain," he replied. "I'm off for a month after tonight. My youngest is due to have his baby any day now. Wife and I are going up to lend a hand."

"That's lovely. Pass on my congratulations."

"I'll do that. Castle's already up in the visiting area, you can go on back."

This was routine now, but Tamago could remember the first few nerve-racking times they'd come to the rehab facility where Castle was staying. Even though it was one of the lowest security centers the CHN had on Earth, for Tamago it was a whole new experience.

They spotted Castle on the far side of the visiting area, curled up in one of the comfortable blue chairs. She was looking out the window at the budding trees, but her hands were busily working away at a complicated puzzle Tamago had brought on their last visit.

"Hey, you—how's it going?" they asked, settling into the nearby chair.

"Did you know we had to genetically engineer several species of cherry trees before we could get them to bear fruit again? There's a whole pre-Collapse thing about bananas not really being banana flavored, and sometimes I wonder if that's the case with cherries," she replied, sounding a bit like Jenks in the moment.

"It's possible, I suppose," Tamago said.

"No one around to tell us if we've completely fucked it up, I guess, huh?" Castle looked away from the window. "Sometimes I think it's a good thing my parents are gone and can't see me like this."

"I don't think it's a good thing."

"Man, they'd be disappointed. Can I ask you something?"

Tamago sat forward, forearms resting on their knees. "Of course, I'm here to talk."

"Why save me?" Castle sniffed away the tears that had gathered in her voice. "The commander and senior chief had things well in hand from what I've read. They didn't really need my help. Why contact me at all? Why speak up for me? You could have just let me get on that shuttle. The Interceptor is a bigger and more well-equipped ship than the SEAL shuttles are. It would have been a bit of a dogfight, but probably not much of one. Mak wasn't a very good pilot. It wasn't a stretch of the imagination to think they were the ones surviving that tangle."

It wasn't a stretch at all. "Why did you help?" Tamago asked.

"I didn't want people to die." Castle's eyes were wide in her face. "I didn't go into this wanting to die, not like some of them—Willis and the others, who thought going up in smoke would somehow make the pain go away. Which I suppose, they weren't wrong. I thought making everyone else pay for this would make me feel better, but then I started thinking about how my parents were just out

having dinner and there were people just like that on the
planet below and—

"I don't know why you come to see me, Tama. I'm so
much worse than them. I wanted to see the destruction.
Wanted to see the NeoG and Free Mars, all of you, hurt the
same way. It seemed right."

"And now?"

"Now I don't know. I won't ever know if Willis actually
killed my parents just to get me on board with this. Now
I'm stuck here thinking about cherry trees and how things
change to make something new." Castle laughed bitterly and
shoved both hands in her hair as she folded forward with a
sob. "This hurts so much, Tamago, and I have to live with it,
don't I?"

"You do." Tamago reached out and touched a hand carefully to the woman's back. "We all do."

MAX'S NIGHTMARES CAME AND WENT WITH FRUSTRATING IN-
consistency. The first week after the attack she didn't dream
at all, just fell into a deep sleep every night. Then later, after
they were back at Trappist, the first one had hit with the
same punch as the MOS explosion itself.

She'd been afraid to go to sleep after that.

Sometimes it was Willis thrusting that knife in his hand
into Jenks's chest instead of his own before Max could stop
him. Sometimes she was back in the MOS, fighting nameless,
faceless opponents only to see her friends' sightless eyes staring accusingly at her when she rolled over the corpse.

Tonight she was in Ford's place, walking calmly out into
the black.

Max woke on an inhale, rolling from the bed she shared with Nika as quietly as possible, knowing he'd probably wake regardless. She made it across the dark and still crew quarters by instinct more than anything, and even if anyone had heard her, they'd all learned not to intervene.

The first time it happened she'd nearly broken Jenks's arms, still caught in a wasteland between the nightmare and reality.

What do you see, Max?

Max gripped the sink in both hands and pressed her forehead to the cool surface. "Floor, feet, sink, soap—" She forced herself to look up. "Me."

She flipped the water on and stuck her hand in it. "Faucet, sink, floor, fabric of my tank top. Running water, my own breathing, the AC unit. Blood, why am I smelling blood?"

"There's no blood, Max." Nika's voice was soft, nearly drowned out by her rapid breaths. "Try again."

"I can't." The sharp tang of blood was too hot in her nose and her mouth, and she could see the dead in the Cargo Bay control room overlaid on the bathroom floor. "It's everywhere. All over me. I can taste it, smell it, feel it—"

"Breathe, Max. I'm right here. Breathe. One in, one out. Breathe for me, Max," Nika said. "Can I touch you?"

Max nodded and turned into his embrace, locking her arms around his waist and burying her face against his throat. The shakes followed immediately after, and all she could do was hang on to the sound of Nika's voice as the one solid thing in the dark to keep her from flying apart.

"I'm right here, Max. You're right here. You're safe. Keep breathing for me."

She lost track of how long they stood there. Time got

slippery in the middle of these attacks. Everyone said it was normal, but Max hated the loss of control more than anything.

Nika knew it and did everything he could to ground her back into reality. "It's been five minutes," he murmured against her hair. "How are you doing?"

Her breathing had slowed, and now her back protested the weird angle she'd ended up in, leaning against Nika. "I'm okay. I think a shower?"

"All right. I'll get us breakfast if you don't mind me leaving?"

She nodded, even though the thought of food made her stomach jump uncomfortably. They both knew the space was necessary. That Max needed the time to compose herself in private.

Max attempted a smile. "I have therapy today. Good news, I guess?"

He squeezed her hand, then gestured to the showers. "Go on. I'll be right back."

MAX MADE IT THROUGH THE MORNING WITH ONLY ONE SLIPUP, A sharp remark in Saqib's direction that her lieutenant commander had not deserved. Thankfully, she'd been able to flee to her therapy appointment.

The apology would have to come later.

When Max emerged from her therapist's office, Jenks was waiting in the hallway, legs crossed, and leaning easily against the wall as she read something on her DD.

Doge was sitting patiently at her side, but he got to his feet and nosed at Max, who dropped her hand on the cool metal of his head. "Morning, buddy," she said. "What are you doing here?" she asked Jenks.

"I work here," Jenks replied, the easy calm on her face didn't match the worry in her eyes.

"Aren't you supposed to go on vacation?" She hadn't meant it to be quite so sharp of a question, but it was too late to stop the words.

Jenks was unfazed by the bite in Max's voice. "I'll get around to it. The boys' schedules have to align first. Besides, this is more important."

"I'm fine."

"Sure you are." Jenks flicked her eyes down to where Max's hands had curled into fists. "You gonna take a swing at me right here in the hallway, Commander?"

What she should do is unclench her fists, apologize, and ask for help. It's what she'd just spent an hour talking about with her therapist. However, Max couldn't make herself do any of it. "I might, Senior Chief, so why don't you back off and leave me alone?"

Doge's soft whine as he eased in Jenks's direction almost broke her.

"I leave you alone and it'll just fester. Let it crawl back under your skin after you did all that work with your therapist to pull that part of yourself free." Jenks shrugged. "You can throw a punch if you think it'll make you feel better, but I know you, Max, and fighting isn't what you need right now."

"Fighting is all that I'm good at. Fighting. Killing."

"No it's not."

"Why do you keep poking, then?"

"Because you keep lying to me about being fine." This

time it was Jenks's voice that was sharp, and Max couldn't stop the guilty flinch. "And I know how watching people you care about die can open up a wound in the very heart of you. I know that killing people is bad enough when it's the only choice you have to keep yourself and others alive, but it's a thousand times worse when you realize you are pleased to have been the one to make them stop breathing. To make them pay for what they did.

"I keep poking because I love you and I'm not going to let you go through this alone." Now there were tears in Jenks's eyes, but she was smiling as easily as if they were talking about her kids and not Max falling apart in front of her.

"How do you do it?" Max whispered. "How are you so relentlessly cheerful in this terrible world?"

It was hard to keep the other woman's gaze, even more so when Jenks said her name on a soft exhale. But then her hands were on Max's face, pulling her down into a hug and she collapsed against the shorter woman with a sob.

"Because I have my family. Luis and Tivo and the kids and my brother . . . and my *sister*. Max, I get through every day because I have found you all and you have found me in turn. If I could take this pain from you, I would," Jenks whispered against her hair. "I'm so sorry. It doesn't get easier, ever. Except . . . it kind of does. I am, as you say, relentlessly cheerful because it's the best fuck you I can think of to this terrible world."

"I'm not as strong as you," Max said, holding on with all her might. "I never have been."

"First off, that's bullshit, and you know it. Secondly, it's not about being strong. I simply refuse to let being broken keep me from seeing the world like this because I'm spiteful and too stubborn for my own good. I will pick up the pieces of myself over and over, put it back together, and die with as much love in my heart as I can hold because I don't see the point in doing anything else." Her arms tightened around Max.

"I'm so scared."

"I know. And I won't tell you that it's just going to magically go away one day. This changed you. What I can tell you is you're not alone and you don't have to go through this alone. Not now, not ever. It's not going to be quick and it's not going to be easy, but it is going to be okay."

And because it was Jenks, who never lied about the important things, Max knew that she could believe it.

ACKNOWLEDGMENTS

To my family, friends, and cats for keeping me (mostly) on track and providing snuggles and distractions as needed, including when I thought I didn't need them. "Thank you for everything" will never be enough appreciation but I'll keep saying it anyway. Blue, even though our roads have diverged, you are forever my best friend and I love you.

Special thanks as always to Lisa DiDio for your cheering, your presence (your alcohol), and your unfailing belief that I can keep doing this. I love you and am so lucky to have you in my corner. To Kalatanyx, KT Yarrow, and Kat for your excitement and assistance and just being truly lovely people; thanks for being around to cheer me on.

To my friend Jackson Ford. Thanks for letting me space you. You're the best!

Thanks to my agent, Andy Zack, for all your support.

Thank you to David Pomerico, my editor, for your excellent vision of this whole universe and all your incredible contributions along the way and for responding to my "What about *Die Hard* in space?" with an unequivocal "Yes!" And a million thanks to all the people at Harper Voyager who work day in and day out to get books like mine out the door looking like their best version of themselves. I couldn't do this without you.

To all my readers and fans who have checked out from your libraries, bought, read, shouted about, and supported my writing over the last eight years: THANK YOU. You are all amazing and I love you.

ABOUT THE AUTHOR

K. B. Wagers is the author of the NeoG adventures from Harper Voyager and the Indranan and Farian War trilogies from Orbit Books. They are a fan of whiskey and cats, *Jupiter Ascending*, and the Muppets. You can find them on various social media sites, where they engage in political commentary, plant photos, and video game playthroughs, by going to kbwagers.com.

DISCOVER THE NeoG SERIES BY
K. B. WAGERS

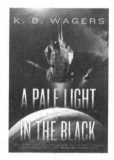

A Pale Light in the Black
The rollicking first installment in a unique science-fiction series that introduces the Near-Earth Orbital Guard—NeoG—a military force patrolling and protecting space, inspired by the real-life mission of the U.S. Coast Guard.

"An unexpected and refreshing twist on military science fiction."
—Library Journal

Hold Fast Through the Fire
The NeoG patrols and protects the solar system. Now the crew of *Zuma's Ghost* must contend with personnel changes and a powerful cabal hell-bent on dominating the trade lanes in this fast-paced, action-packed follow-up to *A Pale Light in the Black*.

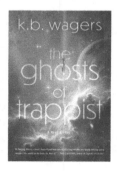

The Ghosts of Trappist
Military sci-fi meets found family space opera when the crew of *Zuma's Ghost* find themselves under attack, shocking truths are about to be exposed, and the NeoG is once again called to action!

Ensign Nell "Sapphi" Zika has been working hard to get past her trauma, but the unnerving pleas for help she's hearing in the Verge and the song she can't get out of her head are making that increasingly difficult. As *Zuma's Ghost* gears up for a final run at the Boarding Games, their expert hacker is feeling anything but confident. Plus, her chief's robot dog, Doge, is acting weird, and the increasing number of missing freighters is putting everyone living on or stationed around Trappist on edge.

Printed in the USA
CPSIA information can be obtained
at www.ICGtesting.com
LVHW030007011124
795343LV00009B/30

9 780063 115248